RUNAWAY BRIDE and PREJUDICE

USA TODAY BESTSELLING AUTHOR

EMMA ST. CLAIR

To my own Robbie Bobby Baby Benjamin Bunny

Thank you for all the cheerleading you do. Also, even if I couldn't work it into the book, please know I was thinking "They're blue too!"

CONTENT WARNINGS

This is a light and funny romcom, but I want to help readers feel safe! Here are some topics that are touched on in the book:

- Parents passing away (past)
- Divorce and parental neglect (past)
- Cheating boyfriends (VERY present)
- Some punching
- Some pinching
- Criticism of Keanu Reeves's body of work

Spoiler alert: No one dies. There is no sex in this book. You will get a happy ending with no cheating and minimal angst.

ABOUT THE APPIES

The Appies is a fictional AHL team located in the also fictional town of Harvest Hollow. We wanted to create a hockey team with the vibes of the Savannah Bananas. (If you don't know the Bananas, do yourself a favor and look them up. You're welcome.)

All of the Appies books can be read as standalones, but if you'd like to read in order, this is the reading order: *Just Don't Fall, Absolutely Not in Love, A Groom of One's Own,* and *Romancing the Grump* (with more to come).

While these are hockey books, they are primarily romance books, so at times, some liberties may be taken with some details, hockey and otherwise.

PART ONE- RUNAWAY BRIDE

CHAPTER 1

Van

PEOPLE SAY when one door closes, another one opens. And maybe that's true.

But I wanna know what people say when one door opens and you find the groom hooking up with someone who's *not* the bride—less than an hour before the wedding.

In a church, no less. Classy.

There's some special ring of Dante's Inferno set aside for people who cheat *on their wedding day*. This guy—whose name is so forgettable, I don't remember it, though I probably should—is like whatever insect belongs on the ladder rung beneath cockroaches.

And he's supposed to be marrying my coach's daughter.

Amelia. Even just her name sends a disturbing twinge of *something* through me—something I'd like to ignore. An unfamiliar emotion landing somewhere between jealousy and an irrepressible—and maybe irrational—longing.

Whatever I shouldn't be feeling regarding Amelia, I think I'm pretty safe experiencing rage at the sight of her fiancé with someone else while wearing his wedding tux.

Some guys might have walked right back out of the room.

Pretended they saw nothing.

Kept their mouths shut.

I am not *some guys*.

All I wanted was to take a leak before the ceremony in case it was one of those long ones with a lot of readings and singing. I've been dragged to my fair share of weddings, and long ones are the worst if you need the bathroom.

Then, I planned to avoid making eye contact with Amelia for the duration of the wedding, enjoy the open bar, and go home alone to sulk. Or move on. Whatever.

But then, I saw Coach walking toward me in the hallway, eyes on the phone in his hand. He hadn't seen me. Yet.

Considering the fact that I'm *always* on his naughty list, *never* on the nice list, I didn't really want to open myself up to a lecture. Had I stopped to think about it, I might have realized Coach isn't concerned with his least favorite player on the day of his daughter's wedding.

But I didn't stop to think. I ducked into this office—and a situation I can't ignore.

"Guess this isn't the bathroom. Sorry," I say, not sounding sorry at all.

I lean casually on the doorframe, not taking my eyes off the dirtbag adjusting his tux. The woman he was kissing dove behind the large mahogany desk when I walked in, and I can hear her shuffling around back there. Probably trying to fix her dress. Or maybe digging herself a hole to climb into. Solid plan.

The dude has the decency to look sort of apologetic, though it's more like *sorry I got caught* than *sorry for being a trash human*. Quickly, though, his expression turns to irritation.

Like *I'm* the one doing something wrong here. Classic cheater's projection.

"The door was locked," he says. "You shouldn't be in here."

I cock an eyebrow. "It wasn't locked. And you're going to blow by apologies and excuses and skip straight to blame-shifting? Huh."

"I don't owe you an explanation. I don't even know you."

"True. You don't owe me anything." I slide my hands into my pockets. Deceptively casual. "Now—as for what you owe Amelia …"

His face pales at the mention of the woman he's supposed to marry in less than half an hour. So, there's at least *some* shred of humanity in this guy. I remember the way he clasped Amelia's hand last night at the rehearsal dinner, all emotional and moved during the toasts.

He's a good actor—I'll give him that.

I am *not* an actor, which is why my teammates kept giving me a hard time, asking why I was so quiet last night. Why I wasn't drinking. Or flirting with any women.

Guess they haven't noticed it's been a long while since I've actually dated.

Anyway, I told them all nothing was wrong; that I don't have to be ON all the time. That my smart mouth isn't *always* running.

Which is true. It just wasn't true last night. My real reason for being in a mood isn't one I plan to tell them.

Amelia also looked happy last night. But jittery too— unless I was imagining it. It's not like I really know her. I did keep my eyes on her, and I couldn't help but notice the way she kept fidgeting with the stack of bracelets on her arm, never sitting still.

And whenever she wasn't smiling, her face looked … hollow.

Unlike her douche of a fiancé, Amelia didn't seem emotional during the toasts. Not until Coach got choked up talking about how Amelia's mom would be so proud. Which had just about everyone in the room crying. Tucker blew his nose so loudly that a woman at the next table dropped her champagne flute.

Thinking about Coach, about Amelia, about this guy pretending to care last night has me clenching my fists in my pockets.

"Amelia deserves better than this," I grit out.

"How do *you* know Ames?" the dude demands.

Ames must be his nickname for Amelia, and it burns that he thinks he gets to still use a pet name for her. I'm pretty sure he forfeited the right to say her name at all the moment he first hooked up with this woman. Or whatever woman came before her. Because I doubt this is the first. There's usually a long line behind every cheater.

As for how I know Amelia … it's a simple story.

We met randomly. Talked. Thought she might be my soulmate.

Then I realized she was my coach's daughter.

The quintessential Romeo and Juliet story. But with more hockey and hopefully with less death and mayhem.

"How I know Amelia is irrelevant. Consider me the good angel on your shoulder, here to make sure you do what you need to do."

The idea of me as an angel is laughable, but whatever. I

can imagine Alec and Tucker and the guys on the team howling over this comparison.

He scoffs, and I study him. He's got that whole clean-cut, white-collar thing going on. Neatly trimmed hair. White teeth. Eyebrows that look like they get regularly manicured. And he's wearing enough projected anger to fill a stadium.

Is this the kind of guy Amelia likes? The kind of man Coach would approve of?

As opposed to me—a tattooed hockey player with a reputation.

"This is a private matter," he says.

I'm sure he'd *love* to keep it a private matter. As in, a secret, hidden thing.

Protectiveness surges within me. It's an emotion that comes standard with any decent guy who has sisters. I've got three, which amplifies my sense of outrage.

Why can't I remember this guy's name? It starts with a D, but I can only think dude.

But *dude* is too nice.

Douche. I'll go with that. Douche the Groom. Or, more likely about to be Douche Formerly Known as Groom. I don't want to be so happy about this because it means Amelia will be crushed.

Single again. But crushed.

And single.

Irrelevant. Because she's off-limits, dummy. She's the coach's daughter.

The woman hiding behind the desk chooses this moment to stand, smoothing down her dress. Her *bridesmaid's* dress. I'm not super knowledgeable about fashion, but the dress is almost the same style my sister, Alexandra, picked for her bridesmaids a few years ago.

9

Talk about a cliché. The groom and a bridesmaid in the church office—like a game of cheating Clue.

The woman touches his arm with familiarity, telling me this isn't the *start* of something. Not a first-time or one-time thing.

Maybe he's the kind who told himself this would be the last time, that once he said *I do*, this would all be in the past. Faithfulness from this hour—clearly not *day*—forward.

Yeah, right. Cheaters gonna cheat, and they're gonna keep on cheating. Unless someone steps in and stops it.

Someone like me.

"So, how's this going to work?" I ask.

"How's *what* going to work?" Douche snaps.

"Do I need to escort you physically to tell Amelia about this, or can I trust you to walk yourself?"

"The door was locked," he stammers, going back to his original response. Like the main problem here is faulty hardware. Not his actions.

I snap my fingers. "Catch up. We've moved on, and you're burying the lede. The headline is *Douchebag Groom Cheats Less Than an Hour before the Wedding with a Bridesmaid.*"

"Maid of honor," the woman corrects, almost like a reflex. Immediately, she seems to realize what she's said, or maybe what she's *done*. Her eyes go wide, and then she bursts into tears.

Normally, I'd hate seeing a woman cry, but in this case, I have zero pity for either of these two.

"Don't cry, baby. We'll figure this out." Douche the Groom has the audacity to pull her into his arms. "Like I promised."

"Just a hunch, but I'm not sure I'd trust any promises he makes," I say.

"You don't know anything," Douche says.

"You made *her* promises"—I point to the woman sniffling in his arms—"but you're about to make vows to *Amelia?* I guess the plan was to keep on cheating after the wedding with your fiancée's best friend?"

"Her cousin," the woman says, again like the words just kind of escaped without her meaning for them to.

I suck in a breath through my teeth. Cheating with a friend is bad. Cheating with family is worse.

"And how do you think Amelia's *dad* will feel about this?"

That sobers them *both* right up.

"You're one of the hockey players," the woman says through a wet sniffle.

Douche appraises me, suddenly looking less confident. Hockey players are a brutal bunch. Though the Appies are less so than most. We rely on skill, not sheer force or dirty plays. I don't take my gloves off if I can help it. But I won't run away from a fight either. If they come my way, they come my way.

Okay, and *maybe* I've been known to instigate sometimes. Whatever. It's part of the game.

"This is all just a misunderstanding," Douche says.

"Cool. Then let's go clear it up with your *fiancée.*"

"You can't tell her," the woman whispers. "It will kill Milly."

Milly—another nickname. How many does Amelia have? And why do I hate both of the ones I've heard? Maybe they're tainted by the people saying them.

I open the door and gesture for them to walk out.

"This would probably go down better if she hears it from you *both*." I tilt my head toward the hallway behind me. "Come on, lovebirds. No time to waste. I think I hear the string quartet warming up."

"Where have you been?" Alec whispers as I slide back into my pew with my teammates.

I shrug, giving a little twist of my lips that hopefully hints I was somewhere more fun than marching Douche the Groom and the Maid of Dishonor down the hallway. I left them right outside the door of the bridal room, both of them looking like they were going to hurl.

Maybe I should have gone in with them. But I couldn't risk seeing Amelia. I don't think I could have walked away, not when I knew she was about to hear devastating news. And it's not like I'm the person she'd turn to for comfort.

Douche was right about one thing: I barely know Amelia.

"Van probably found a woman," Tucker whispers, leaning down from his spot at the end of the aisle.

"And a coat closet," Wyatt mutters, shaking his head. The man is a monk, rarely going out with us and, as far as we know, *never* dating. But this means he always assumes everyone else is hooking up.

"Nah," Dumbo says, eyeing me. "He doesn't look happy enough. My vote is diarrhea."

Alec snorts, and Parker turns around to poke me in the shoulder with one of her pink-painted nails. "Hush!"

"Ow!" I whisper-shout. "I'm not the one who said *diarrhea.*"

"You just did," she says. "Now, pipe down back there. All of you. They're about to start."

They aren't. But I'm the only one in this room who knows that right now, so I mutter "Yes, Boss" along with the rest of the guys.

Parker may be the social media manager, not our actual boss, but she keeps us all in line. Partly because we like and

12

respect her. Partly because she can be surprisingly scary for someone so upbeat. Beside her, Logan tilts his head enough for us to see his smug grin. I think he gets intense pleasure from watching his fiancée force us into submission.

I smooth a hand over my hair, which will go right back to being messy in two minutes. Any minute now, someone will be walking in the sanctuary to announce that the wedding is canceled. Glancing around the room, everything still seems to be normal.

My gaze stops at our group. I'm seated by Tucker, Dumbo, Wyatt, Camden, and Alec, our captain. The single guys. The row in front of us has all the couples: Eli and Bailey, Logan and Parker, and Felix, who's saving a spot on the end for Gracie, who's playing in the string quartet. Nathan is also up there, even though Summer, his new girlfriend and the newest member of the Appies' legal team, is out of town.

The influx of serious relationships—and one marriage in Eli's case—this season has shifted things a bit. Now our team has an adult table and kid table vibe going on. I know which table—or row, in this case—I'll probably never be in.

And what I witnessed a few minutes ago is exactly why. I've had a front-row seat to my parents' unhappily ever afters proving what I already know: monogamy isn't easy. Vows are too often broken.

My whole childhood was like a cautionary tale against marriage.

No shade to my teammates, who all seem like they're in good, healthy relationships. But I know how it goes. First comes the sunshine and rainbows and heart-eye emojis. Then comes the fighting. The cheating. The inevitable, messy breakup. The aftermath.

It's the circle of love. And it's one ride I doubt I'll ever get on. Not unless I meet someone I couldn't imagine living without. Someone worth risking it all for. So far, no one's come close.

Except maybe one woman—the very one who should never have made me entertain those kinds of thoughts.

Tucker leans close. "Dude. Did you know how hot Coach's daughter is?"

"Probably why he kept her away from us," Dumbo says.

"Stop talking about her," I grumble.

Alec eyes me with a little too much interest. "When do you ever *not* want to discuss a hot woman?"

The comment bugs me. Maybe I've leaned into the bad-boy image a little too hard. It bothers me to think my closest friends might really just think of me as some superficial womanizer.

"It's Coach's daughter," I say, going with the only explanation that won't beg more questions. I clench my jaw and face forward.

"Do you know her or something?" Alec asks. "You're being weird. Even for you."

"No."

It's not a lie. But it's also not the truth.

Amelia and I met exactly one time before this weekend. I was picking up a to-go order at the restaurant bar. She was meeting her dad for dinner, and he was running late.

I'll be honest—I started talking to her because she was hot. Honey-colored hair in a perky ponytail, striking blue eyes, and a smile that tugged me to a stop where I stood.

But I stayed and *kept* talking to her because she made me laugh. I wish I could remember now what she said. Whatever it was, I choked out a surprised guffaw, the kind of laugh that sounded like some kind of weird drunk donkey. It made her giggle.

The next thing I knew, I was sitting beside her at the bar,

sharing my burger and fries right from the styrofoam to-go container. We talked like we'd known each other our whole lives. I talked about my favorite sci-fi books, and she mentioned secretly wanting to be a writer. I touched briefly on my parents' messy divorces and she told me how hard it was losing her mom.

We laughed. We flirted. I started to think maybe this could be something—the kind of something I'd never had.

I mean, it was way too fast and definitely stupid to think about that, but Amelia stirred to life the kinds of feelings I've never had. The kind of easy enjoyment mixed with potent attraction that left me feeling woozy.

My parents' excessive failings at monogamy might have left me barricaded behind a No Entry zone for relationships, but Amelia hit me like a runaway truck barreling down a mountain road with cut brakes.

I went to the bathroom and dunked my face in the sink, hoping cold water would settle me. It didn't. So, I decided to march back out there and ask her out. Only one way to see if this could be something real.

And then, I walked out of the bathroom and saw her with Coach.

Her *dad*. My *coach*.

And like a total coward, I hid in the hallway until they went into the restaurant area, grateful I'd introduced myself as Robbie, not Van. If she didn't recognize my face, which she obviously didn't, she might have heard her dad mention my name. Probably not in a good way.

Only my sisters call me Robbie. But when I met Amelia, that's how I introduced myself for some reason.

The only topic I avoided was playing hockey for the Appies. It was kind of nice to have that be an epilogue and not the opening for once.

Except in this situation, we happened to be connected through hockey in the worst possible way. The last thing I need is Coach catching wind of me with his daughter.

The one he'd said in no uncertain terms none of us were to go near. Ever.

So, for months I tried to forget her. I tried dating her out of my system, but it's like meeting Amelia altered my brain chemistry. I compared every woman to the one with the sweet smile who stole my fries and made me feel like I was the living embodiment of a Taylor Swift song.

One of the happy ones, not the breakup ones.

Whatever. I never told anyone. I hoped that watching Amelia marry some other dude would finally get her out of my system. Factory reset me back to standard settings as a guy who kept things casual and didn't ponder things like instalove with my own personal Juliet.

Instead, this week and the weeks leading up to it have been torture. I've played like crap, and Coach actually switched Dominik to my place the last few games. Whatever. I figured this weekend would be the end of it. I'd get her out of my system, get my spot in the line back for playoffs, and go on with my life.

But now …

Guests are still buzzing in the sanctuary, the anticipation practically visible in the air. They're waiting for the typical processional music: *Pachelbel's Canon in D Major*. This is the kind of factoid I picked up by my parents' third respective weddings.

And as I'm thinking it, those familiar notes begin playing from Gracie and the other musicians. The hairs on my arms stand at attention under my sleeves. A prickle of unease washes through me. *Uh-oh.*

"Oh, good—they're starting," Alec says, leaning close as a

man in a black robe walks from a side door to the front of the room.

Not good, I think.

"The faster we get through this, the sooner we get to the open bar," Dumbo says. Tucker gives him a fist bump. Parker turns and glares.

My gut is twisting uncomfortably. Because the officiant doesn't announce that the wedding is off like I hoped he might. He stands there at the front of the room, smiling. His is the face of a guy about to pronounce two people *man and wife*.

There's the smallest chance Amelia would have said her groom's unfaithfulness didn't matter and decided to get married anyway. I don't know many women who would stand for that, though it's a possibility.

But there's a bigger chance that after I left, Douche the Groom tucked tail and ran away without confessing the truth. I should have dragged him into the room myself.

Maybe it's not too late to do just that.

I'm on my feet and heading out of the sanctuary before I can think twice about it.

"Where are you going now?" Alec hisses.

I don't miss the way Parker's head whips around, *Exorcist*-like, her eyes narrowed. I know I'll get an earful later.

But I'm doing the right thing. Whether it's for Amelia's sake or selfish reasons or both, I'm not about to let her marry Douche the Groom.

The last thing I hear before I push out of the room and into the hallway is Dumbo smugly saying, "Told you it was diarrhea."

CHAPTER 2

Amelia

"Your mother would be so proud." Dad's smile caves in at the corners, but he's trying so hard to keep it together.

I wish he'd stop talking about Mom. At the rehearsal dinner last night, it was hard enough. Now, when I have a very strong urge to confess I'd like to call the whole thing off, I can't take the thought of disappointing Mom. Or Dad.

Would Mom be proud?

Because from where I sit at a makeup table in the bride's room, I'm not feeling so sure.

While Dad has missed any sign of my doubts—last night or today or over the past eight months while planning the wedding—Mom wouldn't have. She'd have taken one look at me and *known*.

The same way she knew the moment I walked in the door after the eighth grade boy-girl party where I had my first kiss. And just like then, she would have said, "Spill," and then listened as I told her everything, supporting me no matter what.

With Dad ... I'm not sure why, but I can't be honest. Maybe because he's such a fan of Drew and so excited about me getting married?

On paper, Drew is all the things I thought I wanted. Handsome, hardworking, and steady. No drama but also not boring, despite what my best friend, Morgan, said after meeting him the first time.

She says boring; I say dependable.

Plus, he got Dad's hearty stamp of approval, which means more to me than anything else.

But ... maybe it shouldn't.

"Thanks, Daddy," I say, patting his hand instead of voicing my whispered doubts. Because talking about them won't bring Mom back. Or change anything. It's not like I'm going to cancel the wedding because of my so-cold-they're-frostbitten feet.

Though canceling actually sounds really nice...

I swear, thinking about making Mom proud has me actually considering the words. What if I told my dad I wasn't sure? Would he try to convince me it's just nerves?

Or would he ask why and open the door for a real conversation about why this feels like impending doom rather than the start of a happily ever after?

I'm exhausted from stamping out my feelings of disquiet like so many tiny fires. The doubts have twined with guilt over having doubts, and I've felt a big ball of ick in my stomach for a long while now.

A lot of people might say trust your gut. But usually when I think my gut is saying something, it's just hunger.

Before I can dredge up the courage to ask Dad how he

knew *he* was sure about marrying Mom, he pulls something from his pocket.

"I know you already have something blue, but here's one more. It was your mother's."

He places a silver ring in my palm. I turn it over in my hand, swallowing down my words and a huge lump that's lodged in my throat. I don't remember ever seeing this ring, a simple design with a striking blue stone. It's dark and rich, threaded with a lighter color, almost like the night sky.

"Lapis Lazuli," Dad says, his voice gruff. "With, uh, pyrite mixed in. That's why it's colored like that. She called it her wish-upon-a-star ring."

I love it. The ring, the name—even the stone, which makes me think of *The Vampire Diaries*. I almost crack a joke about being able to walk in the sunlight now, but Dad scoffed at the show and any other teen drama I used to love. He's more of a Sports Center and game show kind of guy. Also, discussing vampires on your wedding day is probably bad luck.

"Does it fit?" Dad asks.

I slide the ring onto the pinky of my right hand. It's an almost perfect fit, though I bet Mom wore it on a different finger. She was petite, barely above five feet. Dad always called her his pocket Patti. I'm only average height, but even in eighth grade, the year Mom died, I was two inches taller than her.

My nose stings, and I fight back tears. Again.

I really wish Dad had kept the ring for another occasion. It could have been a present for high school or college graduation. A random birthday. National Hug Your Daughter Day.

But on this day, my wedding day, the sentimental gift only ratchets up my guilt and the ugly bramble of emotions choking out the light.

"Thank you. This will remind me of her every day," I tell him. Not that I need the ring as a reminder.

"I wish she were here." His normally strong voice is a whisper.

"Me too," I say.

Because if she were here, she would find a way to fix this. To draw out the words I can't seem to voice.

She wouldn't let me walk down that aisle—or any aisle—until I was *sure*.

"You're going to be so happy. Just like we were. Marrying your mother young was the best decision I ever made. You never know how much time you'll have, so—"

"Enjoy every moment," I finish. Dad's philosophy, one he adopted after losing Mom, is pretty much branded into me.

Once again, I try to draw on my own strength to speak. Now, I've got Mom's ring like a talisman. I almost tell him I'm scared. I'm unsure. I think this might be a mistake.

But then I see Dad's wide smile, his crinkled eyes. The head he shaved just for the wedding when I kept insisting it would be better than the wispy combover he's been rocking for years.

My words evaporate as the door opens, and my cousin, Becky, walks in. There's a flash of dark hair in a black tux in the hallway that looks an awful lot like Drew, but I know he's with the guys in their room on the other side of the church. Probably just another guest.

Still—my unsettled feeling grows.

"Hey," Becky says, standing by the door uncertainly.

Dad gives my shoulder a last squeeze. "See you in a few minutes?"

I nod, then watch as he gives Becky a quick kiss on the cheek. Her smile is thin, and she glances down as he whispers something to her. Then he ducks out of the room and I draw in a deep breath, the pressure on my chest easing slightly.

"You look beautiful." Becky sounds wistful, her voice a little wobbly. "Are you doing okay?"

The pressure snaps right back like it was only bungeed away.

"Just feeling the normal nervousness," I say, meeting Becky's eyes in the mirror. "It *is* normal, right?"

"I wouldn't know." For a moment, she sounds bitter. But then she smiles too brightly and says, "But yes—totally normal!"

Grabbing a makeup brush, Becky swipes another layer of bronzer on her cheeks. She's going to look like an Oompa Loompa if she doesn't stop. Her eyes are red. Has she been crying?

I frown. What's there for her to cry about *before* the ceremony? Maybe she's also thinking of her mom, who died a few years before mine. Her dad and my dad supported each other through their losses, though Becky and I have never been close.

That bond between our dads is why Becky wears the official maid of honor title. It's a thing they decided for us—that we'd be involved in each other's weddings this way, even if we aren't really in each other's lives.

It's definitely a title only thing. Becky was barely present during the wedding planning and hasn't even been around most of the morning today. Morgan effectively took over all the big duties, which I'm grateful for. I'd much rather have my best friend helping than Becky.

Maybe if we were closer, I'd ask my cousin if she's okay. But right now, my only job is to warm up my cold feet, kick my nerves to the curb, and get my lace-underwear-clad butt out the door.

"Where's Morgan?" I ask, touching the stone on Mom's ring.

Becky shrugs. "No idea."

My best friend and cousin can't stand each other, which has made all of this more fun with a capital NOPE—it's not fun when your bestie and maid of honor fight like feral cats.

"I thought you were all taking last-minute pictures," I say, and Becky's gaze slips away from mine.

"We were. I had to go to the bathroom. They're probably just finishing up," she says, still going at it with the bronzer.

I stand from the dressing table and walk to the full-length mirror, doing a final assessment. My foundation is even, covering my freckles; my lips are painted a Taylor Swift red; and my eyes are lined without me looking like a raccoon. My hair is halfway pinned up with natural curls spilling over my shoulders.

Perfect. It's all ... perfect.

Then why don't I *feel* perfect?

The urge to run hits me again, and I eye the door leading to the parking lot. So tempting.

But Amelia Davenport Davis doesn't quit things. Or people. Cold feet or nerves or whatever, I *will* walk down the aisle very soon, recite my vows, kiss my groom, and become Amelia Davenport Tilly.

A.k.a. Milly Tilly.

I can't help it. I burst out laughing, bending over to clutch my stomach.

"Careful!" Becky scolds. "You don't want to rip the seams."

My laughter trails off and I turn back to the mirror. "Do you think my dress is too tight?"

I couldn't force myself to do the whole bride diet thing. But I told myself it was fine because I didn't want to get married looking like some skeletal version of myself just because society seems to equate status with skinny. Years down the road, I wouldn't want my kids to be like, "Who's that lady?" when looking at my wedding photos. Drew fell for me *with* my curves, and he'll marry me with my curves.

But no woman wants any part of her popping out of her wedding dress. Or to rip the seams during a bout of maniacal, possibly unhinged, laughter over a terrible last name.

"No! Sorry. You look fine. The dress is perfect," Becky says quickly. Her words sound even less convincing than my own thoughts. "You're perfect. Your marriage will be perfect."

Perfect. That word again. After a lifetime of being followed by the idea of perfection—or maybe chasing after it?—I wouldn't mind trading it in for a little messy reality.

Becky sniffs, turning away to wipe her eyes. Again, what's with all the crying? I don't know what's up with her, but *something* is off. I'm just about to ask when the door bursts open.

Becky jumps, but I'm used to the way Morgan enters every room—like a cyclone hopped up on speed. My best friend is soft and pretty like a peony, but is more of a Venus flytrap.

"The time is at hand," Morgan says with a dramatic flourish and a grin.

The wedding coordinator follows Morgan into the room. With her pouf of white hair, the stopwatch around her neck, and the flask she must think we don't see, the woman feels more like a caricature than an actual person.

I muster up a smile for Morgan. "Hey. I think I'm ready."

My out-loud words are followed in quick succession by silent ones: *I'm not ready. I'll never be ready. I can't do this.*

I press a hand to my throat.

Morgan tilts her head. "You good, Milly?"

With her lips painted an uncharacteristic light pink and her normally wild white-blond hair secured in an updo, Morgan looks like a muted version of herself. I promised her she can take her hair down and go back to her trademark red lips for the reception. For the ceremony, Morgan insisted I be the only one sporting red lipstick for maximum dramatic impact. It looks good, but also like we're both playing dress-up.

"The time is actually past," the church coordinator says. "We're six minutes past schedule."

The woman looks ready to take a ruler to my knuckles. Instead, she frowns down at the stopwatch around her neck. I briefly consider asking if I can have a sip from her flask. Though I've never particularly found much courage in the liquid variety. The effect alcohol has on me is less bravery and more stupidity. I'm a lightweight who goes from stone-cold sober to making impulsive decisions in a flash.

Morgan must see something in my expression—probably a pure shot of panic—because instantly, she's across the room, elbowing Becky out of the way so she can peer more intently into my soul.

"Why do you look like you just got fired instead of like you're about to get married?"

"She's just nervous," Becky says, fluttering around us like some kind of gnat.

Morgan swats her away without sparing her a glance. "What can I do?"

I appreciate that she doesn't just try to reassure me or blow off how I'm feeling.

Instead of answering, since there *is* no answer, I start spouting facts. "Google says that planning a wedding is one of the top most stress-inducing activities on the planet. I mean, aside from actual life-and-death stressors like safety and starvation."

"What have I told you about googling things?" Morgan asks.

"That TikTok is the new Google?"

Morgan rolls her eyes. "No. That you of all people should not be googling. You'll end up in a death spiral. You're supposed to call *me* instead. Now, what's up?"

I twist Mom's ring on my finger. So much smaller than the diamond Drew gave me, which feels like a shiny, weighty anchor.

"Dad gave me this," I say, holding out my hand to show her the ring.

Morgan softens. "Your mom's?"

"Yep."

"Aw, my sweet little Milly. Bring it in." Morgan draws me into a hug, and I giggle. "Shh—there, there. Shut up, boy."

This is a quote from *The Simpsons*, Morgan's favorite show. I never quite understood the appeal, but I know her most-used quotes from it, which include this one and something about being a Viking in your sleep.

Her hug does make me feel better. Sort of. It doesn't take away the weird, sinking feeling, but I don't feel so alone and panicked.

For about five seconds. Then my eyes start to burn, and I have trouble breathing.

Morgan's eyes narrow, and she waves Becky toward the door. "Out."

"You can't kick me out. I'm the maid of honor!"

"Seven minutes past," the wedding coordinator says. We all ignore her.

"Stop trying to pull that trump card like it's anything

more than a title for today," Morgan snaps at Becky. "I need to talk to my *best friend*. Alone. Now."

My cousin, for whatever reason, seems ready to put up a fight, wringing her hands and not moving even an inch away. "I think—"

But before Becky can finish whatever she was going to say, the door bursts open again. Even harder than the dramatic entrance Morgan made minutes ago.

If she was a cyclone on speed, this is a typhoon on bath salts.

The door actually crashes into the wall behind it, making all three of us jump and stare at the two figures entering the room, one of whom isn't coming willingly.

"Drew?"

My fiancé is being dragged by a dark-haired man at least six inches taller and so broad he barely fits through the doorway. When he looks up and our eyes catch, I'm too stunned to speak. I know that face.

Robbie—a man I've met only once but couldn't forget.

Hard to do when you have a great conversation with a stranger, the sparks flew so hard they almost singed the roof off the building, and then the guy heads to the bathroom and … never returns.

Not that I've been harboring bitterness about it for the past year or anything.

Last night when I saw Robbie at the rehearsal dinner and realized he's one of my dad's players, it only left me with more questions.

Like … did Robbie know who I was the whole time we were talking?

Or maybe he *didn't* know, saw my dad come into the restaurant, and then bailed.

If I had to guess, I'd go with the second one. My dad has

always kept me from the teams he coached in a sort of no-crossing-the-streams situation. Dad might not be above murder or maybe just some light mutilation if one of his players so much as touched me. I'm sure he's made this known to them. He's been doing it with every team he's ever coached. It's never bothered me as I'm not into athletes.

Or, I didn't *think* I was. But I liked Robbie. A lot.

Until he ghosted me. I met Drew a few weeks later and, well, did my best not to think about the one who got away.

Now, though, I have *new* questions.

Why is Robbie *here?* And why is he dragging Drew by his jacket?

"Yum," Morgan whispers, clearly not as bothered by the whole fiancé-being-manhandled thing.

I ignore her. "What's going on?" As I step closer, Robbie releases Drew and gives him a light shove my way.

To my surprise, Becky darts over, steadying Drew as he stumbles.

"Oh, good. You're both here," Robbie says, glancing between them.

Both?

Becky is still holding Drew's arms, and they are standing *way* too close together. With the kind of body language that screams this isn't the first time they've been this close.

Or *closer.*

My stomach gives a sudden and violent lurch to the left. Morgan stiffens beside me. Yep, she noticed too. She emits a low growling sound, and I grab her hand. Partly for comfort. And partly to hold her back since we still don't know what's going on here.

Though I'm beginning to think I have a good idea.

Noticing the tension in the room—or maybe hearing Morgan's growl—Becky and Drew jump apart. But it's the guilty expressions on their faces that cement the picture forming in my mind.

Becky and Drew? My fiancé and my cousin?

Okay, who dropped me into my own reality show? I did not sign consent forms for this.

Swallowing, I glance quickly at Robbie, still standing inside the room with his arms crossed and a thunderous look on his face. I still don't know why *he's* here, but he's apparently not going anywhere.

"Your fiancé has something to confess," Robbie says, emphasizing *fiancé* in a way that makes it sound like he's talking about dog poop. The sneer on his lips adds to the effect.

They're nice lips. The night we met I couldn't stop looking at them as we talked. But I really should not be distracted by them right *now*. Not when what he's saying has nausea curling in my gut.

"I'm sorry, but why are you here?" I ask him.

"My question exactly," Drew mutters.

"Because I couldn't stand by and watch—"

Robbie stops himself, taking the smallest step back and looking, for the first time since he barreled into the room, a little unsure.

For a moment, I'm shuttled back to the night we met, when I mentioned losing my mom. *That must have been so hard,* he said, which trumped the simple *I'm sorry* people usually offer up. His dark brown eyes met mine with a tug I felt travel up my spine like I was being unzipped and had stepped out of myself into something new. When he covered my hand with his, brushing his thumb across my palm, I felt the caress everywhere.

Then he left me, I remind myself. I turn back to the situation at hand. One I'm really getting impatient to resolve.

29

"Just say it," I tell Drew. "Whatever this is, *say it*."

His cheeks are red, his eyes apologetic but with a slight edge of anger, reminding me of a kid who's been caught but is still blaming his little brother. Or the family dog.

Drew shoves his hands in his suit pockets and looks at Becky, who bites her lip and stares down at her pink shoes like she's hoping if she clicks them together three times she'll be sent anywhere but this room.

"Why don't we all just calm down," Drew says in a firm voice, clearly meant to placate and soothe.

Which is funny considering no one is really freaking out. Yet.

But his words turn the tension in the room up to the broil setting.

For a man who apparently has been maintaining relationships with multiple women, Drew sure doesn't understand us very well. Anyone with a frontal lobe knows telling women to calm down is the equivalent of waving a whole barrage of red flags at an angry bull. I bristle, feeling my nostrils flare and my lip curl.

Becky stamps her stupid Petal Pink shoe and gives a little, outraged scream. "Calm down?" she screeches.

"Babe—" Drew starts, then swings wide, deer-in-the-headlights eyes toward me when he realizes the confirmation in that one little word.

I sort of wish Drew *were* a deer and in my headlights. I'd happily mow him down.

Actually, maybe I'd swerve to avoid him, let him live his stupid deer life. Because I realize in this moment, as one angle in a lopsided love triangle, that it's not a huge loss.

"So, you two have been …" I trail off, not able to stomach the words.

Neither Drew nor Becky seem inclined to finish my sentence either.

It's Robbie who speaks. "I found them together in some office twenty minutes ago." He clears his throat, looking apologetic but also angry. "Like, *together* together."

"I get the picture," I snap, my face heating.

Am I humiliated? Sure.

Betrayed? Check.

Relieved? Yes. More than any other feeling, this one rises to the top.

Which makes me feel strangely guilty and giddy in almost equal measure.

"It's over," Drew says, not specifying which of us he's talking to.

The man is such a coward. I can see exactly how intentional his vagueness is. It's basically the equivalent of relationship roulette, and he's trying to place bets on both red and black to see which one earns him more.

He probably figured he'd throw those words out and see where things landed. So passive he doesn't have to make the choice himself.

You know what? I can make the choice easy for him.

"I agree," I say calmly. Every head in the room swivels toward me. "It *is* over."

Drew looks stunned and a little hurt, which he has no right to feel. Becky's mouth hangs open, and the church lady frowns at me like she's about to protest about messing up the schedule.

Robbie—well, he looks impressed. One corner of his mouth —which I *still* should not be noticing in this moment—curves up in a way that I can best describe as approval. But also *trouble*.

I turn away from him and that bad-idea smile, facing

Morgan. She looks like she wants to give me a high five, then later tell me *I told you so*. Because she totally *did* tell me so way back at the start of my relationship with Drew. "He's too meh for you," I think were her exact words. My response was that *meh* wasn't a word, and then she and I fought about slang and the devolving of language, and she let me make my choice. My bad one.

Maybe I'll buy her a cake later and have them write "You Told Me So" in red icing, and we can eat the whole thing together while re-watching *New Girl* for the hundredth time.

"Can we talk for a sec, Ames?" Drew steps closer to me, and Robbie crosses the room to stand beside me.

Correction: to tower over me.

I'm not sure who dubbed him my protector, but he's clearly taking on that role. While I should tell him to get lost, I find myself shifting closer. If for no other reason than to use him as a physical barrier. The dude is huge, and will definitely make a good fiancé blocker should I need one.

"Pass." In a quick move, I take off the engagement ring and set it on a table, not wanting to touch him. He opens his big, dumb mouth to ask a question, but I keep going. "Unless you want to tell me how long you've been messing around with my cousin?"

No matter how relieved I am to be walking away from this, my own question makes me feel queasy. I can't think about the two of them together.

The wedding coordinator clears her throat and glances at her stopwatch. "If we're not going to proceed, we really should make an announcement."

"Is that what you want, Ames?" Drew asks. "To end this?"

And I swear, the man looks almost wistful, like he's

hoping I'll say no. I don't get it. He doesn't want to make a decision, but he also doesn't want me to walk away.

I'm not the only one who notices this. Becky makes a strangled sort of shriek but is blocked from coming closer by Morgan. Robbie's low, throaty rumble makes me shiver.

"Becky, I am not your biggest fan right now, believe me," I tell my cousin. "But because you're family, I'll tell you that this is not a man you should waste any of your time on."

"Now hang on." Drew frowns and takes a step closer, reaching for me for some stupid reason. The man is honestly a walking and talking nominee for being naturally selected out of existence.

And then he does something even dumber.

Drew grabs my arm.

He circles his hand around my wrist just as my dad and Uncle Bobby walk in, just as Becky picks up an angel statue off a table and lobs it across the room.

This also happens to be the moment Robbie yanks Drew away from me.

I'm not sure who Becky was aiming for—maybe Drew and me both—but Robbie is the one who takes an angel right to the face.

CHAPTER 3

Van

My ears are ringing. My head throbs. And the chaos breaking out in the room around me only makes it worse.

There's shouting, a crash, and a few outraged screams, like I've been dumped into the set of a *Real Housewives* filming. Minus the housewives.

But I can't say exactly what's unfolding because my eyes are squeezed closed as I breathe through the pain.

It felt like I took a puck to the face with no helmet. Or maybe a boulder. A wrecking ball?

"Here," a soft voice says.

A hand cups the good side of my jaw. Something solid and cold lightly presses against my cheek.

I crack open my eyes, and the first thing I see are red lips, curved in a smile. A blinding white wedding dress. And pale blue irises, like the sky in early spring when there's still frost some mornings.

Amelia wears her emotions like they're a flag unfurled, visible for anyone to see. I remember that about her the night we met—the unguardedness that made me feel like I could be vulnerable too.

Right now, her eyes hold an apology with a side of gratefulness. And if I'm not mistaken, there's a glint there too, telling me she didn't forget the way I ghosted her.

Amelia. In the midst of all this drama, centered around her wedding day, she's checking on *me*. And pressing ice—no, I realize as I finally tear my gaze away from her, a bottle of champagne—to my face.

"Thanks," I say, then wince, because talking doesn't feel so great.

I've been hit in the face more times than I can count. But there's a difference between taking a hit on the ice when I'm prepared for the possibility, with adrenaline and endorphins pumping through me, versus a random blow with whatever hit me.

I glance down. See a small statue on the floor.

Of course—I *would* get knocked in the face by an angel.

Feels like a colossal sign that maybe I should have minded my own business.

But no, I think, glancing at Amelia again, who's watching me while keeping the champagne pressed to my cheek. I would do it all over again.

I start to speak, but Amelia shakes her head. "Shhh," she murmurs, and it doesn't grate the way it might if a normal person shushed me.

It's soothing, and as she lifts her other hand to my hair, running her fingers gently over my scalp, I hold back a groan.

Because if I'm being perfectly honest, I've imagined this exact thing.

Amelia with her hands in my hair, I mean. Not so much the scuffle happening behind us or the cheating groom.

I'm suddenly yanked backwards and away from Amelia. My normally good reflexes are clearly on break, and I land hard on my butt.

"Take your hands off my fiancée!" the groom shouts, looming over me.

This guy.

How did *he* end up with not one but two women hooked on his line?

I glare up at the man whose name I now know is Drew. Which is just *so* perfect. He's a total *Drew*.

"*Former* fiancée," Amelia says, stepping in between us, hands on her hips and eyes blazing.

"Will someone please have the decency to tell me what the hell is going on here?" Coach shouts.

That's Coach. And he's pulled out the rare voice he uses when we're all being stupid on the ice and about to lose a game if we don't pull it together. Everyone in the room goes still. He has that effect.

I finally take in the scene around us. The cheating maid of honor is caught mid-tussle with the other bridesmaid a few feet away. A man with the same round baby face as Coach—his brother, if I had to hazard a guess—seems like he paused in the middle of trying to break up that fight. He's got a bridesmaid in each arm.

The short, white-haired church lady with a stopwatch around her neck takes a sip from a silver flask with a cross on it.

Okay, then.

Coach's gaze lands on me, and his eyes narrow. "This *can't* be good if you're involved, Van."

Great. Appreciate the vote of confidence, Coach.

I know I'm not the guy's favorite, but seriously?!

"It's not him you should be mad at," Amelia says, and Drew's eyes start darting around the room, clearly looking for an escape route.

Amelia holds out her hand to me, the one not still curled around the champagne bottle. Not that I need her help, but I let her pretend like she pulled me to my feet.

Drew surges forward again, and Amelia wields the bottle like a cattle prod, shoving him back.

"It's over. So, don't call me your fiancée and *don't you touch him.*"

She punctuates this by shoving the bottle into his chest again.

This is a side of Amelia I only saw slivers of the night we met. Like when she and I argued over whether rereading a book should count toward your reading goals for the year. She nearly took my head off arguing about keeping your reading tally "pure" with only first-time reads.

Probably the only other person I could argue something like that with is Felix. But our bookworm of a goaltender has no idea I read as much as I do. He's got a massive library at his place, while I mostly stick to ebooks and audio. I definitely never had fighting about books in a restaurant bar with a beautiful woman on my bucket list.

And she's wrong, by the way. Rereads totally count. So do audiobooks—but at least we agreed on that point.

Amelia's grip tightens on the champagne bottle, and I start to worry. Because I get the sneaking suspicion Drew is the kind of guy who would sue for assault if she takes a swing.

I gently pry the bottle from Amelia's fingers.

She glances up at me in surprise, then offers me a small smile before turning a glare back at the idiot posturing in front of her. He puffs up even more seeing Amelia smile at me.

Coach glares at Drew and me in turn, like I hold an equal —or *any*—responsibility for this mess.

"It's just a misunderstanding, sir," Drew says, and I snort. He shoots me a withering look.

"I still don't understand why *you're* here," Coach says, his gaze hard on me.

I've always known I'm not Coach's favorite player on the ice. Maybe off the ice too. Just one of the reasons I ran from Amelia the night we met. It saved me from being chased out with a barstool by her dad.

I get it. I'm too mouthy. I start things. Don't walk away when I should. Play around sometimes when I should be serious. Coach's approval or lack thereof never bothered me.

Until now.

Maybe I should step away from Amelia and walk right out of this room.

But I don't.

"Robbie—or *Van*, I guess," Amelia amends with a quick narrow-eyed glance my way, "is the one who made Drew come in here and confess he's been cheating on me." She winces as she adds, "With Becky."

"Becky?" Coach rears back.

"*My* Becky?" the maybe-brother echoes. Becky's dress is ripped at the shoulder, one strap limply hanging down.

The other bridesmaid looks like she has a small clump of bleached hair in her fist. *Good for her!*

"I didn't mean to, Daddy," Becky says, bursting into dramatic tears.

"It sure didn't look *accidental* when I walked in on the two of you earlier."

Like I said: too mouthy.

Coach blinks rapidly for a few seconds, his gaze bouncing between me, Amelia, Drew, Becky, and Becky's father, whom she's cowering behind. The other bridesmaid is now sharing the flask with the older woman.

"I can't believe this," Coach says, and I feel for the guy. Not as much as I do for Amelia, but it would totally suck to have your niece be the one ruining your daughter's wedding day by sleeping with the groom. "And *you*."

His voice takes on a hard edge when he rounds on Drew. I recognize the look in Coach's eyes. I've never seen this expression on *his* face, but I've seen it plenty of times on the ice. And it means someone's about to get a reckoning.

Before Coach can throw a punch, I push past Amelia and attempt to get between him and a decision he may regret.

And for the second time today, I take a blow to the face. This time, it's Coach's fist.

"Daddy!" Amelia exclaims, stepping forward and curling her hand around my elbow tugging me backward.

He looks dazed, like this moment totally got away from him.

Amelia turns to me. "Are you okay?" She lifts her hands to gently touch my cheeks, both of which have now taken a pounding. I'll have matching black eyes in a few days.

"Are you okay, Van?" Coach asks. "I didn't mean to hit you."

Amelia bristles when her father steps closer to me, shoving me behind her, which is really adorable. She can't be more than five-and-a-half feet, which is almost a solid foot shorter than me. But I like the way she keeps trying to protect me.

39

"He'd be better if you hadn't just hit him in the face, Daddy. The only people in this room deserving of any kind of punch are Drew and Becky. And I'm not even sure *they're* worth it."

Out of nowhere, Becky's dad jumps in. "Now, wait just a minute. Don't drag my little girl through the mud just because you're having wedding-day jitters or whatever this is."

No offense to Coach, but his brother seems about as smart as a bag of rocks. He and Drew are cut from the same cloth, purchased at the store that sells stupid by the yard.

"Maybe you should add another name to your list of punchable people," I mutter.

"It seems so," Amelia says.

Becky peeks around her father's bulky frame. "I really didn't mean to hurt anyone. And *I'm* hurt too. Drew said he loved me."

"Drew said a lot of things," Amelia grumbles.

Coach's face has been growing redder by the second, and he steps closer to Drew. This time, keeping his fists by his sides. "You need to leave. Now."

"But I—"

Coach ignores Drew and stomps over to his brother. "I don't want to hear a single word from you in her defense. There is absolutely none. You've spoiled your daughter since the time she was knee-high, and it's time both of you take responsibility for your actions."

Clearly, some old wounds have been opened. As the two men begin yelling with Drew stepping in the middle, I'm made more aware of the pounding in my head.

I groan, and Amelia turns to face me again.

"I'm so sorry you got dragged into my family drama," she

says, glancing over her shoulder where there's a veritable brawl happening. "Though I guess you did insert yourself."

For a moment, she looks like she's going to ask why, but then the non-cheating bridesmaid steps close, holding out the old woman's flask.

"You might need this. Not too much though since you haven't eaten. Can't have you going all savage on us."

Amelia takes a dainty sip, then wrinkles her nose and coughs as she hands it back. "What *is* that?"

"I think Fireball? Cinnamon whisky." Her friend takes a bigger swig, then turns to me. "Hi, I'm Morgan. Milly's best friend. Single. And not a cheater, for the record."

"Van."

"Also known as Robbie," Amelia says.

Morgan's eyes take on a knowing look. "Robbie as in Restaurant Robbie? The guy who—" She makes an oomph as Amelia elbows her. "Right. Nice to meet you, *Robbie*. Or Van."

Clearly, Amelia has talked about me. I'm dying to know what she said, but this isn't the time to ask.

Amelia lifts a brow. I never knew a single eyebrow could hold so much judgment. "Apparently, he's a man of many names."

Before I can explain myself, Morgan takes Amelia by the shoulders.

"Listen. I can handle things here. Do you want to go?"

"As soon as humanly possible."

"Great," Morgan says, then groans. "Hang on. Neither of us drove to the church."

"I've got a car."

Both women swivel to face me, Morgan with a growing smile, and Amelia looking doubtful.

"Really? You wouldn't mind?"

"Nope." I did drive Tucker and Dumbo, but there are a bunch of guys from the team who could get them home. They'll get over it.

"Van," Morgan says, turning to me, face serious even as her eyes still dance. "Or Robbie. Whatever your name is— you've heard that with great power comes great responsibility?"

I chuckle. "I've seen *Spiderman* a time or two."

"The quote comes from Voltaire," Amelia corrects, reminding me of our long-ago book debate. "Not Marvel."

Again, Morgan glances between us. "Okay, then. We're all familiar with the quote. Good. Van—will you take responsibility for Milly while I make sure they don't set the church on fire?"

I glance behind her, where Drew and Becky are now shouting at each other. Coach and his brother are embroiled in an all-out brawl. I should care more than I do.

Maybe if Coach hadn't thought the worst of me and then accidentally decked me, I'd help him out.

But I'd rather stay with Amelia.

There's a crash as Coach and his brother fall through a coffee table, now rolling around on the floor throwing ineffective punches. It's the worst fight I've ever seen. And that includes the time I saw two players get into it after one licked the other one's face.

"That's our signal." Morgan ushers us toward a door at the back of the room, which appears to lead directly to the parking lot.

"You might want to grab some of my teammates from the sanctuary," I tell Morgan. "They'll keep Coach from hurting someone—or himself."

"Are any of them single?" Morgan asks.

"Plenty."

"Great." She grins, gives Amelia a quick kiss on the cheek, whispers, "Love you, Milly. You're going to get through this."

"Take care of my dad," Amelia says. "And the grandmas. And Aunt Sally."

"Will do. But I'll let your dad beat up Uncle Bobby a bit first, okay?"

"Agreed."

Morgan gives Amelia a quick hug before giving Drew a sharp kick to the shins as she heads out into the hallway.

Amelia snorts, then turns her ice-blue eyes up to me. For someone whose life just imploded and is literally standing among the fallout, she seems way too calm. But it's there in her eyes—a gathering storm.

"Are you sure you don't mind helping me escape?" Amelia asks, and the way she bites her lip has me thinking things I shouldn't be thinking. Not when she's wearing a wedding dress.

And not when there has to be a whole maelstrom of emotions underneath the surprising calm she's wearing now. I hope by the time the storm comes she has someone with her to walk her through.

I wish it could be me.

Unlikely.

Especially not when she's gone from pressing a champagne bottle to my aching face to looking suspicious when she heard Coach call me by a different name.

At some point, I'll explain why I ran out like a coward that night. But first, we need to get out of here.

Especially before Coach sees her leaving with me. I have a

feeling he would *not* approve. Even if I'm just playing the chauffeur.

I force my gaze back up to her eyes. "I always wanted to be someone's getaway car."

When she hesitates, hazarding a gaze toward the chaos behind us, I take her hand. "Come on. I've got you."

CHAPTER 4

Amelia

"Where to?" Robbie asks, the engine of his SUV purring to life with the push of a button.

Some people might be in awe of artificial intelligence or advancements in biotech. Me? I'm forever astounded by starting a car with the press of a finger. Maybe because my dad is of the opinion that cars should be driven into the ground. And since Toyotas never die, my little Camry may outlive me. I certainly don't see a push-button ignition in my near future.

Robbie—or Van?—clears his throat.

"Right. Where to, where to, where to," I mutter, like Dorothy clicking her heels together. As though chanting the words will give me an answer. It doesn't. My brain feels like it's been bleached. "Um, I don't know. I guess I didn't plan my escape very well."

"I think you're doing just fine." He glances over, a wry grin on his lips. "You got out. That's the important part. Keep thinking, and for now, I'll just get us out of here. You know, in case your idiot ex-fiancé tries to chase after you." He puts the car in reverse, then pauses, turning to fully look at me, his dark eyes intense. "Unless … you *want* him to chase after you?"

"If he does, will you run him over?" I deadpan.

"Yes," he says. No hesitation. And a small, pleased smile. A wicked one.

I love it.

I mean, *assuming* we're both kidding. I wouldn't literally commit homicide or ask anyone else to do so over *Drew*. He's totally not worth the jail time.

But I do think there should be laws in place over this kind of thing. Fines. Legal ramifications. A scarlet letter. Just not … vehicular homicide.

Would he *actually* run Drew over?

I study Robbie's—*Van's*—profile as he turns out of the church parking lot, headed west toward the mountains. When we met his head was almost shaved. I even reached up to run my fingers over the rough stubble at one point that night. Now, it's longer and softer. A bit unruly.

It suits him.

He has a wide, square jaw covered with a neatly trimmed beard; a nose that's either been broken a lot or is naturally somewhat crooked; and a scar threading through his eyebrow, extending down near the outside corner of one eye.

And let's not forget the hint of a tattoo peeking out where his shirt's unbuttoned.

It drove me nuts the night we met, and I spent too long trying to figure out what the ink peeking out of his V-neck was.

Now, his suit jacket is in the back, tossed casually like the man dares wrinkles to defy him, and he's unbuttoned the top few buttons of his shirt. I still can't get a good look at the tattoo though.

I realize with a hot flush of shame that I'm staring. Admiring him, if I'm being honest. Then my gaze snags on the swelling in his face. Tomorrow, it will be worse. Guilt pricks me.

He took not one but *two* hits on my account. And he barely knows me.

"Your face." I start to reach out, then drop my hand to my lap in a fist. "Does it hurt?"

He shoots me a quick glance, as though my words or maybe the shift in my tone surprised him. "Nah. I mean, it's a little sore, but no biggie. I get hit all the time. Just usually not by an angel statue and my coach's fist."

He chuckles, a low sound that makes my skin hum like a plucked string.

"I'm sorry," I say with a wince, studying the red mark on his cheek. There's a tiny scrape too, one that might scab over tomorrow. "Sorry about everything."

Van frowns. "None of this was your fault. No apologies from you. It's a rule."

"I didn't realize there were rules for being a runaway bride."

"Oh, absolutely."

"Yeah?" I ask. "Whose rules are they? Is there a list somewhere?"

"The rules are yours to make." He shoots me a quick look and an even quicker smile.

"But *you're* the one who said no apologies is a rule."

"Fine," he concedes. "That's *my* rule. The rest are up to you."

I like this idea. New rules for what will be a new chapter in my life.

Though I'm not at all ready to think about that new chapter too hard. Because there are a whole lot of wayward sections of my old life I have to deal with first. Wedding gifts to return, finding a place to live since I moved in with my dad temporarily, and—*ugh*—finding a new job.

Because a few months ago, I made the ill-fated decision to apply at Drew's company. We don't work in the same department, but the company is small enough I won't be able to avoid him. I can't go back. It was a realization I had the moment I took off his ring.

"Are you comfortable?" Robbie asks. "Do you have enough room?"

"As comfortable as I can be. This thing isn't exactly made for car trips."

I gesture toward my dress, the skirt puffing up around me like spray foam insulation in a crawlspace. The gown is gorgeous if not horribly uncomfortable. My ribs ache from the bodice, which has some serious boning, and is seriously oppressive. It is definitely not a dress meant for car rides. Even in SUVs as spacious—and surprisingly clean—as this one.

I shouldn't have made the assumption that all hockey players would have messy cars that smelled like stank hockey gear. The interior of this car actually smells fantastic. Or maybe that's him?

I manage *not* to lean over and sniff him, though I'd like to know if the clean, masculine scent is him or some kind of hidden Sexy Dude Smell air freshener inside the car.

He notices my not-so-subtle perusal of his vehicle, frowning as he glances around the car. Hopefully he didn't notice me sniffing.

I swallow down a laugh because I cannot believe I'm sitting here in my wedding dress, thinking about how good he *smells*.

"What?" he asks.

"Your car is clean." A stupid thing to say. Especially because it reveals that I expected it not to be.

"I have two," he says with a grin. "My Jeep has all the hockey gear." He pauses. "And all the mud."

Mud? Okay, I guess he's one of those guys who does the whole off-roading thing. And he's also a guy who does the whole two-cars thing. I know Dad's team has reached some kind of superstar level for AHL in the past few years, but maybe I didn't realize how well the Appies were doing. Or maybe Robbie—*Van*—has family money.

I might have gotten along with him from the very moment we met, but I know almost nothing about him. Including his actual name.

"Important question: what should I call you? Robbie or Van?"

"You can call me whatever."

"Should I add that to the rules?" I tease.

"Totally."

"But what would you prefer?"

"Van is what I go by. Almost no one calls me Robbie. Or even knows that's my real name."

Interesting. Because the night we met, he said his name was Robbie. I immediately want to ask who "almost no one" is, but I don't.

"Did you introduce yourself with a different name the night we met because you knew who I was?"

He winces. "No. I had no idea you were Coach's daughter. Not until I saw him with you, put the pieces together, and—"

"Then ran away like a coward?" I suggest cheerfully.

I wait for him to bristle. To bluster and argue the way Drew would at being told he was cowardly.

But Van only chuckles. "That about sums it up. I'm sorry. It was stupid. I should have come back over and dealt with the fallout." He pauses, then glances over. No hint of a smile this time. "I don't think I'm your dad's favorite."

"I *have* heard your name from him before—Van."

His dark brows practically hit his hairline. "Yeah? He's talked about me?"

"No. He uses your name as a curse word. You know, like, he'll stub his toe and yell, *Van it!* Or call things a *Van* shame."

This earns me a laugh, deep and husky. I catch myself grinning, then force my face back to neutral. Nothing should be funny right now. I definitely shouldn't be enjoying myself with some guy right after running from a wedding with another guy.

You make the rules, I remind myself, and it makes me feel slightly better. Because it feels good to laugh right now.

"I was kidding by the way. About my dad using your name as a curse."

Mostly. I mean, Dad doesn't use Van as a curse but I definitely have heard him muttering about Van before. He tries not to bring work home with him, which I think is mostly due to him wanting to keep me disconnected from his hockey guys.

And now ... I'm running away from my wedding with one of the players he likes the least.

"Oh." Van seems relieved. "If you were serious, I'd be a little more worried about having you in my car right now."

"You might still need to be worried."

"Too late. I'm committed to seeing this thing through."

Though most of the conversation is light and teasing, Van's words have a warm bubble of happiness buoying my mood. He makes me feel less alone, like we're partners or a tiny team.

A comfortable silence falls between us as Van heads west, toward the rolling hills at the edge of town, feeding into the Appalachian mountains that surround Harvest Hollow. Something eases in me the farther we get from the church and today's events. I shuffle the skirt of my dress around so I can sink more comfortably into the seat.

"Are you taking me to an isolated spot to murder me?" I ask. "Because my dad would definitely murder you back. And my phone shares my location with Morgan, who is like the Liam Neeson of best friends."

"I have no murderous plans, aside from the one to run over your ex."

My ex. That is going to take some getting used to. Not as much in the emotional sense as the realization that I am now a woman who had a fiancé, almost had a wedding, and now has an ex. It says a lot about how I felt—or *didn't* feel—about Drew that I'm more concerned about the titles and the practical details than the person I lost.

Good freaking riddance.

"So, where are we?"

"This is a route I drive when I need to think," Van says. "Or if I'm in the middle of an audiobook, sometimes I'll just drive and listen. It's pretty."

It's more than pretty. The road loops and winds like a line of cursive written through the hills. It's late spring and the trees are lush and heavy with green. Every so often, we get a perfect view of Harvest Hollow down below, looking quaint and adorable. Which, really, it is. The sky also seems somehow closer up here, the colors richer, even as the sun lowers, casting longer shadows from the trees and hills.

I can almost picture what the sunset must be like—a

whispered outline of gold edging the darkness as the stars blink awake. Then I imagine Van driving this way alone, an audiobook playing over the speakers. The thought makes my chest pinch, and I'm not sure why.

"Do you want to listen to an audiobook now?" I ask.

"Nah. I'm in the middle of a space opera. It would be weird to drop you into the middle of that."

I yawn. "I don't mind."

"You want to nap?" Van asks. "Nothing like a good angry nap when you need one."

"You take angry naps?" I ask.

"Oh, yeah. I also post-game nap, sleepy nap, sad nap— you name it, I'll nap it."

I can't stop a giggle from escaping. This seems to please Van, who offers me a crooked grin.

"Good to know you have a plethora of naps at your disposal. I think I'm too keyed up to sleep."

My blood feels carbonated, a jittery edginess that fizzes through me. It reminds me of the time Morgan and I were up late cramming for exams and I thought it would be a good idea to take one of those six-hour energy drinks.

Spoiler alert: it was *not* a good idea.

I was too wired to focus on studying, then conked out with my face on my notebook. Morgan barely woke me up in time, and I had to sprint to class and take the exam with a spiral notebook mark on my cheek.

Right now, I'm feeling the same effervescence in my blood and am probably about six-degrees of separation from mild— or possibly medium—hysteria.

"You don't have to talk about it, but how are you doing? Today was a lot. And you seem surprisingly okay."

"I might be in temporary denial. I don't know exactly how I'm feeling," I admit. "But definitely not how I'm *supposed* to feel. I don't think? I wish there were some kind of guidebook."

"There probably is," Van says. "But you could write your own with the rules you make up. You told me you're a writer, yeah?"

He remembers. Such a small thing, but it feels bigger. Or maybe I'm attaching meaning to things I shouldn't. Getting attached to a man I hardly know who just so happened to play my hero for the day.

"I write," I hedge.

"Then you're a writer."

"But they're not, like, published things."

Just dreams. Aspirations I haven't quite pinned down yet. A Substack account with about seventy-two followers. Three of whom I suspect are Morgan using different email addresses.

"Can I ask a nosy question? One that's none of my business," Van adds.

"Oh, you're asking for permission now?" I tease. "After basically diving nose-first into my business today?"

"Not gonna apologize."

"I wasn't asking you to. By the way—thank you."

He waves off my thanks. "So, that's a yes to my nosy question?"

I laugh. "Sure."

"What did you see in that guy, anyway? Like, is he your type? The dream guy? Because he just seems so beneath you. No offense."

"Why would that offend me?"

His lips quirk. "Because I implied you have terrible taste."

"Okay, *now* I'm offended." But I'm not really, and Van clearly hears the lightness in my tone.

Which disappears when I start to think about Van's question. What *did* I see in Drew?

I fold my hands in my lap, feeling the absence of my engagement ring like a bruise. But I have Mom's ring, and I twist it on my finger while debating how to answer this.

In the end, I decide this is one topic I'd rather not examine too closely right now. And I definitely don't want to talk about it with Van.

"I plead the fifth."

"This car isn't a courtroom."

"Then I plead temporary insanity."

"Makes more sense," Van says.

Van goes quiet, either a sign of a good listener or a man who's wishing he never got involved with all this. With me. Or maybe he's disappointed I clearly dodged answering his question.

The trees lace their fingers over the road, dipping us in shadows, quieting the buzz under my skin. Slightly. I don't think it's going away anytime soon.

"I'm sorry," I start. "I just—Ow!" I rub my arm where Van just pinched me. *Pinched* me! "What was that for?"

"Whenever you say you're sorry, I'm pinching you. Got it?"

"New rule—I'm banning pinching."

"Impossible to ban. Pinching is a clause under my no-apologies rule."

"Any other clauses I need to know about?"

"I'll let you know," he says.

"At least don't pinch so *hard*." I rub my arm, which has a tiny red splotch now. "I'm going to bruise."

"It wasn't *that* hard," he says. Then his smile drops. "Was it?"

"No," I admit. "I won't bruise. It's fine. Is pinching a

hockey thing? I thought y'all punched each other. Not *pinched* each other."

"It's an *I have three sisters* thing."

"Three? That's … wow." I stare at Van's profile, processing this information. "I think you told me that, but I don't remember. Older or younger?"

"One older. Two younger."

"This must be where this whole protective vibe comes from. I bet you chased off so many boys."

"Too many," he growls, his eyebrows lowering like he's thinking of each and every boy who wronged each and every sister.

I think of him marching Drew into the bride's room, the same expression on his face. I didn't allow myself to think so then, but it's a good look on Van.

I smile. "Well, thanks for extending your services to a non-sister."

"You're Coach's daughter," he says, like it's a given.

Like that's the reason he's here.

Disappointment is a metal vise squeezing my ribs. Or maybe my dress has some kind of tripwire, where if you don't actually get married in it, the bodice becomes like a bear trap, squeezing the life out of you. Especially if you start getting any kind of ideas about a man other than the one you were supposed to marry.

It's stupid to be disappointed. To think Van's actions today had anything to do with *me*.

Just like when he ghosted me at the restaurant, his decisions are about my *dad*.

"Right. My dad is your coach," I say, appointing myself Captain of the Obvious.

"I would have done something anyway," Van says. "I hate cheating. And cheaters."

I want to ask more questions. About his sisters, about why the mention of cheating has his hands curling tightly around the wheel until I fear it might break off in his hands.

But I chicken out.

"Can I borrow your phone?" I ask instead.

"Here."

I think Van's about to hand me his phone, but instead he reaches over, takes my hand, and places it on the steering wheel.

It takes me entirely too long to realize he expects me to steer. That his hands are no longer on the wheel as he lifts his hips and starts digging around for his phone in his back pocket.

"What—no! I can't steer like this!"

Especially not on a winding road. I am not known for my driving prowess. Just ask Dad's exorbitant insurance from my teen years. As if to prove the point, my grip tightens, jerking the wheel a little to the right.

"Just hold the wheel steady," Van says, somehow sounding still unconcerned.

But I am anything but steady. And I *am* concerned. What if a squirrel runs out into the road? Or a deer! Or a bear! I can't run over nature!

"Is your phone in some kind of locked pants-vault?" I say, my voice coming out squeaky and panicked. "You need to take the wheel!"

We're climbing uphill, a nasty curve coming up.

"Nah, I trust you."

The bend in the road is closer. Van isn't even slowing yet. I stomp on an imaginary brake.

"But you shouldn't! You barely know me! *I* don't trust me!"

I practically shriek this last part.

"You've got this," he says with far more confidence than I deserve.

He won't think this when I wrap his shiny SUV around a pine tree.

"And I've got you." Van locates his phone and tosses it in my lap, taking control of the car once more. My palm is sweaty when I peel it off the wheel. But I didn't kill us, so ... celebrate the small victories?

Another un-wedding rule I can add to the list: always celebrate the little things.

"Nice steering," he says.

"Bad driving," I snap back. He only grins. "What's your passcode?" I ask, trying not to sound like I'm still breathing heavily from my anxiety about steering his car.

"Never give this out," he warns.

I scoff. "Who would I possibly give it to?"

"Anyone. But especially your dad. Or my teammates."

"Why? What's on here? Loads of blackmail material?" I realize after I ask that maybe I don't want to know.

Van gives me a sidelong glance. "Nah. I just don't want them all up in my business. *You* can look through whatever you want."

I would love to snoop to my nosy heart's content. Especially considering Drew *never* let me look at his phone.

Now, of course, I know why he didn't. I'd like to find his phone and smash it with a sledgehammer. Then run over it. Then shove it down a garbage disposal. I try not to think at all about Becky. Because that betrayal, even if she and I weren't ever very close, cuts deeper. You don't do that to family.

"The passcode is ten-ten-ten." Van's voice shakes me free of a dark mental path and I'm glad.

"October tenth, 2010?" I ask.

"Nah," Van says with a smirk. "It's perfect tens. Like me."

"Oh my *gosh*," I say. "Are you for real right now?"

He totally is. I can tell by the way he's grinning unapologetically. Smugly.

Okay, so Van has a mad case of overconfidence. He scores a perfect ten on the self-esteem scale. And, okay, fine— maybe close to ten in terms of looks. But he's edging pretty far into cocky territory.

Today at least, I don't mind overly confident. Or even cocky.

Maybe I just don't mind *Van*. Whether it's his protectiveness or the unapologetic way he barged into someone else's business just to do the right thing or maybe it's the allure of the tiny bit of ink creeping out of his shirt collar, I like him. I feel comfortable and safe around him, like we've known each other for years.

A strange reality, but there it is.

"You've got a whole lot of missed texts," I tell him. "What's the Dream Team?"

"Ah," he says. "That's a group text with some of the guys. A reporter called our line that once and it stuck."

"Your *line?*"

He laughs. "You really don't know hockey, huh—even with your dad as a coach?"

"I really don't know hockey."

"A line is the guys you're usually out on the ice with. Technically, my line is only offense with Logan and Eli, but the Dream Team is all the guys who start: Alec and Nathan on defense and Felix in the goal. We also just added two new guys to the thread: Camden and Wyatt."

"Okay, well, they're still blowing up your phone." Texts are coming through even while the phone's in my hand. Too fast for me to even read them.

Though I'd like to.

"Can you mute the conversation? They won't stop anytime soon."

I do, catching only a glimpse of texts asking Van if he ran off with the bride and if he thinks this will get him his starting spot back. Did he lose his starting spot? Another question I wonder but don't ask.

I tap in Morgan's number, one of the only ones I've got memorized. Before I call my dad, I need some intel. I can only hope she answers. I never pick up when it's numbers I don't know. Despite putting myself on a Do Not Call list, I get daily calls asking me to donate to all kinds of things or scammers telling me I have a computer virus and need to download their software.

"Hello?" she says, sounding slightly breathless.

"It's me. I'm on Van's phone."

"Oh, hey, Julia."

I wrinkle my nose. "Julia? It's me, Amelia."

"I meant Julia Roberts, a la *Runaway Bride*," Morgan says. "Too soon?"

I laugh. "No. It's fine. The shoe fits, I guess."

I actually prefer thinking about this situation as something active I did—running away—than the passive idea of me being a jilted bride.

"How are things? I wanted to call my dad but thought I'd check in with you first to see how things are."

Morgan whistles. "You missed quite a show."

"What kind of show?" I glance at Van, then say, "Hang on. Putting you on speaker. What happened?"

"Basically, a team of hot hockey players in suits stormed into the bride's room, pulled your dad off Uncle Bobby, then proceeded to both cause chaos and also create order. They booted Bobby, Becky, and Drew right out of the church, then one of them—the pretty one—"

Van snorts. "That would be Alec."

"Yeah, him. Alec went and made an announcement in the church about it. He's very professional and well-spoken in addition to being pretty. Then the woman who runs all the social media stuff—"

"Parker," Van supplies.

"Yeah—Parker. She helped your dad deal with all the aftermath. Basically, the team saved the day. It was awesome. Your dad is loved."

My dad is loved. Right. That's why they were helping, not because they know or care about *me*.

Dad is also probably the reason Van is still driving aimlessly through the darkness. Not because of *me*.

That thought makes me a little sad, and so I push it away. I've got enough sad for a few dozen Amelias.

In the grand scheme of things, Van being here for my dad —not me—shouldn't even be on a top ten list of terrible things to be upset about today. And yet it's this I fixate on, my thoughts circling around and around it like a dirty drain.

"So, you think I should call him?" I ask.

"Honestly," Morgan says slowly, "I wouldn't right now. I mean text him you're okay, and I can tell him in person. But he's still breaking stuff."

"My dad is breaking stuff?"

"Like a toddler hopped up on juice boxes being told it's time to leave Chuck E. Cheese." She pauses. "He threw a chair through a window."

"Of the *church?*"

"Of the church. At least it wasn't stained glass," Morgan adds. "It'll cost less to replace. Is this kind of thing covered when you book a wedding?"

"Doubtful," I say. "I still can't believe this. I've never even seen him get that mad coming home after losing a game."

"He does get mad," Van says. "But he's never thrown a chair through a window. I think this situation warrants it."

"Take me off speaker for a sec," Morgan says, and I comply, putting the phone back up to my ear.

"Just me now. What is it?"

"I have an idea," Morgan says. "I just want you to think about it before you say no."

"Your caveat already makes me want to say no."

She ignores this. "You've got the reservations all set up for the honeymoon, right?"

"Ugh, don't remind me. More money lost." Drew and I split it half and half. He did most of the planning for our Florida trip, and then we traded off paying for reservations. Dollar signs dance like sugar plums through my head and leave me a little lightheaded.

"You should go," Morgan says.

I almost drop the phone. "What?" I *hiss*. I glance over at Van, who's trying very hard to pretend like he's not listening. And failing.

"I would go with you, but you know how my work is this time of year."

Morgan does something with accounting and right now is a particularly busy season. Honestly, it seems like *all* the seasons are busy for her. I wish right now she had some normal job that would let her take a last-minute trip with her best friend whose world just crashed.

Oh. My. Gosh. My world totally just crashed, didn't it?

It feels like someone just gave my corset strings a vicious yank.

Morgan continues. "Going alone would be a chance to, I don't know, come to grips with things. Make your plans for the future. Or the opposite: drink a thousand piña coladas with absolutely zero guilt and zero thought to the future."

I can see the allure. There's a tug of desire at the idea of escaping, for sure. Especially right now, when Van's large SUV feels like a tiny clown car and the bodice of my dress just keeps tightening as Morgan keeps talking.

Suddenly I remember Becky's comment about splitting my seams and there's a sharp pain in my abdomen.

"Say something," Morgan urges.

"I don't know."

Going on the honeymoon trip Drew and I—okay, mostly Drew—planned … *alone?*

While there are plenty of introverted people in the world who might love the idea of a solo vacation, the idea of even having dinner alone makes me break out in metaphorical hives. My circle might be small, but I like being around people.

Plus, it would feel like a slap-in-the-face reminder of being rejected by Drew. Being glad it's over between us doesn't take the edge off the humiliation of how it happened.

"You could always ask Restaurant Robbie to go with you," Morgan suggests, her voice sounding sly. "He certainly seemed keen on helping out earlier. Almost like he *wanted* to go with you."

"That was different—he was just—I mean. No. That's one thing. This would be … another."

My face flushes. Not just my face—my neck and my chest too. I lean forward, yanking the temperature dial on my side of the car down. Van frowns and adjusts the vents to be blowing more in my direction. The tiny, thoughtful gesture has me biting the inside of my cheek.

"Suit yourself. But if it were me? I'd be asking that hunk of man to be my plus-one. I mean, the team has a break now, right? That's why you and your dad picked this date—to work around your dad's schedule?"

"Yeah, but … I don't know."

Dad actually put pressure on the team owner for this mini-break in hockey stuff before the playoffs. It served a dual purpose: leaving him time to enjoy my wedding but also giving the guys a much-needed break right before the last few games and then playoffs. Apparently, the team's social media success means a lot of extra events on top of regular season games, and more than once, Dad has come home grumbling about them being overworked and overscheduled.

"My ticket isn't until tomorrow," I say.

"Get them to switch it. You can get out tonight. There's one more flight leaving in three hours. You can make that."

"I can't pay to change the ticket," I admit, though Morgan already knows my financial situation, which is categorically not great.

"I'll happily help with anything. Call me. I'll charge it to my card and you can pay me back. *Do not argue*," she orders in a sharp voice as I start to protest. "I'll help if you need it, and you've got enough to cover food, drinks, tips, whatever. Everything else is reserved and paid for, right?"

She knows it is. Because she knows too much about me. "You've really thought this through," I say dryly.

"I'm not going to push you," Morgan says.

I laugh, and it sounds just slightly tinged with hysteria. "Isn't that exactly what you're doing—pushing me? It's kind of your trademark."

"Look. I'm morally opposed to the idea of using another person as a rebound," she says. "So, it's not like I'm saying you need to go get wild with the Appies' resident bad boy. But I think you'd be safer with him. And maybe have a better time than you would by yourself. I don't like thinking of you alone. Van definitely seems like he'd bring the party. He'd keep you from wallowing, that's for sure. What have you got to lose by asking?"

Nothing. I've already lost it all.

"I'll meet you on the way to the airport. I'll send a text to this number telling you where." Morgan hangs up.

I drop Van's phone back in the cupholder. He glances over, but I can't look at him. How must I look right now? I'm sure my hair is falling out of its careful updo. My dress takes up half the car.

I'm suddenly aware of the garter, cutting into my upper thigh.

I hate the garter tradition and tried to talk Drew out of it, but he has a bunch of friends who think the garter toss is the best moment of any wedding. He joked that they were training for it like some kind of Olympic event. I'm sure it would have devolved into a drunken wrestling match.

Hoisting my skirt up, I manage to wrangle an arm inside without flashing my underwear to Van. "Can you roll down the windows?" I ask.

"Um, yeah. Are you sure you're okay?"

"No. But I will be." I yank the garter down my leg. I might end up with a little fabric burn.

Worth it.

The wind whips my hair around my face as I line the garter up on my finger like I'm shooting rubber bands at someone across the elementary school lunch table. This doesn't count as littering, right?

Who cares, I tell myself. Some squirrel will make it into a very nice nest.

I aim for the woods and let the garter fly.

It immediately gets sucked right back into the open back

window like some kind of bad boomerang. I twist around but can't see where it went.

Does this mean Van technically won the garter toss?

I start to laugh. What starts as a little giggle erupts into a hearty guffaw, awkward and loud. Van keeps shooting me glances like he's fully expecting my head to start spinning around, *Exorcist*-style. Wouldn't be all that surprising.

I feel a little possessed. All the fizzy bubbles in my blood have been shaken, and I can feel the pressure on my figurative cork.

"Can I do anything?" Van asks.

The question is sweet, and cuts right through my freak-out. I think about what Morgan suggested—almost demanded. Could I ask Van? The idea feels preposterous. So stupid.

He wouldn't want to go.

Would he?

Would I want to spend the next four days with a man I barely know on the honeymoon I was supposed to take with a man I thought I knew?

Yes, I think, glancing over at Van.

He makes me feel safe. It's like I've known him for years, even though we're practically strangers. I trust him. And even though I shouldn't have any kind of even mild feelings of attraction toward another man today of all days, I do. That's probably a reason not to have Van go.

But I can't ignore the pull toward him. We could just be friends. Totally. Friends who are taking a supposed-to-be honeymoon together. It could be totally fine and platonic.

And really, really fun.

When Van reaches across to touch my hand, wild abandon takes over.

"How would you like an all-expenses-paid tropical vacation—with me?"

CHAPTER 5

Van

"You want me to go with you?" I ask, not sure I heard her correctly. I couldn't have. "On your …"

I swallow the word *honeymoon* rather than say it.

"I mean, not like *that*. You're not just a replacement groom or something. Obviously."

Her hands disappear as she twists them into the fabric of her dress, swallowed up in soft white. I watch as she starts to slump, her smile falling.

Up until a few minutes ago, Amelia was holding it together pretty well, all things considered. Now, she's like a sheet of ice over the top of a pond, spiderwebbed with cracks. I'm afraid any word I say might break the whole surface. So I shut up.

"Just as, like, a vacation. One I planned with someone else," she mutters, almost an afterthought. "But it could be fun, right—a free beach trip? I know the team has a few days off. We'll be back Wednesday. It's barely four days."

The smile she turns my way is a little off. As in, paired with the too-bright eyes, she looks a little … feral.

"So, what do you think—want to extend this little trip all the way to Florida?"

Warning bells go off in my mind.

Given all that's happened today, falling apart is totally to be expected. I've been surprised how calm she's been. How poised. How *normal*. Then she got off the phone with her friend, attempted to toss her garter out the window, and now asked me to go on a trip she planned with her ex-fiancé.

It's a total trick question. A trap. The kind of invitation with no right answer. A quiz designed to make you fail. The song of a siren perched up on a rock, leading a ship and its men toward doom and ruin.

This particular siren has a vulnerable look in her blue eyes and about a hundred yards of white fabric bunched up around her as she blinks over at me, waiting for my answer. She looks like a wounded marshmallow.

But, like, a really *attractive* wounded marshmallow. One I definitely shouldn't eat.

Or go on vacation with.

Amelia is beautiful. *Hot*, really, though I don't typically look at women in their wedding dresses and think about their hotness.

Actually, maybe *hot* doesn't quite work. It's a descriptor based solely on physical attributes.

But if we are talking about looks, Amelia is, objectively speaking, hot.

Her hair is the color of the local honey I bought at the farmer's market while doing a charity event with the team. Amber blond—a deep, rich color. Her eyes are an icy blue—

piercing—but despite the cool color, the expression there is soft and warm. Not cold. Even back at the church in the middle of everything, I noticed the way her eyes stayed *kind*.

It's the way her kindness and whatever else shines through her physical beauty that makes her offer *so* tempting.

Because when I look at Amelia, I see *more*. I *feel* more.

More than what I usually feel when I'm around a hot woman.

More than I've wanted to have with another woman.

More, more, more.

The night we met, I remember feeling like I could talk to her for hours. Maybe I would have if her dad hadn't shown up. I definitely would have asked her out.

Amelia is fun. Spunky. Sweet. Open and honest in a way not many people seem to be these days. The way I wish I could be. She's the kind of woman my sisters would love. I mean, they'd love for me to settle down, *period*, but only with someone who earned a stamp of approval from all three of them, which is a near impossibility since they're so different.

Yet somehow, I know Amelia would immediately have all three sisters' endorsement.

Actually, I have a sort of half endorsement from them already.

The night Amelia and I met, I sent a message to our sibling group text. A simple: *I met someone.*

But since I never talk to them about dating, this was an event. I barely told them anything about her, not even her name, so it was a little easier to quell their excitement when later I had to text them that it wasn't going to work out. For months after, they hounded me about the woman from the restaurant who got away, which only made it harder for me to forget Amelia.

None of these thoughts should be crossing my mind. Not

when we're barely an hour past the moment she would have said "I do" to some other guy.

In short, Amelia is not someone I should be taking any kind of overnight vacation with. Not with her fragile emotional state.

And not with how much I enjoy her company.

Definitely not with the low hum of attraction inappropriately buzzing along my skin.

Oh, and let's not forget the kicker: she's Coach's daughter.

He would destroy me if I made a move on Amelia. Maybe even for thinking about her being hot. He'd murder me, then have my body dragged behind the zamboni at The Summit as a cautionary tale.

That's if my teammates didn't kill me first. I think even Parker might advocate for my murder. And then find a way to plan social media content around it.

All things considered, the fact that Coach is her dad takes Amelia's offer from *probably a bad idea* to *run far away and run fast*.

I lift a hand from the wheel to scratch at my stubble. How can I let her down easy—without hurting her feelings or making her feel rejected?

Or worse, unwanted?

Especially when that's the opposite of the problem I'm having here. I want to go too much.

"I probably shouldn't. I mean, I can't."

Any pretense of an excuse zips right out of my brain. Leaving me to sound like a first-class jerk. I think even the dog ate my homework would have sounded better than just *I can't*. Full stop.

"No problem," Amelia says quickly, *too* quickly, waving a

hand. "Kind of a silly idea. Morgan suggested it. Just so I wouldn't be ..."

Alone. She doesn't say the word out loud, but she doesn't have to. It's right there between us, making me feel like the scum of the earth for saying no.

Amelia just found out her fiancé was cheating with her cousin. Now all she wants is to *not* take their intended honeymoon by herself.

I drop my hand to my chest, which feels tight at the thought.

Coach's daughter, I remind myself. *On the heels of an epic breakup.*

Coach's daughter. Whom you're absurdly attracted to.

Amelia is like a bad idea sandwich. Or no—a bad idea *buffet*.

Nope, nope, and more nope.

Amelia struggles with her dress, finally managing to shove enough of it up out of the way to release her feet. She puts them up on the dash. "Is this okay? My toes on your nice car?"

I glance over. Normally, I don't love people messing with my stuff. Putting their hands—much less their feet—on my gear, my place, my car. But for some reason, I don't mind Amelia's small feet with their light pink toenails on my dash. I'm not, like, a foot guy or anything, but her toes are cute.

"It's fine."

I reach a stop sign at the bottom of the hill. We're at the end of my thinking and audiobook route. Instead, I ask, "If you're going on your trip, should I drive you to the airport? Do you have bags packed somewhere?"

"Morgan has them. But I could always buy new stuff if I need to. I have Drew's credit card. Would it be bad to max it out?"

"He'd deserve it if you did. And then some."

"I'll think of some more creative form of justice," she says, making me smile. "I just need time."

"Let me know if you need help. I'll happily help you deliver creative justice."

Ameila tilts her head back and laughs. It's tinged with a little bit of hysteria. "Good to know. Do your services extend past getaway driver and creative justice wielder?"

"You'll never know the extent of my skills." I say it in an over-the-top flirty way. Trying to keep things light and teasing.

"Wow," she says dryly. "Do these kinds of lines work on women?"

"Typically, I don't need lines."

It's true. But I'm leaning into this a little harder than necessary. Am I trying to show off or scare her off? Unsure.

"You do know that's gross, right?" She tilts her head toward me, toes curling a little on the dash.

"You do know I'm kidding, right?" I ask.

She arches an eyebrow. It's cute. "Are you? Because I heard you're the bad boy of the Appies."

"Who told you that?" I feign shock even though I'm very aware of the reputation I've earned—no, more like *cultivated* —on my team. It's not really true, especially considering some of the real bad boys in professional sports, but I lean into the label anyway.

It's an easy recipe: keep all talk to surface-level stuff, act like you don't really care about anything, and flirt with any woman who breathes. Place in the oven at 350 for an hour, and you've baked yourself a bad boy.

"A reputable source." She pauses. "Is it true?"

"Eh. Not exactly. I guess it depends on what you mean by bad boy."

72

Something about Amelia losing respect for me doesn't sit right. I don't love the look she's giving me now. Like she believes whatever she's heard, and it really *does* bother her.

Given the way her day turned out, I suddenly want to dispel any notion she has of me being a bad guy. I'm for sure nothing like Drew and don't want to get lumped in with his kind.

"I mean, maybe *comparatively* I guess I could be considered a bad boy. Only because we've got some legit Boy Scouts on the team."

The Appies is a different kind of organization. I've played for a handful of teams, and I could feel something new the first time I walked into the Appies' locker room. The guys and the whole organization, really, isn't like anything else I've known. People talk about teams forming a brotherhood, but often it's just talk. A bullet point on a press release.

With the Appies, it's the framework underpinning the whole group and the reason why so many guys don't want to get called up to our affiliate team and are happy to sign contracts here long-term.

I mean, sure—the money's better than most minor league teams too. That doesn't hurt. But there's money elsewhere. We stay for the team.

I'm not sure how or why or when the Appies became this way. The vibe definitely doesn't trickle down from Larry Jensen, the owner. Total douchey dudebro who sees things—and people—in terms of dollar signs. Which we earn him plenty of.

Maybe the vibe comes from the players or the other staff or just the right combination of personalities. Coach is a big part of it. The assistant coaches too, who take their cues from him.

Then there's Parker, whose social media strategy crafted

an image that maybe in turn crafted us into something differ-ent. Something bigger. Better. She's a good influence and adds her own happy brand of sunshine to any room she walks in.

Unless any of us are out of line, and then the Boss comes out.

If I happen to embrace being the bad boy of the Appies, it's just an easy fit. Ever since I was a kid, I was the one most likely to be sent to the principal's office. For talking out of turn or talking back or just talking too much. Maybe for the odd prank here and there, but what kid hasn't put plastic wrap over a toilet seat or rigged a bucket of water over a doorway?

Until now with Amelia, I've never really minded the label. A bad boy on our team is still better than the best behaved player anywhere else. Plus, I honestly follow the same sort of rules the guys and I set out for each other, which includes respecting women. I just happen to have dated a lot of women. Respectfully.

"And you're not a Boy Scout?" she teases, but I can hear the question underneath her words. "Why the bad boy label then? Is it the tattoos?"

"It's probably because I run my mouth a lot."

She gasps dramatically. "You?"

"And … I've dated a lot," I admit.

"Ah." One syllable. Then she glances away from me.

"I won't get serious unless I find someone I want to be serious about." *Someone like you*, I think. Definitely not the time to mention how I thought this the night I met Amelia. "But I'm not, like, some kind of serial player. I don't, like, date and dash."

She snorts, but a tiny smile returns. "Never heard that one before."

"I just made it up. But it's true." I pause. "I don't want to give you the wrong idea about me."

"You don't have to explain."

But I *want* to. "I'm not a bad guy. I wouldn't be here if I were."

"I know." Her voice is soft, barely more than a whisper. Then she reaches over and brushes her fingertips across my arm.

Even with my cotton shirt between us, her touch hits me like an electric current, a jolt zipping up my arm and making goose bumps rise on my skin.

"Thank you for being my getaway driver," she says.

When she starts to lift her hand away, I cover it with my big one, holding her there. I like the way it feels, having her small hand wrapped in mine.

"Look—what you've been through today is really hard. Not everyone would sail through it unscathed. But I can already tell that you can. You will. You *are*. You're going to make it out just fine."

"Yeah?" she asks, glancing over at me. "You think?"

"I *know*," I tell her, reluctantly removing my hand and putting it back on the wheel.

She gives my arm a last squeeze before curling her hands back in her lap. I drag my fingers through my hair, suddenly feeling hot.

"Whatever, Mills," I say. "It's not a big deal."

"It is, though. Everything you did for me today—it means a lot. Most people wouldn't do this for a stranger."

Amelia doesn't feel like a stranger to me. And I'm not sure what to make of that. Or why it bugs me to hear her say it.

"Wait," she says, turning to face me. "Did you just give me a nickname? You called me Mills."

I think back. "So I did." It just kind of slipped out. But I like it. "Is that okay? You already have a bunch of nicknames."

"New rules, new nickname." She grins over at me. "Mills is great. Do you have any other names or nicknames I should know about? Besides Robbie and Van."

"The guys sometimes call me Vanity."

This makes her cackle. "I can see why."

I reach over like I'm about to pinch her again, and she swats my hand away. "Better than Ego, which is what they call Alec. He's way too pretty for his own good. Also, I'm not vain. Just … confident."

"Right. That's what we're calling it these days. Where does Van come from?"

"My full name is Robert Chaplain Van de Kamp."

"That sounds very fancy. Is your family …" She trails off, and I can almost see her wrestling with how to ask politely if my family is as snooty as it sounds.

"Are they filthy rich snobs?" I suggest.

She laughs. "Yes, that."

"Some of the Van de Kamps are big players in oil and gas. There's a company in Houston, but my branch of the family is only loosely tied to it."

"How does your oil and gas family feel about you playing hockey?"

"My sisters are supportive," I say. "And I don't really care about what my parents—or their spouses of the month think."

I can tell she wants to ask more questions, and I'm relieved when she doesn't. Talking about my parents' many marriages would definitely ruin the mood. Mine, anyway.

"So, we're meeting up with Morgan to get your bags, and then I'll take you to the airport?"

"I guess that's the plan." Amelia deflates a little. "But Van —you don't need to drive me. I can get an Uber or … pick up my car." She pauses, drops her gaze to her lap. "I think it might be decorated. You know with *Just Married* in the windows and stuff. That will be fun."

She laughs but doesn't sound amused.

"I can see it now—me pulling up to the airport in that and getting out in my wedding dress. Alone."

I hate that idea. And the way she seems to have deflated, even though I can tell she's trying to hide it.

"I'll take you to the airport," I tell her, trying to keep my voice both firm but light. "I'm seeing this through. Yeah?"

Amelia nods quickly, but she doesn't lift her head. Still sad. I want to distract her. To drag her out of whatever thought dungeon she's locked herself up in. My stomach rumbling gives me an idea.

"What's your getaway meal going to be?"

"Huh?" Finally, she lifts her chin, looking over at me with wide eyes.

"It's another rule. You get to pick a getaway meal. The opposite kind of food from wedding food. Like … ribs. Or wings."

"So far, you're making all the rules."

"They're good rules. And feel free to add your own any time. So, what'll it be?"

Amelia huffs a laugh, looking at all the fabric bunched in her lap. "Food sounds …"

I wait, feeling like my heart is beating in my throat. It's a dumb idea. But no one's ever accused me of having brilliant ones. I'm winging it here.

"It sounds great," Amelia finally says, grinning. "And I want pizza rolls. With marinara and ranch. And a soft serve cone from McDonald's—the kind with the hard chocolate shell. Do they still make those?"

"Only one way to find out. Let's go see about those dipped cones."

———

Thirty minutes later, my previously pristine car smells like garlic and pizza grease. Normally, my eye would be twitching. I don't usually even eat in this car. But there was something so satisfying about watching Mills dig in, tearing into a pepperoni roll with the ferocity of a starving lion. And then devouring a dipped cone, which it turns out is still on the McDonald's menu. They're shockingly good, if a little messy.

"There she is," Amelia says, pointing.

I recognize her friend with the wild blond hair, standing by a small hatchback and waving animatedly. I'm barely parked when Amelia hops out and the two hurl themselves into a hug that almost looks painful.

I wonder why Morgan's not going with Amelia on the trip. She must have some valid reason—work or something else. Because she definitely seems like a committed friend.

I fiddle with the radio, stealing quick glances but trying not to be too nosy. Even though in reality I'm basically like a teenage girl when it comes to other people's business.

Both women turn, looking my way. Are they talking about me? I lift a hand, and Amelia waves back, then shakes her head vehemently at something Morgan says before they hug one more time. When Morgan opens the back of her car, starting to unload Amelia's bags, I hop out.

"I've got these." I grab the two rolling bags, placing them in the back of my SUV. Amelia hugs Morgan one last time, sniffling, and then stuffs herself and the wedding dress back in the front. When I close the back hatch, I find Morgan standing there, arms crossed.

"Hey," I say a little uneasily.

She narrows her eyes and lowers her voice. "Thanks for taking her to the airport."

The most unthankful sounding thank-you I've ever heard. In fact, she sounds suspicious. She doesn't give me time to respond before she jumps back in.

"But *why* are you doing it? Why did you do any of this—forcing Drew to own up, driving Milly around, taking her to the airport? You barely know her."

I don't really have an answer for this. I mean, at the start, I was just thinking about making sure Douche the Groom didn't get away with cheating.

Then, I was concerned because I didn't want to see Coach's daughter marrying a guy like that.

I became the getaway driver because I had a car. And maybe also because I wanted to.

Now … it's more personal. But I can't really explain *why* I feel this connection with Amelia. Probably because I don't understand it myself.

What's more—I don't really *want* to explain it or examine it too closely. Today is a very go-with-the-flow kind of day. And this flow is taking me and the runaway bride to the airport.

"It's the right thing to do," I say, scratching my cheek. This answer earns me a suspicious look. "Plus, I respect Coach. Which means, by extension, his daughter falls under my protection. Why all the questions? Weren't you the one who told Amelia I should go with her on her honeymoon?"

"That doesn't mean I trust you."

I chuckle. "Okay. You just want me to take a trip with her."

"She said you said no."

"I … did."

Her gaze is assessing. And frankly, a little terrifying. So is the way her red lips peel back in a smile. "But you're thinking about it."

I glance toward the front seat. Amelia is twisted in her seat, watching us through the back window. I offer her a shrug. Glancing at Morgan, Amelia rolls her eyes and turns back around.

"Look," Morgan says, lowering her voice. "I'm just concerned about her. She seems okay right now, but that's what worries me. And I'm afraid if she goes alone, when she cracks, no one will be there to help pick up the pieces."

"So, you don't trust me, but you also want me to be that person?"

She purses her lips. "If I could, I'd go. But I can't leave work. And I'm going to do my best to take care of all the un-fun stuff while she's gone, so when she comes back, there will be less for her to do. It'll be like the wedding never almost happened." She pauses and purses her lips. "You stepped in when a lot of guys would have walked away."

"Thanks."

"Also, you're the only one I can think of."

"I take back the thanks."

"I don't need it. I only need your assurance Amelia will be okay—*if* you change your mind and decide to go."

"I won't."

"Okay." She definitely doesn't believe me.

Honestly, I'm not sure *I* believe me. I remember Amelia's face when she tried to toss her garter out the window. The wide eyes and the slight shake in her hands. I think of how she keeps twisting the blue ring on her finger and burying her hands in her dress.

Then I try to imagine leaving her alone in front of the airport.

"But … if I *did* happen to go, she'd be safe with me."

The five seconds—I count them—while Morgan watches me with cool gray eyes stretch long, making my fight or flight instincts pick up. I remember Amelia comparing Morgan to Liam Neeson earlier.

Finally, she nods. "Cool. Because I'd hate to have to hunt you down and make you suffer."

"You and Coach both," I mutter.

We stand there, both nodding at each other for a few seconds before I say, "Cool. So, um, can I go?"

Morgan steps back, waving her hand in a go ahead motion. "Yep."

A tension I didn't realize I've been holding releases with a slow exhale. Maybe too soon, as her dismissive wave turns into dragging her thumb across her neck in a terrifying warning.

Just as I'm about to open up the door, she says, "Oh, and keep her away from alcohol."

"She's a lightweight?"

Morgan laughs. "More than a lightweight. Treat her like a Gremlin. Except it's not feeding after midnight; it's anything more than a few sips of alcohol."

"A Gremlin?" I frown, sure I'm missing a reference.

"Dude—I'm a little concerned if you don't know basic pop culture references."

"I'll google it," I tell her, then hop in the car.

"What are you googling?" Amelia eyes me curiously.

"Gremlins?"

"Classic movie," Amelia says through a yawn. "Don't get them wet or feed them after midnight."

"Apparently," I mutter, wondering how I'm the only one

who doesn't have an awareness of *Gremlins*.

Amelia dozes off on the way to the airport while my mind won't stop racing, weighing the merits of going with her against the merits of not ticking off my coach by putting myself in a situation designed to test my self-control.

It feels stupid to go.

It feels cruel not to.

I wouldn't let any of my sisters go alone.

But I don't feel particularly *sisterly* about Amelia.

Will I be able to resist Amelia if I spend days on end with her?

Will I be able to live with myself knowing she's possibly breaking down when she's all alone?

By the time I pull up to the curb, my stomach feels like I've been downing shots of battery acid.

Amelia wakes up with a wide yawn, looking adorably sleep-rumpled. "Are we there already? I must have fallen asleep."

"My dad always used to call that time traveling. When you'd fall asleep while driving or flying and then wake up at your destination."

Amelia grins. "Time traveling. I love it."

Her smile fades as she glances up at the airport doors. They slide open as a woman with two children and ten bags waddles through. A woman follows, and is swept off her feet and into a passionate kiss by a man holding up a sign.

"Well. I guess this is it."

"I'll help with your bags," I say, needing something to do.

But when I get the bags up on the curb, I realize Amelia hasn't gotten out of the car. I step closer to her window, then gesture for her to roll it down. She does, but she won't meet my gaze.

"What's up, Mills?" I ask, leaning on the car.

"I don't know about this," she says, glancing past me toward the various travelers saying their goodbyes and filing into the airport with their bags.

"Which part? Talk me through it."

She nibbles at her bottom lip, and I force my gaze away from her mouth.

"The part where I'm about to get out of your car wearing a wedding dress and look like the jilted bride traveling alone. And the whole idea—I mean, I should probably stay and help Morgan and my dad sort through the mess. Taking a vacation right now feels … weird."

The tightness returns to my chest. No one has ever accused me of being a bleeding heart. But maybe it's because I don't choose to show that side to many people. Just my sisters, who know all my secrets. And hold them over my head often. With glee.

Which might be why I don't share with many other people.

"Hey." I touch Amelia's chin, lifting it until she meets my eyes. I don't like the indecision I see there. "There's nothing jilted about you. Okay? What happened today had zero to do with you and everything to do with Drew's poor choices. You get that?"

She nods, but her eyes only gain a fraction of the brightness they held before. "Yeah. You're right."

She still doesn't get out of the car, and I see her fiddling with her ring again. Walking into the airport in a wedding dress will certainly draw attention. Attention and questions to answer. Which is probably the last thing she wants right now.

"Hang tight," I say. Tossing her bags back into the car, I jog around to my seat and then follow signs for the parking decks.

"Where are we going?" she asks.

I snag a ticket from the machine on the way into the lot, then find a spot between two parked trucks. I cut off the engine and turn to Amelia. "You can change in here. The windows are tinted, and now you've got cover on both sides. I'll stand guard in back, just in case."

"Thank you." She reaches across, squeezing my arm again. "Could you maybe bring me my clothes? I have what I was planning to wear after the reception on top in the smaller rolling suitcase."

"Yep."

I open the back again, unzip the smaller rolling back and see a skirt and folded shirt ... with a bra and underwear right on top that I'm desperately trying to ignore.

Nothing to see here, I tell myself. *Nothing to* think about. *Nope. Nothing at all. Block it from memory.*

I tuck the undergarments between the shirt and skirt, then hand them through Amelia's open window without making eye contact. Then, I wait, leaning against the bumper and ignoring the way the car bounces as Amelia must be wiggling in and out of her dress.

I imagine Coach standing a few feet away, glaring at me. It helps.

After a few minutes, Amelia emerges from the car, saying "Ta-da!"

She's dressed in a flowery skirt that brushes her knees and a soft t-shirt, her hair fully loose around her shoulders, a darker gold glow in the dim lights of the parking deck. She looks great. I swallow.

"What about the dress?" I ask.

She wrinkles her nose. "Do you mind if I leave it in your car while I'm gone?"

"Nope. Let me know if you want me to burn it."

"Not without me," she says with a laugh, then she turns pensive. "I'm not sure what I'll do with it, but I have some ideas. Later. If you get tired of keeping it, you can always give it to my dad."

I can only imagine the kinds of looks and comments I'd get from the team if I showed up at The Summit with her wedding dress. I'm already afraid to check my text thread.

"Thanks for everything, Van."

With no warning, Amelia leans forward, giving me a tight hug. She smells like fresh, clean linen with a hint of lemon. I take the tiniest sniff, lowering my nose to her soft hair. The hug is so brief I don't have time to hug her back before she lets go.

She clears her throat when I'm just standing there, blinking at her.

"My bags?" she says.

"Right."

I pull the rolling bags from the car and then shove my hands in my suit pockets, where my phone starts to buzz.

"Thanks again," she says. "I'll, um, see you around?"

Unlikely. I don't know when or if our paths will cross again. Despite living in the same town and having her dad in common, we've only met twice.

The thought makes me sad, and I remind myself I barely know her. Somehow, this situation has left me feeling a false sense of connection. Like a trauma bond, but a little lighter. A *light* trauma bond. I'm sure it will fade.

"Take care of yourself, Mills," I tell her. "And remember— if you need help with revenge …"

"You're my guy."

I like the way those words sound on her lips. More than I have a right to.

She looks like she wants to say something else, then turns

and walks away, head held high and bags rolling behind her. I wait by the back of my SUV until she's safely on the elevator in the corner of the parking deck, giving me what looks like a forced smile as the doors slide closed.

I feel sadder than I have any reason to be when Amelia's out of sight.

And as I climb into my SUV, feeling my phone buzzing again in my pocket, I'm struck by an unease I can't shake.

It feels wrong to leave Amelia alone right now, after everything. I think of the offer to go with her, my pulse quickening at the thought. Then I remind myself of all the reasons it's a bad idea.

But … it's also a bad idea to let her go alone.

Maybe an even *worse* idea.

I mean, if I go, it's not like I'm going to *do* anything. Amelia's attractive, yeah, but it would be a friend thing. She's certainly not looking for something right now, and I've been on a dating hiatus for a while. It won't be an issue.

I'm not sure if I believe my own words, but either way, I find myself jogging across the parking deck and pounding down the stairs. I need to find her. There's just no way I'm letting Mills spend a honeymoon alone.

My phone has been buzzing almost nonstop since I helped get Amelia's bags out of the car. Maybe the guys are calling now that the texts are muted.

As I reach the ground level, I finally pull out my phone. It's Coach.

I pause, lingering on the sidewalk and watching the front doors of the airport slide open and closed as people move in and out. "Coach," I say.

"Van de Kamp," he says. "Is Milly around?"

"Not at the moment. We're at the airport. You want to talk with her?"

"That's not why I called. Look—I wanted to say I'm sorry."

"I've had a black eye before. I'll live."

"No," he says. "I mean, for assuming you had something to do with that mess. That was wrong of me."

My throat suddenly feels tight. I tug at the open collar of my shirt. "Ah, thanks."

"After everything you did today, I hate asking one more thing."

I start to move again, weaving through idling cars at the dropoff area in front of the airport. I scan the big windows inside, finally relaxing a little when I catch sight of Amelia waiting in a long line at the counter.

"Morgan says Milly's going on their honeymoon alone." He almost growls the word *their,* and I try to picture him throwing a chair through a church window. "She said she asked you to go with Milly."

I wait for a series of threats.

"I want you to go with her."

I slow to a stop just outside the automatic doors, which get confused and whoosh open. Then halfway close. Then open again as I drag a hand through my hair.

He's asking me to do what I was already planning to do, so I'm not sure why the request gives me pause. It should feel like a free pass. A stamp of approval.

Weirdly, it feels like as much of a trap as it did when Amelia asked.

If I tell him I was already planning to go, will he forget his apology and assume the worst again?

And if I don't tell him, is it bad to let him think it's his idea?

I guess so long as Amelia doesn't think that's why, it

87

doesn't matter. I wouldn't want her to assume I'm here because of her dad.

"Uh, you want me to go with her?" I ask, then add, "Sir."

"I know it's a lot to ask," Coach says. "I'll reimburse you and—"

"No need. I wouldn't feel right about taking your money."

That would be way too much like Coach paying me to go with Amelia.

"Obviously, I'll expect you to stay in your own room, and if I hear so much as a rumor of you touching—"

"No touching. My own room."

"Thank you," he says, relief palpable through the phone. "I can't tell you enough how much this means. I hope you know if I had anyone else to call, I would."

I shake my head. And *there* it is. Just when I think I'm making a tiny smidge of forward progress, he reminds me that I'm still his least favorite.

"And Van? I'm trusting you with my girl. You understand?"

I do. And I hear the unspoken threat in his voice. "Understood, sir."

And I have every intention of keeping his trust. I'll go with Amelia and watch out for her. Be her friend, though I'm always the guy arguing against guy-girl friendships in the long-term. This is short-term. Special circumstances.

Totally fine.

But as I hang up, Amelia suddenly appears on the other side of the sliding doors. She pauses and glances at me—first in confusion and then with a wide smile. I have to swallow hard. Wondering exactly what Coach's trust entails. And if I'm breaking it right now staring at Amelia's smile the way I am.

I stride through the doors, passing a few feet from where Amelia stands, still smiling up at me.

"Hey," I say.

"Why are you here?" she asks. "Miss me already?"

Oddly, I did.

"Is the offer still open?" I ask, crossing my arms. "For the free vacation?"

Her eyes brighten. "Seriously? You want to come?"

I nod, and then she's launching herself at me, practically hanging off my neck. "You won't regret this," she says.

Somehow, I think she's wrong about that.

CHAPTER 6

Amelia

FLYING first class really is top-notch. But our seats and the exorbitant price Van paid to get us in them is not why we've had such *excellent* service. We've barely taken off and the flight attendant has been hovering better than any helicopter mom at the playground.

"Are you sure you don't need anything?"

I'm all set to tell the toothy woman looking only at Van that no, for the third time, we don't need any overpriced airplane food or beverages. What we—okay, I—*need* is for her to stop trying to flirt with the famous hockey player she recognized the moment we stepped on the plane.

But she hasn't been getting my hints. Or Van's hints, which consist of leaning against the window pretending to be asleep. She's the reason I took the aisle seat to begin with—

to keep Van out of reach after she kept trying to help him find his clearly marked seat when we boarded.

Before I can tell her again that we don't need anything, Van gives a dramatically loud yawn and stretches. Leaning away from the window and giving me a wink, he puts one big hand on the seat in front of me and the other behind my head until I'm caged in.

A proprietary move. One that has my stomach cartwheeling toward a cliff.

He's close enough to give me a slight buzz from whatever cologne he's wearing. And to get a peek at the tattoo on his chest, which is a little easier since he undid two more buttons on his dress shirt. I suppose this is his version of travel casual when you came straight from a wedding: black pants, belt, and a shirt unbuttoned halfway to his navel.

I still can't see the whole tattoo, but now I know the lines curling up out of his shirt collar are flames. Black outlines; no color. But as for the full image, I'm still not sure.

"We'd like two glasses of champagne, please," Van says, his eyes never leaving mine.

I normally hate when men order for a woman. If they ask first—sure. Or if they want to make a recommendation, that's great. Maybe in those cases, a woman *might* find this romantic. But most of the time, it just comes across as the pinnacle of mansplaining. Like, *I'll help the little lady out because reading a menu is hard work and decisions such as this are best left to the men-folk.*

I'm not sure why Mr. Misogyny speaks in my head with a cowboy's drawl, but he always does. No offense to cowboys.

Drew ordered for me all the time. And what's worse—I let him. It should have been written down in a list of red flags. Instead, it was one of many things I tried to ignore through a gritted-teeth smile.

Somewhere along the way, I told myself that love was about compromise … which I guess only applied to *me*, since Drew *never* compromised.

Somewhere along the way, I also told myself I was in love. An even worse mistake.

Just as I'm about to protest out of principle—even though champagne sounds perfect right now—Van's fingers land lightly on the back of my neck. He cocks an eyebrow as he glances at me.

"Unless you want a different drink?" he says. "Maybe something harder?"

Earlier in the car, Van said he didn't need lines to pick up women. I think he was trying to be funny, pushing a certain narrative that may not be accurate. But it's clearly based in *some* truth. Because I, for one, am practically ready to eat out of Van's hand.

The man is *potent*. Even when he's not trying to be.

And if this is him *not* trying, him just *pretending* so we can ditch the overzealous flight attendant, I'd hate to see Van's charm dialed up to even a medium setting. I'd melt right into this lovely faux leather seat.

When his fingertip strokes my neck, I'm a goner.

"I'm sorry—what was the question?" I ask as Van slowly, lightly trails his fingers down my neck to my shoulder, stopping when he reaches the collar of my shirt.

He toys with the fabric, and I swear, it's like his touch has some kind of direct line to my heart. The effect is not unlike jumper cables or those paddles they're always using in medical dramas. Though I'm not sure if he's shocking me to life or frying my engine.

"Is champagne good, or would you like something else, Mills?" he asks, his brown eyes warm. Amused. Alluring.

The scar through his eyebrow adds a delicious edge of danger to the whole look.

Bad boy, indeed.

A tiny shiver flows through me. "Champagne is great," I say, my voice wobbling a little. It'll pair perfectly with the bubbles still coursing through my blood.

"Are you celebrating something?" I'm jarred by the flight attendant's voice. I forgot for a moment she was here. And when I glance up, I see her big smile has gone slightly brittle with Van's show.

Clearly, I'm not the only one affected by the potent powder keg of man seated beside me.

The man who leans even closer, his smile curling up on one side in a way that has my stomach clenching. One finger drags slowly back up my neck and pauses at my hairline.

He's like a genetically engineered apex predator—all the languid, powerful movements of a jungle cat mixed with the paralyzing venom of a snake bite. That's the only explanation for the way I'm sitting here, slack-jawed and totally unable to do more than blink.

"You could say that," Van murmurs, his gaze on my mouth.

Say what? What did she ask?

Oh, right—are we celebrating? Yes, we are. *Pretending* to celebrate, that is. Because at the front counter, Van managed to sweet-talk his way into two first class seats next to each other on a mostly full flight—the last one of the night—to Tampa because we're newlyweds.

Considering the events of the day, it's only like, an eighth of a lie. Not a white one but maybe just a little greige. Technically, we did come straight from a wedding where one of us was—supposed to be—the bride. And we *are* heading toward a honeymoon.

For the record, I thought playing newlyweds was a terrible idea and, had he warned me, I would have stopped him. For a whole host of reasons—not the least of which being how much I loved the way Van wrapped a possessive arm around my waist, staring down at me with pure, unadulterated adoration.

Correction: fake, *manufactured* adoration.

But Van already committed us to the lie by the time I realized what was happening. I figured it wasn't a huge deal since we're under no obligation to keep up now. It's not like airports are known for communication between the front desks and the people working the gate or the flight crew. I seriously doubt Thomas radioed ahead and told Jill at the gate to welcome the newlyweds.

This flight attendant clearly did *not* get a memo. Still—we boarded together. Shouldn't she have at least assumed we *could* be together and not tried to get Van's attention every five seconds? Guess not.

"Great," she says, sounding like she's dry-swallowing a bitter pill of disappointment. "Be right back with your drinks."

The moment she's gone, I manage to shake off whatever spell Van has me under. Leaning forward, I use two fingers to pluck his hand off of my person and drop it in his lap.

"What was all that?" I hiss.

Clearly unperturbed, Van shrugs and pulls out the in-flight magazine and starts flipping through. "What was all what?"

"You—with the leaning and the touching and the sexy voice."

Van pauses his magazine perusal and gives me a flirty side eye, which I don't think I knew was even possible. "You think my voice is sexy?"

His pitch is low, the tone gritty. As though he's taken the sexy dial and cranked that puppy up a few more notches.

I poke him in the chest, careful to avoid bare skin. "You stop it right now."

"Stop what?" He grins, but then it drops and his expression turns sincere. "Look—she was clearly not giving up. And you were clearly getting jealous—"

"I was not jealous! Just annoyed. On principle. For all she knows, we could be together. And you being some *famous hockey player*"—I put this in finger quotes, which makes Van snort—"doesn't make you property for public consumption."

"Fine. Since you were clearly getting *annoyed on principle*" —he finger quotes me right back—"I thought I'd make sure she knows I'm not available. Is that okay?"

"Yes. But there's no need to be so ..." His grin grows, and my words sputter out.

"So ... what?" he teases. "I'm just being myself."

Slowly, and with the devilish smirk to measure all other devilish smirks against, Van lifts one finger to his mouth. Slowly, his tongue darts out and he licks the tip, and then uses it to turn the next page of the magazine. Which he is not even pretending to read.

I need some kind of Van vaccine. Just a little injection of the real thing so my body can train to fight him off. Otherwise, I'm honestly in trouble here. You'd think, given my very recent breakup of an engagement, attraction to another man wouldn't even come into play.

And it probably wouldn't under any other circumstance with any other person.

But my travel companion happens to be the one exception.

Even last night at the rehearsal dinner—which now feels like it took place centuries ago—my stomach dropped and

95

then I felt a whole body *something* when I caught sight of Van —a.k.a. Restaurant Robbie at a table across the room. There was a flash of hope, followed immediately by disappointment and guilt for feeling anything at all when my fiancé was seated beside me.

Whatever connection we felt the night we met snapped right back into place when Van drove me away from the church. But I refuse to fall prey to some weird rebound second-chance crush. It's a terrible idea.

Morgan would disagree. She'd cheer me on while watching with a bowl of popcorn in her lap.

But I'm not Morgan. I'm *me*. The woman who was wearing a wedding dress until an hour and a half ago. And who is now fending off inappropriate feelings inspired by the ridiculous flirt sitting next to me.

I snatch the magazine from Van's hands, quickly roll it up, and whack him in the shoulder. "No!" I say firmly, like I'm scolding a dog. Not that I'd actually hit a dog with a rolled up magazine. But Van can take it. "Bad. No!"

He actually giggles. Which only makes me swat him harder. Because it's kind of adorable. And that makes me angrier.

"Why are you—ow!" he says. "This is worse than my pinching!"

"I'll stop if you stop with all the flirting and the touching and the pretending!"

Van's face shifts, and before I can blink, he's trapped my magazine-wielding hand in his. Our faces are much too close as he says, "Who said anything about pretending?"

A throat clears. "Sorry for interrupting, but here's your champagne."

At the sound of the flight attendant's voice, I pull my

hand away from Van. The magazine slips from my fingers and falls somewhere below our feet.

Van, whose brain hasn't shorted out like mine, takes the champagne flutes. "Thank you."

I don't miss the way the flight attendant shoots her shot. Rather than just letting go quickly, she releases slowly, dragging her fingernails over Van's hand. This happens literally right in front of my face.

The nerve! Van made it clear we're together, and she's still trying? I find myself with a violent urge to rip those gel tips right off her nails.

What is happening to me?

I am not a person who believes in physical violence. And here I am—beating Van with a magazine and wanting to rip off our flight attendant's gel nails. I'm not quite unhinged— yet—but I'm getting there.

Van pulls back, a little champagne sloshing over the top of one flute and landing on my lap. He clears his throat, for the first time all day seeming uncomfortable. It only fuels my rage.

I turn to the flight attendant.

"I'm sorry, but are you hitting on my *husband?* The one who vowed for better or for worse to *me* just a few hours ago?"

Don't know where *those* words came from.

Actually, I do. They come from the part of me who was *supposed* to be married. Who had planned to recite those vows a few hours ago, even if not to *this* man.

And if I had taken those vows, I would absolutely say something if some rando was hitting on my man.

I am doing women everywhere a service by calling this lady out.

The woman's cheeks flame, and she quickly steps back. "I'm sorry."

I don't look at Van. Instead, I watch as she walks away in her navy suit.

A head with soft white curls appears over the top of the seat in front of us, and an older woman grins at me. "Good for you, honey."

I smile weakly before she drops back down in her seat. "Thanks?"

A champagne flute appears in front of me, and I take it with a shaking hand. Van's fingers close around mine, steadying me.

"You okay?" he asks.

"Fine." My voice is a coiled spring. "Does this happen often?"

He gives a little shrug. "Sometimes."

Which I'll take to mean more often than I want to know. I also don't want to know if Van would have brushed the woman off had I not been here. He did say he dates a lot. I swallow.

Still cupping my hand, Van leans close, his lips brushing my ear. "For the record, jealousy looks hot on you, Mills. Even if you're pretending."

He leans away, dropping his hand, and I take a quick swallow of champagne. I feel the cool liquid travel all the way down my throat.

The problem is I'm *not* pretending. The part about marrying Van may have been a straight-up lie, but the desire to do bodily harm to the flight attendant—or at least settle for a verbal beatdown—is viscerally real.

I'm not possessive so much as I'm *possessed*. I can practically taste my own jealousy underneath the dry fizz of the champagne. It's sickly sweet and heady. Maybe in shoving down my feelings about what happened with Drew and Becky, I'm forcing all of my other emotions to the surface. Like I can only hold *so many* feelings back at one time.

Or maybe I'm just … not myself.

"You started it with your lies," I mutter, which is also true.

Van takes a slow sip of champagne. "When did I lie?"

"At the counter. You told the man we were newlyweds."

"No, I didn't. I simply walked up to the counter and said *newlyweds*. Not *we are newlyweds*," he says. "Was the implication there? Yes. But I didn't outright lie."

I think back to the exchange and realize he's right. His ability to be so casually deceptive—and believable—terrifies me.

"Oh, you're good," I tell him. Meaning, of course, very, very bad.

"So, did you change your mind about keeping up the charade?" He lowers his voice. Not like anyone could hear us over the plane's engine. "You want to stay married to me, Mills?"

My cheeks flush at the mere idea of Van and me and marriage. "No."

"You sure? It might come in handy now and again." He finishes his champagne, watching me.

I lift the flute to my lips and let the smallest amount roll over my tongue while I consider. While I do, I feel Van's attention on me. It's oppressive. Not in a wholly bad way, but more like an unignorable presence, a barometric pressure shift.

"It's probably a bad idea," I tell him.

"Okay," he agrees easily. "But if you change your mind,

we can always pull the married card when it suits us. You know—for upgrades, free stuff." He grins. "Scaring off handsy flight attendants."

I roll my eyes. "Fine." Eyeing the glass in my hand, I say, "I probably shouldn't have much more of this or I might start an actual cat fight."

Van smiles. "You can cat fight if you want to. You can pretend to be my wife. Or not. You get to make the rules, Mills."

I lift my half-full glass and clink it against his empty one, holding his gaze as I say, "Cheers to rewriting the rules."

Moments after he finishes the champagne, the flight attendant reappears—of course—and I practically throw the glasses at her with a glare. Van chuckles, winks at me, and then leans his head against the window.

I cross my arms. "You can just… sleep like that?" I grumble.

Before I have time to protest, Van sits up, lifts the arm rest between us and puts his arm around me, pulling me over until I'm leaning on his chest. Beneath my cheek, his muscles are firm, but somehow perfectly snuggleable. His hand slides gently up and down my back, and just like that—I'm back to being totally paralyzed by him. Or maybe just so relaxed I don't *want* to move.

"One of the perks of having me as a travel buddy is that you don't have to get a crick in your neck while sleeping. Consider my pec your personal pillow."

"A pectoral pillow," I mutter, and he chuckles.

"You got it. Now, you've had a helluva day, Mills. Rest."

Maybe I should be bothered by this too—Van's bossiness. Him telling me to rest. But Van seems to perfectly anticipate my needs. He isn't being controlling but considerate.

His command to sleep—along with the pec pillow and his

gentle hand stroking my back—has an almost instant effect, and I find my eyelids heavy and my mind drifting away.

"Thanks, Van. For ... everything."

He says something in a low voice, but I only hear a rumble, and I fall asleep thinking about purring jungle cats.

CHAPTER 7

Amelia

So warm. Soooo nice and warm.

Was that my alarm? I groan. Definitely don't want to get up. Five more minutes. Maybe ten.

I burrow my face deeper into my pillow, reaching for another one to put over my head. But my hand closes around something not so soft instead.

I thought I got rid of this stupid pillow—the memory foam one that I ordered off an infomercial and turned out to be as heavy as a boulder. I squeeze.

Not memory foam.

Not ... a pillow?

More like—

"Time to wake up, gorgeous."

The sound of Van's low, gritty voice instantly floods me

with memories of the day's events. I tense and go completely still. Like maybe if I don't move and don't open my eyes, this won't be real.

Because I am *not* in bed, being woken up by my alarm.

I'm on a plane after I did *not* get married. A plane that is no longer moving.

And even before I open my eyes to survey the damage, I'm *very* aware of how I'm practically lying on top of Van, my head nestled into his chest, lips brushing the bare skin between the open buttons of his shirt. One hand fisted in the material and the other … the other is not squeezing an infomercial pillow but *his leg*.

Not just his leg—his upper thigh. Like, *way* upper thigh. Almost to his hip.

I snatch my hand away and sit up so fast the edges of my vision go black. All I can see for a few seconds are Van's amused brown eyes and his upturned mouth.

And did the stubble on his face grow while we were en route? Because it already seems darker, and fuller. Sexier.

No! *Not* sexier.

Okay, objectively, yes—sexy. It's not even a point up for debate.

But I can't have feelings about his objective attractiveness. It's simply a truth universally acknowledged.

MOVING ON.

"We shall never speak of this," I whisper, wiping a hand over my mouth just in case I drooled. "*Never.*"

"You don't kiss and tell—got it."

My cheeks are flaming. "I don't—we didn't. There was *no kissing*," I hiss, really hoping I'm right. I may have slept through thigh groping, but I wouldn't sleep through a kiss. "And nothing to tell."

Van says nothing. His widening smirk—says a lot.

Wait. Did I … do more than just snuggle him in my sleep?

"No," I whisper. "I didn't. I wouldn't!" Blood surges to my cheeks. Panic claws at my chest. I grab Van's arm and squeeze as I lower my voice. "Did I kiss you in my sleep?"

For a long moment, Van says nothing, and I wonder if it's possible to literally die of embarrassment. The way my heart is sputtering in my chest and the air is struggling to pass through my lungs, I think maybe it is. They keep defibrillators on planes, right?

Then Van's smile shifts to something less devilish and more soft. Almost … tender. He reaches out, fingertips grazing my cheek as he tucks a strand of hair behind my ear.

"Relax, Mills. I'm just messing with you. I'm the one who pulled you over here and said to rest. You needed it. We're fine. There was no kissing. Okay?"

I nod dumbly, grateful for the easy out he just gave me.

But then he leans closer, his breath hot on my neck as he says, "Besides, kissing me is not the kind of experience you'd be able to sleep through. Though you might dream about it …"

I poke him in the chest, *hard*, and he laughs and allows me to shove him away. "Shut up, you."

But as I sit up and start to gather my things, I catch sight of a red smudge peeking out of Van's open shirt right next to his tattoo.

A perfect imprint of my lips on his skin.

———

"You don't need to do this," I repeat, but the stubborn man

I'm calling my travel companion for the next four days doesn't listen.

"I'll take the Range Rover," he says to the man with the nametag. "Always wanted to drive one of those."

I want to scream.

After we got off the plane, we ran into trouble. Starting with—my bags not making it to Tampa. It's late, and there was nary a person at any counter to help us, only an automated number to call and report the missing bags.

Which means now Van and I are both only wearing the clothing on our backs. Between us, we have one phone and two wallets, though mine isn't particularly helpful considering my financial situation.

Then we got to the rental car counter, where it turns out I can't pick up the car we reserved. Or should I say Drew reserved. In only his name.

The issue isn't that I'm a day early to pick up the car. The issue is that Drew didn't put my name on the reservation. Guess he assumed he'd be the only one driving it.

The man behind the counter refused to give me information on our reservation or any credit toward a new vehicle. Nothing. It's like I don't exist.

Because I'm not Drew.

At that point, Van whipped out his black credit card for the second time tonight. I'm keeping a mental tally in my head of how much I owe him, and it's already too much. A last-minute, first-class airline ticket and now he's renting a high-end car? I'll be paying him back forever.

Espccially since I'll have to look for a new job.

Oh, and did I mention I used up my pretty meager savings and last paycheck to cover the final payment of my credit card?

Someone should really explain to college kids how those

cards work. Especially considering the way companies pass them out on college campuses like parade candy or Oprah in that one meme: *You've been preapproved! And you've been preapproved! You've all been preapproved!!!!*

Okay, so my dad *did* explain them to me. I half listened, then ignored all his advice in lieu of things like ordering pizza, upgrading to a new laptop, buying new, adult clothes right after graduation. Plus any wedding stuff over the past year that Dad deemed "unnecessary."

I didn't go nuts. But I also paid the minimum most months, falling right into the credit card company's clutches until I was up to my eyeballs in stupid debt, growing steadily because of the thing I wish I'd listened to my dad about: *interest.*

Dumb. So dumb. But I learned my lesson, paid off the card little by little and then dumped all my remaining money into paying it off this week so I could get married debt-free.

Which would have been fine. Except now I'm *not* married, which means I'm all debt-free with nowhere to go and no money to not go there with.

My lease ended this week, with my stuff in boxes at Drew's place. Now, living with Dad will be more long-term until I can find something else. And my bank account is sitting pretty with a big fat three-figure sum total.

I don't even have the option of starting a whole new mountain of mini-debt with the credit card I just finished paying off. Because I cut it up.

My whole life right now feels like a collection of tiny bad decisions all stacked up in a Jenga tower. And Drew pulled out a key piece right at the bottom, sending everything crashing down.

"Mills." Van's big hand lands on my shoulder. Squeezes twice.

"What?" This comes out a little snappier than I meant it to. I sigh, my shoulders slumping. "Sorry."

"No apologies, remember?"

"Right. The rules." His fingers gently knead my shoulder, then slide up to the back of my neck. I'm not even into massages—usually I'm too ticklish—but Van's strong fingers almost have me groaning right here at the Avis counter.

"What's the deal?" Van asks. "Are you okay?"

"I just hate that you're paying for stuff. But …" I swallow, then work up the courage to meet Van's eyes. "I'm kind of in a bad financial place right now. All things considered."

"Look—I was thinking about taking a trip during this break anyway. And I would have spent money on that. So, stop worrying. I'd probably have spent way more in Vegas."

"What were you going to do in Vegas?" I ask.

I'm immediately sorry because the kinds of reasons men might go to Vegas aren't all ones I want to think about.

He shrugs. "Maybe catch a few hockey games. A show or two."

I'm immediately dying to know what kinds of shows Van would attend. Music? Magic? One of those sexy revues where the women do high kicks with feathers and sequins?

"But mostly blackjack," Van says, and the sudden tight-ness in my chest eases.

"You like blackjack?"

"I do. And it does *not* love me back. So, really, you're saving me from myself. And from the house taking all my money."

I don't know if any of this is true or if Van's lying, but I find myself happy to believe him. And then I find myself saying, "I've never played."

It's the thinnest of veiled requests. Me basically begging him to teach me.

Van grins and says, "Guess we'll have to pick up a deck of cards with the rest of our supplies."

Right. Because now neither of us has any other clothes than the ones we're wearing. No toiletries either.

So we stop at a Walmart before we get to the tiny island resort, which is separated enough from the mainland to make leaving to buy things a pain. I'm sure everything at the resort will be way overpriced.

But I draw the line at letting Van buy me underwear. It's embarrassing enough that he's paying for my clothes—bad enough that we're buying Walmart clothes. I have not shopped at Walmart in years. While it's greatly improved from what I remember, it is not my typical style. If I could afford it, I'd buy everything from Anthropologie. As it is, I cannot without the power of my credit card, so my typical style is pairing one nice, special piece with bargain finds from Ross or H&M.

Tonight, *all* my finds are bargain. And I may burn them when I get my actual bags. If I had to describe this style it's very bright. And very rayon.

They carry a few of the makeup brands I use, and I try to stick to the essentials: face wash, moisturizer with SPF, foundation, concealer, blush, and mascara. I don't want to appear too high maintenance, though if I'm being honest, I'm *medium* maintenance. If it weren't for the ridiculous amount of freckles I have always hated, I probably wouldn't wear more than moisturizer and mascara. But I *do* have freckles. And some PTSD from being constantly teased about them when I was little.

I also grab a new notebook in a cheerful yellow with a honeycomb design and a pack of pens in case I have ideas and need to write. I'm never without a notebook and feel better once it's in the cart along with a pair of flip-flops, sunscreen, a fluffy towel, and a beachy book in case I feel like reading.

It bothers me that Van is going to have to pay for all this. But I'll allow it.

I will not allow him to pay for the bras and underwear.

"Just put your stuff in the cart, Mills," he says. "We've been over this. I've got the money. I'll cover it, and I don't want you to worry about it."

"I'm not worried. Look! I did put some stuff in the cart. But I'm buying these," I argue stubbornly, clutching the multipack of cotton boy shorts to my chest, which hopefully hide most of the two bras.

"Your loss." Van looks like an oversized mutant child as he puts one foot on the cart and pushes off with the other to glide down the aisle.

"You're going to get us kicked out," I call. He only laughs.

Somehow, Van looks totally in his element here. Not that Walmart specifically is his element. He is absolutely not a People of Walmart kind of person.

It's more that I have yet to see Van look uncomfortable today. In every situation he's been thrown in, he lands on his feet, adapting and going with the flow like wherever he is, he's meant to be there. Despite the fact it's ten o'clock at night and he's in Walmart wearing dress shoes, suit pants, and a shirt that seems to get unbuttoned a little more each hour. I'm less distracted by his tattoo now that his very defined six-pack is partially visible.

Not that I'm looking!

No. I'm really not. I'm staring at the pack of panties and the two bras in my hand—wondering if the sixteen-dollar bra is really that much better than the three-dollar one. Heck, I should get them both and then do a test. Then again, the airport will probably find my bags tomorrow, so I don't need two bras but just in case—

"Gimme." Van's hand reaches out, snatching the underwear and bras right out of my hands and tossing them at the cart. He misses, and now two bras and a pack of neon underwear skitter across the tile floor.

I didn't even notice him coming back down the aisle.

I scramble to grab the underwear, pulling them to my chest again. Van eyes me, hands on his hips and eyebrows raised.

"You don't need to be weird about this. It's just underwear, Mills. We all wear it."

"You wear bras?" I deadpan, and he laughs.

"No. I don't wear bras." He reaches in the cart and plucks out a package of boxer briefs, holding them up and waving them. "See! Underwear. Everybody wears it."

Okay. I did *not* need this visual.

He's chosen dark colored boxer briefs—black, navy, charcoal gray—and all I can think about is the fact that the shirtless dude modeling them on the package has got nothing on Van.

"Don't make it a big deal." Van says, tossing the briefs in the cart. This time, he makes it.

He's right, of course. It's just … okay, maybe I'm a little uptight about some things. Including underwear. Uptight is such a negative word.

Private. That's better.

"Sorry if I don't go flashing my panties to every Tom, Dick, and Harry hanging out in Walmart."

"I'm sorry, did you say my name?" A man with bushy gray eyebrows and a circa-2000s soul patch steps into the aisle, holding a blender in one hand and a pair of work boots in the other.

As one does in Walmart.

"What?" I say.

"I'm Harry," he says, tapping his chest with the blender. "I thought I heard you say my name and something about … panties?"

Van snorts, and the man—Harry—drops his gaze to the underwear and bras still clutched to my chest. This feels like a strange sort of life lesson, like the reason why no one should walk around Walmart holding—and arguing about—undergarments.

Had I just put them in the cart like Van asked, we would not be having this conversation.

"I'm sorry," I tell him. "I did say your name, but I was talking about the metaphorical Harry."

"The who-what now?" Actual Harry asks, his bushy brows drawing together in consternation.

"Sorry—just a bit of confusion here." Van tugs the undergarments from my hands for the second time and drops them into the cart.

"Hop on," he says, tipping his chin toward the back of the cart.

And even though I was just chastising him for riding on the cart, I grab the handle and step up with both feet. I'm not quite prepared for the heat of Van's body against my back as his hands grasp the handle next to mine. He pushes us down the aisle and away from Actual Harry.

I find myself giggling as Van picks up speed. "This has to be against store policy," I tell him, even as I'm grinning.

His voice rumbles near my ear. "Do you always follow the rules, Mills?"

Yes. Honestly, I do.

I follow the rules, but what's more, I think I often treat other people's expectations of me—especially my dad's, but also Drew's—like rules as well. The thought starts to make my stomach sour.

But then Van gives us another push and we're flying, laughter bubbling up out of me.

"Like I've been saying, it's time to make your own rules," Van says, then swerves to avoid a woman with a cart full of canned goods, not slowing down at all. Not bothered by her glare.

Van's words send my brain humming, the idea for a new post taking shape. I should write about this experience— what to do when you find your fiancé cheating on the day of your wedding.

The rules for being a runaway bride.

Then I give my head a little shake. Who am I kidding? This is the Saturated-with-Information Age—there are likely thousands of books *and* blogs about this very thing. I bet someone has already penned a *Runaway Bride for Dummies* book.

But even if it's already been written, the college professor in the one creative writing class I took once said that every story has been told but not by *you* in *your* words. Seth Godin says only you have your distinctive voice and that hoarding it is toxic.

So ... why not?

My fingers itch to open the package of pens and start writing in the yellow notebook.

Later.

Because now, I'm busy leaning into a very warm, sturdy chest of a man encouraging me to fly.

"We're definitely going to get kicked out," I say, gasping for breath as my giggles turn into full-blown laughter.

"They'd have to catch us first. And I'd like to see them try."

As I grip the handles for dear life, my cheeks start to ache from smiling so big. I can't remember the last time I felt *this* happy.

With a cart full of bargain clothes, rolling at a quick pace through Walmart, with Van pressed close to my back, his laughter in my ear. Breaking so many rules and for once, thinking about making my own.

CHAPTER 8

THE DREAM TEAM

Alec: Mind telling us what exactly happened with the groom, Van? Is it true you stole the bride?

Logan: Parker wants to have a word when you get back.

Alec: Oooh someone's in trouble...

Eli: Dude! Sounds to me like he saved Coach's daughter from marrying a giant turd. If the rumors are to be believed.

Logan: I didn't say Parker was MAD.

Alec: We all know what it means when Parker wants to "have a word."

Logan: Watch it.

Alec: Hey, I didn't say anything bad.

Eli: ANYWAY. TELL US WHAT HAPPENED!

Felix: Did you really walk in on the groom and someone hooking up? That's so not cool.

Alec: I guess that means you weren't having diarrhea.

Nathan: How did we get from point A to point poop?

Alec: Dumbo said Van had diarrhea.

Eli: [laughing emoji] [crying emoji] [poop emoji]

Wyatt: Why am I on this text thread?

Camden: Right?!?! This feels more like punishment than reward.

Alec: You guys would rather be on the thread with Tucker, Dumbo, or Dominik?

Wyatt: Carry on

Felix: Don't mess things up with Coach's daughter.

Eli: Are you, like, babysitting her? Or …

Felix: There best not be any kind of OR.

Nathan: I'd kind of like to see Coach beat Van with his skates.

Logan: Why so violent? I'd like Coach to have nothing but happy, easy times from now on. He deserves it after that mess.

Logan: So don't do anything to make things worse, V.

Alec: This is VAN we're talking about. What do you expect to happen?

Logan: Maybe just don't break her heart. Again. Because Coach definitely WOULD break you.

Felix: The woman just walked away from her wedding. I doubt she's looking for a new guy.

Alec: I'll say it again: this is VAN we're talking about.

Nathan: Don't give Vanity a bigger head than he's already got.

Felix: Van, be good.

Eli: [laughing emoji] [dancing lady emoji] [skull emoji]

Van: Hey

Eli: VAN!

Alec: Send proof of life.

Logan: Nice picture.

Eli: Dude, who decked you?

Felix: Button up your shirt. I can see your belly button lint.

Wyatt: Why are you in a Walmart bathroom?

Van: Long story

115

Van: Several people hit me today

Nathan: More than one?

Alec: How about give us the short story???

Van: First I was struck by an angel

Wyatt: Unlikely

Van: Second hit was Coach

Felix: Okay, I'm going to need the long story.

Nathan: At least medium length.

Van: Caught the groom cheating with the bride's cousin aka the maid of honor. Forced him to confess. Chaos ensued. Maid of honor threw an angel statue at my face. Maybe accidentally. Coach punched me. Definitely accidentally. Became the bride's getaway ride.

Van: Did NOT have diarrhea.

Eli: That's good because a Walmart bathroom is not the place you want to have stomach trouble.

Alec: Come over to Felix's. You can give us the long story in person. This is too good.

Van: Can't. I'm in Florida.

Wyatt: What's in Florida?

Van: Me

Eli: [eye roll emoji] [angry emoji]

Logan: I thought you were going to Vegas for the break.

Van: I was thinking about it

Alec: Did you go straight from the church to the airport? It's only been like six hours.

Van: Basically yeah

Logan: So why Florida

Van: I got an offer I couldn't refuse

Alec: Is it just me or is Van being deliberately vague.

Nathan: Not just you.

Felix: Stop dancing around the question. Why are you in Florida?

Wyatt: What part of Florida?

Logan: Don't you dare ghost us. I'll send Parker after you.

Alec: Stop trying to use Parker as a weapon.

Felix: Van. Why are you in Florida and why aren't you answering the question?

Van: Jeez.

Van: I'm in Florida with Amelia. She wanted to get out of town and already had the trip planned

Eli: Um

Alec: That's ... wow.

Logan: I'm definitely not telling Parker.

Logan: Yet.

Felix: Have you buttoned up your shirt yet? If not, please do so NOW.

Camden: Forget what I said earlier. I like this text thread.

Nathan: Does Coach know?

Van: He asked me to go

Logan: Coach ASKED you to go?

Eli: Coach asked YOU to go?

Alec: I'm offended.

Van: He wanted me to make sure Amelia's okay

Van: It's fine

Van: We're having fun

Eli: Uh-oh

Alec: Define fun

Logan: Fun or "fun"?

Van: Do you guys not trust me at ALL?

Alec: No

Felix: Unlikely.

Eli: Maybe?

Wyatt: Jury's still out

Nathan: Not with Coach's daughter.

Van: Good to know where I stand

Van: Gotta run

Logan: Be careful

Alec: Be GOOD

Eli: [laughing emoji] [smiling with halo emoji]

Felix: BUTTON UP YOUR SHIRT.

CHAPTER 9

Van

I'VE NEVER BEEN a good chess player, thinking multiple moves ahead. I tend to go with the flow, living in the current moment. Choosing to live spontaneously, according to my changing moods or shifting circumstances.

All this lack of forward thinking has led me to this moment, where I'm actually starting to worry about the sleeping arrangements for this impromptu getaway.

Separate rooms, Coach said.

No problem, I agreed.

Only—it *might be* a problem. Because the hotel is packed, and there is an issue with Amelia's reservation. For now, I'm choosing not to panic, standing by the counter with a bunch of Walmart bags at my feet while Amelia argues with the woman at the desk.

It's almost midnight, but the lobby is still lively. I wander away from the counter, sensing Amelia's need to handle this herself. If she can.

Music spills out of a restaurant on one side, and on the other, a bar is playing several sports games at full volume. Leafy tropical plants and flowers in oversized pots ring the room, making it feel almost like we're outside. The back of the building is a row of doors, all open, letting in a breeze and the faint sounds of a band outside. The ocean isn't visible, but I can see couples swaying under hanging lights.

It's a nice place.

Would be nicer if we could get a room.

Correction: *two* rooms.

I wander back to the counter, sliding a hand around Amelia's waist. She tenses, then sighs and relaxes into my touch. I tug her closer.

"How's it going?" I ask, not wanting to overstep but also itching to hand over my card, see if money and a charming smile can solve this problem, and move on.

"The suite isn't available tonight," Amelia says, gritting her teeth. "And the reservation isn't in my name, so even tomorrow, I can't check into it."

I look down, noting the tiredness around her eyes. "How about we worry about tomorrow tomorrow. Will you let me take care of tonight?"

Amelia hesitates. I wait until she nods, then pull out my wallet and manage to extract my card with one hand, keeping Amelia close with the other. For her sake or for mine, I'm not sure.

"Two rooms, please."

"Unfortunately, we're almost completely booked." The employee's dark hair is pulled back in a tight knot, and I swear, the uptightness in her manner is rivaling the severity of her hairdo. Or maybe the hairdo is causing it? I wonder if she took it down and shook it out if it would ease the pinched expression on her face. "But you're in luck. We do have one room with a king-sized bed. Not a beach view I'm afraid ..."

She goes on about the room, but I stopped really hearing her when she said king-sized bed. It takes me a moment to realize she's stopped speaking and is holding my card, poised to swipe it.

"Will that be okay?"

No. It will not be okay.

But Amelia smiles—a little bit of a wild look in her eyes—and says, "Sounds great."

No. It does not sound great.

What if Coach calls? What will I say when the guys text?

How will I share a room—and a bed—with Amelia?

And is *she* really okay with this?

I study her while signing my name to the receipt, agreeing to the hold charges, and whatever else the woman is saying. Standard hotel stuff. Amelia's eyes scan the room a little too quickly, like she's searching for an exit.

"Hey," I say, leaning close. "If you want, we can—"

But my suggestion about leaving this hotel and going back to the mainland where there were dozens of hotels dies when there's a commotion at the back of the room.

A large group enters from the open patio doors, laughing and talking, the sounds echoing off the marble floors. The people at the front of the group part, revealing a man in a suit holding the hand of a woman in a white dress and veil.

A wedding party. Amelia stiffens.

They stop in the center of the lobby and the whole group cheers as the groom dips the bride and kisses her.

And kisses her.

And ... *kisses* her.

I don't think Amelia is even breathing. I give her a light squeeze, my palm curled at her waist, but she doesn't move.

"Here you go," the woman at the counter says.

When I reach for my card, Amelia slips from my arm.

"I just need to use the bathroom," she blurts out.

My chest compresses as her face crumples and she scampers across the lobby, her fists curled tight by her sides. I slip my card back in my wallet, ask the woman at the desk if she can watch our Walmart bags for a moment, and then I jog toward the bathroom.

I walk right into the women's bathroom.

Okay—so I should have knocked. A woman washing her hands at the sink jumps at the sight of me, eyes wide.

"Sorry," I say, though I'm not. "I'm looking for a friend—"

"Van?" Amelia's voice, a little tremulous, sounds from one of the stalls.

The woman washing her hands makes a hasty exit as I stride down to the next-to-last stall, which is the only one fully closed. It's also the only one with someone sniffling behind it.

I rap my knuckles against the white wood door. "Mills? You in there?"

"Maybe. Why are *you* in here?"

I lean against the door, crossing my arms. "Open up."

"What if I'm pooping?"

I snort. "Are you?"

A pause. "No."

"Then let me in."

A longer pause. Then I hear the shuffle of movement and the solid clack of the lock sliding open. Amelia cracks the door open, meeting my eyes with red-rimmed ones of her own. My stomach dips.

I have a knee-jerk visceral reaction to tears, stemming straight from childhood and three sisters.

Callie, my older sister, swears she never cries, but I've seen it. Once. She made me swear it never happened. It was beyond terrifying to see the sister who seems made of indestructible material break down over a particularly horrendous breakup.

I've tried but couldn't quite forget the way her normally impermeable facade cracked and fell.

Alexandra cries when she's happy, when she's sad, when greeting card commercials come on or when a sports team or athlete shines. "I just love seeing people succeed with their gifts," Lex told me once while wiping her eyes after watching an Olympic gymnast's floor routine.

And while my youngest sister, Grey—short for Greyson—isn't quite to Lex's level, she cries a normal amount and also whenever anyone else is crying. But Grey hardly ever stops smiling—even if she's also crying.

The sight of tears immediately cloaks me in an overwhelming sense of powerlessness. Combined with an irrational and powerful urge to fix whatever it is. Whether that's scaring the pants off a stupid boy who hurt Callie or turning off the TV so that Alexandra won't cry over someone dying in "Grey's Anatomy," a show all of my sisters obsess over and in which a main character seems to die every other episode.

With Amelia, the tears hit me harder, though it makes no sense. I both want to pull her into my arms and also go hunt down Drew and tear his head off. Probably but not definitely metaphorically speaking.

I choose the hug instead.

"Come here."

I tug Amelia into my chest, dropping my chin to the top of her head. She doesn't hug me back, her arms hanging limply by her sides. Her whole body trembles, and my hands tighten into fists, my knuckles brushing against her spine.

When I hear what sounds like someone approaching the bathroom, I duck further into the stall, spinning us until Amelia's back is to the door, which I lock.

She sucks in a breath.

Not two seconds later, a woman walks inside and the water starts running. Amelia and I both hold still. I'm glad these stalls have fancy doors that extend all the way to the floor. Because it would be really obvious two people are inside this one.

The woman washes her hands for an excessively long time, and when she starts humming a One Direction song Amelia makes a small sound—stifling a laugh by the sound of it. I bite my lip, trying to hold in a laugh. She shakes in my arms.

I give her the tiniest pinch. She shakes harder.

I pull back so I can see Amelia's face, which makes it worse. When her eyes meet mine, she almost loses it. I cover her mouth with my hand, still biting my lip, and her eyes dance even as a leftover tear drips down the slope of her nose.

The moment the woman turns off the water and exits the room, still humming "Best Song Ever" under her breath, we both lose it.

Amelia clutches my shirt as she cackles, pressing her forehead to my chest. I love the sound of her laugh and the feel of her happiness.

It's like holding sunshine cupped in my palms.

When Amelia finally looks up at me, my laughter stills. Her smile fades, replaced with something totally different as the moment between us shifts.

Remembering why I'm here, I ask, "You okay, Mills?"

Her teeth worry her top lip, and I refuse to let my gaze fall there. Instead, I keep my eyes on her crystal blue ones. But as I watch, they fill with tears again.

I shouldn't have opened my stupid mouth. Should have stuck with laughter, pulled her out of the stall and taken her to dinner, pretending like I never found her crying in the bathroom to begin with.

"Hey," I say softly. "You know it's okay if you're *not* okay right now? Because you're going to get through this."

"Yeah?" she demands. "How do you know? You barely know me."

It doesn't feel that way. It didn't even feel that way on the night we met. More like … we'd known each other forever and just reconnected after a long absence, with lots of catching up to do.

The hours today have only added to that feeling. It's as though our time together runs on a different plane, slow and languid like taffy, stretching minutes into years.

"I know not many people would be able to make it through a day like this. And you did. You *are*," I tell her. "There will be hard days to come. But I can already tell that you will sail through them, Mills. You *will*. You hear me?"

She nods, the tiniest of smiles curling her lips up at the corners. But two tears slip from her eyes, rolling slowly over her cheeks. Without questioning the impulse, I lift my hands to cup her face, brushing the tears away with my thumbs.

"I hate seeing you sad," I whisper.

She shakes her head, still cupped within my hands. "I'm not sad," she says, even as another tear spills over.

I wait, biting the inside of my cheek so I don't fill the silence with something stupid. A trick I learned after years of doing it wrong with my sisters, making bad jokes or offering ill-fitting advice. "You just need to shut up," Callie told me once. It was Lex who had her heart broken, and I'd just said something ridiculous I don't even remember now.

"Okay, I'm a little sad," Amelia amends. "But not because I wish things turned out differently with Drew. I'm not sad about losing *him*."

It shouldn't make me so happy to hear how vehemently she says this, and how his name comes out of her mouth like a curse. But it does.

"I'm more sad about the idea," she goes on. "My parents had this amazing marriage ..." She pauses, draws in a deep breath, then continues. "They wanted more kids, but Mom couldn't get pregnant. So, we had this little, happy family of three. Until we lost her. It was important to my dad—you know, seeing me married and happy like he had been. He wants that for me. *I* want that for me."

Her words crack something open in me. I can almost imagine it. The picture of a perfect little family, and then Amelia in that white dress, beaming as she walks down the aisle on her father's arm.

Why she's beaming and walking toward *me* in this image, I don't know. Clearly, I'm not marriage material.

I let my hands fall from her face, sliding them down her arms to squeeze her hands. When I should let go, I don't. So we stand here, chest to chest in the bathroom stall, hands clasped together.

"So, you were marrying him to make your dad happy?"

"Not completely. I mean, I am a people pleaser. But it wasn't just because of my dad. It all kind of spiraled away from me. Drew ticked all the boxes," she says with a shrug. "I did *like* him. I convinced myself I loved him."

"You didn't?"

"No."

The word comes out with conviction. And it makes something buoy up inside me.

"Maybe it makes me sound crazy to say that when I was supposed to be marrying him today—"

"It doesn't." I squeeze her hands.

"It makes me *feel* crazy," she says. "Like, how could I not know how I felt before? Or how did I not have any signs he was cheating? I think I realized it the second you dragged him in there. I was so relieved. Disappointed and humiliated and angry, but relieved."

"Sometimes I think we see what we want to see," I say. "What we hope for."

She nods. "I definitely saw something other than reality. Especially when I had my dad right there, encouraging and supporting my choice to marry him." I frown, and she speaks quickly. "He didn't push me. You have to understand—losing Mom so young made Dad a huge proponent of doing things *now* and *soon*. Before it's too late. It's why he and I take big trips in the off-seasons, why he's been sky-diving and wants to climb Kilimanjaro. He even tried to convince me to swim with sharks in Australia."

"You don't want to have quality time with Jaws?" I ask.

"I'd like to keep my legs and arms, thank you very much."

"Good choice."

Amelia sighs and drops her forehead to my chest. "I can't believe I'm talking to you about all this. In a bathroom stall, no less."

"Overall, the ambience isn't so bad."

She giggles, lifting her head to look at me again. Without asking any kind of permission, my heart decides to kick into a higher gear.

"Thank you," she whispers. "You're a good listener."

"The guys would be shocked to hear you say that. They're always telling me to shut up."

"Don't shut up. I like what you have to say."

"Good," I say lightly. "Because you're stuck with me."

Her stomach chooses that moment to let out an unholy growl. She squeaks, yanking her hands away from mine and pressing them over her abdomen.

"How embarrassing," she says, but she's smiling. "I mean, we didn't eat that long ago. Did we?"

"It's been hours. The hotel restaurant was still open."

"Are you hungry?" she asks.

"I'm always hungry. Now, come on," I tell her, unlocking the stall door and stepping out. When I hold out my hand, she takes it with no hesitation. "Let's get you fed, Mills."

CHAPTER 10

Amelia

AFTER A VERY BRIEF meal as the restaurant was closing, Van and I ride the elevator in silence up to our room.

Our *one* room.

Though I started yawning heavily and almost fell asleep while eating my grilled shrimp salad, I am suddenly wide awake and tense. For the first time pretty much all day, aside from when he was listening to me in the bathroom, Van is quiet. Other than the crinkle of the plastic bags carrying all of our current worldly possessions, the elevator ride is painfully silent. I almost wish for terrible instrumental versions of pop songs to play through the speakers.

Twisting Mom's ring, I try to look at Van without turning my head, but I can only see his black dress shoes, winking as he shifts his weight.

Is he as nervous about this as I am?

Because despite how comfortable I feel with Van, we're about to share a single hotel room with a single bed.

Both of which turn out to be even smaller than I expected.

I mean, I knew it wouldn't be the suite Drew showed me pictures of when he booked the resort. But I also didn't expect a space barely big enough to fit a bed and a couch.

"That's not a king bed," I blurt. "Is it?"

Van is frozen just outside the door, like he's a vampire, needing an invitation to enter. His eyes scan the room, landing on the bed. "No," he agrees. "Not unless there's such a thing as a Florida king, which is somewhere between a twin and a double."

"It's fine," I say, as much to myself as to him. "We'll try to get a manager or something to move us to the suite tomorrow."

"Right," he says. "Tomorrow." He's still standing just outside, keeping the door propped open with one dress shoe.

"Are you coming in?" I ask.

He starts to step inside, then hesitates, his eyes meeting mine. "Are you sure you're okay with this?"

I wonder which part of *this* he means. The *this* where I'm sharing a room with a man I've spent a sum-total of less than twenty-four hours with in my whole life?

Or the *this* where we're practically going to be sleeping on top of each other?

Probably *not* the *this* where I'm feeling an unsettling attraction toward him.

I can only hope he can't tell. Because the last thing I want is for Van to think I'm looking for some kind of rebound hookup. Or *any* kind of rebound.

"We're both adults," I tell him, but the crack in my voice

undermines my words, making me sound like a teenage boy in the middle of puberty.

"Right," he agrees.

When he still doesn't move, I drop my bags on the bed and stride the four steps it takes to get to the door, dragging Van inside by his shirt sleeve. It seems important right now that I touch fabric, not skin.

The door slams behind him. A very final sound. One that has me swallowing hard and smiling too wide. Because the room suddenly feels like a trash compactor, the walls inching closer and closer as all oxygen seeps from the room.

We are standing in the narrowest part of the room, between the bathroom door and a tiny closet. Only one lamp near the bed offers any light in the room. Should have thought of that before I yanked him in here. Van's face looks dangerously handsome cast in shadow, his eyes inky and dark as they hold my gaze with an intensity I can't quite read.

Whatever exhaustion I felt during our meal downstairs has evaporated completely. I am now wired. It feels as though every cell in my body has been activated, and they're all tiny satellites, tuned to Van.

"Night swimming," I blurt, and he blinks like I've broken him out of a trance.

"What?"

"We should go swimming. Now."

"You're not tired?" he asks.

"Not anymore. Are you?"

Slowly, he shakes his head. When he speaks, it's in a rough rasp. "Not even a little."

"Then it's settled." I dart back to the bed, grab the two bags with my new Walmart digs, and sidestep Van on my way to the bathroom.

Before I can step inside, his fingers curl around my wrist.

"Hey," he says, whatever expression his face held moments before replaced with a divot between his brows and concern in his dark eyes. "Are you sure you don't want to sleep? You practically face-planted into your salad at dinner."

"I …"

Glancing around at anything but Van—the watercolor of a beach scene, the little metal sprinkler in the ceiling, the emergency exit map on the back of the door—I try to locate an answer. I'd rather not admit how uncomfortable I feel. Which has nothing to do with not trusting Van and everything to do with not trusting my feelings. Or my decisions. Or my hands, which practically shake with the desire to touch him.

"I don't want to sleep," I say finally.

Van waits, like he can tell there's more. And there is.

"Because when I wake up tomorrow, I think this all might hurt more," I whisper.

While I am nervous about sharing this tiny space with the big man still clasping my wrist, I'm surprised by this truth, which I just confessed so easily.

"Today is like a weird bubble," I continue, my words gathering momentum as they fall out of me like a long line of dominoes tipping into one another. "Doesn't it feel like it's been ten days?"

"It does. And also like it went by really quickly."

"Tomorrow is the start of a whole new chapter. It will all be real," I explain. "And I'm not ready."

Van nods, though I'm not even sure if this makes sense and is a very deep thought or if it's pure nonsense stemming from emotional overwhelm and the late hour. His fingertip brushes over the inside of my wrist before he releases me, and the champagne bubbles in my blood return with a vengeance. I'm practically drowning in them.

It's not a bad way to go.

"Then we put off tomorrow in favor of today," Van says with a grin. "Suit up, Mills. I'll race ya."

———

The only problem with this is that the water of today is much colder than I suspect the water of tomorrow will be.

"It's freezing!" I shriek.

Van only smirks, backing deeper into the water, his expression a clear challenge. "If you put more than your pinky toe in, maybe you'd get used to it."

"Shut up. You skate on ice for a living. Do you even *feel* cold?"

"I feel nothing," he says.

I roll my eyes, taking the tiniest of steps forward, sucking in a breath as a wave submerges me up to my ankles. Surprisingly, we aren't the only late-night beachgoers. A few other couples walk hand-in-hand along the shore, and there are two people making out in a lounge chair. Just down the beach, employees are cleaning up after a wedding. I have to swallow down a knee-jerk emotional reaction as a man on a stepladder takes down flowers draped over an archway.

Forcing my eyes away, my gaze snags on Van. It's a much better view.

I tried not to stare when he dropped his shirt in the sand a few minutes before, but now, I look my fill. He's broad and bulky. Solid and strong. And I can finally see his full tattoo, which is a dragon tattooed across one of his pecs and extending down his ribs.

Flames shoot from his open mouth, and thin plumes of smoke curl out of his nostrils almost to his collarbone. It's all done in delicate black lines, save the golden eye of the dragon, which is done so that no matter where I move, it's always watching me.

The whole thing is gorgeous.

If we were living in a fantasy novel, the tattoo would be some kind of enchanted creature. Like a familiar—a magical guardian that would be able to peel itself away from Van's body and come to life. An inky companion.

"Come on, Mills. Don't be scared."

Van cups his hand and arcs a spray of water my way. I squeal and jump back. But when he laughs, a deep, low sound of amusement I can feel all the way down in my toes, something snaps.

I practically rip the thin coverup over my head and sprint into the water.

Running into a much-too-cold ocean while sporting a neon-green Walmart bikini whose seams I don't quite trust?

Not on my bucket list.

More like on my *nope* list.

But Van's teasing, his challenge, and most especially, his laughter, emboldens me. He has that effect, like he is somehow able to reach in and tug at the heart of me. I can feel something shifting, lighting up as Van sends sparks of life into what was cold and dead.

Okay—that's a little dramatic. Into what was *dormant*. Not dead.

"Uh oh," Van says, backing up until he's waist-deep, just past where the waves curl and break. "Looks like I woke the beast."

"Are you calling *me* a beast?" I ask, feigning outrage. I stop a few feet away, hands on my hips, rocking a little as waves slap gently at my middle.

His smile widens. "Are you fishing for a compliment, Mills?"

"No." *Was I?* "But I'd prefer not to think of myself as beastly."

Especially on a day like today. I barely swallow rather than say those last words. Maybe I am fishing for compliments.

Or just a sense of being wanted, being desired. Even if, in the end, I didn't want Drew, he didn't want me first.

There's something about having a man choose someone else over you, or even choose someone else along with you in my case, that's shaking my confidence down to its roots. It sends thought cockroaches scurrying across my mind, the sort of worries and ideas that creep out in the darkness when you're lying in bed.

And I don't need Van seeing any more of my vulnerabilities when he's already been witness to so much humiliation.

There's a tight pinch in my chest, and suddenly, it's hard to catch my breath.

I may not have spoken the words, but I swear, Van knows. The smile slips from his space, and the crease reappears between his brows.

"Mills—" Van starts.

Before he can finish whatever pitying words he's about to say, I dive beneath the surface.

The shock is exactly what I need to zap away the icky feelings. I can't give weight to the unwanted emotions when all I can feel is *cold.*

Kicking off the sandy bottom, I swim toward where Van stood, hands outstretched. Almost immediately, my fingertips brush Van's calf.

He has the reflexes of a cat—or, I guess, or of a hockey player—and darts to the left. But not quickly enough. I wrap both arms around his knees and push off the bottom, lifting his legs off the ground and sending him toppling backwards as I surface.

Thank you, buoyancy and the Archimedes principle. And high school physics, I guess, for teaching me these terms I've never thought about until now.

The moment Van tips over, I release him and duck back under water, kicking away. When I come up for air, he's already back on his feet, sputtering and gasping, frantically scanning the water. His eyes land on me, and I can visibly see his shoulders sink with what looks like relief.

Was he worried about me?

Just as quickly, his eyes narrow and his expression shifts to something darker and dangerous. Keeping his gaze pinned on me, he shakes water from his hair, tilting his head to one side then the other, like he's clearing out water from his ears.

I grin. *Sorry, not sorry, big guy.*

"Quite a display of strength there, Mills. And subterfuge."

"Quite a display of vocabulary."

"I told you; I like to read," Van says, and before I start to pick that statement apart with a million questions about his reading, he speaks again. "Have you been lifting weights, Mills? Is wrestling your sport of choice?"

"Neither. I simply used the element of surprise combined with the effects of buoyancy against you. It's what happens when people call me a beast."

Van narrows his eyes and takes a step forward, his movement predatory. I take a step backward, my heart starting to hammer in my chest.

"You didn't let me finish," Van says, continuing to advance.

Slowly. Steadily. My heart feels as though it might fling itself right out of my chest as I continue to back away, needing to take two steps for each one of his.

"Oh? Did you have another insult to add?" I ask.

"Hardly."

But Van doesn't tell me whatever else he planned to say, and I can tell from the gleam of his smile that he knows it's driving me mad. I realize too late that Van has changed his angle, sidestepping until he's now between me and the shore, putting the deep water at my back. Which means I can only go so far. I'm already almost shoulder deep as he advances toward me.

I have no idea how well Van swims, but he's without a doubt more athletic than I am. I don't need to watch the droplets of water tracing a slow path over his pecs and down the start of his blocky abs to know how fit he is. My swimming prowess extends to some third- and fourth-place swim team ribbons when I was a kid. Somehow, I don't think breaststroke is going to help me now.

I may not *need* to watch, but I find myself mesmerized for just a moment by the ridges of muscle and—wait. Is he flexing his pecs on purpose?

My steps have slowed while I was distracted, allowing Van to get almost within reach.

I dart back and a little to the side, water sloshing up to my chin. "Stop that!"

"Stop what?" He laughs. "Chasing you? Or distracting you with my pecs?"

"Both."

"Maybe if you stopped ogling me—"

"I wasn't ogling!" When he arches one dark brow, teeth gleaming in the moonlight, I splash him. "Fine! But I was—"

Van leaps forward, cutting off my words as his hands grasp my waist. I shriek.

"Calm down or someone will think I'm murdering you," he says through a laugh, then lifts me like he's going to toss me.

"No! Please!" I beg, trying to find a handhold on his body.

Aside from attaching myself to his torso like I'm a barnacle and he's the prow of a boat, I can't hold on. My fingers slip over his slick skin, struggling to hold onto the swell of his shoulders.

"*No please*, what?" Van asks, eyes gleaming and lips curving up in a smile.

"No, please don't throw me," I say, not even caring that I'm begging.

"Who said anything about throwing you?"

But even as the question is leaving his mouth, Van jerks me higher, loosening his grip like he's going to toss me, only to tighten it again. Such a tease. He pulls me back to his chest, laughing. I start to scream and one of his hands releases my waist to cover my mouth.

"No screaming," he says. I nip at his finger and he drops his hand, going back to gripping my waist. "And no biting."

"I make no promises," I tell him.

"Fine. If you don't like being tossed, how do you feel about spinning?"

Without waiting for my answer, Van adjusts his grip and starts to spin us. Tight circles pinwheeling through the water. My own personal spinning teacup ride.

Okay, *this* I don't mind.

I tilt my head back, reveling in the dizzying feeling of motion and the closeness of Van's solid body, the warmth and strength of his hands on me. There's too much light pollution to see many stars, but there are scattered pinpricks of light against the curtain of black sky.

It's a beautiful night, and I want to wrap it around me like a shawl. To revel in the lightness and joy sparking deep in my chest.

And to think—I was supposed to be married tonight.

Had my life gone according to plan, I would be here with Drew. Though, not *here*. Our flight was supposed to be tomorrow, and Drew is not a night swimming kind of guy.

And until now, I don't think I would have considered myself a night swimming kind of woman. Whatever we would have been doing, I'm so grateful I'm *here* instead.

As Van slows down and comes to a stop, staggering dramatically as though too dizzy to keep his balance—okay, maybe he actually is too dizzy to stay still—I brush his wet hair back from his forehead.

"Thank you," I tell him, tasting salt on my lips.

He tilts his head. "For not throwing you?"

"No. For making this fun instead of miserable. For giving up Vegas or whatever else you could have done on this break. I know your schedule will be ridiculous when you get back. You're giving up your time to be with someone you barely know."

"It doesn't feel that way," Van says.

"You mean it doesn't feel like you barely know me?"

It's the same for me. From the very start, Van felt like he wasn't new to me. Like he'd always been there, like an invisible seed making itself known in spring when shoots break through the surface, the roots already spreading wide.

"That—and giving up. This isn't a sacrifice, Mills. I'm having fun too."

There's an instant shift in the air between us, reminding me of the way a cold front blows in from the mountains, dropping the temperature rapidly with a few strong gusts of wind.

Now, we're staring at each other as though our gazes snagged and are linked together.

A lush headiness diffuses through my limbs as Van

continues to stare. Because the way he's looking at me, it's almost like—

No.

He can't want to kiss me.

He can't be feeling the same strong tug I am, a riptide drawing me out to sea.

The best way to fight a riptide, I remind myself, *is not to fight.*

You let it draw you away from shore, then when the riptide ceases, you swim parallel to the shore until you can come back in. My dad drilled that into me every beach trip we took. Which wasn't many. He had an irrational fear about riptides or, more likely, just about me drowning.

Is it bad to think about Van like a riptide? To stop fighting this pull?

If I let it take me out, when this attraction ends or when we go home or when he stops being so sweet and looking at me like he wants to kiss me, I can swim away and head back to shore. And to normalcy.

Then again, if he keeps looking at me like this, I'm not sure I'll survive it.

Maybe the rules of riptides should not apply here. I have a sneaking suspicion I'll be dragged out to sea, then left without the strength to get myself back to shore at all.

Fueled by a sudden sense of self-preservation—along with the need to *not* kiss this man on the day I was supposed to marry another one—I break the moment, shoving at his chest lightly.

"Shut up."

His gaze snaps from my mouth back to my eyes, and he loosens his grip on me, allowing my feet to touch sand again. I back away one step. Two.

"I didn't say anything," he says.

"You were thinking about it. Stop."

His smile is brighter than any star I can see. "You've got it. Whatever you ask for, Mills."

And I shiver, not because the cold of the water is finally seeping through my bones, but because I realize that in his simple offer of whatever *I* want, Van just gave me more than Drew ever did.

CHAPTER 11

Van

I WAKE WITH A GROAN, feeling the telltale ache that comes with hotel travel. Even though the Appies' accommodations got a major upgrade in the last eighteen months, a hotel bed is a hotel bed is a hotel bed.

And a hotel couch is a hotel couch.

I'm sprawled out shirtless on a sofa, one knee bent and the other leg dangling over the side, my foot flat on the floor. I barely fit—why am I sleeping here? My jaw aches and as I blink, I can feel swelling in one eye and the other cheek.

Did I get in a fight last night? I don't even remember the game.

Do we have a game today? What city are we in?

Is that coffee I smell?

How did I not make it into bed?

The answers, along with memories, come to me in a rush when I hear a voice say, "Morning, sunshine. Nice hair."

I glance over to see Amelia, sitting cross-legged with a paper cup on the definitely not king-size bed. Which is close enough to the couch that I could nudge her with my foot.

Her honey hair is down and wild, like she got out of bed, gave her head a good shake, and called it good. She's fresh-faced without even a hint of makeup and wearing the Batman pajama pants and black tank she picked out at Walmart last night.

Not gonna lie—it's a good look on her.

I rub the grit from my eyes, not even bothering to straighten out my hair, which likes to do its own thing in the mornings. "What time is it?"

My voice still sounds like it's been through a paper shredder, which is about how I sound for the first hour I'm up every morning. Usually, no one's around to hear it, and I feel slightly self-conscious. At least it didn't crack.

"A little after ten."

Amelia laughs at my expression, which is probably horrified. I can't remember the last time I slept this late, even on days we don't have morning practice. A little coffee sloshes over the paper cup she's holding.

"Oops." She lifts the mug and licks the droplets of coffee right off the side. I can't look away from her mouth.

Taking a deep inhale through my nose, I squeeze my eyes closed. It's far too early to be thinking the kinds of things I'm thinking about *the coach's daughter*.

Those three words are as effective as any cold shower. Or they should be. Repeating this phrase in my head worked most of yesterday.

Up until the moment I almost kissed her in the ocean.

That memory slams into me with the weight of a building

collapse. I can hardly believe I let things get to that point. It wasn't my intention.

One minute we were playing, and I was feeling good about making her smile after a terrible day. I didn't realize the urge to kiss her was coming until I found my eyes dropping to her lips and my whole body swaying toward her.

If Amelia hadn't said something, I might have actually done it. I might have kissed her.

And while this memory should serve as a cautionary tale to me in the bright light of morning, it doesn't. Instead, thinking about the almost kiss, about the way Amelia felt in my arms, only makes the blood cycle faster through me. It's a challenge to keep my gaze from her mouth as she lifts the cup to her lips.

I am in so. Much. Trouble.

"Your face doesn't look horrible," Amelia says.

I open my eyes. "Best compliment I've had all day."

She laughs, golden hair dancing around her shoulders. "I just mean, you're a little swollen, but the black eye isn't so bad."

"Yet," I say. "Tomorrow it will look worse. Trust me."

My phone buzzes on the little table next to the couch. It's plugged into the charger I bought last night. I sit up, reaching for it. Needing a distraction.

And ... it's Coach Davis. What perfect, poetic, terrible timing.

I don't answer, though I'll need to call him back soon. Can't have him imagining the worst. Or knowing the reality. Which means maybe calling him back after we figure out this rooming situation. If Amelia can move into the suite she and her ex booked, then I'll stay here, keeping my separate rooms promise to Coach.

"Are the guys texting you again?" Amelia asks.

They probably are, but I still have their thread muted so I can have some amount of peace. "It's your dad."

"Oh." She takes a measured sip of her coffee. "I'm sure Morgan told him I'm with you. Think he'll freak out?"

This is the perfect opportunity to tell her that not only was her father on board, but asked me to come.

I'm not sure why I don't.

Coach said not to, but it's not for fear of him that I don't tell Amelia. I mean, letting him think I'm helping him out is a chance to get in his better graces. But I've survived being his least liked player this long. He didn't take me off my line for personal reasons—it wasn't until my performance started sucking. And there's no way he could have guessed it had to do with my complicated feelings about his daughter's upcoming wedding.

Ultimately, I think I don't want Amelia to think I'm here because of her dad. Like some kind of bodyguard slash babysitter who was hired to do what I'm doing.

I'm here for her. That's it.

I don't want her overthinking or rethinking my every move, doubting my reasons for being here. Doubting my words. Doubting *me*.

"If so, I'll handle it. Is there any more coffee where that came from?" I grumble, needing caffeine about as much as I need a new direction for our conversation to go in.

"Coming right up!"

Amelia's too-bright voice tells me she is the most *morning* of morning people.

Of course she is. The sunshine to my dark morning cloud. I'm glad, though, happy she seems to have been wrong about waking up with a painful crash into her new reality.

She sets her mug down and hops off the bed and into the

bathroom, where I guess the coffee pot is? I didn't notice much last night aside from how small this room is.

After swimming, we took turns changing in the bathroom, where I also took a cold shower just as a reminder of where my brain needs to stay. When I emerged, wearing the athletic shorts I'm using as pajamas, Amelia had her back turned to me and was already asleep. Locating a coffee pot was the last thing on my mind.

"How do you take your coffee?" she calls. "No—wait. Let me guess." She leans out of the bathroom door, tapping her lips with a finger. "Black."

"Close." I make her wait a few seconds, mostly because I like seeing her riled up. When her eyes narrow and she starts drumming her fingers on the door fame, I answer. "Two creams, no sugar. Maybe three creams."

Amelia whistles. "Three creams? Wow. Want some coffee with your milk?"

"It's the perfect ratio. How do you drink yours?"

"Black. One sugar in the raw. If it's available."

I wrinkle my nose. "That's *one* choice you can make."

"Shut up, Mr. Cream."

"That is *not* going to be my nickname, Mills."

"We'll see. You gave me one without asking how I felt about it."

"I thought you liked Mills."

Instead of answering, she ducks into the bathroom again, where I hear the last drips landing in the cup. Didn't she say she liked it? Did I overstep? But when she comes back out, her smile is smug, like she knew I was suffering while I waited for her answer.

"Don't worry," she tells me, handing me my coffee. "I love it."

Relieved, I settle back on the couch, hearing a few loud

pops in my back. Amelia returns to the bed fluffing a pillow in her lap as she sips her coffee.

"Good. Now we can work on finding one for me that I approve of."

"We'll see, Mr. Cream."

"*No.*"

"I'm open to your suggestions," she says with a laugh.

"Romeo? Casanova? Handsome?" I tease.

She makes a buzzer sound. "No way. I could always just go with Vanity."

I groan. "Not that. Please not that."

"Okay, hotshot." Her eyes widen and she bounces a little on the bed, sending more coffee dripping over the rim of her cup. This time she doesn't lick it off. "That's it! Hotshot. Like *Speed*." When I stare blankly, she gives me an incredulous look. "You know—the movie with Sandra Bullock."

"Is that the one with the witches?"

"No." She looks aghast.

I yawn. "Was she the FBI agent pretending to be a beauty pageant contestant?"

"No—that's *Miss Congeniality*."

"Hm. Then I don't think I saw *Speed*."

Amelia's eyes go wide. "You've never seen it? Are you serious?"

"When did it come out?"

"Sometime in the nineties? I don't know exactly." When I shake my head, she leaves the coffee and rummages around the room until she finds the remote. "We should watch it."

"What—like now?"

"Why not? I'm sure we can find it streaming somewhere."

I take a sip of coffee. It tastes like what you'd expect from coffee made in a bathroom. "We're staying at a fancy resort and you want to watch a movie?"

A flush rises in her cheeks, and I feel bad about my comment. I also realize she has freckles. I'd never noticed them, and I wonder if she covered them with makeup the times I'd seen her before. They're light, barely visible now that she's blushing, but they cover her cheeks and the bridge of her nose.

"I mean, we can do whatever we want," she says, looking down. "And you don't have to hang out with me all the time."

"What if my only plans for this trip are to hang out with you every moment of every day?"

The pink in her cheeks deepens, but now she smiles. "I'd be okay with that. But I don't want you to get sick of me."

"I'm afraid you're stuck with me, Mills. But first order of business: we should call about your luggage and also see about getting your suite."

"Was the couch terrible? I tried to make you take the bed!"

I wasn't about to make her sleep on the couch. Even if it would have been a better fit for her than me. "Nonsense. I'm fine. But I wouldn't be opposed to booking a massage at some point."

"That can be arranged."

We decide to split up. I stay in the room and call the airline about her luggage, while she heads down to the lobby —still in pajamas, which I love—to ask about the suite she and Drew booked for tonight.

After I get hung up on twice and end up leaving a voice message I'm sure no one will ever hear, I pull a shirt on and head down to see what's keeping Amelia. Even if the reservation was in her ex's name, the suite will likely be at least available tonight.

Or not.

"You already booked the suite?" Amelia sounds half a breath away from pure panic. "How is that possible? I was supposed to be staying there tonight. We had a reservation."

This morning, the woman with the tight bun has been replaced with a guy who looks barely old enough to vote.

"We did keep the reservation," he says, clearing his throat and tapping on the computer keys.

"But you *didn't*," Amelia says as I reach her. "Obviously." She shakes her head at me as if silently saying, *can you believe this?* Honestly, with her luck the past twenty-four hours, I can believe it. "I'm right here, and you're telling me the suite is taken. So, how did you honor the reservation? Please. Explain."

Her voice is almost banshee-like and she punctuates her words by tapping her finger on the counter. I step closer, wrapping an arm around her shoulders. She relaxes into me with a soft exhale, and it instantly makes me feel better.

"Obviously, there's some confusion," I say.

The boy-man stops tapping at the computer and cracks his knuckles before answering. "As I've previously stated several times, the honeymoon suite is currently occupied."

I can feel Amelia coiling tightly with tension. Hoping to prevent a total nuclear meltdown, I angle her away from the counter as I lean closer.

"We understand someone was in the room last night. But check out is at"—I glance around, finally spotting a small sign behind the counter— "eleven. So, once the occupants check out, she would like the room she reserved."

"Months ago," Amelia adds. "We reserved it *months* ago."

The boy-man nods slowly, with exaggerated patience. "Yes. There was a reservation. And while I can't give out any information about guests, the person who made the reservation just checked in early."

Amelia and I both go still, and it's as though twin light bulbs go off above our heads. The honeymoon suite is occupied—*by the person who reserved it.*

As in, Drew the Douchebag Groom.

"Check-in isn't until three," Amelia whispers, as though this is the most unbelievable part of all this.

Or maybe the only thing she can process right now is hotel policy. Because thinking about everything else is *worse.*

The boy-man behind the counter has the decency to look apologetic.

I'm not sure how this is possible, but it sounds like Drew managed to swoop in—or fly in, I guess—and claim the suite already this morning. How? Why?

But it doesn't matter. Only two things do.

The first is that we're going to be stuck in the tiny room with all the nearly combustible tension between us.

The second is that Amelia's ex fiancé is here. In this hotel. Right now.

Coach had the right idea throwing a chair through a window. I'd like to do the same thing now. Except maybe substitute Drew for a chair. I imagine how satisfying it would be to toss him through a window or a wall, leaving a douche-shaped outline like in a cartoon.

"I wish you had run him over," Amelia says softly. She sounds like she's in shock.

I wish I'd agreed to her movie idea. It's way too early for all this.

It's also too early for anything worse, and when the boy-man's eyes go wide, focusing on something—or *someone*—behind us, I know something absolutely worse is happening.

There aren't enough curse words in the world to use as Amelia and I turn to see Drew walking out of the elevator. He's wearing swim trunks, one hand holding a hotel towel held under one arm … and he has the other wrapped around Amelia's cousin.

I'm striding across the lobby before logical and rational thoughts can stop me, ignoring Amelia as she calls my name. I don't stop until I reach the Douche.

There are a few gasps from people nearby as I grab him by the back of the shirt collar, yank him away from Amelia's cousin, and haul him inside the elevator just before the doors close. Barely giving the panel a glance, I hit a random button near the top.

Then I let go of Drew's collar and step into his space.

"Hey—" he starts.

"You do not get to speak right now. What you're going to do is listen very carefully. I will not repeat myself. But I will make myself clear without words if you don't hear me the first time. Got it?"

Drew opens and closes his mouth, but as I step closer, looming over him, he nods. But he's glaring, looking like a kid who got caught lying to his parents and is trying to blame *them* for his bad behavior. Whatever. I can't make him do the work he needs if he wants to be a decent human.

But I can make him do one thing.

"My team and I, we have rules."

He snorts, and I close all the distance between us until we're chest to chest. I've got a good six inches on him and even more in bulk. I almost never throw my weight around off the ice—unless my sisters are involved.

Or, I guess, Amelia.

Before I can continue, the elevator dings and the doors slide open. Not stepping away from Drew, I glance back, hoping to scare off whoever it is with a look.

But the older woman stepping into the elevator wearing a

151

blue coverup and a beach bag doesn't seem to read the room —or, in this case, the elevator—because she steps inside.

"I'm kind of in the middle of something here," I tell her.

The woman sniffs, then raises one sculpted eyebrow. "I don't mind."

Okay, then.

Turning back to Drew, I tilt my head, cracking my neck. Always a good intimidation move. It also helps slightly with the crick I have from sleeping on the plane.

"When we get back down to the lobby, you are going to walk right over to the front desk and give up the honeymoon suite."

"But I—"

"No."

I stop just short of grabbing him by his scrawny neck. I already risked enough dragging him onto the elevator. Pressing assault charges would fit right into his whole wimpy aesthetic. He flinches, even as my finger hovers inches from his chest, pointing at him but not touching.

"There is no *but* that could possibly excuse you sleeping with the maid of honor who is also your ex-fiancée's cousin, then coming here and claiming the honeymoon suite for the two of you."

"I paid for it," he sneers.

"I don't care. I'll happily foot the bill as soon as you turn over the room to us. You'll need to save your money anyway. Because you are going to pay Coach and Amelia back every single cent they spent on the wedding. Because you know what?"

I lean closer until our foreheads are inches apart.

"It's the right thing to do. You don't seem to have any concept of right or wrong, so consider this my way of helping you out. Explain the situation to the front desk. Then get your stuff out. Preferably, take it to another hotel. Or another state."

"I'm not—"

The woman, whom I'd forgotten about until now, speaks. "Young man, are you really trying to argue?"

I take a step back from Drew as he stutters a response.

"Uh, y-yes ma'am."

She shakes her head at him and turns to me. "I'm a lawyer." She pulls out an embossed card from her beach bag and hands it to me. "And I specialize in civil cases much like this one. I wish I could say this is a one-off, but there are plenty of bad fish in the sea."

I take the woman's card, sliding it into my pocket. Not a bad idea to put her on call. The team has lawyers but I don't know if they'll help with something like this.

"And there aren't enough men like you." She pats my arm, then steps back, waving a hand. "Continue. We're almost back down to the lobby."

I glare at Drew. "Do we understand each other?"

For a moment, I really think he's going to argue. The woman clears her throat, and in my peripheral vision, I see her shaking her head.

"Fine," Drew spits out.

"Good." While I feel like I've taken some small slice of justice, it's not nearly enough as I feel the elevator slowing. "Last thing. I'd ask you to apologize to Amelia, but it's clear you don't have the proper understanding of what you've done wrong. So, don't talk to her. Don't call her or text her. Don't look at her. Because she deserves better. She deserves the kind of man you could never hope to be."

"Let me guess," Drew says, narrowing his eyes. "You think *you're* that man?"

I raise my voice, as obviously, he has a hearing problem.

"I don't come close to being good enough for Amelia. But if she were mine? I would never let her go. I would spend every waking day and every single breath just hoping I could show her the love she deserves."

I don't realize the elevator is stopped and the doors are open until I hear clapping. It starts with the lawyer still standing a few feet away but she's quickly joined by most of the lobby by the time I've turned around.

Everyone *but* Amelia and her cheating cousin. They aren't standing anywhere near each other, but share the same shocked expression. Amelia blinks at me like I've just announced I'm an alien, here on a mission to destroy the earth.

Ignoring everyone but her, I cross the lobby and lace my fingers through Amelia's before I can rethink it. I hope she doesn't feel the way my hand is shaking.

"Let's go pack up your things. I think by the time we get back down here, our room situation will be straightened out."

CHAPTER 12

Amelia

"LET ME GET THIS STRAIGHT," Morgan says. "Drew and Becky checked into the honeymoon suite this morning but Restaurant Robbie drove them out with a pitchfork?"

"Van. Yes. But without the pitchfork."

"A flaming torch?" she asks hopefully. "A sword?"

"Just with words. And possibly some threats."

"Okay," Morgan says. "I can believe it. But now you're sharing the honeymoon suite with Restaurant Robbie—"

"*Van.*"

"—because they didn't have any other rooms."

"Correct."

Morgan is quiet for a beat. I'm sitting on the balcony, still in my pajamas, watching the beach below. Sweating a little because even in the shade with a fan overhead, it's a hot, cloudless day. A beautiful, ripe peach of a day, ready for the plucking.

But I'm alone in the gorgeous, airy honeymoon suite, hanging on the balcony watching other people living resort lives down below while I'm huddled out here on a call with my best friend. In somewhat of a panic, I might add.

Van left almost an hour ago for the fitness center, claiming he needed to get in a quick workout.

Which could be true. It probably is. I mean, hockey is his job, so needing to work out makes logical sense.

But he was quiet after we left the lobby. After what he said to Drew in the lobby.

Quiet on the ride back up to the tiny room we shared last night. Quiet while I packed. *Really* quiet when the front desk called up to say he would need to check out of this room as the hotel is completely booked. Quiet as we moved all of our stuff—still in Walmart bags—up to this suite, which is like five times the size of where we stayed last night.

Despite that, when the door closed behind us, I swear the room felt more like a closet.

Because after what Van said to Drew in front of half the hotel, something shifted for me, but also based on his uncharacteristic silence, for him. For us.

Or maybe he regrets what he said? Or regrets that I overheard?

If Amelia were mine? I'd never let her go.

The tug of longing in my chest nearly bowled me over as I listened to Van's words.

Yesterday, he asked if I was just marrying Drew because my dad wanted me to, and I said no. And it's true. Drew's bad behavior didn't strangle out my desire for marriage. I still want to have what Dad and Mom did—almost as badly as Dad wants that for me.

156

I think I wanted it so badly in fact, I focused on the *what* and picked the wrong *who*.

And now ... I don't think I'm stupid to imagine Van as a potential *who*. I felt it the night we met—this instant connection, a spark of something bigger. There was something different between us then, and the same something is different now.

The problem isn't the *who*; it's the *when*.

How can I trust my feelings after they've been put through a wood chipper?

I know I'm a complete mess. Even if I don't feel it yet.

"I'm not sure whether I should warn you away from having a rebound or cheer you on," Morgan says, almost like she portaled into my brain and rooted around in my thoughts.

I flinch at the word *rebound*. That's not who Van is. Not who I want him to be, anyway.

"What if," I ask slowly, glancing behind me at the empty suite just to be sure Van hasn't returned. "What if Van is more than a rebound?"

Another, longer pause. "You think you feel something real, Milly?" she asks. Carefully, like I'm a hardboiled egg she's trying to peel in one go. "Already? I'm not trying to be rude. It's just ... you were supposed to get married yesterday."

"I *know*."

"I mean, I'm all for you taking some risks. Blowing off some steam. You deserve to have a few days of a sort of fantasy life."

Sure. All that sounds good. Only, I don't agree that this is just a fantasy or blowing off steam. Is it?

"But I would be a bad friend if I didn't tell you it sounds totally out of character for you to fall hard for someone right after your engagement and wedding fell apart. I mean, this isn't you. It sounds like maybe denial or transference or something."

"It's not so ridiculous," I say, sounding more defensive than I feel. What I actually feel is hurt. Deeply wounded. And afraid of what truth might be in her words. I touch Mom's ring and take a slow breath before I continue. "I told you the night I met him how different it was. I talked about him for weeks. Wondered why he left and what could have been. Remember?"

"Oh, I remember. You were a mess. Then Drew happened. He was basically a rebound for a relationship that never even happened. Listen, I'm not saying your feelings for Van aren't real."

"You're not?"

"No. I'm saying they might not be. And I don't know how you'll actually know in the span of a few days on vacation with him. Which is why I think you should be very careful," Morgan says, shocking me.

I would have assumed the wild child to my rule-following people-pleasing self would tell me to let loose and go for it.

Her warning is not what I want to hear. And like Van said, I get to make the rules here.

"But when you suggested I come here, you said I should have a good time."

"Right. But you're talking about *more* than a good time. If you think that there's something real here, potential for more with Van, then you don't want to act on it. Not now."

"Why not?" I know I sound stubborn. Borderline whiny. Because my best friend is telling me I can look at a cake, but I can't have it and I certainly can't eat it too.

No cake. No eating.

No *fair*.

"Because you've been through something huge, Milly. You're probably still processing. Or in denial. Right now, you're probably not feeling like yourself."

She's right about that. But it's not a bad thing. I feel free. Hopeful. Curious and actually excited to see what comes next. Relieved I didn't make the biggest mistake of my life. I feel itchy to write. Brave, like maybe instead of looking for another boring office job dictated by my degree, I'll look for something to do with what I actually love instead.

I worried that waking up today would be a shock. That I'd crack open my eyes, remember the whole horrible ordeal with Drew, and collapse.

Instead, I woke up and saw Van, sprawled out on the couch. I smiled. Remembered the day we had. How he cared enough to force Drew to confess. Cared enough to be my getaway driver and then my travel companion. He made me smile. Even laugh. He wiped tears from my cheeks in a bathroom stall.

Who does that?

The kind of guy you *keep*. That's who.

Now Morgan is saying to ignore that. She's telling me not to act on the things I feel just because of what I've gone through in the last day.

Okay. Fine. It *is* very logical. I see where she's coming from. It's good advice. Best friend advice.

Normally, it's the advice I would be giving *her*.

But I don't want to hear it. I certainly don't want to take it.

The sound of a door closing has me turning around again, peering through the glass.

What I *want* is the man who glances everywhere until he sees me on the balcony. A man whose whole body relaxes when his eyes find mine. A man whose sweat-soaked shirt sticks to his body like a second skin. Whose dark hair is a mess. Whose smile sends my insides veering off a cliff and into a freefall.

"Milly?" Morgan says.

I'm still watching Van, who points toward the bathroom, lifting his brows in question. When I nod, he grins, then peels off his shirt, leaving it on the floor as he walks into the bathroom. Okay—a little gross. But the man has to have some flaws. The last thing I see is his smooth, muscular back, the ink of his dragon's tail curling over his ribs.

What Morgan's saying is smart. I should definitely take her advice. Totally.

"I've got to go," I say, getting to my feet.

"Are you sure you're okay?"

"No," I tell her. "But I will be."

Of this one thing, I'm absolutely sure. Everything else? As the Magic 8-Ball would say, *Ask again later*.

———

"You're writing." A pleased smile accompanies the statement.

A shirtless chest accompanies Van.

I glance away lest I get caught ogling him again and stretch out my hand. It's cramping around the pen from twenty or so minutes of nonstop writing.

The moment I hung up with Morgan, I came inside, opened up the new notebook I bought, and put pen to paper. I'm a little surprised to see that while Van was showering, I've filled four pages front and back about how to survive your wedding falling apart. It's a mix of rules, inspired by Van's suggestion yesterday, and stream-of-consciousness feelings.

"I guess I am."

"Awesome." He rubs a small, white towel over his hair, then tosses it in the general direction of the bathroom.

"For a man whose car is ridiculously neat, you seem to have a different approach to living spaces." I nod toward the sweaty shirt, still on the floor, and then the towel.

Van picks up both. "I'm in vacation mode," he says. "Or maybe I'm just leaving breadcrumbs behind so you can find me."

I laugh, and as he approaches, I close my notebook, suddenly feeling shy.

"I don't want to interrupt you," he says.

"Yeah you do."

"Yeah. I do." He grins, nudging my bare foot with his own. "But seriously, if you're in the middle of something, I'll go out again. Give you peace. Or wander to another end of this giant suite and you'll never know I was here."

"Other than your *breadcrumbs*."

He laughs. "Other than that."

Honestly, the suite is big enough to share with another person and not know they're here. This living area is bigger than the one in Dad's house, and though the kitchen doesn't have more than a sink, fridge, and some appliances, the dining table seats twelve. The sectional sofa could hold almost that many and there are a few chairs around as well.

The bedroom has its own seating area, and the bathroom is the size of my bedroom at home. I think the walk-in shower is the size of my whole bathroom.

Everything is done in pale pinks and turquoise, an upscale beachy feel with potted palms and flowers every-where, gauzy curtains hang over the sliding doors in here and the private balcony off the master bedroom.

It's gorgeous. But I couldn't help but feel a tiny pinch of

regret that it means now there will be a whole room and a closed door between Van and me. I won't wake up a few feet from him, able to reach out and touch him if I wanted.

Sheesh. One night and I'm already thinking about withdrawal. Maybe Morgan was right.

I set down the pen and shake out my hand. "I need a break. My fingers might permanently freeze in this position otherwise. How was your workout?"

His eyes cut away. "Okay. The fitness center is decent."

"But?"

He gives me a sheepish grin. "I ran into some Appies fans, which meant cutting things short."

I remember the woman on the plane and her blatant overtures. I almost ask if they were male or female fans but restrain myself. "Does that happen often?"

Van plops down on the couch and rests his feet on the coffee table near my notebook. "More and more. Things changed a lot in the last eighteen months. It happened fast. The power of social media, I guess. Have you met Parker?"

I shake my head. "I know who she is. But Dad pretty much keeps me from his work world."

"Is that who you were talking to when I got back? Your dad?" he asks, voice carefully and uncharacteristically neutral.

I have a brief moment of panic as I realize one more logical reason to tread carefully with Van, one Morgan didn't realize. My dad. He's kept me away from hockey players because he doesn't want my heart broken by some athlete. And now, I'm falling for the guy on his team he apparently likes the least.

"That was Morgan," I say. "She said she'd tell him I'm fine. He's still pretty upset, and she thought it might make me upset."

"How *are* you feeling?" Van asks.

I grin. "Shockingly good. Though I feel bad about feeling good, if that makes sense."

He reaches over and gives me a little pinch. "No guilt. It's in the rules."

I tap the notebook. "I actually added that in."

"That's what you were writing?" He looks pleased, and warmth fills my chest.

"I had an idea for a blog post. One that's funny, but also touches on real stuff. A mix of humor and advice. Who knows? Maybe you'll even get a little credit, considering you keep trying to make the rules."

He holds up both hands. "I'll stop. I swear. The rules are up to you. And so is our agenda. So, what are you thinking about doing today?"

I hesitate, remembering the way it felt to see Drew and Becky in the lobby. I may be completely and one hundred percent glad I didn't marry him, but it doesn't remove the sting of the whole thing. Or the awkwardness of standing near my cousin while listening to Van shout at my ex-fiancé, who is now apparently Becky's new *official* boyfriend.

I'm not sure if they're still here or if they left, and I'd kind of rather not find out.

I pick up the remote. "While you were showering, I happened to find *Speed*."

Van's lips twist. "We're at a fancy resort on the ocean, and you want to watch a movie in your pajamas?"

"With room service," I add, wishing this didn't sound as lame as it does. I set the remote back on the table. "You can do whatever. It's not like you have to babysit me."

He stiffens at this, his jaw tensing underneath a layer of dark stubble. "That's not what I'm doing, Mills. As long as you want me around, I'm here. Is watching a movie what you really want to do?"

I hesitate. I'm physically and emotionally wrung out. Escaping into a movie sounds phenomenal. So does sharing a couch and a meal with a shirtless Van.

I'd also prefer not seeing Drew and Becky. Ever again. But definitely not today.

"For now. Yes."

"Okay." Van picks up the remote, then tosses me the leather room service menu with the hotel logo embossed on the front. "Then a movie and room service it is."

———

Two hours and one blown-up bus later, Van and I are reclining on the couch, surrounded by the remnants of half the room service menu, and arguing over whether Keanu Reeves can act or not.

Van is operating under the misguided assumption that Keanu is some kind of robot clone, delivering all of his lines with the same tone and facial expression.

Clearly, he's incorrect.

"Have you even read about his tragic life?" I press a hand to my chest. "So much pain."

"No. I have not read about his tragic life. And that's not what's in question. It's his ability to *act*."

"I think we're just going to have to agree to disagree. Or maybe we need more data points!" I reach over and smack him on the thigh. Momentarily get distracted by the width of it. The firmness. Shake my head and drag myself back to the topic at hand. "There's *The Lake House*, which also has Sandra Bullock and—"

"Or the *John Wick* movies, where he maintains the same

expression the whole time while killing everyone involved in the killing of his dog."

"His dog dies?" I whisper. "That's awful."

"We could also watch *The Matrix* movies where he maintains the same expression while knowing Kung Fu. Because the man can't act."

"I don't get it. What do you have against Keanu Reeves? The only thing I can think of is jealousy."

"You think I'm jealous? I'm not jealous. I just think he sucks at his job."

I navigate to the search area, driven by a crazed need for Van to understand the error of his ways, but he plucks the remote from my hand and holds it up. I reach for it, but he lifts his arm above his head.

"Van."

"Mills."

"Give me the remote."

"No."

Without stopping to consider any of the consequences, I launch myself into his lap, holding his arm still with one hand and grasping for the remote in the other.

"Mills," he says, too easily passing the remote from one hand to the other. He grunts when I lean over, my knee going into his stomach. "No more Keanu. You're cut off."

Just as I grab his other arm, he flicks his wrist and sends the remote skittering over the tile floor. The back pops off and the batteries fall out. One rolls under the armchair as we both watch, me still sprawled over him, one hand still curled around his forearm.

But when our heads turn back to each other, we seem to realize at the same time how close we are.

I am draped over his lap, one hand still gripping his

forearm while the other is flat on his bare chest. Our faces are just inches apart.

And just like the brief moment in the ocean last night where the tension spun a tight web around us, everything slips away. There's only Van, his breath catching as his gaze drops to my lips. And me, trying to ignore the rising heat making me think stupid thoughts.

Thoughts about kissing him.

Thoughts about rebounds and what Morgan said about timing.

Thoughts about almost making a huge mistake marrying the wrong person.

Van's eyes meet mine, and I swear, I see conflict there, mirroring my own.

Is he afraid of my dad? Worried about the timing of this as well?

Or maybe this is just physical attraction for him, not the bigger thing I'm feeling.

In a move so quick I don't have time to react, Van flips us. I'm on my back, hands pinned above my head as he hovers a safe distance above me.

Too safe.

I want him closer. I want his mouth on mine. I want to not worry about whether this is too much or too soon.

"What do you want to do?" he rasps.

My brain has a mild aneurysm at the thought of answering him honestly. "W-what?"

"Today. We've done enough Keanu-ing today. Time to venture out into the real world. I know I've said you get to make the rules and this is all your choice, but you need a nudge out of the nest."

"Are you a mama bird in this analogy?"

He ignores me. "We're going to get out of this room and do something you want to do. Tell me what you want."

I'm sure he doesn't intend for his words to have double meaning, but I can't stop my thoughts from spiraling out into a lot of things I want ... but probably shouldn't have.

"Do you think they have zip lining around here? I've always wanted to go. Drew has a thing about heights so he vetoed it."

"Of course he did," Van mutters, and I want to kick myself because the mention of Drew shifted the air in the room.

Van releases me. Stands. Holds out a hand to pull me up. "Come on, Mills. I want to see you fly."

CHAPTER 13

Van

Zip lining sounded all well and good until we're up on the wooden platform, gearing up. It's not the height. It's the alligators.

"Look at this view!" Amelia says, breathless and bright-eyed. She tugs on the end of her braid, and I barely resist doing the same.

I know she wouldn't mind. We've been playfully touching each other practically since she hopped in my car. But I think if I tug on her hair, it will be pulling her into me. And that's a very bad idea.

And not because of the alligators.

"I am looking at the view," I mutter, forcing myself to look past her pretty face and her tempting braid, past the treeline to the pond below where dozens and dozens of alligators rest motionless like so many armored logs.

Armored logs with snappy teeth.

While Amelia was showering and I was trying not to think about her showering, I went downstairs and picked up a stack of flyers from the concierge on nearby activities, most of which are back on the mainland. Apparently, the only zip lining place with open slots today was this one. Which is an add-on excursion with your ticket to the alligator park.

Amelia's and my opinions on reptiles are as disparate as our feelings on Keanu Reeves's acting abilities. Amelia got even *more* excited about this when she realized we would get to see alligators.

"They're so cute," she said, which made me question her judgment even more than her faith in Keanu or choosing someone like Drew.

"Let's get you strapped in," the guide says, and my eyes snap to him just in time to see him wink at Amelia.

I frown. *Could he have made that sound more like an innuendo?*

"Hope you don't mind me getting a little up close and personal for a moment," the guy says, winking again, laying the innuendo on even thicker as he starts to help Amelia into her harness.

I check his nametag: Wave. Someone either had parents who were high when they picked out his name or he picked the nickname all by himself. As he kneels in front of Amelia, tightening the straps around her waist and, in my view, touching her a lot more than necessary, I find myself stepping closer.

Amelia doesn't seem to pick up on his intentions, which should tell the guy she's not interested, but when he stands back up, he does so right in her personal space, practically dragging his chest along hers on the way up. There's no way for Amelia to miss *that*, and she laughs nervously, backing up until she's pressed up against the railing.

"How's this feeling?" Wave asks, his voice low and throaty.

Pretty awkward, I'd like to say.

Instead, I forget about all the murder logs down below and sidle up next to Amelia, wrapping my arm around her shoulders and brushing a kiss to her temple. Time to reprise our honeymoon role-play.

"Hey, baby," I murmur, running my nose down her cheek to her jaw.

Amelia turns slowly, blinking up at me with slightly parted lips. Underneath her freckles, which I'm happy she didn't cover with makeup today, her cheeks flush a pretty pink. I was going to wink just to clue her in but even if Wave hadn't just ruined winking, the look Amelia's giving me makes me forget for a moment.

Forget why we're here.

Forget she's not mine.

Forget my own name.

"Hi," she whispers, like we're sharing a legitimate moment.

And then, we are.

I reach up and brush back a strand of hair that's escaped her braid. When my knuckles graze her neck, she shivers.

"You good, Mills?"

Because I'm not. In fact, I'm starting to suspect Amelia is going to ruin me.

But I sure am enjoying the ride.

Amelia smiles and my ribs suddenly feel tight.

"Yeah, I'm good, hotshot."

Wave clears his throat. "So everybody's all good, then?"

His eyes bounce between the two of us, and he takes the smallest step back. Still too close. I'm ready to get off this platform and to have Mills to myself again. Which isn't how today or any of this is supposed to go.

Wave clears his throat again and I take a step back from Amelia, trying to clear my head. But the only thing it does is make me want to go right back to having my arm around Amelia.

It also allows Wave to step back in. Dude doesn't seem to take hints.

Read the room, pal. Or, as it were, read the platform.

Now I clear my throat. Dramatically. Amelia giggles as I pin a glare on Wave. "Are you going to make sure my harness is tight enough?" I ask him.

"Looks good," he says, giving me barely more than a cursory glance.

"But you've got to check, right? Standard procedure and all that. Preventing lawsuits."

Do I really want a man called Wave getting all up close and personal in my *very* personal space? No. I really don't.

But I suspect he'll like it even less. And though maybe it *is* a standard practice and not just something he did to get close to Amelia, it's clear he had zero intention of doing the same for me.

Guess Wave doesn't care if I fall into a gator pond.

"Wait," Amelia says, her fingertips brushing my arm. "Are you allowed to zip line?"

Wave's head snaps up. He's frowning, but I swear the guy looks hopeful. Probably at the idea of separating Amelia and me.

"Heart problems? Medical issues? Did you even read the waiver?"

"No medical issues." Though I do seem to have a heart problem. One that got me up on this platform to begin with.

"He plays hockey," Amelia explains.

"Ah. That explains the black eye," Wave says.

I glare at him. "That's not where I got the black eye. Are you going to check my equipment or not?"

Amelia tugs at my arm again, and I turn toward her as Wave crouches, checking my harness a little more enthusiastically than necessary.

"Would my dad be okay with this?" Amelia asks. "I don't want you to get in trouble."

"Nothing in my contract says I can't zip line." There are a lot of other stipulations about what I do, especially during the season. Some of which *might* actually extend to include something like this. But I'm not letting Amelia go by herself.

"Don't worry about me," I tell her. "Are you nervous?"

"Can't wait," she says, beaming.

Wave pulls something a little tighter than necessary and I grunt, glaring down at him. "Hey, pal. I'm all for safety, but I'd also like to have children at some point in the future, so let's not tighten things too much down there."

"You want to have kids?" Amelia asks softly, and the hopeful look she's trying to hide has me feeling a surge of hope too.

Swallowing around the tightness in my throat, I say, "Someday."

It's not something I think about often, mostly because I haven't been in any serious relationships and I haven't been in a hurry. There were times I swore I'd never want to have kids, not after what my parents put us through.

At the same time, I love my sisters. I love the idea of growing a big, nosy, stepping-over-boundaries family. Of having my own chance to do things differently than my parents did. I've thought about having kids with the same distant sense of *maybe one day* that I've thought about having a wife and a life after hockey.

Which is to say, I haven't thought about it much. Or often.

The very first time I considered it with any kind of concrete idea was the night I met Amelia. Before I realized who she was. Then I tried to shove all those thoughts into a storage bin in the attic of my mind.

Until yesterday, when thoughts I shouldn't have started plaguing me again.

Until now, when I'm absolutely wondering about possibilities.

Though I certainly didn't mean to lead our conversation here at this exact moment. I really just wanted Wave to stop messing with straps so close to my crotch.

But as Amelia's pale blue eyes search mine, I find myself imagining me on my hands and knees as I play monster the same way my dad did with me and my sisters—on the very rare occasions he wasn't working. Before our parents' divorce and the carousel ride of new partners, new spouses, new exes.

I won't do that to my kids. It won't be rare to play with them. Not an exception. It will be the *norm*. If I'm going to do the family thing someday, I'll be home more, play with them more, have laughter and squeals of delight be my new soundtrack, replacing the slice and swish of blades on ice and the resounding thump of a puck hitting the boards.

Another sound exists in this vision too, jarring me when I realize it's Amelia's laugh.

I blink, and then I can see her there too.

We're in a backyard in summer, the scent of grass and something grilling close by. Dirt pressing into my knees and palms as I chase a little blond girl with pigtails, sudden weight digging into my back as a boy tries to tackle me. Amelia's laughter rises over soft music playing from somewhere. She's watching me with a wide smile, sitting in an Adirondack chair, a baby curled up against her chest, a tuft of dark hair like downy duck fluff on top of her head. I don't know how I know it's a baby girl, but I just do.

The vision is so clear, so vivid, that for a moment I am completely frozen. It feels like I've been pummeled into the boards by a huge defenseman and had the wind knocked out of me.

This is ... I don't know what this is. Unfamiliar. Terrifying.

Considering our present circumstances, a *terrible* idea.

Yet I find myself wanting to call my sisters and ask for advice. Which would be the first time I've *ever* done that.

"Van?"

Amelia's right now voice pulls me back to the moment. Where we're standing on a platform above a bunch of prehistoric dinosaurs who hopefully can't jump high enough to chomp us. I suck in a breath, my heart thrashing wildly and sweat gathering at my temples and my lower back. Her face puckers in concern, and even Wave picks up on it as he stands, finally done messing with my harness. I'm sorry I ever asked.

"It's normal to be nervous, but if you need to barf, do it over the railing. It's not easy to clean all the way up here. And the fish will eat it." He points to the pond below and laughs.

"Ew," Amelia whispers.

"I'm not nervous," I tell him with a glare, then turn back to Amelia. "I'm fine. Just ... remembered something I forgot to do before I left home."

"What?" Amelia asks.

"Uh …" I search for some logical explanation because there's no way I'm telling her I just got the wind knocked out of me while imagining her as my actual wife and the mother of my children. "I forgot to feed my fish."

"You have fish?" she asks.

No.

"One. It's a betta." I did have a betta once. Super easy to take care of. I could have one again if needed.

Like, if Amelia came to my place. It would be easy to pick one up. I think they sell them at every pet store. The harder thing would be getting Amelia to my house to prove the existence of my currently nonexistent fish.

"Who's watching him while you're gone?" she asks.

"Who?"

"Your betta."

"Oh. It's a fish. He's fine. We're only gone for four days."

Wave claps his hands. "Well, if you're not going to hurl, we can go ahead and get started," he says.

He explains how the harnesses hook to the cables, the way we'll end up at the platform we can see in the distance. Across from the gator pond. I try not to watch one of the alligators swimming below, its whole body motionless save for the powerful, slow sweep of its tail through the water.

I don't know much about alligators other than to know they're reptiles, which I avoid as a general rule, and they might look mostly lazy and slow, but they can jump out of the water and run faster than a person on land. I've seen enough TikTok videos to know that.

"Who's starting off?" Wave asks, and I immediately tap Amelia on the shoulders.

"Ladies first," I say. "Unless you'd rather follow me."

I really don't want to leave her on the platform alone with

Wave for any length of time, so I'd prefer to send her on and hope the next employee doesn't try hitting on her while I'm still making my way across.

"I'll go," Amelia says, and the next thing I know, Wave is clipping her onto the cable. She stands with her toes on the edge of the platform and glances back at me. "See you on the other side, hotshot."

The grin she sends my way makes something clench inside my chest, reminding me of the growing pains I used to get as a kid, a deep throbbing ache just above my knees before I grew an inch almost overnight.

And then Amelia kicks off the platform and is gone, screaming happily as she goes.

I can't help but keep one eye on the gators as I watch her go, my fingernails cutting into my palms.

"Don't worry," Wave says with the fakest smile I've ever seen. "You'll be okay."

Amelia tilts her head back to the sky, stretching her arms wide.

No. No, I'm actually not sure I will be okay.

And when it's my turn and I step off the platform, hurtling toward the next station, I hardly feel the drop in my stomach.

Because inside, I was already in free fall.

———

Amelia licks a drip from the side of her ice cream cone. "Tell me about your sisters."

My focus on her mouth is jarred away by the mention of my sisters. It almost feels as though they've been deposited on either side of Amelia. We're strolling through the park, enjoying a post-zip line snack.

Or, as I like to think of it, a yay-we-weren't-eaten-by-gators celebratory ice cream.

No gators attacked us, and no more employees hit on Amelia. Possibly because every time I joined her at the next platform, I glared at any male nearby, and she greeted me with a huge hug, eyes shining and smile wide.

Because she's having a good time zip lining, I kept reminding myself. *Not because of you.*

Now, we're back on the ground and have been wandering the park. It feels way too much like a legit date. Aside from the alligators, which should never be on a date. Even so, it's the best one I've ever been on.

"My sisters?" Hopefully, she didn't just see me fixated on her mouth.

"Yes," she says. "You said you have three of them?"

"Yes. One older—Callie—and two younger, Alexandra and Greyson. Lex and Grey."

She licks her cone again and I look down, scooping up a spoonful of vanilla because I was smart and got a cup. Less messy. Less licking involved.

"And?" Amelia says.

"And what?"

She punches me in the arm. "Tell me about them, dummy. Realize you're talking to an only here." When I stare blankly, she says, "As in, only child. I live vicariously through other people's sibling stories."

I feel slightly queasy thinking about Amelia and Coach in a big house alone. No siblings. No mom and wife. Just the two of them.

Then I think about Coach punching me in the face again if he saw me watching Amelia eating ice cream.

Right. Always a good reminder.

"Yeah, so my sisters are both the best and the worst.

Bossing me around, ganging up on me, but also helping when I need it. They're independent, but come to me when they have issues they can't solve themselves. Or one or two of them will come to me when one of them needs help but is too stubborn to admit it."

She doesn't seem to pick up on my tension. "Do they ever come watch you skate? I'd like to meet them."

This makes my skin start to prickle, a low buzz of longing along my skin. "You don't even come to our games, do you?"

"I might start."

"Really?"

"Yes. I think I'd like to see what all the fuss is about. So, will I ever see them at a game? Are they fans?"

My lips quirk. "Callie had to be escorted out of my last game for the things she was yelling at the ref. And other fans."

"I love it." The wistfulness in her voice makes me hurt, and so I keep talking.

I tell her about how they dress up and paint their faces when they come to my games, making best friends with our fans while also nearly getting into fights. I talk about Grey and her music. Lex and the struggles she and her husband are having with fertility. Callie defending her dissertation on British literature in a few months.

"She's going to make us call her *doctor* the second she gets her PhD. I just know it," I say.

I realize I've been talking for a solid ten minutes. My ice cream is long gone, and we're back near the start of the park, and Amelia sits down on a bench shaded by lush foliage. She pats the space next to her, and I sit. A breeze cools my neck, which I'm thinking might be getting sunburned.

"I bet they get all up in your business about your dating life," she says casually.

A little too casually—almost like she's trying *not* to sound interested in broaching the dating topic.

"Not really."

She glances up in surprise from her cone. "No?"

"Mostly because I've never talked to them about anyone."

"I thought you said you dated a lot," she says.

"I have, but not anyone serious enough to bring up to my sisters."

"Ah. Right—you're Mr. Casual."

The words bother me. Partly because I don't want Amelia to think of me that way. And partly because that tends to be how *everyone* sees me: casual. Fun. The truth is, I'm not sure I've ever dated a woman who wanted more. Or thought I was capable of giving more.

I've heard some of my teammates complain about women who tried to get things more serious, tried to lock them down. Dumbo once got a whole new phone number and changed apartments to get away from a woman who wanted to be exclusive.

I've never had that problem.

It's almost enough to give a guy a complex. Up until now, I took note, but didn't really care. Because I'd rather not have to let someone down easy who got the wrong idea.

Now, sitting on a bench with Amelia's thigh brushing mine, I'm thinking about it. Wondering if I could be more than just a fun, casual guy for Amelia. If she ever wanted to date me, that is.

"That's me—Mr. Casual Goodtime Guy." My words are dry. Paired with the jazz hands I pull out of I don't even know where, I sound way more bitter than I feel.

"I didn't mean it like that." Amelia nudges me with her shoulder. When I don't respond right away, she pauses mid-lick and turns to me. "You know you're more than that, right?"

"Sure. It's nothing. I was just being dumb."

Amelia hums, like she sees right through me. "You're more, hotshot. Much more."

I have to look away for a few seconds to compose myself. From both her words and the sight of her tongue licking up the side of the cone. Together, it's a lethal combo.

"They'd like you," I admit. The words sound far more vulnerable than I want them to.

"Your sisters? I thought you didn't talk to them about women," she teases.

I've backed myself into a corner here. I can say that we're not dating, which feels harsh. Even if we're not. We're … I don't know what.

But I don't know what Amelia would think if I tell her I planned to tell them about her.

Would she read too much significance into that? Would it put too much pressure on me?

I know with certainty, all three of my sisters would have a few choice words to say if they were here now. They would recognize in half a second how I feel about Amelia, and I would never hear the end of it. No doubt they'd love her.

But at least one if not all of them would slap me in the back of the head and tell me this is not the time in Amelia's life to have some chump falling all over her. They'd tell me to give this space. Not to put too much significance into anything. Definitely not to think about kissing her when her feelings are likely all over the map. They'd tell me not to add any pressure to Amelia.

They would be right.

I glance at Amelia, like her face will somehow give me the right response. Instead, I lose myself in the warmth of her cool blue eyes, the spray of freckles on her cheeks, the way sunlight spins her hair into gold.

One side of her mouth lifts in the smallest of smiles. "What?"

I can't stop myself from reaching over, sliding a strand of her silky hair between my fingertips. "I'd like to tell them about you. If … that's something you'd like."

So much for not adding pressure.

From a hidden speaker above our heads, a booming voice announces the gator feeding in five minutes. We both jump. Amelia almost drops her cone.

I'm both relieved and disappointed by the way it ripped away the mounting tension of the moment. I drop Amelia's hair. She giggles and bites her lip.

"Let me guess—you want to go to the gator feeding?"

"Can we?" Amelia asks, eyes so bright there's no way I could say no to her.

"As long as they're not feeding *us* to the gators."

"I think it's raw chicken," she says.

Gross. But for her, *fine.*

We get up, and maybe I shouldn't, but I toss my empty cup in the trash and take her hand, sliding my fingers between hers. They're sticky from the ice cream, and I don't even mind.

"You are the slowest ice cream eater I've ever seen," I say.

"It's a gift. You and your sisters are close," Amelia says. "What about your parents?"

Now there's a conversational land mine. I try not to stiffen. Because I might have siblings where Amelia has none and I might have two living parents, but she has something I don't. A parent who *cares.*

Shrugging, I watch a family walk past, their littlest child in a plastic alligator stroller. "There's not much to say. They got divorced when we were young. Got remarried and divorced again and again to other people in a steady rotation. Bounced the four of us between houses in a constant battle of one-upmanship."

"Wow." Her voice and her eyes soften. "So they had joint custody?"

"At first, we split time between them—literally alternating every day—and we mostly fended for ourselves at both houses. Later on my dad got a new job in another state and we all moved in permanently with my mom. He'd fly us out sometimes at holidays, taking us on extravagant trips with his woman of the moment, all as a way of getting back at my mom. Totally toxic."

"I'm sorry." Amelia squeezes my fingers and rests her head on my arm. Her touch smooths over the years of stock-piled hurt. Not like a touch could fix it or anything, but she makes me feel somehow less sad about the whole situation.

But while she's looking at me, not what's left of her cone, a big drip runs right down the cone and halfway down her wrist.

"Shoot," she says, dropping my hand.

Before I've given any thought to it—clearly—I grasp her arm. "I got it."

And then I press my lips to her skin and follow the path of sticky sweetness all the way to the cone. Our eyes locked the whole time. My heart a pounding drum. A single bead of sweat racing down the center of my back.

Amelia watches with heavy eyelids and parted lips. I pull back, keeping my fingers wrapped around her arm, clearly a sucker for punishment.

"Thank you," she says, just as I say, "I'm sorry."

"No apologies. Remember?" Her voice sounds strained but soft, like she's worked hard to get this whisper out.

"Those are your rules," I tell her.

"Maybe we should make some for you, hotshot."

We probably should. And my rules would start with: *Stop falling for a woman who was supposed to marry someone else yesterday.*

Followed by: *Keep your hands—and mouth—to yourself.*

But I've always been horrible at following the rules.

CHAPTER 14

Van

BY THE END of this little vacation, my chiropractor is going to have to use a croquet mallet to knock my spine back into alignment. I vow never to sleep on a couch again. I've already booked an appointment for next week. As well as a massage. I might need to soak in an ice bath for an hour. Or two.

As for what's going to help knock my heart back into alignment, well … I don't know who to call about that. And I don't want it set back to where it was.

"Morning, hotshot."

The words, soft and slow and sleepy, are punctuated with the sound of a coffee mug being set down on the coffee table. I grumble, but I'm smiling as I lift my head to look at Amelia.

Or, I *try* to lift my head.

I drop it back onto my pillow with a groan. This is definitely the worst it's been. I think I pinched something. It makes me feel a hundred years old.

"Awww," Amelia says, and I hear her shifting around before she settles on the couch next to me. "Your neck?"

I mumble something like a yes just as her hand finds my neck and begins to knead my muscles. I hiss when she reaches a sensitive place. Her fingers gentle but don't stop.

"I told you not to sleep on the couch," she scolds. "Why are you so stubborn?"

No sense answering that one.

Her fingers locate a knot in my neck, and I groan. "Right there," I mumble through the pillow. My speech sounds thick and slow like I've been drinking.

But the only chemical hitting my bloodstream is *her*.

"I've got you," she says.

She absolutely *has* got me. More than she probably realizes.

"Just relax. It's raining anyway, so we're in for a lazy day."

Now that she mentions it, I hear the soft patter of rain on the balcony, the low growl of thunder. It's soothing, and as Amelia rhythmically rubs my neck, I fall in and out of consciousness, finally waking sometime later to find Amelia stretched out beside me, practically hanging off the side of the couch, her arm across my back anchoring her in place.

Coach's daughter, I try to remind myself. But that's not working anymore. Coach isn't here. And I'm done worrying about what he'd do if he were.

I shift, rolling over and gently tugging Amelia until she's curled into me, her face in the crook of my neck and my nose in her hair. She smells like fresh laundry and citrus. I thought she smelled like lemon before, but it's more complex, tart and fruity. Maybe grapefruit?

I stifle a groan. Because I am now a man who smells a

woman's hair and overanalyzes scent profiles. If that's even the right term.

Flavor profiles deals with food, so—

"You make a nice pillow," Amelia murmurs, and her lips graze my skin. She sighs. "Warm."

"Thanks for the massage. I think I might actually be able to look both ways before crossing the street now."

She giggles, her hand finding mine as she links our fingers together.

"What do you want to do today?" I ask.

"We did what I wanted yesterday," Amelia says, propping up on an elbow to look at me. Her eyes are heavy-lidded, sleepy. The lopsided bun piled on her head looks like it will fall out any second.

She's so beautiful. Just like this.

But her elbow is in my gut. I grunt and reposition us so that she's looking up at me but not stabbing my organs.

"This is your week, Mills."

She's already shaking her head. "*Our* week." I like the way that sounds. She must too because she smiles and bites her lip. "So, how should we spend *our* day?"

I slide my fingers from hers and reach out to tap her nose. "I like your freckles."

She makes a face. "Really? I hate them."

"Why?"

"Maybe if I just had a few, it would be fine. But I have so many."

It's true. She does have a lot. I could see how this might make a person self-conscious. But they suit her.

"I wouldn't change a thing about you, Mills."

The words come out husky and low, carrying the full weight of my sincerity. As I watch, the freckles in question fade under the rush of red in her cheeks.

"Same." One side of her mouth curls up in a tiny smile. "But don't let it go to your head, hotshot. Although"—she sinks her hand into my hair and my eyelids fall halfway shut — "I don't think you're half as cocky as you want people to think you are."

"That so?"

She starts to rub my head, her nails lightly scratching my scalp. If I could purr, I would. I want to keep my eyes on her but they flutter closed.

"I don't think you're such a bad boy either. In fact, you're kind of a sweetheart."

She's wrong, but I'll play along. "Mm-hm. Don't tell the guys."

"Oh, I plan to tell everyone," she says. "I'm going to have it tattooed on my body somewhere."

My eyes crack open. "Your first tattoo will be for me? I'm flattered." When she doesn't say anything, my eyes open wider. "Wait—do you already have a tattoo?

"Maybe."

I haven't noticed any, and I've seen her in two bathing suits this week. The turn in conversation has my blood thumping. "Yeah? Where?"

"Wouldn't you like to know."

I would. Very much. And it must be written all over my face because she giggles and pushes off me to stand up, stretching her arms overhead.

"I'm kidding. No tattoos. I'm not against them or anything. I just haven't found a design I love. Plus, my dad …" She trails off, catching herself.

"Your dad isn't into tattoos?"

"Nope. He hates them."

A lovely and grim reminder that I am the last man who would earn Coach Davis's approval.

"But I think maybe I'd like to get one sometime. Would you go with me?"

The question hangs there for a moment, looming in the air between us. It's the first real mention we've had of being home. Together. Of whatever this is—the teasing, easy friends that also includes snuggling and a very heated attraction—lasting beyond the plane ride home.

"Yes," I tell her. "Anytime."

She smiles. "Before we venture out for the day, can I borrow your phone? I was thinking about drafting a blog post."

I grin. "You feel ready to put your notebook thoughts out into the world?"

"Yeah. I've got that impatient feeling, like the words are trying to push their way out."

"Good. You can have my phone. I'll go work out. But be thinking about what you want to do today."

"Okay," she says easily. "You too. Because we're in this together."

I really, really like the sound of that.

———

She's still writing when I get back from working out, barely lifting a hand in greeting as her thumbs fly over the screen. When I emerge from the shower in shorts and an unbuttoned Hawaiian shirt, she's still going.

I lean in the doorway, just watching her. She's sitting cross-legged on the floor, still in her Batman pajamas. Her elbows rest on the coffee table, and her gaze is locked on my phone as she taps something out with both thumbs, the tiniest crease between her brows.

Beautiful. The kind of unsettling beauty that leaves me off-kilter and struggling for breath.

Amelia must sense me in the doorway because she looks up from my phone, smiles, then her eyes go a little unfocused as she scans my torso, on display under my unbuttoned shirt.

I grin. "Take a picture; it'll last longer."

"I don't have my phone. But I can—" She pauses, frowning down at my phone in her hands, then drops it. The sound of it hitting the tile makes me flinch.

"Whoops," she says. "Sorry."

Amelia and I both jump when a female voice speaks from my phone. My sister's voice. "Robbie? Do you have a *woman* with you? Scandal!"

Amelia's eyebrows shoot up practically to her hairline. I make a mental note to plan my sisters' demise. I'm not sure if they called and Amelia inadvertently answered, or if she somehow called while fumbling with my phone.

Doesn't really matter now because we are on speakerphone with one or possibly more of my sisters, since they tend to travel in packs.

"Hey, Lex." I clear my throat and button one button, like my sister can see me through the phone.

"And Grey," another voice chirps. "I'm here too. But seriously—who is that? Identify yourself, woman!"

The two of them break into laughter. Amelia's eyes go wide, and I give what I hope is a reassuring smile as I cross the room and pluck the phone from her hand, noting a tiny crack in the glass protector.

"Now, now, now," I tell my sisters. "That information's going to cost you. What's the current standing?"

Alexandra groans. I know it's Lex not Grey because Grey

189

never grumbles. She's a spinning pinwheel of joy even when we're settling scores. I plop down on the couch, and Amelia climbs up next to me, keeping space between us until I narrow my eyes and then she scoots closer.

Not close enough. But I'm not sure we're at the point where I can just haul her into my lap. Yet.

"You're ahead by forty," Grey says cheerfully.

"Hm," I say, watching Amelia watch me. "Then how about another thirty for information."

"Thirty?!" Alexandra practically shouts. "Outrageous."

"Cool. We'll just go," I say. "I can catch you up later. Maybe."

Grey jumps in. "I'll cover it."

I finally take pity on Amelia, who has a million questions flashing across her face. "We have a point system," I explain.

"Paid in cheese," Lex says.

"Cheese?" Amelia repeats.

"Cheese," I confirm.

"And right now, Robbie's smoking us," Grey says.

Lex grumbles. "Because he always has the best secrets."

"So, you trade points for secrets?" Amelia asks. "What's the currency for points? How do you keep track? Is there a spreadsheet?"

"Ooh, she sounds smart," Grey says. "You sound smart, woman whose name we don't yet know."

"And you sound surprised," I say dryly.

"I guess we didn't think you normally chose women based on their ... brains," Lex says.

I clear my throat and squeeze Amelia's knee. She suddenly looks uncomfortable though she's trying to keep her face even. "The price just went up," I say. "Now it's fifty."

"Ugh, Lex! Shut up," Grey says. In a more cheerful voice, she goes on. "To answer your question, smart mystery woman, the points are traded for secrets or favors or just about anything. Blackmail included. And they are cashed in for cheese."

"Cheese?" Amelia laughs. "I don't understand. How? Why?"

"We're a big cheese family," Grey says. "Each point is an ounce. The one cashing in gets to choose the kind of cheese. And Robbie here has expensive taste."

"Thank you. That's nicer than what you said a moment ago."

"I said what I said." Lex clears her throat. "Name?"

"Wait," Grey chimes in. "We're not trading fifty points *just* for a name. We need more intel. Where you are and how long this has been going on and how serious it is."

"I'll tell you who and where for fifty."

"Forty," Alexandra counters.

"Seventy."

"Shut *up*, Lex," Grey says. "Who and where for fifty. Now, spill it."

"I'm with Amelia," I say. "Say hi to my younger two sisters, Mills."

"Hi," Amelia says. "Good to sort of meet you both. You call him Robbie?"

"He says he hates it, but he loves us best." I can see the wheels turning in Amelia's head as she remembers the night we met and how I introduced myself. It's like I knew even from the first few minutes that she would be someone special to me.

I both want and don't want Amelia to know that. It feels freakishly vulnerable, like I'm out on the ice with no pads, no helmet, no stick. Ready and waiting for everyone to take a shot at me.

"What he hates is when we call him by his other nickname," Lex says.

I drop my head. "Don't you do it."

They do it.

"Robbie Bobby Baby Benjamin Bunny," they chorus, then die in a fit of laughter.

Amelia joins them. But she also runs her fingers through my hair, as though offering an apology. When I crack open an eye, she's grinning at me. "That has to be the longest nickname ever," she says.

"It's the worst," I say.

"How did you even come up with that?"

"I don't know," Grey says. "I was, like, five."

"She said it one time, and we immortalized it forever," says Lex. "And your name is Mills?"

"Amelia," she says.

Grey jumps back in. "Getting to the important stuff. Now, where are you? It's still morning. Is this like a brunch situation or an adult sleepover—"

A blush rockets up over Amelia's face before I can interrupt my sister.

"Kind of a long story, but we're in Florida at a resort."

This is met with dead silence from my sisters. As in, so silent they could be dead.

"Still there?" I ask. "Because I just earned a lot of cheese."

"No, we're here," Lex says. "Just … processing. You're on vacation. With a woman."

"Yes." I don't ask if this is so hard to believe because I know it is. A few dates is my longest relationship, unless we're counting high school. Which I don't. I've definitely never taken a trip with a woman.

192

I can't tell from Amelia's face if she's upset thinking of my past—which my sisters are making sound way worse—or if she's pleased.

"Amelia." Alexandra's tone is crisp and businesslike. "Don't take this the wrong way because we'd love to talk to you and ask questions—"

"*So* many questions," Grey adds.

"—but could we have a moment alone with our brother? You sound lovely, and I don't want to offend you when this barely counts as a meeting, and I sure hope we *do* get to meet you in person."

Amelia meets my gaze then gets to her feet. "I hope so too. I'll go shower and get ready. Snorkeling sound good? It's cleared up and there's a group leaving in an hour."

"Sounds great."

Amelia heads to the bathroom, and I walk out to the balcony and collapse into a chair. "Okay. You've got two minutes of points-free answers. Fire away."

But instead of launching into a string of nosy questions, Lex and Grey speak in unison, a freaky thing they've done their whole lives. It drives me and especially Callie nuts.

"You found the one."

I drag a hand down my face. "Don't be ridiculous."

"I thought it was going to be the woman from the restaurant. Remember the one you texted us about?" Grey says in a rush. "I thought maybe you'd meet again and—"

"Actually," I interrupt, "Amelia *is* the woman from the restaurant."

I have to pull the phone away from my face when Grey shrieks. And shrieks. I wait until I can just hear Lex yelling at her.

"—my eardrums," Lex is saying when I rejoin the conversation.

"Sorry," Grey says. "But this is *huge*."

"It is," Lex repeats.

"The clock is ticking on your free pass of questions."

"Oh, he's got it *so* bad," Grey says. "It's adorable. I love seeing you like this."

"You can't actually *see* me, Grey."

"I called it," Lex says. "Didn't I say this *years* ago—when Robbie falls, he's going to fall hard."

"You totally did. Callie was the one who didn't believe it."

"I can't wait to tell her."

"Wait—we have to tell her together. Should we call now?" Grey asks.

"No," Lex and I say at the same time.

"Tick tock," I add. "I can't believe you're not taking advantage of your free pass."

"How long has this been going on?" Lex asks.

"Not very."

"You can't answer everything vaguely," Grey says.

"Fine. It's not even officially going on. We sort of … reconnected," I say, though what happened at her wedding is likely not what my sisters will picture with this description.

"Is it like *wedding* serious?" Grey whispers, like she thinks Amelia is in earshot. Or maybe like this is such a serious question it must be whispered.

"I … don't know."

"That's a yes." Lex sounds shocked.

Grey says, "No, that's the sound of a man who's terrified because he only just realized he's in deep."

She's not wrong.

"Aw, poor baby brother," Lex says.

"You know I'm older than you both, right?"

"How can we help?" asks Grey. "Because if there's one

thing you don't know how to do, it's maintain a serious relationship."

"Maintain?" Lex laughs. "I'm shocked he knew how to *start* one."

"Amen."

"Hey," I protest even though, once again, they're not wrong. It's refreshing to hear their voices, even to hear their assumptions and their statements about me.

As well as the guys on my team know me, there are large parts I've kept hidden from them. Or maybe it's more that I've only chosen to show them one side of myself, using trick mirrors to stay two-dimensional in their eyes. To them, I'm a caricature. Exactly like Amelia said earlier: Mr. Casual Fun.

But then she called me more.

Eli might be one of the few who sees more. When he was just starting to date his now-wife, he called me—not any of the other guys, but *me*—when he wanted help. I ended up being the one who walked Bailey down the aisle when they got married.

By now, my role with the guys personally is about as cemented as my role as center on the ice. Breaking out, being different than how I've always been, is hard.

"For real, though," Grey says, "How can we help? We'll butt out if you want but—"

"Don't butt out." The words are hard to form. Probably because I'm not used to asking for—or needing—help. But with this? With Amelia? I absolutely do. "I mean, I don't know what I need or how you can help, but I … I don't want to screw this up."

"Aw," Lex says with a sniffle.

"Are you crying?" Grey asks, and I hear a wobble in her voice.

"I'm going to hang up if you both start crying. I'll call Callie instead."

"NO!" they both say in unison.

"We'll stop," Grey says, clearly struggling to keep her voice even.

"Fine. But I need to tell you the whole story," I say. "And I don't have long."

CHAPTER 15

Amelia

A GIRL COULD GET USED to this. Sweat resulting from straight-up sunshine, a Diet Dr Pepper delivered poolside, and Van on the lounge chair next to me with his eyes closed, which allows me to unabashedly stare at him any time I want to.

And anyone who might judge me for how often I stare hasn't seen the man shirtless. Or even with a shirt. The man is just plain stareable.

His physical prowess aside, I'm trying to figure how he managed to make me smile more in the past two days than I ever have before. Like, *ever*. Or maybe as far back as childhood when I still had two parents and my days consisted of cartoons and playing on playgrounds and I hadn't yet seen any signs of how cruel life could be.

Van has a magic about him. And it's definitely *him*, not

just the fun things we've done, the new experiences, the ease of a resort vacation.

Though I have really been living out one of the new rules I scrawled for myself in the yellow notebook: *Try something new every day.*

I didn't think anything could top zip lining, which turned out to be one of my favorite things *ever*. But hooking my arm through Van's and dragging him through the park to look at alligators is a close second. When I asked Van how he could have a dragon living on his chest full-time and not like alligators, he didn't have a good answer.

The highlight of that day I'll never, ever admit, even under threat of waterboarding, is when Van licked ice cream off my arm.

I'll also never admit how often I've replayed that moment in my mind. Or how, whenever I happen to glance at his mouth, all I'm thinking about is how warm it felt on my skin.

If I close my eyes, I swear, I can still feel his lips there.

In short, alligator parks are a ten out of ten stars. Would recommend.

Yesterday, after I briefly and accidentally got to "meet" two of Van's sisters, we did a snorkeling expedition at midday. It was fun despite being too murky to see much. We spent the later afternoon on the beach, where I half-heartedly skimmed the book I bought and Van took a nap. The man wasn't kidding about liking his naps.

When I asked if it was an angry or sad nap, he smiled and said it was a happy nap.

While he was happy napping, a wedding took place a few hundred yards away from our lounge chairs. And because I'm a sucker for punishment, I forced myself to watch. I thought it might be upsetting but was surprised when I felt wistful longing rather than sad regret.

In fact, my eyes kept darting from the bride and groom to the man softly snoring next to me, one big arm thrown over his face. Wondering. Imagining. Dreaming.

Then chastising myself for being so foolish.

I'm not sure what it says about me that I could almost marry one man on a Saturday and by Monday, I'm picturing a wedding with a different man.

But here we are.

Maybe if Van was only attractive and charming in that flirtatious way, I would just have a crush. One easily shed when we go our separate ways.

But he's not only that. And, as quick and reckless and unbelievable as it sounds to admit, this is more than a crush. Just like I told him: he's *more*.

I glance at Van again, smiling when I see the faint outline of a lopsided smiley face on his abs. Yesterday, I drew it carefully in sunscreen while he softly snored. He slept just long enough for it to work.

When he woke up and saw it, he threw me over his shoulder, marched into the ocean, and tossed me. Which led to me begging him to launch me again and again. I loved the moments when I was in the air, suspended and about to come down.

I loved being in Van's arms before he threw me even more.

We capped off last night with a sunset cruise full of couples, where we resumed our roles as newly married to fit in. At least, that's the excuse I gave myself to allow Van to spend dinner touching me, his hand heavy on my knee under the table, his arm around my waist as we watched the sun set. His lips on my cheek as we stood at the rail, a pod of dolphins swimming beside the boat.

"I think they're showing off for you," he said then, his

whiskers a delicious scrape on my neck. "Can't say I blame them."

For those hours, I didn't just pretend for the sake of people around us. I allowed myself to sink into the lie. To imagine what it would be like to have him staying close to me because he wanted to. Because he was mine.

The thing is … it was easy to believe.

When Van looked at me with those dark brown eyes, the warmth there felt real. His flirting also fooled my body, which has been in a constant state of heightened awareness for days. I swear, Van shifts his weight from one foot to the other, and my body adjusts too.

When he touches me? Forget it. I instantly become like one of those static balls with all the electricity inside, every electron in me shooting toward the place where Van's finger or his mouth or even his arm brushes mine.

Things were never like this with Drew. Never with anyone else either.

It's ridiculous to think Van and I could really have something. Reckless. Maybe stupid.

I'm trying to internalize Morgan's words. To wait.

To tell myself if it's really this good, if it's really something that could be real, I should wait until I'm in a better place. I'm attempting to just enjoy being drenched in an unexpected happiness. While also ignoring the thread of guilt that keeps weaving through me because I shouldn't feel this way, right?

I mean, my whole life arguably just fell apart. I'll be picking up the pieces when I get back for months. I should be heartbroken. A mess.

And yet—I'm at the complete opposite pole. My heart never broke over Drew, despite being battered around and covered in the slick film of humiliation whenever I think about everything. It's helped that we haven't seen him or Becky. Maybe they checked out and moved to a new hotel. Hopefully in Antarctica.

But being with Van this week has, if anything, inflated and expanded my heart, like it's pumping stronger and steadier than before. As though his presence hasn't simply had a healing effect but one that multiplies me.

I keep trying not to examine what that means, but my mind keeps hovering around it, returning like a memory.

What I do know for sure is that I don't want it to end. I want to tell the front desk we're staying another week. Or that we're staying forever. We'll be the squatters in the honeymoon suite.

But I already know this is an impossibility. Though I've largely been able to forget what's going on at home, texting Morgan a few times for the barest updates, I know it's waiting for me. Late tomorrow.

And with our trip almost over, dread has taken hold in my stomach like a tapeworm.

I expected things to get awkward at some point. For Van to get sick of me or me to get sick of him. Instead, the more of him I get, the more I want. I *crave* him.

We talk, we laugh, we tease. Playfully … but an undercurrent of something sweeter and headier is growing. I can feel it in the way our touches linger, in the heat clambering up my spine when he's near me, in the way his eyes darken when we stare too long.

Not just his charm, I tell myself. *It's got to be me.*

Doesn't it?

The only time we spend apart is when he's working out or one of us is in the bathroom or when we're sleeping. More like when I'm lying in bed, imagining him on the couch, wondering what would happen if I invited him to share my bed. Just to sleep.

I've offered more than once, but he's adamant. He won't.

I know I'm not imagining the shift between us. I think it started the first night in the ocean, his warm hands on my ocean-chilled skin. Or maybe it goes back to the bathroom stall, when he wiped my tears away with his thumbs.

Every little moment, from him licking ice cream off my wrist to arguing about Keanu to allowing me the freedom to make my own choices.

Earlier this afternoon I almost confessed how I felt when he got back from a dip in the pool and told the half-drunk man hitting on me to stay away from *his wife*.

The way he said *my wife* gave my goose bumps goose bumps.

Every step of the way, Van has been my cheerleader, my safety net, and my challenger.

Fly, he told me when we were zip lining.

Want to see what's at the edge of the reef? he asked when we were snorkeling.

Don't miss this, he said, nudging me, as the sun was just about to dip below the horizon and I had been looking at him instead.

I've never felt happier, nor so safe, nor so … *loved.*

That's the one word that fits. Against all odds, all logic, all reason. I can barely think it to myself without cringing.

Because … it can't be.

Right?

I shake my head a little, a physical attempt to shake off my hopes, married with my worries. *Enjoy it*, I tell myself. *Don't think too hard about what it means.*

Or what it will be like returning home.

Now, I reach across the little table between our lounge

chairs and pinch Van's arm. We've been at the resort's adults only pool since lunch, and I'm not sure if he's awake, his dark eyes hidden by mirrored Walmart aviators. They look every bit as good on him as any name brand would.

Van leans on an elbow and pushes up the sunglasses, shooting me a mock glare with his dark eyes. The look zings through me like a pinball shot from a cannon.

"What was that for, Mills?"

I grin. "Paying you back for the other day."

"That was for breaking the rules. Did I break a rule I don't know about?"

"Nope."

"When are you going to share your rules with me, Mills?"

He's been asking every day when he catches me scribbling in the yellow notebook. More since I started borrowing his phone to draft not one but a few Substack posts, which are nowhere near ready to publish. Yet.

I'm not just working on the rules. Everything about this experience has opened me up, like Drew's actions cracked open a locked safe. And now ... I'm exploring the contents.

I have a million ideas for posts and even some job ideas to look for when I get back and am reunited with my phone and computer. While it's super strange not to have a phone and to share Van's, it's honestly refreshing and has been a boon to my creativity. It's also been fun to look through his reading apps, though we share almost none of the same books. The man needs more romance novels in his life.

As supportive as Van has been, I'm still not ready to share my words. Also, a good deal of my journaling has been me processing my feelings. Many of which center around *him*.

"Soon," I promise.

Suddenly feeling shy, I shrug, playing with the strap of my bathing suit. This is the one I like the best—a pink one-piece with side cutouts and ruffles along the bust. It's pretty wholesome with just a nod of sexy where my sides are exposed and in the low dip of the back. I've gotten used to my new wardrobe, which is a good thing as the airline has no idea where my bags are. Maybe in Antarctica with Drew.

Van's dark gaze tracks the movement of my fingers, and then he drops his glasses back in place and reclines again. I swear I can almost feel the echo of his gaze lingering on me like a physical caress, a heated whisper tracing my skin.

"Well," Van says, "how about we stick to the no waking sleeping dragons rule, yeah?" he says, the corners of his mouth lifting in a smirk.

"You're a dragon now?"

He taps the extensive ink on his chest, which I've studied at length in the many hours he's spent shirtless the past few days. Because apparently, Van prefers to wear as little clothing as possible while on vacation.

You won't hear me complaining.

I jump when Van makes a rumbling growl in his chest. The low sound sends a sharp tug of want through me. Then again, pretty much everything Van does has a similar effect.

From the way he listens so intently and watches me just as carefully, like he wants to make sure I'm telling the truth and uses my body language as a lie detector test. He's good too. Always able to sense where I'm hesitating. Abruptly, I stand up, stretching and relishing in the warm lick of sun on my skin. "I'm going for a swim."

"I'll join you in a minute," Van says, but then he yawns, and I suspect his eyes have already closed behind the mirrored lenses of his sunglasses. His dragon, though, is still watching.

The faint outline of the lopsided smiley face I drew in

sunscreen is still visible on Van's abs, making me chuckle as I walk away.

I don't bother with the steps or lowering myself down and getting used to the water in stages. I hold my breath and jump right into the deep end, blowing bubbles until my feet touch the concrete at the bottom.

I pause here, eyes closed, the world muted around me, allowing myself a weightless, peaceful moment.

Well. *Almost* peaceful. Because my brain seems intent on playing a slideshow featuring Van front and center. His cocky smile as he perfectly landed on a platform earlier when zip lining. The teasing smile he gave me when we were playing in the ocean the first night. The way he looks when arguing vehemently about Keanu Reeves—even when he's dead wrong about Keanu's talent.

The way his mouth grazed my skin on the sunset cruise as we stood at the railing, the sway of the boat and Van's nearness making me unsteady. His kindness. His attentiveness. His taut, inked skin on display where he's lying on the lounge chair.

My lungs are burning, along with the rest of me. I push off the bottom, propelling myself toward the surface. Gasping as my face breaks free, I'm instantly warmed by the sun as I take in a few quick breaths, my fingers finding the edge of the pool. I cross my arms on the concrete and rest my chin on them, my body floating behind me as I gently kick my legs.

But then I frown, noticing a bevy of women surrounding Van's lounge chair. It looks like they're trying to get him to sign things—no, to sign *them*. The woman closest to him is leaning over at an uncomfortable angle, gesturing to her chest, a permanent marker in her hand.

Who even brings a permanent marker to a pool?

For a few seconds I just gape, processing. Only a few people this week recognized Van. Almost all of them were harmless. A little kid had Van sign a t-shirt. A couple wanted a picture with him. All a little starstruck. No one—aside from our flight attendant—stepped over any lines.

But these ladies sailed right over any lines of decency.

Van smiles, but it's not any of the ones I've grown used to —not the cocky smirk or the teasing half smile or the full, genuine one. It looks more like he's baring his teeth. He holds up both palms in a gesture clearly meant as a polite *no*. I can read it from here. But the woman with the Sharpie is undeterred.

I swallow down the acidic taste of jealousy, telling myself I have zero claim on this man. But then I see the tightness around his mouth and the way his whole body has gone rigid, and jealousy bleeds into protective anger.

Van turns his face away from the woman thrusting her chest in his face while waving the marker at him. But this leaves him face-to-thigh with another woman.

His sunglasses are still hiding his eyes, but I swear when he glances my way, I can feel his eyes lock with mine.

And maybe I'm imagining it, but I also sense him sending out an S.O.S. over the concrete pool deck.

I've hoisted myself out of the pool and am marching over before I've even thought about it. Still dripping as I reach Van and his cluster of unwanted ladyfans, I nudge my way between them and then plop right down on the lounge chair next to him. It's a thin sliver of space, and I practically plaster my wet body to his.

His arm curls around my back and he shifts, making enough room so I don't fall off, but not so much that there's even an inch between us. I feel him relax against me.

"I'm cold," I say in a whiny, baby voice. The kind I

suspect is right in the middle of these women's repertoire, though I'm currently pretending they don't exist. I let my fingers walk a path up his chest, tracing the dragon's scales, until I reach Van's chin, where I run my fingers over his bristly, two-days' growth of stubble.

"Do you want to go back up to the room?" he asks, one dark brow arching above his sunglasses.

"Maybe. It's awfully crowded out here." I lean closer, letting my lips brush his jaw close to his ear. Not quite a kiss. Not quite not a kiss either. "I wouldn't mind some privacy."

I didn't mean the words, already charged with double meaning, to come out so huskily. But I can't be sorry when they have the effect of scattering the women. One by one, their shadows over us disappear, letting the sun beat down on me again.

"That was quite a performance," Van says.

Honestly? It wasn't a performance at all.

I was *totally* jealous, and can't even deny it to myself. But sure—let's go with that. I'm performing. And I'm only curled up against Van to help him escape the women. Yep. That's why.

"I learned everything I know from Keanu Reeves," I say, and this makes him laugh. Head thrown back, smile wide, chest bouncing beneath me. If it weren't for his arm anchoring me, I think it would have thrown me off the chair. "I hope it's okay that I stepped in. You looked uncomfortable or I wouldn't have interrupted."

Van doesn't miss the shift in my tone. "I appreciate the rescue," he says, tugging me closer.

But I feel a chill, one deeper than the cold water still dripping from my hair and suit. Because we've existed mostly in a bubble, Van and I. These women were a slap in the face reminder of what life is like at home for Van—the well-known hockey player who only casually dates. The one who has promised me nothing.

I start to get up, but Van's arm tightens and he angles his head back so he can see my face. With his sunglasses in place, I can't tell where he's looking. Not until he pulls them up with his free hand, revealing those expressive dark eyes.

"What is it?" he asks.

"I don't want to share you," I say. "It's selfish."

He laughs. "You don't need to share me. And it's not selfish." When he sees the expression on my face, his laughter dies and his brows pull together. "Mills?"

"I just … kind of forgot about reality. Or about you maybe wanting to meet someone here. Someone who isn't me."

He tightens his grip on me. "The thought didn't even cross my mind. Not with them or anyone else."

I scoff. "Says the guy who told me he doesn't need pickup lines."

Van sits up a little straighter, tugging me with him and not giving me even an inch of reprieve. "Maybe I should clarify a few things."

"Maybe it's not my business," I mutter.

"I have a reputation," he continues, ignoring me. "Partly earned and partly encouraged. It's true I've dated a lot. And if I don't want to use lines, I don't need them. I'm a hockey player with an active social media following. My DMs are full of offers if I want them."

This makes me swallow hard, the jealousy from a few minutes ago rearing its roaring head again along with a sick twist in my gut. I know this. And I know he isn't bragging. He's not even saying it like it's a good thing. More like listing out the things that come standard with a job: a cubicle, bad coffee in the break room, and Monday morning meetings at nine.

"I've kept things casual in the past," he continues. "But casual isn't the same as *careless*. And I've had plenty of dates that didn't end in bed, Mills. Just dates." He touches my chin gently, tilting my face up toward his. "If I've kept things light, it's because I take commitment seriously. And I hadn't found the right woman for that."

He *hadn't*.

As in … past tense?

As in … he's found that woman now?

"Do you understand what I'm telling you?" he asks.

I can't read the expression in his eyes, other than to know he's being sincere. It seems important to him that I understand, and he scans my face, waiting until I nod. I understand.

I *think* I understand.

He smiles—a real, full one that lightens something in me.

Van gets to his feet in a swift motion, then gently tugs me up with him, wrapping a soft towel completely around me, holding it closed at my chin. It's kind of adorable.

It also puts his face close to mine.

"Come on then, Mills. Let's head back up to the room and decide what's next on our menu."

He means activities—the jet ski rental or the dolphin excursion we discussed earlier. But the ache in my belly is for something else. For promises and declarations. Confessions, maybe. A whole different menu.

Too soon, I chide myself, but holding back is starting to hurt.

———

As though me thinking about not seeing Drew conjured him into place, he and Becky are at the restaurant. The resort has three inside: a rooftop restaurant we chose for tonight, two off the lobby, plus a sports bar and then an outside casual grill we've frequented. It seems we've been picking different places the last few days. Until now.

"I thought maybe they left," I say.

"We can go." Van's hand lands on my lower back as though ready to steer me right back out the door.

I watch Drew with Becky for a moment since they haven't seen us, taking a sort of internal temperature of how I feel. There are vestiges of anger and hurt, especially where Becky is concerned. The family connection will make her actions more difficult to manage. There are still wisps of humiliation and embarrassment, and I can trace my sudden insecurities at the pool to the two of them.

But mostly, I just feel relieved that I'm here, standing with Van instead of seated with Drew. And based on their tense expressions and the way Becky is practically using her menu as a shield, I think they'd rather be somewhere else too. There is almost a twinge of sadness for Becky. Because Drew is *not* a catch. And if she can't see that—well, I guess that's the bed she made for herself.

Van's fingertips press into my back, his touch making me draw my spine up straight. "Mills?"

"No," I tell him. "We'll stay."

"Are you sure?"

I watch his brown eyes as they scan my face, feeling a hot bloom of pleasure at his attentiveness. When I grin, his eyes dart briefly to my mouth, then up to meet my gaze.

"I'm good. Promise."

He nods, then splays his palm wide over my back as he gently urges me forward to the hostess stand.

"Two, please," he says, and we're led to a table in a row of others, a long booth-like seat running along one side, chairs on the other side of the tables. Usually, this is where people would argue over the more comfortable booth side, but this table happens to be right in Drew's line of sight. With a sigh, I start to pull out the chair, which would keep my ex at my back.

But Van tugs my hand until I realize he's suggesting we both sit on the same side of the table on the booth seat.

Nuzzling my neck as we sit, he tells the hostess, "I hope it's no trouble if we both sit here." His lips drag over my shoulder, and my eyelids flutter closed as he speaks against my skin. "I just can't get enough of her."

If Van ever said those words for *real* about me, I wouldn't survive them. I tuck them away to replay later.

I think about his words at the pool. *Do you understand?*

I hope so.

"Of course," the woman says, quickly adjusting the plates and silverware before rushing away.

I angle my head slightly, giving Van a hefty dose of side eye along with a half smile. "Is this how it's going to be?" I ask. "We're going to give them a show?"

Van presses a quick kiss to my jaw, close enough to my mouth to make it water. It's not the first time he's done this. But it's getting harder and harder to think of this as just something he does when he's playing the part of pretend husband.

The urge to pull him closer and press my lips to his grows stronger each and every time. Right now, it's almost unbearable.

He leans back—seemingly not struggling the same way I am—and offers me a full, wicked smile. "No."

"No? But you wanted to sit on the same side of the table. Right in their line of sight. And now you're being so …

touchy." I trail off, unsure how to describe the physical affection.

His smile is gone, and his eyes are warm and soft. "If you want to change seats, we can. But I know sometimes it can help to face things. Just to look right at them. I wanted you to be able to do that." Under the table, he finds my hand. Squeezes. "And I didn't want you to do it alone."

"Oh." I swallow, then link our fingers.

Once again, Van is challenging me, telling me to fly. Offering a safe space to land.

His lips brush my jaw.

While also torturing me.

"The rest of it," he murmurs, "is just because I want to. I don't care what he thinks. I only care about you. Do you want me to stop being so"—I feel his smile against my skin—"touchy?"

"Nope," I say, fighting to sound normal and not completely breathless. "All that makes sense."

"If you hadn't guessed, physical touch is my love language," he says.

"What's a love language?"

"It comes from a book. I'll see if I can share it through one of the reading apps you use when you've got your phone again."

I shiver, a feeling like goose bumps rising but on my *insides*. A reaction to Van's simple statement about a book, about sharing, about phones, about the future. About *love* languages.

Calm down, I tell myself. But I am a tempest.

"So, this is okay?" he asks, pulling back to meet my eyes.

"Yes," I whisper.

Because I need a moment to compose myself, physically

and emotionally, I pick up the menus, slapping one to Van's chest with a little more force than needed. Then I pretend to read my own while I'm actually working to slow my heartbeat to a steady rhythm again.

Throughout the dinner with our easy conversation and Van's easy touches, I feel Drew staring—glaring, probably. But I refuse to look his way. Van offers up plenty of distraction. True to what he told the hostess, he can't seem to stop touching me—tugging the ends of my hair, letting his fingertips graze the bare skin of my arm, tapping his foot against mine under the table.

Drew probably thinks we're doing it to show off.

The thing is: I don't care if Drew is watching.

I wouldn't care if Drew was making out with Becky right in front of me.

I don't care about Drew.

"We leave tomorrow," I say, after our waitress has cleared the dinner plates and we've ordered dessert.

Van's lips twitch, a slight downward turn he corrects almost immediately. "We do."

The words I want to say swirl in my head, a string of sentences and questions twisting into a tangled snarl.

"I ..." Words gather at the tip of my tongue, then dissipate like fog.

Be brave, I tell myself. *Ask for what you want. Tell him.*

Why is honesty so hard?

And what, exactly, do I want? I think of Morgan's warning about rebounds.

Is that all this is? I force myself to think about this again. Though I have. Daily. Maybe hourly. At the least, I've thought about it every time Van looks at me with the intensity in his eyes right now.

No. I *know* it's more, almost on a seismic level, as though plates are shifting beneath my skin. Reshaping. Changing my landscape.

The timing might make this suspicious or even ridiculous, and maybe I couldn't find a way to articulate to Morgan or my father or anyone else how this is different, but it is.

But there is the tiniest sliver of doubt, making me wonder if the intensity of my feelings is brought on by a mania I'm in denial about. I haven't felt like myself for lots of reasons this week. And Van and I have been inside of a bubble, a setting that isn't real life for either of us.

It would be like growing some kind of plant inside of a covered terrarium. Who's to say transplanting it outside would make it thrive?

I glide a fingertip through the condensation on my glass, watching beads of water form then fall slowly down the side like crystal tears. "I didn't need to face Drew," I say finally. Not the words I want. But a start.

Van lifts his drink, like he needs a pause before responding. I watch through my periphery as his throat bobs with each swallow.

"No?" he asks finally, one side of his lips quirked up in a smile.

I shake my head, holding his gaze. "I'm sure there will be more to process about the whole situation, but I don't have feelings for *him*."

Van's eyes spark at my emphasis on the word him.

"But I do have a lot of feelings," I whisper, the very vague confession tearing out of me like it's the most specific and unforgivable sin ever.

"You're not the only one," Van says, and the way he's looking at me makes me see spots, as though I'm staring directly into the sun.

I blink, and he comes back into focus, just as bright as before. My heart feels like it's quivering in my chest, over-loaded with adrenaline or endorphins or something else. Something I can't name.

Van hums, hand tightening around my waist as he ducks his mouth close to my ear. I close my eyes.

"What do you want, Mills?"

The directness of his question should make it easier. He's opened the door and invited me in. I just need to walk through.

Somehow, the opening has the opposite effect, and I find my wants—and more, my words—paralyzed. Lodged in my throat.

I want to tell Van the truth—that I'm having very real feelings for him. Not new feelings either. A reprise of what I felt the very first night we met. Like the hope and the excite-ment and the rush of being around him simply paused all those months until it had a chance to breathe again.

Feelings that have nothing to do with Drew or my canceled wedding, and have everything to do with Van. Who he is. How he makes me feel.

And how I want to do the same for him. How I suspect from the things he's told me here and there, that people expect too little from him, and he lets them. That no one except maybe his sisters support him the way he's supported me this week.

But maybe I need more time. Big things aren't always easy for me to process in the moment.

Like when Mom died. My body felt like scorched earth, cracking but never releasing. I cried, sure—but it felt like I never could access the main area of grief. A few years later, I burst into tears at the gas pump when the screen asked if I wanted a car wash. A happy memory of Mom had bubbled to the surface, the two of us going through the car wash, "Bohemian Rhapsody" blasting through the speakers as we sang-shouted in our best singing voices.

I was crying too hard to drive home, and Morgan had to come pick me up. We left my car parked there overnight, and I wept on her couch until dawn.

Maybe I need space and distance to process. But for the first time in my life, I find myself wanting to be risky. Wanting to simply go for what I want. Wanting to speak up for myself.

"Here is your dessert." We scoot back from the table to give the waitress room, the moment broken as a single plate of dark chocolate ganache cake is set before us.

Van keeps his gaze on me even as the waitress lingers to refill our water glasses. But I can't bring myself to look back at him. Finally, when she's gone and it's just us and an untouched piece of chocolate cake, I clear my throat, testing my words.

They come out as a whisper. "I don't know what I want."

More like … I know what I want. But I'm scared to want it and even *more* scared to say it out loud.

He doesn't seem surprised. He doesn't seem hurt. Almost like he expected this to be too hard.

Instead, he nods once and says, "Tell me when you do. I'll be waiting," and then removes his arm from around my waist. But only so he can pick up his fork.

I do the same, though I'm disappointed with myself, disappointed with the lack of his touch. Disappointed that Van chose this time to give me space rather than to push me.

Even though it says so much about his character to give me what he seems to know I need.

But when I lean my thigh against his, he doesn't shift

away. He gives me a sidelong look and smiles. Sweet. Not sad. Patient.

And when we get up to leave, I realize Drew and Becky left at some point without me even noticing them go.

CHAPTER 16

Amelia

AFTER DINNER, the scent of the ocean draws me toward the open patio doors along the back of the building. The breeze lifts my hair from my neck as I tug Van along with me. I stop just outside the doors and take a deep inhale. There's music spilling out, another wedding happening in the same spot where they seem to happen daily at ten, two, and six.

A familiar weight lands on my shoulders. I open my eyes to see Van watching me with a tiny smile, amusement sparkling in his brown eyes.

"I'm going for a walk on the beach," I tell him, feeling suddenly exposed. "You don't have to come if you don't want to."

"Are you sick of me?" he asks, gasping dramatically and pressing a hand to his chest.

I smile. "Not even a little."

He leans close, lips grazing my ear. "Then stop trying to get rid of me. Want to stop for a drink first?"

I've avoided drinking alcohol almost the whole week, aside from the half a glass of champagne on the plane. I'm usually a total lightweight, but that didn't affect me. Normally, a beer or a glass of wine and I get loopy.

But it's the last night. It feels right. Celebratory.

So we stop by the little thatched roof bar by the beach and I order a piña colada.

Van looks surprised. "No Diet Dr Pepper tonight?"

I love that he knows my drink. Though I guess he watched me guzzle it all week long. "Feels like a good night for a piña colada."

"I didn't think you liked drinking."

"More like … drinking doesn't like me."

"Morgan said something about that," Van says, taking his beer and handing me my drink.

It has a little umbrella and a slice of fresh pineapple, which is delicious. "I'll probably give half to you," I tell him, taking a sip as we wander away from the lights and the noise.

But it's like a frozen dessert, and I suck down almost half before a brain freeze makes me pause in the sand, groaning. "That's it. You get the rest."

But Van sets both drinks down on a table near some lounge chairs. He takes my hand, tugging me toward the water. When he slides his hand out of mine, a surge of disappointment rises. At least until he wraps an arm around my shoulders, pulling me close. I rest my head against his chest, breathing in his sharp, masculine scent.

We reach the damp, packed sand and start along it. A little shorebird out past his bedtime zips ahead of us, chasing the waves in and running back out.

Van gives me the side closest to the ocean, and the water

rushes over my feet and up my ankles, then recedes so it can do so again. It's cold, but invigorating.

I'm going to miss this when we're back in the mountains. I wish I could scrunch up North Carolina like an accordion so Harvest Hollow could keep its charming mountains but also not be such a long drive to the Outer Banks or other beaches.

I lean into Van, also wishing we had the technology to bottle up moments like this, revisiting them whenever we'd like to. The reality of tomorrow being our last night hangs heavy over me.

I'm going to miss this. Miss him.

You don't have to miss him, I remind myself. *You just need to admit what you want and see if he wants the same thing.*

I *think* he does. But it's hard to imagine this man with the larger-than-life personality and the very busy and very public job wanting the same thing. Wanting me.

There's attraction, sure, but would Van want more with me? Even thinking it makes me feel like the pick-me girl— like I'm somehow different from all the other girls before.

But he introduced himself as Robbie. I'm not sure why my brain circles back to this fact. Maybe because of his sisters? Who also seemed shocked when he said he was on vacation with me. So ... maybe this is something real for him too.

I struggle to picture this easy banter, this physical closeness at home in Harvest Hollow. It's hard. And I definitely have trouble imagining the conversation with my dad in which I explain how I fell in love with a man I barely met in less than a week. I know there are people who have this kind of story, or even a faster love at first sight kind of relationship. But it has to be so rare.

And it sounds ... impossible. Improbable. Imagined.

I curl my hand around Van's back, sliding it up his

untucked polo shirt until my palm finds his warm skin. We walk in silence, the water rushing over our feet, then back out.

Everything seems heightened. The stars, brighter. The crash of waves, deeper. Van's muscles rippling under my hand as he walks. The sense of loss knowing we leave tomorrow, weightier.

"Permission to speak freely?" Van asks after a moment.

I hesitate. "Yes?"

"Don't sound so sure, Mills."

"It's just ... usually people are about to say something rude when they ask that. You know like, don't take this the wrong way but I hate your face."

"You hate my face?"

I poke him in the ribs and he laughs. "No, dummy. It was an example."

"So, you admit you *like* my face?"

A little *too* much.

"How about we get back to what you were going to say originally. Permission granted, by the way. Speak freely."

Van is quiet for so long I forget he wanted to say anything at all. Then I get nervous again about whatever he wanted to say.

"Well?" I ask. "Are you going to speak freely or not?"

His fingertips trail over my arm, making me shiver. Even my legs feel shaky.

"This has been the best few days I can remember," he says finally, voice gruff, and I trip over an uneven place in the sand.

Or maybe I tripped over his words, because they're not at all what I expected. He steadies me, his hand warm and strong on my shoulder. He pulls me closer, sliding his hand down to the curve of my hip.

"Seriously?" I ask.

He nods, then shoots me a sideways look, his smile soft. "Yep."

"Maybe you just needed a break from hockey?" I ask. "I know from Dad the schedule is brutal."

The Appies work *hard*. During the season, I barely see Dad, and the players have extra press and charity events and things I don't even know about.

But I immediately wish I hadn't brought up my father. Van stiffens, his fingers tightening on my hip. It's easy to forget out here that they have their own relationship apart from me. Not a great one.

What would Dad say if I brought Van home?

No—what will Dad say *when* I bring Van home?

Because I realize in this moment, despite Morgan's warnings and my own doubts and the ludicrousness of the last few days, this is something. It's real.

And it's big.

If Dad has an issue with Van, he can get over it.

And if I can't bring myself to be brave enough to tell Van how I feel, this all may be a nonissue.

"I think it's more about the company," Van says, and my heart takes this as its cue to run amok, beating wildly in my chest.

I don't know how to respond, so I go with teasing. Trying to play it off while also tucking it away into my core memories. "All those ladies at the pool today, huh?"

He snorts, but when I glance over, his expression is sincere. Vulnerable. Definitely not his typical cocky mask. I sway on my feet, thoughts humming.

"It's *you*, Mills."

"Oh," is all I can manage.

Van bumps his hip into mine. "Now's the time when you say, 'Me too, Van. I love having you around too!'"

I laugh at his high-pitched impression of me. "That's not how I sound."

"It's a *little bit* how you sound."

"Shut up."

"I will. But only after you tell me how much you enjoy my company." Van drops his hand and takes a few quick steps ahead, then turns to face me, walking backward with his eyes fixed on mine. "I'm waiting."

He's teasing. But our conversation has shifted to encompass something larger than companionship and a walk on the beach.

My mouth goes dry. This is it—another opportunity to speak up. To tell him how I'm really feeling. A second chance after I froze in the restaurant and couldn't form the words. But I'm still processing how it's possible to feel so much for someone I've only just met in such a short time.

How did I get so addicted in so short a time?

How will things change when we go back home?

The idea fills me with a deep and echoing emptiness. An ache that has me pressing one hand to my chest, like I can shove all these big feelings I shouldn't be having back inside my body. Or down a mineshaft.

As the silence stretches, Van's smile falls, and he turns around, giving me his back. He pauses, waiting for me to catch up. I do, stumbling again over every divot in the sand until Van hears me struggling, and turns with a frown to wait.

But his expression is closed. His hands hang limp and loose at his sides.

"It's okay," he says, and though I can see the corner of his mouth curling up, there's no smile in his voice. "You don't have to say anything. I promised myself I wouldn't push."

"No, Van. That's not it."

I place my palm flat against his chest, my fingertips ending up just inside the V of his shirt collar. They rest on the plume of smoke curling up from his dragon's mouth and I'm momentarily distracted by the crisp ink. My fingers curl, grasping the hem of his shirt as my gaze snaps up to his.

I open my mouth, but words vanish at the tempest brewing in Van's dark eyes.

I *do* have something I want to say. But I'm still struggling with getting the words from my head to my mouth. They're getting lost in translation somewhere in the short space between.

So, I decide to forgo words and go all in with one risky move.

I lift up on my toes and press my lips to his.

It's a tiny kiss. Short, soft, a little bit awkward and a whole lot hesitant, as though I'm fourteen and this is my first-ever kiss. And it feels that way to me—like this one brief touch erased any kiss before it. The press of his mouth to mine hits some kind of reset button in me, leaving me new and naive and innocent.

Van's whole body goes still. Underneath my palm, still splayed over his chest and half inside his shirt, he's not even breathing.

Did his heart stop? No—there it is, a faint pulse barely registering under my fingertips.

But more importantly, I realize—his mouth does not move.

He isn't kissing me back.

As my heels settle once more on the sand, the drop back

down feels like a freefall from a tall building. Ending with a splat on the sidewalk.

My hand falls away from Van's chest. I stare down at my bare toes, still perfectly pedicured from an appointment the day before the wedding. The heaviness in my stomach moves from an ache to more of a cramp.

"I'm sorry," I whisper. "I thought—"

Van's hands curl around my upper arms, tugging me closer, and when I look up, his eyes are wild, his lips are parted, and his breath is coming in short pants.

"What did we say about apologies?" he whispers. "Because I refuse to be sorry about this."

And then he's the one kissing me.

Only it's not a quick, chaste press. There is nothing awkward or innocent or hesitant here.

It's a claiming, a confession, completely consuming. His mouth is hot, the press of his lips firm as one hand travels up my arm and tunnels into my hair. Like he's been dying for days to do this.

His other hand finds my waist, sliding around until he's nudging me closer, fingertips along my spine.

No space between us, breaths mingled, and our words spoken solely through motion.

I grip the front of his shirt so tightly a button pops off. He must feel it because he chuckles. I swallow the sound, hungry for it, for him.

I don't want this moment to end, and at the same time, I want to have five thousand more moments just like this one.

A lifetime of this.

"Van," I murmur.

"Mills."

His lips drag away from my mouth, reluctantly, like it's work to pull back. But then he kisses across the swell of my cheek and along my jaw and just beneath it, as he nibbles my neck.

The firm press of his lips and the insistent scratch of his facial hair is the perfect combination. It leaves my legs shaky and my skin buzzing. I'm holding onto him now not because I'm desperate for him—though I am—but to keep my knees from buckling.

The slap of a rogue wave high against our legs sends us both stumbling. I'm almost certain it's the only thing that could have pulled us apart short of an alien invasion or maybe the jaws of life.

My dress is soaked up to my thighs and so are Van's shorts, though only the very bottom. The perks of being tall. We stare at one another, then burst out laughing. He sends an arc of water my way. I gasp as even more of my dress gets drenched.

"You looked like you needed to cool off," he says.

I gape at him. The man I was just kissing. Who seamlessly transitioned back into our playful back-and-forth without missing a beat.

"Me?" I can't even find words to splutter out a comeback so I scoop up water in my hands and splash it his way.

I didn't aim, but all the water manages to hit the crotch of his shorts, instantly making him look like he wet his pants. He glances down, propping his hands on his hips. When he looks back up, the glint in his eyes has me taking a few steps back, my heart taking off at a dead sprint.

"Is this how you wanna play, Mills—dirty?"

His words, or maybe the throaty tone of his voice, makes me tremble. I've never been like this with anyone—embracing passion and playfulness like two sides of the same coin. It only works because the currency is trust.

The only way I'm able to be this way with Van, to be so myself, is because I trust him.

"I'll play any way you'd like," I tell him, my own voice a ragged whisper. "But … you'll have to catch me first!"

I'm already running before I finish, tripping over my feet and the tangle of my wet dress. Van reaches me in seconds, hoisting me up and helicoptering me around on his shoulders until I'm gasping for breath while laughing, my damp dress sending out sprays of water.

When Van sets me on my feet again, I'm so dizzy, he has to hold me up. His rough hands cup my cheeks as he bends to kiss me again and again and again.

Light, playful kisses with him smiling against my mouth. He pulls back, thumbs sweeping my cheekbones the way he did the other night. Only now, there are no tears to wipe away.

"Is this okay?" he asks, eyes fixed on my mouth as one thumb brushes the corner.

I press a quick kiss there. "I started it."

"And you're under no obligation to continue," he says. "If you were just testing the waters or if you're feeling some kind of way about the wedding—"

I interrupt Van with a kiss. Slow and lingering.

"This is about no one but us," I tell him, finding his eyes but not pulling away enough to see them as more than a too-close blur. "You and me, hotshot. It has nothing to do with him or everything that happened. Other than the fact that those events led us here."

And I'm so glad they did.

"I don't want you to feel rushed," Van says. "But also …" He drops his voice to a rough whisper, leaning his forehead on mine and shifting his hands from my cheeks to my neck.

"This means something to me, Mills. The way I feel about you is not casual."

My hands had been loosely curled around his waist, and I lift them now, cupping his prickly jaw in my palms.

"It's not casual for me either. More like … monumental. And I'll be honest—it scares me."

"The last thing I want is to scare you."

"It's the good kind of fear. Like zip lining when I first stepped off the platform."

Van smiles, and I trace his Cupid's bow with a fingertip, dodging when he tries to nip me. "I'd prefer an analogy with fewer reptiles, please."

"Frisky's going to get offended at some point."

"Frisky?"

"Your dragon. I named him."

"You named him *Frisky?* Why not, like, Killer or Draco or Brutus?"

I drop one hand, tracing the lines on his skin, more visible now that I've ripped the button off his shirt. "He likes his name." I switch to a baby voice. "Don't you, Frisky? Don't you just love your name like a good dragon? Yes, you do!"

Van growls and hoists me up again, this time throwing me over a shoulder so I'm hanging down his back. I don't mind the view of his muscular backside as he strides across the sand.

"Where are you taking me?"

"Not sure yet."

I lift my head, drawn by music and laughter from the wedding in the distance. With fairy lights strung up over the sand and an actual acoustic band playing beach music punctuated by the pounding waves, it's magical.

I tap Van on the back. "Might I make a request? Look over there."

Van turns, pausing as he sees the wedding I'm pointing to. "The wedding?" He sounds confused. Maybe a little concerned.

"Why not crash the reception? Maybe just for one dance."

Van hesitates. I can feel tension coiling in his back. "Are you sure you're okay with this?"

The funny thing is that my own failed wedding didn't even occur to me. Which feels like a massive step. And further confirmation that what's happening between me and Van isn't some kind of emotional rebound.

I smile. "Positive."

A moment later, Van sets me back on my feet and takes my hand in his. I'm glad because I'm so overwhelmed with emotion and maybe exhaustion and possibly the effects of the piña colada that I need his steadying presence.

My brain feels like a mix between a spinning top and one of those kaleidoscopes you turn as a kid, the colors bursting and shifting against a backdrop of light.

There's no security or any kind of barrier outside the designated wedding area, and no one notices as we slip into the crowd. The moment we do, however, the song changes from something slow and romantic, with couples swaying on the small dance floor, to "Shout" by the Isley Brothers.

Van raises his eyebrows, a clear challenge as the swaying couples turn to boogeying couples all around us. With a grin, I throw my hands up.

This is how we spend the next hour, laughing and touching and kissing as we dance at someone else's wedding until my feet are sore.

And then, feeling warm and loose and euphoric from the

sum total of this evening and the last few days, I lift on my toes, tugging Van down until I can whisper in his ear.

"I have an idea," I tell him, heart jackhammering away. A bad idea or a great one—I don't know. It may be *right*—it *feels* right—but what I'm absolutely sure of is that it's reckless.

A big, scary thing for the day. A stepping off the platform in order to fly.

And I want it more than I've wanted anything. "Pop quiz, hotshot?"

He presses a kiss to my mouth before putting his lips to my ear. There's no reason to whisper, but we're both doing it anyway, and it makes me laugh. "Okay. Shoot."

"Yes or no."

"Yes or no *what?*"

"That's the quiz," I tell him.

"Are you going to tell me what I'm saying yes or no to first?"

"Nope. Yes or no, hotshot. In or out."

He hesitates for a moment, and my heart beats so fast I almost change my mind. But then he flashes me a grin and says, "Yes. Whatever it is, I'm in."

CHAPTER 17

Van

I WAKE up to the feeling of cold stealing over me, like someone just ripped a blanket away from me, leaving me bare. Wouldn't be the first time. I shiver and turn, reaching for something or someone and finding nothing.

"Eli, is that you? Not funny, man."

He would be the one to do it. Maybe Alec? He seems to enjoy sneaking in people's hotel rooms to mess with them. He's done it to Nathan more than once when he slept through alarms.

But when I crack open my bleary eyes, I realize I'm not on the road with the guys. I'm at the beachfront resort. And I have no reason to be cold because the bed sheets are pulled up to my chin.

The bed sheets.

Not the blanket from the couch, where I spent most of the week sleeping.

No—I'm in the massive bed.

Amelia's bed.

My head jerks to the side, painfully letting me know I have a crick in my neck. Another crick. The same crick. Who knows at this point.

The other side of the bed is empty. There's an indentation in the pillow next to mine, and the sheets are pulled back like Amelia got out in a hurry. When I set my palm down, the sheets are cold.

My brain is still foggy, but the events of the night before come back to me, a flood of happy memories. Kissing Amelia on the beach. Dancing with the wedding party.

And then …

I bite my lip over a smile.

"Mills?" I call, my voice a gruff morning rumble.

The last few mornings, I woke to the smell of coffee, but it's not there now. Just the faint citrus scent from Amelia's pillow. I lean over, inhaling as my eyes flutter closed.

"Amelia?" I call again, even as I notice the unnatural stillness, the reverberating quiet.

A hazy dread settles over me like smog as I climb out of bed, pulling a pair of shorts on over my briefs. The bathroom door is ajar, and my unease settles slightly as I see Amelia's toiletries still on the counter.

She hasn't left.

Why would I assume she had?

I shake my head. She wouldn't go. Not after this week, after last night. She probably went to get us breakfast. A surprise for our last morning.

Our last morning.

Yesterday, I woke up with dread thinking about leaving.

Now ... hope buoys me. There will be complications, of course, like talking to Coach—Amelia's dad—whom I've been ignoring now for days, other than quick texts saying things are fine. He won't be happy but ... I'll make it work. I'll tell him how I feel, convince him it's not some kind of fluke. Amelia will help.

It will be fine.

When I pick up my phone, opening our text thread, I'm surprised to see a new one from him. It didn't show up as unread, so I must have opened it last night.

Thanks for babysitting Amelia, it reads. *I owe you one. Consider your old spot yours again. I'm putting Dominik back in his line.*

That's ... good, I guess. But I'm surprised to find I don't actually care about my position. What I really don't like is him still thinking this week was me *babysitting*. I'll have to tell him that too—I didn't come here for him.

I came for *her*.

Thoughts of Amelia have my stomach swooping happily. I need to see her. To have my fingertips on her skin, my mouth on hers again. When she gets back, I hope she doesn't mind if breakfast is not what I'm in the mood for.

Feeling better with every step, I saunter out of the bedroom, scratching my stomach with a yawn. I scan the room, heading for the table, where I can see a folded paper, ripped right from Amelia's yellow notebook by the looks of it.

Smiling, I pick up the folded paper with *Van* in loopy cursive across the front. Even her handwriting is cute. I shake my head grinning as I wonder how she turned me into a sentimental schmuck so fast. The guys will *never* let me live this down.

No regrets.

Other than waking up alone. If it were me, spending the

day in bed with room service sounds better than getting dressed to hunt down breakfast.

But Amelia probably has some surprise in store, something to celebrate—

My thoughts skid to a halt and my smile slips away as I read the note.

Van,

Didn't mean to snoop but saw my dad's text. You can consider your babysitting job officially over. Enjoy having your spot back. Last night was clearly a mistake.

Don't worry about me. I'll get home and find a way to pay you back everything I owe you.

-A

My jaw clenches as I read it a second time, understanding washing over me. Amelia read her dad's text and assumed his words were true.

That I came here on her father's orders to win back my spot on the line with Eli and Logan.

Bitterness rises like a stench in my nostrils. Shouldn't she have woken me up to ask if it's true?

Would you have? a voice retorts in my head. *Or would you have believed the words of a man you've known your whole life, trusted him over a man you spent a few days with?*

I'm hurt and angry, but I also don't blame Amelia. Only myself. I should have told her father no. Told him I was already coming with Amelia, even if that risked his ire.

Then I should have told Amelia he asked. Whatever impact it would have had on the two of them, that's their issue to work out.

I don't regret any of my other actions. Not even last night.

But she called it a *mistake*.

My fist crumples the paper before I read it a third time. I hurl it toward the balcony, but even balled up, the paper is light and barely clears the end of the table, rolling unevenly to a stop somewhere underneath the sofa.

I work to unclench my fists, then breathe deeply, slowly, placing my hands on the table and spreading my fingertips wide.

She's gone. Amelia's gone, leaving me behind like a skin she's shed.

Deep breaths, I remind myself, but they're ragged. Unsteady. A stitch forms in my side as though I've been sprinting with no warmup. *You can fix this when you get back.*

But it doesn't feel very fixable. Maybe because it was so delicate to begin with. I scrub a hand down my face.

What can I expect after only a few days together? Especially considering the way those days started.

But I'm not ready to give up.

I always said if I found the right woman, I'd make it work. I won't give up.

I can come up with a plan.

I can …

I can …

My mind is blank. Because I'm not a planner. And I have no idea how to fix the mess I made. The mess *we* made, Mills and I.

My hands clench again. I need something else to throw. Something more substantial than a little ball of paper.

This moment feels like the *gotcha* at the end of a prank. The *I told you so* after not listening to good advice.

It's the worst case of *I should have known better* of my life—and there have been a lot of those.

My stomach sours, a bitter taste coating my tongue as I work to swallow.

This shouldn't matter so much, I tell myself. But it does. It's *all* that matters.

And just how much it matters hits me as I slide the ring off my left hand, narrowing my eyes at the cheap gold band, like it's somehow to blame.

I won't be needing this anymore.

Only, I can't set the ring down. I don't want to.

So, I stare at the wedding band Amelia and I picked out at the only place open late last night--the most touristy gift shop in the resort, barely a step above the stores selling spray-painted shirts and hermit crabs. Instead of buying Amelia a matching one, she asked me to switch her mother's ring to her other hand. I remember the way her hand shook when I did it and her brilliant smile afterward.

Swallowing down a knot in my throat, I grab my suitcase and start to pack.

Guess it's a good thing we didn't go out and get matching tattoos.

PART TWO- PREJUDICE

RULES FOR RUNAWAY BRIDES
BY AMELIA DAVIS

Step aside, Julia Roberts—there's a new runaway bride in town.

Actually, there are *dozens* of us. Women who have stayed silent, tucked away into the shadows like secrets.

Because there is deep shame in calling off a wedding, whether it's moments before walking down the aisle (in my case) or days, weeks, or months before. Even if it's not your fault.

Even if the groom is caught with the maid of honor minutes before the wedding (also in my case).

It takes strength and courage to call off a wedding. Whether it's due to infidelity or realizing it's the wrong decision, there should be no shame. Better to realize now and have to deal with the logistics of returning dozens of wedding gifts than to say "I do" and then untangle two whole lives.

So, gather round, runaway brides! Here are some tips for your journey.

1. **Don't be afraid to walk away.** You might have already taken this step, but if you're reading and suddenly recognize a twisting in your gut of real, true doubt—it's okay to call off your wedding.
2. **Phone a friend.** Or ten. Whether it's driving you away from the church or helping return gifts, you can't do this alone. Ask for help. Repeatedly.
3. **Get out of town.** Take some time for yourself, whether that's literally or figuratively out of town. Back off from your normal routine. Breathe.
4. **Take forward steps.** Don't get stuck, though the temptation might be strong to live in regret or memories. Move forward, not back. Even if you start with baby steps.
5. **Do something that scares you every day.** Take risks—the healthy kind. Challenge yourself. And make sure some of those friends from #2 are there to keep you safe.
6. **Don't fall into a guilt trap.** You've heard of a guilt trip, but a guilt trap is when you fall into a pattern of feeling like this is your fault. It's not, so keep moving and don't fall into the trap!
7. **Don't fall for a rebound.** You might find yourself tempted to attach all those unmoored emotions to another, new person. Resist. Give yourself time to heal first, to make sure your feelings are real. Otherwise … you might find yourself running away from one relationship to another.

Runaway brides out there, I see you! And I've been in your shoes. Follow for more tips and share if anyone you know has run or *needs* to run. My inbox is open if you need to talk. <3

CHAPTER 18

Amelia

I'm sitting at the kitchen table, staring down at a piece of toast buttered so well it glistens, when Dad drops a kiss on my head. I try to arrange my face into a smile that doesn't look deranged or clownish. Or like a deranged clown.

He's pretending things are normal, I think in an attempt to help me heal from what happened with Drew.

I'm pretending I don't know about his deal with Van. And also like I didn't *marry* Van.

It's been almost two weeks since I left him in Florida and it still feels like someone took a rusty chainsaw to my heart.

Finding out my dad essentially traded a spot on a line—whatever *that* is—to one of his players in exchange for "babysitting" me is tough to stomach.

I mean, I *know* Dad had my best interests at heart. Always. Even in this.

Morgan told me all the things he did for me while I was gone, from calling lawyers to see if it's possible to legally hold Drew accountable for wedding costs to returning gifts to fielding phone calls—and all this at his busiest time of the year with playoffs around the corner.

I also know it's killing Dad to be at odds with his brother. And to see Becky, a niece he'd always adored, do something so disloyal and awful. He's hurting. I know he doesn't want me to see his pain. To worry about him when he's worried about me.

It makes me sad.

I am also still mad.

Which makes me feel guilty.

I am a quagmire of messy, ugly feelings. And that's without taking into consideration all the conflicting emotions I have about Van.

So, Dad and I are riding this weird carousel around and around. Playing parts, keeping secrets. Pretending we're both fine.

"I packed you a lunch," Dad says, pulling an insulated bag from the fridge. One I've never seen before and I bet he bought just for this occasion. It has Taylor Swift on it and sparkles as he sets it down in front of me.

A few months ago, I'd have laughed and tried to explain that loving Taylor's music and respecting her business savvy does *not* mean I want a Taylor Swift lunch bag. Especially not on my first day at a new job.

Eventually, though, I would have given up trying to explain, hugged him, and said *Thank you, Daddy* like a good daughter.

Now, my stomach clenches at his attempted kindness. "You didn't need to do that."

"Don't worry—I didn't cook."

242

"Let's hope not."

I'm not amazing in the kitchen, but between the two of us, my dad is the one most likely to start a fire in the microwave. He probably stuck a Lunchables and a cheese stick inside the bag like I'm seven again.

He chuckles, and I find myself smiling back for half a second before it falls. It's hard not to drop back into our normal back and forth. Even when nothing feels normal.

I watch Dad's face as he takes a sip of coffee. As my one little act of passive aggressive retaliation for the deal he made with Van, I've been watering down his coffee. Every day, I add a little more water, a little less coffee.

Stupid, I know. But I take the smallest bit of pleasure in this tiny, immature act. It's not like I'm *hurting* him. It's barely even a prank.

Actually, now that I'm thinking about it, I've never really *played* pranks. Even on April Fool's Day. Pranks are not for rule-followers. *Morgan* is the type to play pranks. *I* am the type to worry about getting caught or the consequences.

A stray thought hits me right in the gut—Van would approve.

Of this prank, of me doing something I've never done. The thought has me holding my breath and using all my mental fortitude to force my tears right back into the ducts from whence they came. I will *not* cry over Van.

Not again. Not this morning.

Dad takes another sip, and I swear he flinches, then frowns at his mug.

I want to have a silent celebration. And I also want to confess and make Dad a fresh pot.

Who even am I anymore? I swear, it's like Van shook something loose in me. As to whether this is a good or bad thing, I'm undecided. For now, my whole life feels like I'm wearing a sweater that went into the dryer one too many times when it was supposed to be air dried. It's familiar, but doesn't quite look or feel the same.

I glance down at my right hand, where I've moved Mom's ring again, and the tears threaten again.

"Excited about your big day?" Dad asks.

"Sure," I say, but my brain snags on his word choice.

My *big day*. You can say that again. But I can't think of "big day" without thinking of weddings, and the last thing I want to be thinking about today is THAT kind of big day.

Unfortunately, my new job is going to be one giant reminder. Because I took a job working for the Appies as a staff writer and content creator.

One can't be choosy when you're jobless and need money to move out of your dad's house as fast as humanly possible. And other than working in the same building as my dad and one particular hockey player I'd rather avoid, this is a dream job.

When Parker called me, gushing, and said I just *had* to work with her at the Appies doing longer form online content, I couldn't say no.

I mean, it's a full-time job *writing*. Finally.

A few weeks ago, I also would have been thrilled to work with my dad. Thrilled to have his approval, which, to my shock, he's freely given.

I thought there would be pushback because one—it's a writing job not a practical business one, and two—it's in the proximity of hockey players. Ironically, coming back seemingly unscathed after being with Van in Florida somehow convinced Dad that his precious daughter can be around hockey players and live to tell the tale.

If he only knew …

Maybe it's because working in the same building means he can keep an eye on me?

As I study him now, I can see it in his expression. It's almost identical to his proud dad smile, one I've grown used to seeing over the years. But ever since I got back from Florida, it's been slightly forced, like he's trying too hard. Like he thinks I might break at any moment, and it's his job to hold me together with extra optimism, super wide smiles, and packed lunches.

His phone rings in his hand, and his expression turns thunderous. Which means it's Uncle Bobby. Again. Dad refuses to talk to him, though Bobby hasn't given up trying.

"What if he wants to apologize?" I ask.

Dad's head snaps up, and he clicks off the ringer, sliding the phone into his pocket. "He doesn't."

"But how do you know if you won't talk to him?"

"He leaves voicemails," Dad says.

"And?"

Dad shakes his head. "Let's just say we both share the same protectiveness when it comes to our daughters."

Becky hasn't tried to reach out. But I wouldn't want to talk to her any more than Dad wants to talk to his brother. They are in the wrong, they're family, and this rift is ugly. It feels wrong. One more addition to the strange tension in my life.

"Are you sure you're okay?" Dad asks. A daily question.

"I will be."

"I'm proud of you, Milly."

Would he still be proud if he knew about Van?

I could be mature and talk to him about it. All of it. I could tell Dad about my time in Florida with Van. And how it all came crashing down because I saw the text Dad sent Van.

How deeply he actually hurt me while he was trying to protect me.

But I won't tell him. I can't. At least for now.

I haven't told anyone what happened the last night in Florida. Not even Morgan. I did tell her Van and I kissed, but not about what else we did.

It's not healthy keeping such a huge secret, but I need time to process. Which means I'm shoving down all the negative emotions, letting my insides rumble and riot like an active volcano just waiting to blow. Dad seems to be chalking up any weirdness on my part to the wedding fiasco and then seeing Drew and Becky in Florida. I'd much rather him think that than know the truth.

You know—that I *married* his least favorite player.

"I'll pop in and see you in your new office later," he says.

"You don't need to do that. And it's a cubicle, not an office. Honestly, I'm surprised you're so excited," I say, keeping my voice level. "Seeing as how you wanted to keep me away from hockey players for so long."

Dad shrugs. "You'll be working with Parker. She'll keep you in line. And maybe I worried a little too much. I mean, you came back from Florida with Van unscathed."

Did I though? I stab my toast with a fork.

"And of all the guys on the team …" He shakes his head, and I decide to cut him off before he starts complaining again about Van's poor performance and attitude to match.

"I'm also surprised you weren't mad he went with me," I say innocently. "Seeing how you're always complaining about him."

Practically ripping the figurative door off the hinges to give him an opening to tell me that he asked Van to go with me.

No—*bribed* him.

"Should we carpool?" Dad asks instead.

Being trapped in a car with my dad and all this awkwardness for a twenty-minute commute? I'd rather be in a car filled with snakes. And the only one who hates snakes more than me is Indiana Jones.

"I'm not sure how my day will look, so I'll drive myself. Plus, you've been staying late," I remind him.

Like he could forget playoffs start at the end of the week. Last year, he was practically a ghost during this time. I'm honestly looking forward to it now.

"Right. Okay."

I can tell he's disappointed, and despite the simmering lava of anger inside me, the tiny part of me used to being daddy's little girl pinches uncomfortably. But only until I remember what he did.

The pain quickly swallows up the pinch.

"In that case, I'll head in a little early," he says. "You'll find me if you need anything?"

Nope, I think.

"Yep," I say.

Still, he hesitates at the door. "Well, I guess I'll see you at work."

Hopefully not. But I force another clenched-jaw smile and wave goodbye. Then he's gone. Leaving me alone to finish getting ready for my first day of a job I'm excited about.

So long as I can avoid my husband.

———

"I'm so excited you're here," Parker squeals.

An actual squeal. Accompanied by a boa constrictor hug, which is followed by a full body shake she gives me with both her hands wrapped around my upper arms.

247

This could be an invasion of personal space, overstepping to the nth degree. But there's something so wholesomely endearing about her that I don't even mind.

She makes it easy to forget all the anger I'm holding onto, which is a feat. But with her wide smile and sparkling, sincere eyes, she's like a black hole of happiness, sucking up all my negativity.

If she could find a way to bottle this up and sell it, she'd make millions.

"Sorry," she says, still beaming as she releases my arms. "I'm just happy to have another woman around here. Before Summer—you'll meet her later—it was just me, choking on the fog of testosterone in this building."

"I'll bet."

Though I also bet she can't mind *too* much. I didn't miss the engagement ring on her finger. Her fiancé is one of the Appies, and I kind of regret not paying more attention so I'd know which one.

We're standing inside the staff entrance to the Summit—a building until now I've just driven past and never actually been inside. Already, my body is on high alert. It was even before I saw a mud-crusted Jeep in the parking lot and remembered a conversation we had about Van having two cars.

He's here. Like I knew he would be. But it's a whole different thing to know it and then be here knowing he is somewhere in the building.

I swear, the little hairs on my arms are standing at attention, like they're just waiting for a sighting.

Thankfully Parker pulls me away from my paranoia when she gives my shoulder a squeeze. "I'm also excited because you're *you*," she says. "Have things calmed down with your articles?"

I shake my head, unable to stop myself from smiling. "It's still out of control. Awesome, but insane."

The silver lining to all the dark clouds in my life lately was having my "Rules for Runaway Brides" article blow up.

I spent the plane ride back from Florida channeling all of my energy into the final draft, writing in my little yellow Walmart notebook through the blur of tears. My forceful handwriting ripped the pages in a few places. That notebook and enough pain to fill a stadium were the only things I took with me when I snuck out of the hotel room. Then, locked in my room at home with Taylor Swift's *Evermore* album on repeat, I edited and hit publish.

What I did not expect was for the post—and my previously unknown little Substack—to go viral.

I mean, it *was* catchy. Full of dark humor and more relatable than I realized it could be. I had no idea how many comments and shares I'd get from women and friends of women who called off a wedding or had been left at the altar or just before a wedding. Even some runaway grooms reached out.

When I posted a storytime article giving the actual details with not real names, the momentum only grew. I had no idea how many people walked away from their weddings.

My inbox is overflowing. I'm trying to answer every single message and each comment, but it might take me a year. Or two.

While I wish so many people didn't relate to my experience or the posts, I'm so happy to help people feel seen and heard. Knowing my *words* did that—well, it's literally a dream.

The best part, though, was the influx of job offers. Some were just temporary things—writing part-time for various publications or penning paid guest articles, some of which I might still do.

But I couldn't turn down this job. An actual, full-time, with-benefits job for an organization that's nationally known. Most AHL teams don't have the kind of clout or name recognition the Appies do. It would be stupid to say no.

Even if it means being in the same building as the two men who are the focus for all of my volcano rage.

It's not lost on me the irony that Drew—the guy who cheated on me throughout our engagement and in the very church we were supposed to get married in—doesn't make the top two of people making me angry. He's barely a blip.

Honestly—while what he did sucks and I'm still hurt about Becky's involvement, I feel like I dodged not just a bullet but a whole firing squad. Marrying Drew would have been a colossal mistake.

Bigger than marrying Van? a tiny, nasty voice in my head asks. I drop-kick the thought right out of my head.

Parker hooks her hand through mine and starts to tug me down the long hallway, our footsteps echoing on the concrete floors. "Well, I am beyond stoked we get to have you. That *I* get to have you," she amends. "I promise not to work you *too* hard."

The evil laugh that accompanies her words makes me wonder if I've misjudged Parker's sweetness. Her enthusiastic smile and brown glossy waves give off cheerleader vibes, but there's clearly a dark little edge hiding under there somewhere.

It only makes me like her more.

"Paperwork first," she says. "Then I'll show you around and then we'll meet everyone."

I stumble a little, and she steadies me. "Everyone?"

She laughs. "I mean, everyone in the office. The players

are kind of on their own schedule. Especially the next few weeks with the playoffs coming up. We'll still do some things with them, but I stockpiled a lot of content so they could focus."

"That's smart." I try to keep my voice even and not betray the thread of panic I'm feeling. "But since I'm focusing more on the writing, I won't need to interact with the players as much … right?"

"Not as much as I do, since you'll be working on posts and longer captions for our socials—stuff we've already done with the guys. Plus, we're a few days away from the first playoff game and your dad is keeping them busy."

"Okay," I say, relieved.

But then she keeps going.

"You will get some hands-on time with them, though, because we've got one project coming up where I'll need you to do some interviews and a few other things."

She waves a hand like this is no big deal. The panic tightening all my muscles would disagree with her about that.

I must not hide my horror well because Parker laughs.

"Don't worry—they'll behave. They're good guys for the most part, and even if not, they're all afraid of me. Plus, you're the coach's daughter. They know he'd kill them if they did anything rude."

She laughs. I pretend to, and my fake laugh sounds a little like a hyena with a case of asthma. I wish Dad hadn't bought me a lunch sack because I could really use a good, old-fashioned paper bag to breathe in right now.

"Anyway. Today will be pretty boring office introductory stuff. But don't worry—soon I'll have you getting hands-on with both the writing and with the guys."

Cue the real panic.

But before I can run through the nearest wall and leave an

Amelia-shaped hole, Parker pulls me through a doorway and into an office area. "Summer has all the boring paperwork ready for you. You'll love her too, despite the aforementioned boring paperwork. If you ever need to sue someone, she's got you covered."

"I already told you," a strong, female voice says. "I don't handle lawsuits."

Parker and I turn to see a woman in a dark suit with a lemon-yellow shirt striding toward us. Her dark hair is pulled into a neat updo, and she somehow manages to look fashionable and effortless at the same time. Approachable, yet like you wouldn't want to tangle with her.

"Are you sure?" Parker asks. "Not even a tiny, baby lawsuit?"

"Nope. Who do you want to *tiny, baby* sue anyway?"

"I've got a list," Parker says. "Summer, this is Amelia. I don't want to sue her."

Summer smiles and steps forward to give me a firm handshake. "Glad to have you on board."

"Thanks," I say, both wanting to bask under the praise and hide under the nearest desk. "Nice to meet you."

"I'm part of the legal team. And while I *do* have your paperwork, I can't help with any lawsuits."

"I think I'm good for now," I tell her.

The moment I say it, I realize I actually *do* need legal advice. Specifically around how to undo a marriage.

It's been on my mind constantly, but I've avoided even a quick Google search. Like if I don't type the word *annulment* or *how to get out of a mistake marriage* into a search bar, the marriage needing to be annulled won't exist.

Similarly, I'm not sure about the validity of the marriage certificate. I didn't really question it when the officiant said they keep them on hand, and the waiting period is only if

252

both bride and groom are Florida residents. That now sounds a little sus to me, but again—I've only gotten so far as to let my fingers hover over the keyboard while *thinking* about looking this up.

I wonder if this is the kind of thing I could ask Summer. But then I shake off the thought. It's my first day, and I don't exactly want to start by confessing to one of the other two women on the Appies' staff how big of a mistake I just made.

With an *Appie* no less.

Parker links her other arm through Summer's and steers us away from the reception desk, which is currently empty. "Come on. Let's get the boring stuff out of the way so we can get to the fun part."

"I resent that," Summer says. "What's boring to you is my Roman Empire."

Parker wrinkles her nose, releasing us so we can all walk through the doorway and into a small office. "Your Roman Empire is paperwork?"

"I do love a good contract." Summer gives a happy little sigh as she sinks down into her chair. Parker and I sit down across from her, leaving the door open. "But that doesn't make me boring, okay? I'm still super fun."

"When you're super fun, you usually don't have to *tell* people you're super fun," Parker points out.

The two of them go back and forth while I'm signing … and signing and signing. Summer briefly explains each document in a way I can understand, telling me I can take my time if I want to read everything. Which I definitely don't. She can keep her paperwork Roman Empire.

I'm just handing back the last page when someone walks right into her office, already talking. A someone whose deep voice makes all those alert hairs on my arms stand straight up.

"Yo, Summer. Got a minute?"

Van steps into the room.

I can't help but turn, like he's at the other end of a tether. One that just yanked me tight. I suck in a breath.

He jerks to a stop, blinking at me like I'm a mirage he hopes will disappear. The way his eyes go flat makes my chest hurt.

I wonder if he knew I was going to be working here. My dad probably told him.

Or, I think, watching a flurry of emotions pass over his face, *maybe not.*

The last time I saw him, he was asleep. Shirtless. I woke up the morning after our wedding draped over him, my cheek pressed to his dragon tattoo. I remember the sudden spike of panic, the *Oh crap what did I do?*

But after a moment of listening to his slow breaths and watching his lashes flutter on his cheeks, the panic subsided into a warm affection. A sense of rightness and peace about it all.

Then I slipped out of bed and saw the text.

Now, he's standing just a few feet away with his dark, messy head of hair. The broad shoulders and a jawline I've traced with both my fingers and my mouth.

He shaved.

Why his smooth, bare jaw feels like a betrayal, I'm not sure. But I remember telling him I loved his facial hair. Remember running my fingers over it. Kissing it.

I remember the way it felt against my skin ...

His eyes slide away from me as his jaw clenches. Something deep inside me sinks, and I grab tightly to my anger with both fists. I've found that anger makes the very best shield against hurt.

As long as I ignore the little ugly voice asking me if Van

might be hurting too. If me leaving while he slept had the same impact on *him* as reading Dad's text had on *me*.

"I already told you, Van," Summer says, rolling her eyes. "We're not going to trademark your face."

Parker snorts.

"Uh, it's not that," he says, already starting to back out of the office. "I'll come back later. When you're not, you know, busy."

"No, it's fine. We're almost done," Parker says, getting to her feet and waving Van toward the empty chair right next to me.

I should get up, but instead, I grip the arms of my chair tighter. Everything in me is screaming that I should run right out of the office. Okay, not *everything*. Because another tiny part—one which clearly suffered a lobotomy—wishes I could run right into his arms.

Van freezes, his mouth opening and then closing again before dropping into the chair next to me. So close I can feel the heat of him and smell the familiar masculine scent.

I wish this chair had an eject button to shoot me straight through the roof of the building and out into space. Apparently, a secret marriage supplies my brain with cartoon solutions—like running through walls and being shot out of my seat.

Actually … tying Van down to a set of train tracks doesn't sound so bad right now.

Summer frowns as she looks between me and Van and then back to Parker. "Do you know Amelia?" Summer asks, gesturing toward me. "She's new, and she's awesome."

Oh, he knows me *all right.*

I will my cheeks not to blush, like I can consciously control the most subconscious reactions.

255

"We've met," I say, trying to smile even though my voice sounds like a blade.

There is a beat of silence. Then Parker blurts out, "They just took a trip together."

Summer startles, glancing between a now-frozen Van and an even more frozen me.

Parker spins to face me and then words start falling out of her mouth like she's a malfunctioning vending machine.

"I'm *so* sorry. I'm not even supposed to know. Your dad slipped up and mentioned it and said not to say anything to anyone but especially not to say anything to you. I was doing so well not talking about that or the wedding or anything wedding-adjacent"—her eyes are now comically, anime wide — "and oh, shoot, now I've said *wedding* twice—*three* times!!! —and I should totally just shut up before I talk about how the trip was supposed to be your honeymoon—"

"*Parker.*" Summer's firm voice, probably her courtroom lawyer voice, has the power to stop the broken dam of words rushing out of Parker's mouth. "Stop talking."

"Sorry," Parker squeaks, slapping a hand over her mouth but continuing to talk around it. "I'm done. I swear. I'm so sorry."

For the briefest moment, my eyes meet Van's. Regret is a rusty anchor sinking down and down and down in my stomach.

"It's fine," I manage.

"Is it?" Van asks, cocking his head and looking at me with a look that's almost lazy and definitely infuriating. Because he knows it's absolutely *not* fine.

Now both Parker and Summer are staring at the two of us. Parker still with wide eyes. Summer with narrowed ones.

"The real question," Summer says, and I just know this is about to go somewhere I don't want it to go, "is how did you survive a trip with the guy who wants to trademark his face?"

"It took a lot of mental fortitude," I say dryly, hazarding another glance his way.

Van's eyes spark with something. Challenge, maybe? It makes me sit up straighter in my seat, something in me shifting awake like a lazy lion suddenly deciding it's no longer nap time but meal time.

"It *is* hard to resist this face." He makes a lazy circle around his head with one hand.

"Yet somehow I managed," I say.

There's the tiniest lift to one side of his mouth. "Did you, though?"

I lift a shoulder. "Looks that way."

"You know what they say about looks being deceiving."

"Does that also apply to *your* looks?"

He smirks, and I wish it didn't have an almost seismic impact on me. "Aw, did you just call me handsome?"

"Definitely not."

"Are you sure? Because I think a compliment was buried in there somewhere."

"Keep digging. Maybe you'll find it."

Van flexes. "These arms were made for digging."

"Digging yourself into a hole?" I suggest sweetly. "What I meant was about your looks being *deceiving*."

"Guess you'd know about that, huh?"

"Nope," I add, with sickening sweetness. "I don't know the first thing about lying right to someone's face."

His neatly shaven jaw hardens at this, and I swear I hear the sound of his teeth grinding.

I won this round of verbal sparring. So … where's the sense of celebration?

"Time out. The two of you"—Summer leans forward in

her chair, dramatically swiveling her head between the two of us— "spent *days* together?"

"Was it like this the whole time—with the fighty words and the snappy back and forth?" Parker asks. "I'm shocked you *both* survived."

Honestly, I'm not so sure I did. Not in one piece, anyway.

"Me too," Van mutters, getting to his feet. "I'll come back another time, Summer."

And then he's gone, and I'm left facing a two-person firing squad which shoots questions, not bullets.

"What was *that*?" Summer asks.

"Do I need to beat Van up?" Parker crosses her arms. "He's got a mouth on him, but he's a good guy underneath all the cocky bluster."

Great. Now I'm thinking about Van's mouth.

And the good guy I *thought* he was underneath it all.

But I was wrong. Again. Now I'm zero for two in picking the right men to marry.

CHAPTER 19

Van

"WE'RE JUST ASKING for a few details. It's not like we're asking you to kiss and tell," Dumbo whines.

"Yeah, because there should have been no kissing of any kind," Felix adds, giving me a look.

The kind that's a little too assessing.

There's no way he knows, I tell myself. But just in case, I turn my attention to my skates.

It's been like this since I got back. I thought they'd let up. But they're like a pack of dogs with a whole skeleton's worth of bones. I was hoping something would happen to distract everyone. Is it too much to hope for a tiny scandal or an accidental pregnancy or ... something? I'd take just about anything to take the spotlight off me. But heading into the playoffs, everyone has been drama free.

It was *just* starting to fade until today—Amelia's first day at work. Now, they're starting back up with the same questions I've already answered.

I really hope I don't crack and spill everything.

What's worse than getting the third degree is that I just came face-to-face with Amelia in Summer's office. Mills looked just as beautiful as she ever has. She also didn't look like she's been put through a blender, followed by a trash compactor, and then set on fire. Which is how I feel.

It's official: today sucks.

"Come on, guys," Alec says. "There was no kissing."

Our captain's confidence—or cockiness, if we're splitting hairs—earned him the nickname Ego. I'd love to tell him exactly how wrong his cockiness is now, to really rub his nose in it.

But I can't.

"We'd know if he kissed Amelia," Alec continues. "One, because Van can't help but run his mouth. Two, because Coach would have already killed him. He wouldn't be at practice but in a shallow grave somewhere."

That part, at least, is true.

And I bet Dominik wishes I was in a shallow grave rather than here. Our newest player, young and with the kind of over-confidence you can only possess when you haven't experienced enough failure, had been enjoying my spot as center on the first line with Eli and Logan.

But that was before Florida.

Without a word of explanation, Coach switched us back to our respective positions my first day back.

Which means Dominik didn't just lose the line but also center, his preferred position. When the Appies picked him up, Coach wanted to try him as a winger but promised at some point he might move him to center. Dominik's been biding his time since he got here, not all that patiently either.

Now that he's had a taste of what he really wants, he's more than a little bitter about losing it. Especially when he's still playing better than me. I can't even argue the point.

And only I know why Coach made the switch.

Normally, I'd feel just fine about putting the youngest and hottest-tempered player in his place. But since I got my spot back through what feels like paying blood money, I can't even gloat.

Guilt seeps through me, a slow-acting poison.

I wonder if, since technically Coach is my father-in-law even if he doesn't know it, this counts as nepotism?

"You guys are hilarious," I say, still messing with my skate to avoid making eye contact. "Nothing happened on the trip."

Lies.

The thing is—they'd *never* believe me even if I told them the truth. That I fell in love and got married, then got ditched by my wife. Who now seems determined to pretend like it never happened.

Summer is the only person in this *state* I planned to tell. And only after she promises me that lawyer confidentiality stuff. I can't risk her telling Nathan, even if he and Wyatt are the quietest, least likely to spill secret guys on the team. Or that I've ever met. Quiet grumps, saying everything they need to with a glare and a body-check.

No one can know what happened. Not even once I get this annulled or … whatever.

I tried googling annulment to see if that's a possibility. The first thing I learned was that I don't know how to spell the word. Doesn't it seem like it should have two Ls?

Anyway. I couldn't quite cut through the legalese and Amelia must have taken the certificate or whatever we signed at the hotel, so I don't even have that for reference. Summer is fluent in paperwork, so I figured between that and confidentiality, talking to her was a safe bet.

Too bad Amelia happened to be in Summer's office when I went to ask. Oh, the irony.

I haven't seen or heard a single word from Amelia since the note she left before running away. I tried texting, but my phone showed a *message not delivered* notification, so I guess she blocked me.

It's even more ironic that after I helped Amelia run away from her first wedding day, she then ran away from *me* on her second.

I hadn't planned to make the effort to speak to her unless it was absolutely required. Like to inform her that I figured out the way to annul our marriage—the one she thought was a huge mistake.

But in Summer's office, I wasn't silent. I couldn't seem to shut up.

This whole thing is going to come crashing down on my head now because there's zero chance Parker and Summer didn't notice the vibe. I saw the way they both frowned, their heads bouncing between the two of us like they were watching the weirdest tennis match they'd ever seen. One where the players were armed with swords as well as rackets and the ball was on fire.

But if *anyone* finds out, there's no way Coach won't also find out.

And then I really *will* be dead.

My career, at least. I don't think Coach would *literally* kill me. Then again, I did miss him throwing a chair through a church window. He's definitely been in a foul mood.

So there's at least a small chance of homicide. Possibly by furniture.

What I'm not sure of is why Amelia didn't spill the second she got home. I doubt it's to protect *me.*

Maybe because she's embarrassed? That's the only logical thing I can think of, and it makes sense. Amelia is, in all senses of the word, a golden girl. She was probably prom queen or valedictorian or something. Pretty and perfect and rule following.

And I'm ... me.

I'm the Deadpool on a team full of Captain Americas. Well, a bunch of Caps and two Wolverines, by way of Nathan and Wyatt.

In any case, I'm the very last guy Amelia should be interested in, much less marry on a whim.

Even if, for a few days, we felt like we were in sync. Like we had something real and special and—

"Dude, how's your stomach?" Dumbo clasps a hand on my shoulder. Wyatt snorts.

"My stomach?"

"You've been off since the wedding." When I say nothing — *because what is he talking about with my stomach?*—Dumbo continues, lowering his voice but not enough so the whole room doesn't hear. "You know—the diarrhea?"

Now several of the guys are laughing. I shake my head and stand, dragging a hand over my face, freshly shaved this morning. I haven't been able to stand the sight of myself with a beard ever since I got back from Florida. I finally took a razor to it today.

Like the facial hair was a reminder of her.

How I looked when I was with her. How I felt. How she made me feel.

"I've got an iron stomach, man." I stand and lift my shirt, patting my abs. Because that's what Normal Van would do. Make jokes. Brag. Wash, rinse, and repeat.

"I think the phrase is supposed to be an iron lung," Tucker says.

"It can be both," Alec says. "Now, how about you stop arguing about semantics and get on the ice before Coach puts us all in shallow graves. The man has been in a *mood* since the wedding that wasn't."

"Can you blame the man?" Logan asks. "Someone broke his daughter's heart. I'd burn the world down."

And … on that note, I'm out the door before any of them.

———

I make it through practice like it's a normal day. Like I didn't run into Mills in Summer's office that morning.

Do I play horribly? You bet.

But I do it smiling and staying in character—smart-mouthed comments, horsing around, generally being the lovable pain I am.

I hang back when the other guys leave the ice, still trying to shake the restlessness I feel. It's in my limbs, but I think it's spreading outward from my heart. I skate a few quick laps, then take shot after shot. Missing them all.

It's like I'm hoping for someone to pin a participation ribbon on my jersey rather than hoping to win the Calder Cup—the AHL's version of the Stanley.

"Van—a word?" Coach calls.

My stick clatters to the ice.

If there's one thing I've succeeded at since getting home, it's avoiding Coach. I didn't want to get caught in a room with him. To have to meet the eyes of the man who is technically my father-in-law. Once, I even ducked into a shower fully clothed to avoid being seen.

Unfortunately, it was also the shower occupied by Dumbo.

Still—to avoid Coach, it was worth getting a little too up close and personal with *all of* Dumbo.

I retrieve my stick, miss one last shot, and skate over to the bench, where Coach now stands, gripping the wall. His expression is unreadable, but he doesn't look like he's about to rip my head from my body, so my secret is probably still safe.

For now.

"I wanted to thank you for your help with Milly," he says.

Hearing the nickname makes my gut twist. Or maybe what I'm feeling is the twist of the knife *Milly* stuck there.

"No problem."

Coach chuckles. "'No problem'? Son, you gave up almost a week to help out someone you barely know."

I try not to flinch. Someone I barely know … but someone I also *married*.

"Though I guess it *was* a free vacation. For the most part." He shifts, and I realize he's pulling out his wallet. "Milly said you ended up having to pay for some things, and I wanted to make that right."

"Don't worry about it."

"I insist," he says. "But if you don't want cash, I can do Venmo. Isn't that what all the kids are doing these days?"

"No, really—"

"Zelle?"

"I don't—"

"Paypal? I don't like the fees, but I can do that as well."

"I don't need your money." The words come out a whole lot sharper than I intended. "It was nothing."

My time with Mills was the furthest thing from nothing. It's the something equivalent of Mount Everest.

265

Coach eyes me warily, but he does slip his wallet back in his pocket. "We're good, then?"

I know what he's asking without asking—if I'm fine having my spot back in exchange for going to Florida with Amelia. An ugly ache moves through me. I especially don't want my spot, not when I don't deserve it. Not when Coach thinks I did him a favor.

Nothing I did with Amelia was to earn back my spot. Not a single thing.

But when I try to tell him that, I find my throat having some kind of spasm.

The whole situation is made more difficult by the fact that this weird deal he struck makes me respect him less. And I've always held him in high regard—even if my way of showing it is by being the token troublemaker. The man with the mouth.

But what he asked of me and what he was willing to trade —it makes me uncomfortable. I guess we all have weaknesses and blind spots. And Coach's weakness is clearly Amelia.

Apparently, it's a weakness we share.

"You spent four days with my daughter. Making sure she was okay, keeping her safe. And after a particularly difficult time."

His jaw clenches, and I wonder if he's thinking about his brother and his niece. Or Douche the Groom. All extra reasons for his problematic choices of late.

I want to argue. To tell Coach to give my spot back to Dominik. To confess that I didn't go to Florida because of some deal, but *only* because of Amelia.

I want to say I wish I'd never answered his call at the airport and simply gotten on the plane with Amelia as I already planned to do all on my own.

I'm afraid if I open my mouth, the secrets will start spilling like an oil leak, leaving everything polluted and toxic. Starting with my career.

Or—depending on how mad Coach is—my face.

And I happen to like both my career *and* my face.

Or—I *did*.

Now, things feel off. I'm off. Ever since Florida, it feels like I've been shrink-wrapped inside my life. I can't move my arms or breathe, but there's a bright yellow sticker slapped on the outside of the package saying, *Doing just fine, Thank you!*

"How do you think she's doing?" Coach asks, his voice quieter now.

I wouldn't have the first clue. Because today is the first time I've seen her in almost two weeks, and it's not like I really got to know her in the time we spent together. I thought I did.

But I was wrong.

I scratch my cheek, where I either cut myself shaving or have an ingrown hair. Either one would be par for the course. "I mean, she seemed ... good while we were on the trip. We haven't talked much since we got back."

Much seems like a nice, vague qualifier. If I say we haven't spoken at all, he might ask why.

"Really?" He cocks his head. "Did you not get along?"

I'm starting to sweat again. "We had a good time. She's a pretty, um, incredible woman."

See? That's not so hard. I can say lots of true things without telling him everything.

Amelia *is* incredible.

Coach Davis just stares. Like he's waiting.

"Um, she's really fun?"

A real barrel of laughs.

"And nice."

267

A good kisser.

"We had a good time."

Oh, and we got married.

Don't worry, sir—it's in name only, and if I figure out the annulment stuff, not even that.

Soon, she'll be nothing but a paperwork memory.

Coach was saying something else and I missed it.

"I'm sorry, sir?"

"I was just asking if you've seen her. She started work here today. I figured she might track you down."

"I did see her. Yep."

He waits for more, and I'm sweating profusely now, like I've caught a sudden fever or am standing in a humid jungle and not beside an ice rink.

"Good. I hope she had a great first day and everyone is nice. But not *too* nice." He laughs.

I fake a laugh, all the while wondering if I should try to secure witness protection for myself. Because I'm pretty sure Amelia and I were *too* nice on our last night.

"Look—just don't ever tell her I asked you to go with her," Coach says. "I'm pretty sure she'd hate us both."

She already hates one of us.

But I have no plans of telling her that or anything else. Other than what I need to get this marriage annulled once Summer can help me out with that.

If Summer can help me out with that.

No, WHEN Summer can help me out with that.

I'm going to choose optimism.

Because I can't stay married to a woman who ran away after waking with morning-after regrets. Even if divorce is the dirtiest of dirty words to me, so ... here we are.

"I promise, sir."

"Good," Coach says. "Now, let's talk about why it looks like you forgot how to play hockey."

CHAPTER 20

Amelia

MY FIRST DAY is over and it didn't kill me. I only saw Van once, managed to successfully dodge Parker and Summer's questions about why things were so weird when I *did* see him, and I only cried in a back stairwell one time.

Okay, so I *went* to the stairwell twice, but the second time, I only breathed through it. No tears.

Now, I'm waiting in my tiny cubicle for the sounds of the building to quiet.

"You've got this," I tell myself, looking at the empty desk. I really need to find some personal items. Because right now, it's the perfect metaphor for my life. Stark. Barren. Empty.

With a wry smile, I add, "Melodramatic."

"Who's dramatic?"

I jump at the sound of Parker's voice. She appears behind me, grinning.

"Oh." I laugh nervously, glancing around. "I thought everyone already left."

I *hoped* everyone left. I stayed late, declining a dinner invite with Dad so I could be sure to avoid running into Van again. In the hallway. Or the parking lot. Or anywhere else he might be in the building. I swear, I walked around today like I was being followed by a ghost. That's for sure how it felt.

The ghost of mistakes past.

But was the bigger mistake marrying Van on our last night in Florida? Or was it leaving without talking to him about why my dad texted him *Thanks for babysitting*?

Maybe both. In equal parts.

"You're coming out with us," Parker says, and I'm shaking my head even as she starts dragging me out of my chair. "No excuses. Sorry. You're all out of them. They're like vacation days, and you have to earn them. It's your first day, so you've got none." Parker's smile is wicked.

Or at least, it *feels* wicked to me. I'm sure Parker doesn't have a bad bone in her body.

"Who's the *us*?" I ask, hoping and also not hoping to hear Van's name. If he'll be there, I'll fight my way out of this.

I'm pretty sure I could take Parker in a physical fight.

"Me and Summer and Gracie and Bailey."

"Have I met Gracie and Bailey?" I ask, grabbing my purse and following Parker out. The names sound familiar, but I don't think they work here. The only women I interacted with today at the Summit were Summer and Parker.

She bites her lip. "Noooo … "

Her tone of voice is off, and it only takes me a second to connect the dots.

"They were at the wedding."

Not the *wedding*, a little voice in my brain corrects. Reminding me that the wedding Parker means wasn't THE wedding. The one that actually took place. Technically, she means the *failed* wedding.

THE wedding was the one where I actually got married.

The one only Van and I know about. For now.

"Sorry to bring it up again," Parker says.

"It's unavoidable," I tell her with a shrug. "And honestly, not all that painful."

Definitely less painful than thinking about the *other* wedding.

Which is really wild when I think about it. Why should a spontaneous wedding with a guy I barely know—as I quickly found out—hurt more than one I planned for almost a year?

Maybe because I didn't care as much about Drew as I do Van.

Did. As much as I *did* care about Van.

"I'm honestly okay with it," I assure her. "Most of it, anyway." I am still struggling with the part where I lost a cousin and a once-beloved uncle.

"Yeah? Well, you can tell us about it over drinks," Parker says.

I have no plans to tell them *anything* about either wedding over drinks. Or to drink at all, considering what happened the *last* time I drank.

No, I wasn't drunk when Van and I got the brilliant idea to get married. Just ... tipsy. Happy.

Foolish.

The alcohol didn't force me to make the choice or make me lose all my inhibitions. But it did soften up my edges and made me feel like it was okay to let loose a little. In that way, it was a little like Van, who did the same thing.

And had I not found the text from my dad, I don't know that I would regret the decision to marry Van on the beach.

That's what I'm really struggling with—my own conflicting feelings about what happened. About Van.

I thought Van was ... trustworthy. I know it was fast—I *know* it. I can't *un*know it. But then—I trusted Drew. And I knew him longer. Better. He still cheated, and I still had no idea.

So, how can I really trust Van?

After Mom died, one of my dad's favorite things was to tell me how they fell in love. They had the same friend group in college and were just that—friends. But somehow, by the time senior year rolled around and people were talking about jobs and futures and some people were even starting to get engaged, the friendship had blossomed into something more.

"We were friends for years by the time we realized we were in love," Dad told me more than once, often with tears shining in his eyes. "Friendship is a great foundation for trust."

Van lost my trust almost as fast as he gained it, proving Dad's point. Too bad I married him before realizing it.

Why didn't I just, like, let things progress at a normal pace?

Why did I suggest getting married?

I know what people would think, and maybe this is part of the reason I haven't even told my best friend. They'd assume I was in a messy emotional place or maybe even that it was some kind of revenge, especially considering the way Drew and Becky showed up at the resort.

But ... it wasn't just an emotional knee-jerk thing or a revenge plot.

I remember how I felt at that moment. Like I had finally learned to let loose in a healthy way. Like Van brought out something in me no one else in my life had seen. I felt safe. Hopeful. Confident.

But if he could marry me without telling me the truth about why he was in Florida, if he could marry me while the deal he and Dad had was between us like a dirty, not-so little secret—I can't trust *him*.

By extension, it means I can't trust what we had.

His deal with my dad cheapens the simple vows we repeated on the beach under string lights with the ocean's rough murmur nearby. Van's failure to come clean undermines everything, casting long shadows of doubt.

Especially considering what Drew did not a week before.

My trust in other people is shaken—including the trust in myself and my decisions.

I can't shake the niggling sense that I screwed up too by leaving. By not giving Van a chance to explain. By ghosting him completely.

Was he hurt when he found my note?

I rarely allow myself to wonder about this. But every time I do, guilt spears through me.

Because two of us said vows on that beach. And though he kept his deal with my dad from me, I *know* Van's feelings were real.

Feelings aren't the problem. It's the lack of foundation, the lack of honesty and trust, and the decision we both made far too quickly.

Now … I just don't know what to do about it. Except maybe get this thing annulled, then consider whether there's something here worth salvaging?

I'm grateful Parker and I drive separately to Mulligans, giving me a chance to mope and think angry thoughts and bathe in regret. Then banish all those things to the dark corners of my mind. No way do I want these slipping out.

I settle at the table next to Parker and order a Diet Dr Pepper, my guilty pleasure when I need a little pick me up.

Dad loves to tell me that the chemicals in soda will kill me one day, but I figure we're all dying anyway. Might as well die drinking something I love.

Parker lifts her glass to mine in a toast. "We're a pair, aren't we? You're drinking Diet Dr Pepper and I'm drinking root beer."

We clink our glasses. "Cheers," I say.

"Gracie and Bailey should be here soon. Summer ended up bailing." Parker sighs. "Playoffs are in a few days. Which means the guys are all in weird places."

I take a sip of my drink. "Like what kinds of weird places?"

"Logan gets in his head and wants to be alone. Because he came from the NHL and the Appies are a minor league team, he has a lot to prove."

"And what does Nathan do that means Summer isn't coming?"

Parker snorts and leans forward, eyes bright. "Nathan, apparently, likes to cuddle."

I burst out laughing at this. I met Nathan today, but I remember seeing him before. Mostly because he is terrifying. He looks like he could rip all the limbs from a man's body over breakfast.

"Who likes to cuddle?"

Two women pull out the empty chairs at our table. The one who asked the question has medium brown hair and freckles. She's carrying a large instrument case and sets it beside the table. "You must be Amelia. I'm Gracie," she says, extending a hand.

"I'm Bailey." The other woman is wearing scrubs and gives me a shy smile as she takes the seat beside me.

"Nice to meet you both."

"I was talking about Nathan cuddling," Parker explains.

Gracie laughs. "It's always the ones with the tough outer shell."

"Nathan?" Bailey asks. "Cuddling?"

"That's why Summer isn't here," Parker says. "All the guys do different things when it's playoff time. What about Felix and Eli?" Parker leans closer to me. "Gracie is dating Felix—the goalie—and Bailey is married to Eli, the blond who looks like he just drank from a firehose of pure sunshine."

Bailey grins at this. "He really does, doesn't he? For playoffs, I'm not sure he does anything different. Not that I'd know since we're still … new." Her cheeks go pink at this. "He likes to play with the dogs. But that's pretty normal for him. I think?"

She thinks? I wonder how long the two of them have been together.

I feel suddenly like I've been shoved just outside of the circle. Everyone but me is paired up with one of the players. I mean, sure—technically, I am too. I've got more legal claim on Van than Gracie or Summer or even Parker. But for all intents and purposes, I am not *with* him. Which makes me the odd woman out.

A tug of longing moves through me. I can picture how easy it would be to slide right into this group, to complain about whatever weird thing Van does during playoffs.

The longing is quickly replaced by anger. Because Van wrecked what we had after it barely began.

The waitress appears and takes Gracie and Bailey's drink orders. Bailey gets fries and a chocolate malt while Gracie chooses a glass of red wine and a wedge salad.

Gracie leans forward and lowers her voice. "Don't tell him I told you, but Felix is baking."

"Baking?" I ask. "Baking what?"

Gracie's smile is soft. "He's baking his way through a box of recipes that were his grandmother's."

Parker groans and drops her head to the table. "How is it that I get the guy who doesn't want to see me so he can focus, and everyone else gets cuddling and puppies and baking?" She sits up, turning her gaze suddenly to me. "What about Van?"

I jolt, knocking over my drink. Bailey jumps up as a tidal wave of Diet Dr Pepper goes her way.

"Sorry! So sorry." I frantically try to stop the flow of liquid, but I'd need a few dozen more napkins to even make a dent.

The waitress reappears and sweeps the mess into a dustpan using a bar rag. "I'll bring you another one," she says with a sigh.

I'm sure my cheeks are flaming, but I do my best to force my face into some kind of normal expression. "Why are you asking me about Van? I have no idea what he does. Or is doing. Van and I are … nothing. We're not anything. So, I have no idea."

I definitely said too much there. There's a brief pause in which the three of them simply stare.

Parker smiles a little too sweetly. "Of course. You're right. I was just testing a theory."

"A theory about Amelia and Van?" Bailey asks, tilting her head curiously.

"There is no me and Van," I say, waving my hands. This time I avoid knocking over any drinks. But I'm still being overly dramatic. Someone might as well plop me into the middle of a Shakespeare play for all the protests I'm *doth*ing too much.

I wait for them to press harder, but thankfully, the tension seems to ease.

"Too bad." Bailey smiles. "He's really misunderstood, I think. Probably intentionally so."

Or not, I think, but I need to back away from this topic—casually and slowly. Like you would from a bear. Or is that what you do if you run into a mountain lion? I can't remember which predator you're supposed to back away from and in which scenario you're supposed to make yourself look bigger.

Honestly, I should just avoid the forest altogether.

Too bad the forest, in this half-baked metaphor, happens to be where I work.

"He's my second favorite," Bailey says. "No offense to Logan and Felix. All the other guys are great too. But Van walked me down the aisle at my wedding," Bailey says, looking at her ring. "It was really sweet. He—ow!"

Parker or Gracie or both must have kicked Bailey under the table. They are clearly trying to silently communicate.

"Oh, shoot," Bailey says, color rising in her cheeks as her wide eyes snap to me. "I ... forgot."

I groan. "I'm going to say this once." I pause and meet each of their gazes briefly. "I promise, I'm okay talking about weddings. My wedding, other people's weddings—whatever. It's not a landmine subject for me, and it's not the kind of topic we can avoid forever. So, please don't walk on eggshells around me or feel bad for saying the word wedding. I'm okay talking about it."

At least about the wedding they *know* about.

"What about Van?" Parker asks.

The waitress returns then with everyone's orders and a new drink for me. "What *about* Van?"

Casual, casual, casual. That's the name of the game. My tone is perfectly even, my face a mask of innocence. My pulse is a totally different story, but unless any of them are vampires and can sense the quicker flow of blood through my veins, I think I'm safe.

"You just seem to have an emotional reaction to talking about him," Parker says. "Or talking *to* him."

Gracie laughs. "Yeah, but it's *Van*. He has a way of riling people up. Pushing their buttons. Especially with your dad," she adds, looking at me. "I swear, Van is the player most likely to inspire your dad to retire early."

"Oh, yeah." I roll my eyes and try not to think of the text from my dad I saw on Van's phone. "Dad uses his name at home like a curse word."

Gracie and Parker laugh, but Bailey looks slightly troubled by this. And I feel sick saying it because I remember saying something similar to Van.

"I'm kidding, of course, but I do know he makes Dad nuts."

"Like father, like daughter," Parker says, and I don't like the assessing look in her gaze. I swear, the woman is like a dog with a very big, very juicy bone. If I'm not careful, she'll figure things out by my second day of work. Which *cannot* happen.

Conversation moves on then, and I'm grateful for it. Because I am barely hanging on by a quickly fraying thread.

CHAPTER 21

Amelia

"I'm not sure this job is worth the emotional strain." I sigh, hearing what sounds either like a laugh or cough coming through the phone. Or possibly a grunt? "I *know* you're not laughing at me right now."

"Not laughing," Morgan says, but there is definitely humor in her tone. "I just can't help but find this new development delightful."

It's the next morning. Dad, again, left before me, and now I'm sitting in my car, staring up at the Summit, trying to will my hands to open the car door and my feet to get out. I tried giving myself a pep talk. It didn't take. So, I called my best friend.

Not sure this is any better.

The *new development* she means is whatever nuclear level of tension now exists between Van and me. I already told

Morgan how, when Van and I saw each other yesterday, it was electric—and not in a good way.

More like an electrical fire set to torch a whole city block.

Sure—there was attraction too—I'd have to be dead not to be attracted to Van. But that only makes the ugly parts of the tension worse. Because what am I supposed to *do* with the attraction?

Nothing. That's what. Absolutely nothing. If I ignore it, I'm sure it will go away.

Hopefully soon.

"Morgan, you're supposed to be my best friend."

"Yes, and best friends—real, *true* best friends—want what's *best* for the other person. It's how you put the best in best friend."

"Your point?"

"My point," she says, "is that maybe this is best for you."

"Being around a man I'd like to never see again?"

Even as I say it, I know it's not true. I only wish it were true. I wish I could take a shovel and excavate all my feelings, leaving them in a heap somewhere outside of town.

There's another noise, a heavy clank this time, and I frown. "What are you doing, by the way?"

"Trying to fix my car engine."

"Is that something you know how to do?"

"YouTube," she says, like this is the most obvious answer in the world. Or that having YouTube necessarily equates having the ability to fix whatever's wrong with her car.

"That's …"

…*not a thing*, I was going to say, but Morgan cuts me off. Clearly, my work-and-Van-related woes take precedence over whatever is wrong with her car.

"Look—your whole life was shaken up. Not by you. Not in a good way. Now, it's being shaken in a new way. A *deli-*

cious way," she adds. "And it's not happening to you. You're in the driver's seat."

Am I, though? I wonder, watching a car pull through the gates and across the parking lot. I can't help but also wonder if telling Morgan the whole truth might garner me some different advice. Though she is correct—I've been shaken up.

While all that freedom and letting loose felt great in Florida with Van, back in my normal Harvest Hollow life, it feels like a costume I tried on for a few days.

One I secretly wish I could put back on and make it my new daily norm.

I honestly have no idea what Morgan—or anyone else who knows me—would say about my impulsive decision to marry Van. My best friend might just as easily say this was the best decision I've made rather than the worst.

I know her better than anyone, but Morgan continues to surprise me. It's her nature. She's like a rare kind of butterfly, unable to be caught and pinned down to a board. This is one of the things I love about her.

But it also means I don't feel like I can tell her this because I can't anticipate her response.

Also, I'm still choosing to believe that the more time I think about marrying Van, the more times I say it out loud, the more I act like it actually happened, the more real and unavoidable it becomes.

I'm a kid with the boogeyman inches from my own nose, and if I don't open my eyes, *he isn't there*.

"I've got an idea," she says. I hear the sound of her hood slamming followed, a moment later, by her engine starting. "Yahtzee! I love you, YouTube!"

"Idea?" I remind her.

"Right. My idea involves Van, a closet, and putting alllll that frustration to good use." When I say nothing—mostly because my mouth has gone completely dry and my insides feel like they're melting—she adds, "I'm talking about making out in a closet at work with the guy you say you can't stand but actually seem to have very strong feelings for and—"

"Hanging up now," I tell her. "Glad you fixed your car. And also? Just letting you know that I'm officially in the market for a new bestie."

I hang up, tracking the SUV that just pulled into the lot a row up and a few spaces over. My heart pounds as I wait for the door to open. When a man who looks like a Swedish assassin, with white blond hair and sharply cut features climbs out of the car, I expect to be relieved that it's not Van.

Instead, the only thing I feel is disappointment.

———

An hour later, I've decided that Parker is on a personal mission to punish me. And also that maybe she and Morgan are conspiring together.

Despite Parker's assurance yesterday—as in, twenty-four hours ago—that I wouldn't be doing as much with the guys this week because of playoffs, she left me with a list of suggested questions and three of the Appies, one of whom I happen to be married to.

As to why I think she's intentionally torturing me, it was the way she patted my shoulder and whispered "Have fun" in a sing-song voice before she left me thirty seconds ago. If she doesn't suspect something already happened between Van and me, she is trying to encourage something between us.

I clear my throat and look everywhere but at Van. I can feel him looking nowhere but at me.

The guys must have come off the ice because they're in

practice gear aside from their helmets. Other than some footage I've watched online in a weak moment, I haven't really seen Van in a jersey and pads.

It's … a really good look on him. Masculine and a little intimidating and—*nope!*

No ogling! Back on track, Mills!

Gah! Van has even poisoned my internal monologue with his nickname.

"So, um, let's get started," I say. "I'll keep it brief. I'm sure you all have important hockey things you'd rather be doing."

Eli laughs, leaning back in his chair. "No way! We don't mind. Your dad is making everyone else do four lines." When I stare blankly back at him, he adds, "It's a drill."

"One that involves a lot of skating back and forth at full speed," Alec says. "A lethal combination of boring and exhausting. So, please take your time."

"I don't know," Van says, "I'm in the mood for a little matrimony. Sorry—I mean *monotony*."

I cannot keep my eyes from him now but immediately wish I hadn't looked. I was doing *so* well before I looked. Okay—*sort of* well. *Semi*-well. Well-*ish*.

His dark hair is a little damp, probably sweat. Which should be gross but is somehow very, very hot instead. There's the tiniest shadow of stubble on the jaw that was bare yesterday. Van's espresso eyes blaze, sparking a matching flame inside me. Just like yesterday in Parker's office, I can practically see him issuing a challenge.

But what does he *want* from me?

"Sorry, no matrimony today." I give him a smile that is both sweet and sharp. "But I'll try to avoid monotony as well."

Van reaches across and taps the paper Parker left. "Just

stick to the questions, and I'm sure it will be fine. It's always a safe bet to color in the lines and follow all the rules."

From my periphery, I can see Eli and Alec exchanging looks at this back-and-forth, which is growing more bizarre by the moment. At least, for them. Van and I are having a whole other conversation, existing firmly in the subtext.

I keep my gaze pinned on his as I snatch the paper from the table. I crumple it in my hands, then toss it toward the trash can in the corner of the room.

I miss.

Van smirks.

I shrug. "Actually, I think I'll just wing it today. I'm in the mood to live on the edge. Make impulsive decisions. Let loose. You know how it is."

Van narrows his eyes. "I don't know if that's a good idea. You might make a choice you regret."

It's on the tip of my tongue to say, *I regret nothing*—which would have been a *huge* mistake—but Eli speaks first.

"Um," he says, scratching the blond scruff on his jaw. "Are we still talking about the interview?"

I straighten in my chair and smile at Eli, then Alec, whose gaze is bouncing between Van and me. He looks like he's about to ask a question I don't want to answer, so I clear my throat. Then realize I didn't even skim the questions Parker left. I can't remember what the focus of this interview was going to be.

Awesome.

"Maybe you could start with the basics," Van suggests. I'm slightly relieved until he follows this with: "Like, our relationship statuses."

I swallow. Before I can disagree, Alec says, "Single. Happily single, I might add."

Eli raises his left hand, a ring glinting in place. "I'm

married," he says with a huge grin. "Heard you met my wife last night."

"I did. She's really great." I can't help but think about what Bailey said about Van walking her down the aisle, and it makes my skin feel tight.

Van leans forward, elbows on the table. "Want to guess my relationship status, Amelia?"

I cross my arms. "I don't see a ring."

Eli claps Van on the back. "Van enjoys the single life. Maybe a little *too* much."

I try not to let my lip curl. The idea of Van, single and enjoying it makes me want to set things on fire.

"He'll probably never settle down," Alec says.

"Wrong on both counts," Van says, inching forward until he's leaning practically halfway across the table. "I don't like being single. And it would only take the right woman to make me put a ring on it."

I say nothing. My brain has gone back in time to a pre-language era. A caveman grunt is about all I can manage.

"Really?" Eli says, looking a little too eager. "Well, we should set you up with someone then. Doesn't Summer have a sister who's single?"

"Not my type," Van says, and I find myself holding my breath. "I prefer lighter hair. Pale blue eyes. A gorgeous smile."

There's a flutter in my belly and my fingers go numb. Van's eyes skate over my face as he speaks. I don't think my smile is particularly gorgeous, but … he *is* talking about me, right?

Despite myself, I think, *Please let him be talking about me.*

"Someone not afraid to take risks. A woman who will stick around and talk things out when they get hard. Good communication is hugely important. It can help avoid misunderstandings and allow someone to say they're sorry when they've made a huge mistake. One they would have explained, had they been given a chance."

I am frozen in my chair. Can't move. Can't breathe. Thankfully, I can blink, which is the only way I'm keeping in the tears right now.

What was a war of words has turned into something else entirely. I'm not exactly sure what this is, but ... it sounds like an apology. As well as a very pointed critique of the way I handled things.

He's not wrong.

Maybe ... I really, really *was*.

"That's oddly specific," Alec says. "Based on your track record, I thought you liked *all* types. Blonds, brunettes, redheads, tall, short, curvy, athletic—"

"Excuse me." I bolt from the room so fast my rolling chair crashes into the wall. I can't even be bothered to make an excuse.

It's all just ... too much.

My favorite crying stairwell is at the end of the hall and I sprint for the door, the red EXIT sign a beacon of welcome. I burst through the door and scamper down the final flight, my footsteps echoing against the cement. On the bottom level, I duck into the shadows under the stairs, breathing heavy and squeezing my eyes closed. A few tears still manage to slip out and down my cheeks.

A moment later, I hear the door open and heavy steps jog down. My heart tries to catapult out of my chest, and I force myself to breathe in and out, slow and steady even as the footfalls stop behind me.

"Mills," Van says, and I turn, not bothering to hide my tears.

Van's face crumples, and before I can react, he's pulling

me into his arms. I fold into his big, warm, and still slightly sweaty jersey. His hand cups the back of my head and I shudder through a few breaths, my arms locked around his waist.

"I'm sorry," he says. "I didn't want to make you cry. I was trying to—I don't know what I was trying to do."

"You were trying to make a point, and you made it." My fists bunch the fabric of his jersey. "So did Alec."

Van sighs and tugs me a little closer. The hand behind my head shifts, his fingers tunneling through my hair, massaging my scalp gently. His other hand moves up and down my back, fingertips lightly dancing over my spine with a gentleness that surprises me. It feels so good, but I can't relax. Every cell in my body is saturated in tension, like I am made up of millions of tiny, coiled springs.

"What happened before you, who I did or didn't date—that doesn't matter."

"Why not?" My voice is tiny.

His head dips, his nose tracing a little path across my cheek until his lips find my ear. "Because I only married *you.*"

The words curl around me, soothing and sweet. I am cocooned in comfort, even though there is still a niggling worry, and a sense that this won't last. It can't.

I barely know Van. I made an impulsive choice after having a hugely emotional thing happen on what was supposed to be my wedding day. Marrying someone I barely know isn't *me.*

I'm a planner. A rule follower. A by the book kind of woman. Van's very opposite.

And while the time in Florida was fun and freeing, and I got to explore a new side to myself—that simply isn't me. I'm not the person Van said he wanted to marry. That was

Vacation Amelia. Just Got Cheated on Amelia. Needs to Blow Off a Little Steam Amelia.

But now, I've come back to the neat and tidy life I know. It's familiar and comfortable, and more than that, it's who I am at my very core.

Isn't it?

I am above my life, looking down on it. Two Amelias are perched on a teeter-totter. One side has Florida Amelia—who I might as well call *Van* Amelia—and the other has Normal Amelia. Solid and Stable Amelia. Boring Amelia.

The two are engaged in a violent teeter-totter battle to the death. The prize and the cost of this war seems to be my sanity.

Van's hands lift away, and I barely hold back a whimper. But they cup my cheeks, and he drops his forehead to mine. This close, his eyes are inky black pools, not totally in focus.

"It's not too late to fix this," he says, and my brain goes straight to annulment.

But his brain is clearly going in a different direction because the next thing I know, he's kissing me.

And I'm kissing him back.

It's like we're on the beach again, and I'm channeling Bad Idea Amelia, Brave Amelia, Stupid Amelia all over again.

This Amelia is actually pretty awesome. Maybe I need to find a way to fit the two halves of me together. To tell them to balance out the teeter-totter instead of trying to throw each other off.

Van's mouth is both familiar and new. He kisses me like he's finally found his way back to me and has been simply starving in the meantime. He kisses me like he owns me, but also like I own him.

I try to memorize the shape of his lips, the curve of his smile. I need to commit them to memory because even as I'm lifting my hands to his neck and pressing in closer, I know this can't happen again.

Not until we untangle the mess we've made, and I'm not sure where to start.

Kissing … probably isn't the wisest place.

I need to figure out how to get out of this marriage and how to be around this man without being drawn into his orbit. But he's a giant planet and I'm just some little bit of space dust. I stand zero chance of escaping his pull.

Van makes a low, rumbling sound that draws out goose bumps on every bit of my exposed skin.

Maybe I don't need to forget about him. I just need to backtrack. To figure out what it would look like to *date* Van in this setting, with this version of me.

The one who doesn't kiss men in a stairwell after a heated subtext-y conversation.

"You know what's totally not fair, hotshot?" I say, pressing a kiss to the corner of his smiling mouth.

He shifts, trailing kisses down the line of my neck. I shiver. "Price gouging during a pandemic?"

I laugh, and he brings his mouth back to mine, swallowing up the sound. "No," I say between kisses. "The fact that you smell good after practicing."

"You think I smell good?" He nips at my lip. Somewhere near my waist, his fingers gently pinch me, bringing back memories.

"I just said so, didn't I?"

"I missed you, Mills," he says.

I'm not sure why it's these words that do it, but they pull me back out of the deep waters and to the surface, gasping for air. Reminding me where we are. I slow down the kiss, pressing one last quick one to his lips before taking a huge step back.

His hands drop. So does his expression.

"We can't keep doing this," I say softly.

Van smiles, but it's forced. So is the lightness in his tone. "What—kissing in stairwells? Or having secret conversations in the middle of public situations? Pretending not to be married?"

I flinch.

"Ah," he says slowly, stepping way back.

But before I get a chance to locate rational thoughts and organize them into words I can say, the door behind Van swings open, and a short man with dark hair and a maintenance uniform steps into the stairwell and stops.

"Oh," he says, a slight trace of an accent. "I'm sorry."

Van gives him a tight smile. "It's fine, Javi. I was just leaving."

Now, Van is the one fleeing the scene, slipping out the door Javi just came through and giving me a small sampling of what it feels like.

Being the one left behind feels just plain awful.

CHAPTER 22
THE DREAM TEAM

Alec: Van. Dude. I don't know if Dumbo's right and your stomach is jacked up, but you have lost your mojo.

Wyatt: Did he ever have mojo?

Logan: Aw, look at one of the newest additions to the text thread—coming in hot with the burns.

Wyatt: It was actually a legit question

Wyatt: I haven't seen him play like anything other than how he's been lately

Wyatt: Which is terrible, by the way

Eli: LOL

Nathan: The best burns are the unintentional ones.

Felix: I think those are just called the truth.

Van: My stomach is fine and you all suck

Van: THAT'S the truth

Felix: IBS isn't anything to be ashamed of.

Van: Will everyone just SHUT UP about my bowels

Alec: We might. If you stopped skating like one giant bowel.

Logan: Maybe he just has IS—Irritable Syndrome.

Logan: Or SASS—Sucks at Skating Syndrome.

Eli: Also, what was up with you and Amelia? Why did she run out of the interview?

Alec: And why did you chase her?

Felix: Uh-oh.

Nathan: Does it have anything to do with why you broke another stick?

Wyatt: He broke a stick?

Eli: He broke ANOTHER stick?

Logan: I'm less interested in sticks and more interested in what Van said to make THE COACH'S DAUGHTER run away.

Logan: And also why neither of you two idiots stopped him.

Eli: I knew something happened on your trip. I KNEW IT. Didn't I tell you guys something happened?

Van: NOTHING HAPPENED

Felix: We warned you not to mess with Amelia. Didn't we warn him?

Nathan: We did.

Alec: We absolutely did. But earlier they were having like some whole other conversation while Eli and I tried to figure out what they were talking about.

Logan: A whole other conversation about what?

Van: NOTHING. It was a normal conversation.

Eli: I will testify to the fact it was NOT normal.

Camden: So what specifically made her run out of the room?

Eli: Nice of you to join us, Cam. I forgot you were on this text thread.

Alec: I think I was talking about Van's dating life.

Logan: That's enough to make any woman run away.

Van: Ha ha

Eli: Maybe Amelia was jealous?

Logan: Did she LOOK jealous?

Eli: She looked like she was about to cry.

Nathan: You can't make the coach's daughter cry. Then he'll make us cry.

Felix: What happened after that?

Van: Nothing

Logan: You didn't find Amelia?

Van: I didn't say that

Logan: Do I need to send Parker to find her?

Van: No

Van: Amelia's just fine

Alec: So you DID find her?

Eli: You guys. When is Van ever not willing to talk about anything? The fact that he won't say anything is as good as an admission of guilt. SOMETHING HAPPENED WITH HIM AND AMELIA.

Felix: Please say it's not true.

Van: It's not true

Logan: Define the "it" in that text.

Alec: Van? You still here?

Eli: Yo Van

Wyatt: I think it's safe to say he left the group text

Felix: This does not bode well …

Eli: Anyone want to tell me what bode means?

Logan: It means get a dictionary and also that Van and the rest of us are all in trouble.

Alec: Maybe it also means we should have shut up and tried to TALK to him instead of giving him a hard time.

Nathan: Sounds like a job for the captain …

CHAPTER 23

Amelia

DAY three of my new job is thankfully and wonderfully boring. Parker checks in and tells me to go through the Google folder she made and work independently. She also wants me to write up the interview from yesterday, which means the guys did not tell her how it ended. I don't have the heart to tell her the only thing I walked away knowing is the three guys' dating statuses.

I'll figure something out.

I spend the morning going through the various documents and spreadsheets all related to content strategy, Appies branding, and more. Parker is efficient and thorough, and it gets me excited about the work. I create my own document of ideas and sketch out a few outlines for longer posts, then do a little research on sports teams who have great captions on their social media posts to get a feel for length, voice, and even the balance between white space and blocks of text.

It's almost enough to distract me from thinking about Van.

Specifically—Van in the stairwell.

Van's mouth on mine.

Him saying he only married *me*.

And … the disappointed, hurt expression on his face when he walked away.

That look has haunted me like my own personal Casper for the last twenty-four hours.

I can't put off dealing with this or I might explode. Van and I need to have an adult conversation. Preferably in public, so we don't end up kissing again. Then again, being seen in public with a figure as public as Van might not be the best idea.

The problem bigger than location for the conversation is what to say. *I'm sorry for leaving like I did* is a start. But after that … I got nothing.

Because I still don't know what I want.

An annulment, for sure.

But then what? I don't want to just walk away completely.

Do we date like normal people? Pretend we didn't exchange the classic vows on the beach as well as other, less eloquent whispered ones in the middle of that night?

I also can't shake the thought of my dad's response. His approval matters to me. And with the stress of playoffs coupled with the Drew and Becky and Uncle Bobby debacle, I'm not sure he could handle one more thing.

"Oh, Amelia!" Parker singsongs my name as she steps into my office. I don't like the smile on her face.

"Afternoon," I say.

"Making progress?" She doesn't even give me a chance to respond. "I have something super fun for you now."

Fun sounds dangerous.

Parker bounces a little and claps her hands. "Are you ready?"

Absolutely not.

Anxiety rolls through me. "Yes?"

She laughs. "I'll pretend you said that with confidence and excitement. Come on."

"Do I need my laptop or anything?"

"Oh," Parker says, like whatever this idea is, she's so excited about it that logistical details are an afterthought. "Actually, yes."

I stuff it in my bag, and follow Parker toward the elevators, my unease increasing with each of her bouncy steps.

When did I become so jaded that someone else's excitement made me wary?

Oh, right—when I started working in the same building as my secret husband.

Parker presses the elevator button no less than six times in quick succession, then spins to face me, her eyes and smile of equal, blinding wattage. "Remember when I said I had a hands-on project coming up?"

I don't, but the last two days have been a blur. However, hands-on sounds like the opposite of what I want to do right now. Namely, duck into my stairwell until I can breathe normally again.

No! No more stairwells. I need to find a new place to hide.

Parker doesn't wait for me to answer as we step into the elevator and head down—down as in where the locker rooms and the rink are. My stomach roils with dread.

I am trapped in my own personal Groundhog Day. Except

instead of reliving the same events over and over, she's finding creative new ways to mess with me.

"The first playoff game is in two days, and I had this brilliant idea a while back." Parker laughs. "I hope it's okay to say that about my own idea."

"It is," I say, hoping she doesn't notice me sweating. I wipe a hand across my forehead. "What's the idea?"

Please say it doesn't involve Van. Please, please, please *say it doesn't involve* me *and Van.*

The elevator doors open and she bounds out into the hallway, linking her arm through mine when she realizes I'm trailing behind. We're headed toward a door marked *Press*.

"Some of the guys have families who are at every game," Parker says, practically dragging me toward the door. "Locals or family who's committed to travel. Others, like Logan, don't have any family support at all."

Her expression grows somber, but she shakes it off and is back to smiling a moment later. I can't help but admire the woman's resilience. I wonder if her bones are made of rubber. At the very least, her spirit is. She has Tigger DNA. And I'm the mopey little Eeyore practically leaving hoofmarks from dragging my feet.

Parker pauses with her hand on the doorknob to the press room, a huge grin on her face. "So ... I did a thing."

She waits. I wait, sweat now congregating on the nape of my neck and my lower back.

"What kind of thing?"

And why do I get the very distinct feeling that I'm going to be a whole lot less excited about this *thing*?

"I invited as many family members as I could to come for the first two playoff games, which are both home games. We're going to surprise the players. We'll do a series on social media, but I'll also have you do blog posts. Deep dives on the players, as told by their families. The goal is to get to the heart behind the players. The importance of support off the ice. The backstory."

That doesn't sound so bad. I relax—a *little*. "It's totally a brilliant idea."

"Thank you!" Parker beams at me. "We're rounding it out with traditional media, and I've got a writer here to do an in-depth piece for a big magazine which shall not be named." She leans closer and drops her voice to a whisper. "But a synonym for its name is *persons*." She winks.

People magazine has a writer coming? That's ... huge. A jolt of excitement zips through me, and I have a brief moment of awe. Two weeks ago, I was set to marry Drew and work at a job with him—one I only tolerated.

Now, I'm living my best life.

Minus ... Van.

"The first family group arrived this morning, and I thought you could work with them. Show them around, ask questions, then be there for the reveal. I'll be back to film that, of course."

"Cool."

Family members, I can do.

Unless—

With a slow-dawning horror, I realize there is one partic-ular set of family members I should absolutely *not* be around.

"Wait," I say.

"This group really wanted to meet you, specifically," Parker says, her fingers starting to turn the doorknob.

Oh, no.

I really only know the *one* player. And I'm positive the family he's close to will *not* want to meet me.

Or ... if they do, it will be to meet *and murder* me. But surely not. I can't be *that* unlucky.

I mean—what are the odds?

Parker throws open the door, revealing three women in the midst of what looks like a heated conversation. Seeing us, they stop. Then all three of their gazes slide from Parker to me.

"Amelia, meet Van's sisters."

The odds, as it turns out, are not zero.

CHAPTER 24

Van

I MANAGE to duck in and out of Coach's office when his back is turned—he's in the hallway outside the locker room talking with Ken, our offensive coach, and Winston, our head trainer. A risky move on my part, but necessary.

Hopefully, Coach won't see what I left until later. Much later.

As I head back into the locker room, I see Parker waiting inside. She doesn't frequent this area—too much danger of hearing or seeing something that might scar her delicate sensibilities, as she likes to say.

What she really *means* is she wants to avoid seeing Dumbo's hairy naked butt. Again. The screams that day were probably heard in Delaware.

When Parker turns toward me, her grin says I'm the one she's looking for. Great.

I groan, hoping it's quiet enough that Parker doesn't hear. Because yesterday when she came looking for me, it was to stick me in a room with Alec, Eli, and Amelia.

Which ended with a kiss that was amazing until it wasn't, me leaving the Dream Team text thread, and a whole lot of suspicious looks today. Alec keeps trying to *captain* me, and I keep avoiding him.

"Van—this is Melinda. She's here to interview you."

Only then do I notice a woman next to Parker with a matching, huge smile.

I scratch the back of my neck. "We've got practice in a bit."

"That's okay," Parker says. "She'll be here all day. We'll do part of it now, while you're getting ready. More later. Okay?"

Glancing around the room, I notice how quiet all the guys are, like if they don't draw attention to themselves, Parker won't ask anything of them. Not one of them wants to volunteer as tribute. The only one not ignoring me is Dominik who, of course, is glaring.

"Have you thought about Alec?" I ask. "He loves being interviewed and I—"

"Nope. Today, it's you." Parker's tone is edged with something sharp, assuring me that any argument is futile.

"Okay, Boss," I say with a sigh, dropping down to my bench. I don't miss the way a few guys smirk.

Parker appears with a padded folding chair with the Appies logo and sets it in front of me, giving barely enough room for me to lace up my skates. The very last thing I want right now is someone asking questions.

I've kept my mouth shut for two weeks, and I'm hanging by a thread here.

Even my sisters don't know the full story. All I told them was Amelia ghosted me. Probably even that much info was a bad idea considering the fact that all three of them have an ironclad sense of loyalty. And a penchant for revenge. I think it's their way of returning the favor for the way I looked out for them. Thankfully, only a few women have ever lasted long enough or done something bad enough to warrant my sisters' attention.

"So, Van," the woman says. "Should I call you Van?"

"Sure."

"But your real name is Robbie—any other nicknames?"

A few guys cough out, *Vanity*. There are chuckles around the room, and even Parker giggles.

"None I want in print," I say.

Normally, I would have added something flirtatious. A wink. A roguish grin. I know how to work my charm in interviews. Especially with female writers. But I'm just … not in the mood. I'd like to get this over with, not spill the secret I'm holding so tightly, and get on the ice where I can hopefully suck less than yesterday.

At least ten percent less. Low but realistic goals—that's me.

"Interesting," the woman says. I already forgot her name. "I heard rumors of a nickname involving … a bunny?"

My head snaps up, and I narrow my eyes at the woman who's sitting too close. I don't love the expression on her face. It's the look of a woman who's hoping for some *private* follow-up time. Off-the-record time. And the question she asked … there are very few possible sources for that nickname.

When I glance at Parker, she's got her arms crossed, shifting her weight from foot to foot. Based on her expression, she also noticed the woman's intent and is torn between being protective of me and finding out the bunny nickname.

The only people who know the godawful nickname my sisters gave me are … my sisters.

And Mills.

I start to sweat.

"No comment," I say, looking back down at my skates. "Next question."

The atmosphere in the room is charged. The rest of the guys are clearly almost ready to get on the ice, but they're lingering. Listening. I watch Tucker pick up and put down his skate three times, doing a horrible job pretending to examine the laces.

"You've got quite the reputation as a charmer," the woman says, and there are a few snorts around the room. "Are you currently single?"

Though this is a common question, one I should be prepared for, it knocks into me with force today. I suck in a breath, squeezing my eyes closed.

For a moment, all I can see is Amelia's eyes. Her smile. The wild abandon on her face when she stepped off the platform while zip-lining. The look on her face just before I kissed her yesterday.

And then the look of apology when she told me we can't keep doing this. Why was I even surprised? I'm the guy you kiss. Not the guy you marry.

I stand. "I'm not dating anyone."

Not a lie. But I bet no one in this room would guess the real truth.

I'm not dating anyone *because I'm married.*

"Are you looking?"

"No." My voice is clipped. "I need to focus on the playoffs right now."

"And on not sucking!" Tucker coughs out this answer, not

very subtly either, and I want nothing more than to get out of the locker room and onto the ice.

"I know some guys find that blowing off a little, uh, steam actually helps their performance and their focus," the woman says.

What kind of interview is *this?* Pointedly ignoring the woman, I tilt my head, giving Parker a look.

She looks stunned and mildly horrified. "Okay!" she says brightly, grabbing the woman's arm. "We've got to let these guys get on the ice. Thanks, Van. Melinda, we'll find a good spot to watch, then continue the interview later. Or another interview with another player."

"I'm free!" Tucker says, raising a hand with a big, stupid grin on his face.

Parker ushers the woman from the locker room like it's on fire. I keep my head down until they're both gone. Then I sink down on the bench, letting my head fall back.

Something smacks me in the side of the face. "That better not be a dirty sock," I say without opening my eyes.

"Dude," Alec says. "Explain. First, you were weird with Amelia yesterday. Then you left the group chat. And now—"

"What group chat?" Dumbo interrupts. "I'm not in a group chat."

I finally open my eyes and yup—someone did throw a dirty sock. I hate these guys sometimes just as much as I love them. I toss it toward the center of the room, and it lands on the Appies logo. No one claims it.

"No," Logan says, ignoring Dumbo. "First he started skating like he has three left feet. Which was about how long ago?"

"Right after you started," Alec says.

"It hasn't been that long," I mutter. But it has been. I know exactly when my performance on the ice started to decline. And it was when Coach handed out Save the Date cards for Amelia's wedding. Thankfully, the guys probably don't remember that detail.

"And now," Alec says, "you didn't do your usual thing with that reporter."

"What's my usual thing?"

This question is met with laughter, and my frustration builds. I want to go home. Not out to practice, where I'll still suck and maybe be dealing with Coach after he goes in his office and sees what I left on his desk. I won't have to hear it from Alec and the guys about my three left feet and inability to make a shot.

I don't want to go out with the guys. I don't want to be interviewed.

But most especially, I don't want to be in a building where I might just happen to run into my wife.

"Your usual thing," Logan says with a smirk. "Would include flirting. Winking. Possibly hitting on and or asking out."

"She didn't just open the door," Eli says, standing up. "She was waving you in for landing."

He does his best impression of a guy standing on an airfield with flares, directing a plane.

I roll my eyes. "Yeah. She wasn't subtle."

"And usually, neither are you," Alec says. "So, what gives?"

"Nothing," I say.

"That wasn't nothing."

"You've lost your game—on and off the ice."

"I never thought I'd see the day. Van not hitting on a hot woman."

"Think she'll want to *interview* me later?"

"Keep dreaming."

"I know you told her you're not dating anyone," Alec says, cutting through the chatter, "but you *have* to be."

"He does have that look," Felix says, and I don't like the way our goaltender watches me.

"I don't have a look."

"He does," Logan says, then shrugs when I glare. "You do."

"It's the look of a man who's in love."

That's Nathan, and I'd like to knock the smug, knowing expression off his face. Even if the defender is the last guy in this room I'd want to tangle with.

He's also usually the last guy to speak up. But he just got together with Summer and probably has love on the brain.

He also isn't wrong, and I'm doing my best not to squirm. Not to reveal just how close they all are.

Because I'm close to breaking.

"Please," Alec says, tugging at his hair like he's about to tear it all out from the roots. "Please tell us it's not Amelia."

"It has to be," Eli says.

"It really, really shouldn't be," Felix says.

Alec steps forward. "Say it. Say it to our faces. Tell us you don't have a thing for the coach's daughter."

Do not react. Do not react.

I roll my eyes and chuckle darkly. "You think I'm stupid enough to mess around with her?"

My wording is careful. I'm proud of myself. See? I didn't reveal a thing. Not my face. Not my words.

But … the guys smell blood in the water.

"We're not talking about messing around," Logan says. "This is different. You're different."

"You know how much trouble you could be in?" Alec asks with a frown. All of his teasing is gone. "How much trouble we would *all* be in?"

"Dude, everyone knows not to go there," Tucker says.

Dumbo adds, "Even if Coach hadn't warned us all a thousand times. It's just hockey logic."

"Never ever ever date the coach's daughter," Eli says. "Like … ever." He's serious for the first part, and then channels Taylor Swift.

"Relax." I'm speaking to myself as much as the guys. "I'm not dating Mills. I mean, Amelia," I quickly amend, but my correction doesn't help.

Nathan drops his head into his hands with a groan.

Alec just stares.

Logan looks mildly impressed and also horrified at the same time. "You're at the nickname stage?"

And Dominik? He catches my eye and smiles.

Panic sets in. I stand up. "Look—it wasn't like that."

These words are an admission. I realize this belatedly. I thought the guys were shocked before, but Tucker actually falls over with a gasp. Eli helps pick him up.

"Van," Alec says, shaking his head, my name sounding like a curse.

"Did you actually, like, make a move?" Eli blinks at me, like he's in shock. "Like, you kissed her but that's it. Or there was some flirtation or an attraction, but you didn't act on it?"

Eli asks this last part hopefully, and whatever expression is now on my face quickly eviscerates that hope.

"I wonder what Coach will think," Dominik says. He's got a smug grin on his face. "Though I guess Amelia's hot. Good for a night, though I'm not sure she's worth the trouble."

Rage descends over me like a red haze.

I'm across the room in a second, his jersey in my fist and my face inches from his.

308

"Don't you talk about her! Don't say her name! Don't you even *think* about her!"

There's shouting and a bunch of hands on me, yanking me back and away from Dominik who's laughing now. Because I've given him exactly what he wants. I know it.

But I couldn't stop myself.

He's lucky all I did was grab him.

"I get it. Like the lady said, everyone needs to blow off steam. Find an easy hook-up."

"Amelia is not some hook-up! She's *everything*. She's my *wife*."

Dead silence in the locker room. The hands tugging me back go still. Even Dominik trades in his hard stare for a gaping look of shock.

"Robert Van de Kamp!"

Coach's bellow hits the room like a sudden, icy freeze.

Hands drop away from me, and the guys who were surrounding me step back, leaving me standing in the middle of the room, facing Coach. Alone.

Thanks for the support, guys. Really.

Did he hear me? I didn't think he did, but he must have. Or Amelia told him. Either way, the mountain lion is out of the bag.

"Coach, I can explain—"

"What is *this?*"

I stop as he waves a paper in my face. Not just a paper—a note. The one I left in his office not twenty minutes ago.

It takes my brain a second.

He doesn't know about Amelia.

Yet.

"Answer me." His voice is deadly quiet. A low hiss as he shoves the note at me.

I take it, glancing down at the words I wrote last night.

309

Took me twenty attempts, but what I landed on was, *It's not right for me to have the position. Not like this. I didn't earn it. Let Dominik have it. Switch us back.*

Short. To the point. Not enough detail to be incriminating about the deal Coach promised me in exchange for watching over Amelia.

I crumple the note in my hand. "I meant what I said. Give Dominik the center position. I don't deserve it."

I don't dare look away from Coach, but I can tell even from my peripheral vision that the guys are trying to follow this conversation with no small amount of confusion. They, like me, were obviously expecting this to be about what I just told them: the fact that I married his daughter.

Now, we're discussing a whole *other* thing, which isn't as surprising, but probably isn't expected either.

What guy wants to give up his spot on the line? Especially for someone like Dominik?

Coach's jaw works. He takes off his hat and runs a hand over his bald head, like he's winding up, trying to find the right words before he really goes off.

I know he won't want to admit he made a deal with me for a position. That's ... unethical at best. With everything else that's happened to him in the last few weeks, he doesn't need to lose respect from the guys or come under fire officially.

"Are you trying to tell me how to run my team?" he demands.

"No, I—"

"Are you questioning my decisions? My leadership? Are you coming for my job? You think you could do it better than me?"

"No, sir."

He and I stare at each other.

No one can move, like we're all frozen in this room—the guys staring between us while Coach and I are locked in a staring match that feels deadly.

My father-in-law, I remember. *I'm having it out right now with my coach ... but also my father-in-law.*

I blink and drop my gaze first. I'm about to apologize when a frantic knocking at the door breaks the tension.

"Um, hey—woman or women entering," Parker calls through a crack in the door. "Kind of an emergency."

The door swings open. I do a double take.

Parker walks in with Amelia, who has a pinched expression on her face, avoiding looking at either me or her father.

The two of them are followed by ... my sisters?

I'm too stunned to speak. Callie, Lex, and Grey look positively murderous.

Well—Callie and Lex do, and the sentiment is aimed right at Amelia. Grey's glare turns to a grin, and she waves at me like it is totally normal that they just busted into my locker room.

Normally, I'd already be hugging them. But nothing about this situation is close to *normal.* We're in *Twilight Zone* territory.

I swallow hard, glancing over at Mills. Her wide blue eyes meet mine and for just a fraction of a second, it feels like we're back in Florida, exchanging glances and understanding.

Like it's us against the world. Like there *is* an us.

She looks unsettled. Panicked, even. I'm not sure if it's because of my sisters—I'm still confused as to how or why they're here—or the clearly uncomfortable scene Amelia just walked in on.

My body sways, like she has created a full-body magnetic current, tugging me toward her. Her panic has activated an auto response in me. The need to protect her is almost primal.

Then I remember how she left. What it felt like to wake up alone, to read her note and know she was already on a plane. I remember how she kissed me yesterday, then told me we couldn't keep doing this.

I force myself to turn away.

"Parker," Coach barks, though I can tell he's trying to soften his tone. "Now really isn't the time."

"Right … it *does* look like a bad time." Parker's eyes bounce around the room, like she's just now realizing whatever tension she brought with her, we already had it in spades. "It's just—I need to see Van."

"Get in line," Alec mutters, and Coach shoots a look at our captain that shuts him right up.

"We're about to start practice," Coach says. "And Van"—he practically spits out my name and turns to glare at me—"isn't in a position to talk to anyone right now. Not after what he pulled."

Amelia sucks in a breath, and immediately, I know she misunderstood Coach's words.

But before I can say anything, she steps forward.

"It's my fault, Daddy. Or, at least, it's both of our faults."

Coach snorts. "I highly doubt that."

"Mills," I start, but she shakes her head and keeps walking toward Coach with a look like, *I've got this.*

"If you're going to be mad at him," she says, her voice pitching higher as she lifts her chin, "you need to be mad at me. *I'm* the one who said we should get married."

There is a beat of silence in which Coach frowns, blinking at Amelia.

Then, he says, "Did you say *married?*"

Amelia shrinks a little. "Isn't that why you're mad—because Van and I got married in Florida?"

The guys heard me say it, but I'm not sure they *believed* it until this moment.

Coach's face turns red first. Then, it turns an alarming shade of eggplant. It reminds me of nature shows I sometimes watch. Animals often have biological warning signs, like the way poison dart frogs are brightly colored as a way to say, *Don't eat me! Run away!*

The color on Coach's face is a very clear sign that anyone around him should probably run. Fast.

But no one moves.

Amelia glances at me, and I give my head a little shake. I can see the moment she realizes what happened.

That's right, Mills—you just dropped the bomb on your dad.

She takes a tiny step back. "I, um ..."

"You ..." Coach sputters. "You got married? To *him?*" He jabs a finger in my general direction, but his gaze remains on Amelia, vacillating between anger and something worse —*hurt.*

It's the same expression I see when I hazard a glance at my sisters. Callie's jaw is clenched tight. Lex is already blinking back tears, and Greyson looks like she's about to pass out.

All I told them was that Amelia left me. And why she left.

They called me stupid. They called her ... some other things. Family will always take your side.

But now that they know what I *failed* to tell them—well. I'm not sure they're on my side anymore.

Amelia doesn't answer her father. She doesn't need to. Her face—and I'm sure mine if he ever looked at me—confirms it.

It's Parker who speaks next, clearly trying to cut through

the tension. "Well, it looks like we've got a lot going on here." She grabs Amelia's arm and starts maneuvering her toward the door. "What I needed to say can probably wait—"

Coach ignores Parker and steps toward Amelia.

"Of all the things you could have done," he starts, and for a moment I set aside the fact that he's my coach. I see the hurt on Amelia's face, and I step between them. "Of all the thoughtless choices."

Amelia flinches.

"Hey," I say, then stop because I have zero plan here. But I don't like the tone he's using with Amelia, and I shift closer. Not quite touching her but apparently too close for Coach.

His eyes blaze. I remember seeing his fury when he found out about Douche the Groom cheating with his niece. That was bad.

This is … worse.

"Daddy—" she starts.

But she doesn't get to finish. Because my sisters rush us both, Callie and Lex clearly torn between yelling at Amelia and yelling at me, and Grey like she's trying to hug her—just as Dominik's laughter rings out and Coach's fist flies toward my face.

CHAPTER 25

Amelia

"YOU CAN'T KEEP HITTING people to solve your problems," I say, handing Dad an ice pack along with the kind of look I remember him giving me as a kid when I did something foolish.

He doesn't like it based on the scowl I get from him in return. But he does snatch the ice from me, placing it on his knuckles with a wince.

We're in his office, though I'd rather be anywhere else.

Like ... a doctor's office waiting room filled with flu-ridden children dripping with snot.

Swimming through a crocodile-infested river in Australia.

Standing naked on a stage and being told I must deliver a speech I didn't prepare for in front of every person I've ever known.

It's entirely possible I'm being a little dramatic.

"In this case, I think my response was deserved," Dad says.

I guess dramatic runs in the family.

"Really?" I ask dryly. "You think hitting one of your players—not by accident this time and inside the team facility instead of a church—was deserved?"

All because you found out I married Van? I want to add.

But I don't. Because my dad still has a bullish look about him. And saying the M-word seems like it would be waving a very red flag.

He does drop his gaze, though, staring at the ice on his knuckles.

I stare at the top of his bald head, remembering how he cheerfully agreed to shave his combover for my wedding, even though the man was nothing if not dedicated to the little wispy hairs.

Was it just a few days ago he was thrilled about me starting work here, handing me a Taylor Swift lunch box?

The thought makes my heart hurt. I feel so far from where we were, where we've always been. Since Mom died, it was always Dad and me, against the world. But I realize now, sitting across the desk feeling much farther away, the cost of our closeness might have been me always agreeing with him. Always falling in line, following his rules.

When was the last time I disagreed with him out loud? I honestly can't remember.

All of my current relationships are in shambles. My dad and I are not okay. I'm keeping a huge secret from Morgan.

And—I almost laugh at the absurdity of this one—my marriage is falling apart.

I don't know how to fix any of them. I mean, telling Morgan the truth is the easiest place to start. But I can't predict how she'll react once she knows I've been lying about something so huge ... or, not lying, exactly. Just keeping it from her.

Just like Van kept something from you?

Ouch. That was rude. True, but rude.

I really hope Van's okay.

It took almost the entire team of hockey players to pull Dad away from Van. Meanwhile, Parker impressed me by single-handedly keeping Van's sisters from tearing me limb from limb.

Alec and Winston, one of dad's assistant coaches, managed to get all the guys out of the room and onto the ice, telling Dad to take a break while they handled practice.

And now ... we're here. Sitting in a silence so awkward and so poignantly painful that the air feels thick and noxious.

As Dad adjusts the ice over his knuckles, I wonder if Van's face is better or worse than it was after my failed wedding. The man has taken one too many blows to the face for me.

"I just cannot believe this," Dad says, startling me out of my thoughts.

"Me neither," I mutter.

"Van. You married *Van*. Of all the bad decisions to make ... you married *him*."

Perhaps I underestimated how much my dad dislikes Van.

"What were you thinking?" Dad demands.

I know I wasn't thinking about Dad or his reaction when I tugged Van toward the wedding reception, managing to find the officiant as well as a pair of very drunk wedding guests who acted as our witnesses.

I was thinking about how Van, more than anyone in my life including my dad, made me feel more like myself. That it was okay to be myself, whoever *myself* happened to be. And it only took a few days for him to do it.

I was also thinking about his lips on mine and how he made me laugh and how much fun we had.

How being with Van felt different than it *ever* had with Drew. Or with anyone. I'm not sure anyone has ever allowed me that kind of freedom to just unapologetically ... be.

Van reminded me of Mom in some strange way. Being around him made me think of how Dad always said when I found the person I want to spend my life with, I shouldn't waste a second. There was an urgency on that beach—the sense that Van was that person, and I really didn't want another second to go by without making it official.

Apparently, this adage of Dad's only applies when it's *not* his least favorite player.

"I guess you realized your mistake and that's why you came back without him. And why you didn't tell me. Milly, the man is arrogant. A hothead. And the mouth on him." Dad shakes his head, the disappointment on his face growing with every word he says. "Let's not get started about his reputation."

"Yes. Let's not," I mutter. Alec's comments from the day before are still stuck in my head.

The idea of Van and anyone else fills me with hot, hot rage.

"If you were looking for a way to hurt me—" Dad starts.

I interrupt, but quietly. "My decision had nothing to do with you. Or at least, not hurting you. And you don't know Van as well as you think."

Dad leans back in his chair, eyes narrowed. "You really believe after a few days at the beach, you know one of my players better than I do?"

"Yes. Because if you've reduced Van to things you just said, you don't know him at all."

"Do you hear yourself?" he asks.

318

"I could say the same to you."

Dad stands, the bag of ice falling from his hands as he places his palms flat on the desk and leans toward me. I've seen the look in his eyes before, but never directed toward me. I do my best not to wither under it, though that's exactly what I want to do. Wither, cower, apologize. Back down.

As uncomfortable as it is not to do any of those things, I sit up tall under Dad's gaze.

I can't make choices based on what he wants for me. Or on what keeps the peace. I won't. Not anymore.

"You married a man I can barely tolerate after knowing him only a few days."

"Let's not forget—you sent him to Florida with me."

"Not for this! I thought you'd be crying in your hotel room all week. I couldn't stand the thought of you alone and hurt. I expected Van to keep an eye on you—from a distance. Not to have his bad influence impact you like this."

"He wasn't a bad influence. The opposite, actually."

Dad shakes his head. "I don't believe that. You made maybe the biggest decision of your life, done on a whim. In some ways, I get it—Drew hurt you and you reacted."

"That's not why either. This wasn't about you *or* Drew."

"Then make it make sense, Milly."

I'm still not sure I can articulate all the reasons an impromptu wedding with Van on the beach seemed like the right choice at the time. But I *do* know it wasn't just a reaction to Drew. It wasn't me lashing out or acting out because I was hurt.

Dad pauses, and it feels like he's winding up for a big explosion. Instead, his next words are whispered. "You got married, and I wasn't there."

He blinks, and something in me twists up tight. The hurt is clear in his voice. Is this really the crux of it—he's hurt because I got married without him? Dad had been so excited to walk me down the aisle on my wedding day, and he wasn't even there. He didn't even know about the wedding at all until I blurted it out in the locker room.

I didn't think the ache in my chest could be any worse. Turns out—it can. A heavy dose of guilt will do that to a person.

"Daddy—"

"Don't *Daddy* me."

It's like he physically reached across the desk and slapped me. I swallow hard, then stand up and take a wobbly step back.

"You made a foolish decision while you were hyped up in an emotional state. Or maybe it was about revenge—getting back at Drew and Becky." He shakes his head. "And you chose the one player who is the epitome of the reason I wanted to keep you away from hockey players. A man who—"

"*That's enough.*"

Maybe I'm still upset with Van for making the deal with dad. For marrying me without telling me the reason he came to Florida in the first place. And maybe I do feel bad about getting married without Dad being there.

But I won't stand by while Dad eviscerates Van's character. Or mine.

"We're done here," I say. "I'm not going to talk to you when you're just lashing out. Maybe later, when you've had time to cool off, we can discuss this rationally."

Dad laughs, a dark chuckle that has absolutely zero humor in it. "You want to talk about being rational? You married a man who must have messed up so quickly that you came home pretending the wedding never even happened."

Tears prick my eyes but I will not let him see me cry. "I

left because I saw your text. The one where you thanked him for *babysitting* me."

Dad should flinch at this. He should be bothered by his actions. By the way he went behind my back and tried to manipulate the situation. Even if he did so because he was trying to protect me.

But he only shakes his head, then waves a hand. "Then, go. Sounds like you and your new *husband* have some issues to work out."

He's not wrong about that. Yesterday, the issue I wanted to work out was an annulment.

Now ... now I don't even know where to start. I just know I need to get out of this office.

As I walk out, just before the door slams, I hear dad say, "Your mother would be so disappointed."

And I guess I need to find a place to stay because I am *not* going home.

CHAPTER 26

Van

I'VE SAID it many times before—Parker is a genius.

But … having my sisters come surprise me?

This falls under the accidental evil genius category.

Parker couldn't have known why this is the absolutely worst possible timing. And the worst idea—to invite my sisters and to leave them in a room alone with Amelia. I'm honestly surprised they all walked out of the room.

My sisters are brutal. Callie and Lex, anyway. Actually, Greyson is the one I'd worry about the most, but it would take a LOT to get her mad enough to exact revenge. And then she'd find a way to ruin your life with a sweet smile on her face.

Knowing what I'm personally in for with my sisters is why I took my sweet time getting home. Now that they know what I didn't tell them—the tiny little detail about my marriage—they will have words for me. A lot of them.

Probably not unlike whatever words Coach had for Amelia. I hope she's okay.

It's why I'm standing on my own porch, hesitating with my forehead against the door of the little craftsman bungalow I started leasing a few months ago.

Because they're in there. Waiting.

I swear, I can hear them breathing.

"No sense just standing there, baby brother." Lex's voice through the Ring doorbell makes me jump.

I take a step back from the door, glaring toward the tiny camera. "I *did* actually hear you breathing, then. I thought I was imagining it."

"Nope." It's Callie this time, and I can hear the smile in her voice. "We've been watching you."

"And listening," Lex adds.

"That doesn't sound terrifying," I mutter. "Wait—and how are you talking to me through my system?"

"Oh, sweet brother," Callie says. "You underestimate my skills."

When she was younger, we sometimes called Callie the computer whisperer. She took apart her first computer when she was nine. Put it back together and in working order—with modifications—the next year. She developed an app at sixteen and hacked into our school's servers her senior year. Not to change her grades but just for—as she put it—funsies.

I guess taking over my own Ring doorbell system shouldn't be surprising.

"Looks like somebody's having a bad day," Alexandra says in a faux pitying tone.

"Or a bad couple of weeks," Callie says. "Maybe you

should come in and talk about the marriage you forgot to tell us about?"

"We'll be nice," Lex says sweetly. *Too* sweetly.

"We're the nicest." Callie's tone suggests otherwise. She sounds like the Big Bad Wolf telling Red that his big eyes are *better to see you with, my dear.*

I snort. "You know this is not making me feel any better about coming in there."

The deadbolt pulls back. I take another step away from the door, the instinct to run *strong*. The doorknob turns and the door creaks open. Just a few inches. Enough to make this feel like my own personal horror movie.

It's stupid. But my heart is speeding along like a runaway train, and my eyes dart from the door to the windows along the front of the house.

I don't see anything. But … they're *there*.

"Don't be silly, Van," Lex says. "Just come inside. We're *family*."

"Yeah. Which means you have fewer lines you won't cross. Because you know I'll forgive you."

"I'm not sure you're the one who should be talking about forgiveness," Callie says. "At least, not about being the one to give it."

"Maybe you should think about *asking* for it," Lex says.

It's then I realize they've been distracting me from what I should have already realized by now.

I swallow, glancing around the porch. "Where's Grey?"

"What do you mean?" Callie asks innocently.

"Greyson hasn't said anything," I say, keeping one eye on the cracked open door but also glancing around. "Where is she?"

"She was just right here," Lex says. "Darn. Where *ever* could she have gone?"

The sound registers just as I feel something hitting me in the back. *Hard.*

Thwap! Thwap! Thwap! Again and again, I'm struck in the back, my butt, and down the backs of my legs.

Instinctively, I cover my face and huddle against the house.

They're just paintballs, I tell myself. Because this would not be the first time. But it's still terrifying when you're not expecting to be shot with them. And direct hits with paintballs aren't exactly pleasant.

"Grey! Enough!" I bellow.

The shots stop. I drop my hands and turn toward the front yard. And jump when one more shot rings out. This one hits way too close to my crotch, leaving a purple splotch just inches to the right of my fly.

"Greyson," I growl. "I swear …"

Movement catches my eye, and Greyson belly crawls out from the bushes between my house and the next door neighbor's wearing a camo suit. Her face is covered in greasepaint, really almost invisible except for the white of her smile. She's even got on some kind of fancy goggles covering her eyes.

This is why Grey is the one people should be the most afraid of.

She stands, slinging the gun over her camo-clad shoulder.

Here's the thing: this is all ridiculous. I'm upset about Amelia and about Coach. My teammates all seem ready to kill me. I should *not* be in the mood for my sisters' teasing or their paintballing.

But this is *so* familiar. Not the specifics of being stalked and shot with paintballs by Grey. In the general sense, though, this is how we operate—all up in each other's business, being supportive and also unrelenting.

325

Maybe my life is still the same mess it was five minutes ago, but there's a sense of lightness now I didn't have before.

"Someone found the army supply store," I say, looking her up and down. "And my paintball gun."

"I actually brought the suit with me. You never know when you might need it." Greyson lifts the goggles, perching them on top of her head as she hops up the steps and gives me a side hug. "I didn't get to do this earlier," she says, like she didn't just shoot me up with a paintball gun. "Good to see you, big brother."

"I guess it's good to see you too." I hug her back, then ruffle her hair, distracting her as I disarm her.

"Hey!" she protests as I take the gun. "No fair."

"All's fair in love and family."

When I glance up, Callie and Lex are in my doorway. I can't tell if they're trying to present a united front or just blocking me from entering my own house.

"Who gave you a key?" I ask.

"Parker told us where you keep it," Grey says cheerfully. "I like her, by the way."

"Yeah, well. I don't think she likes me very much," I say, shaking my head.

"Come on," Grey says, resting her cheek on my chest and getting greasepaint all over my shirt. "Let's go inside and discuss your heartbreak and your quickie marriage—"

"How was it even legal, by the way?" Lex wants to know, ever the lawyer. "Florida isn't Vegas. There are waiting periods and fees."

I've wondered this myself. "The officiant worked for the resort and had a certificate we signed. He said something about residents and non-residents and ... I don't know. Amelia has the paperwork. Unless she threw it away. Which at this point is highly possible," I mutter.

"Come on," Callie says. "Stop standing on the porch."

"Do you promise to be nice? No more paintballs?"

"No promises," Callie says as she and Lex step back, making space for us to enter the house. "But we promise we'll still be family in the end."

"Family first," Grey says, and I drop a kiss on top of her head. She smells like greasepaint and dirt.

"Family first," I echo, then lean down and whisper to Grey, "But I will get you back for this."

"Counting on it," she says with a smile.

———

It's amazing how my sisters, in a few hours, can make my house feel like theirs and *I'm* the visitor. The three of them are lined up on my couch with me in an armchair. They look a little like a tribunal about to come down with a verdict. Except I guess Grey's paintballs satisfied their anger with me over keeping this secret.

Now, they're concerned.

"So, that's it? That's the whole sordid tale?" Callie asks.

Once we sat down and Grey washed her face, I told them everything. Start to finish, from meeting Amelia the very first night in the restaurant—which they knew about, just not the details—to waking up alone and then the kiss in the stairwell followed by Amelia reiterating that it's over.

"That's everything."

Lex sighs. "It would make a good movie. All the drama. The romance."

"All it needs is a happy ending," Grey says with a smile.

"I'm not so sure that's possible," I say, sinking deeper into the chair.

They exchange glances, having the kind of silent conversation I've grown used to watching over the years. We're all close, but the three of them have something a little extra.

I'm not sure if they group themselves by age on purpose, or if they naturally just happen to end up oldest to youngest most of the time. It's also in order of darkest to lightest hair.

A running joke is that Mom and Dad's genes ran out of pigment by the fourth kid. Callie's long hair is almost black, mine only a few shades lighter than hers. Lex's chin-length hair is chestnut brown, and Greyson has wild, golden brown curls.

Seeing them this way, I catalog all the subtle changes since I saw them at Christmas. Lex has dark circles no concealer could touch, and I hope things are okay with her husband.

Greyson looks about the same, though her skin is a little pink from scrubbing off the camo paint. She missed a few spots of dark green, making her complexion look slightly moldy.

Callie's lines all seem harsher somehow, from the firm set of her mouth to the blade-sharp edge of her winged eyeliner. I should check in on her more. I think it's easy for us all to forget that the oldest and toughest one of us isn't impervious to hurt.

It's hard not to worry about the three of them, even when I'm the one currently in crisis.

"I like your house," Grey says brightly. "By the way."

Lex nods. "This is a step up from the last apartment. Still looks like a bachelor pad."

"You got a fish," Callie says. It comes out like an accusation.

I'm run a hand through my hair, trying to figure out how we went from talking about my secret, possibly not-quite-legal marriage to my house and my betta fish.

"He's new," I say.

Theodore is bright green, and when I saw him in the pet store, he immediately reminded me of Alvin and the Chipmunks. As to why I felt the need to go to a pet store and buy a fish after lying to Amelia about having one, I don't know. It just seemed important at the time.

And maybe I was lonely.

Turns out, fish aren't great company, but he is a good listener. We've had some long, one-way conversations lately. The best thing about him? No judgment. Although, I deeply suspect he doesn't care what I tell him so long as I keep the fish food coming.

"I always saw you as more of a dog person than a fish person," Grey says.

"I'm not home enough for a dog. A fish is about the only thing I could handle aside from a pet rock or a Chia Pet."

"Could we please get back on track?" Lex says, leaning forward.

"I think he went off-track two weeks ago." Callie points an accusing finger at me. "You got *married*."

"I did."

"You lied to us," Lex says.

"I didn't *tell* you."

"You lie of omissioned us," Grey says. "The same thing you did to Amelia, by the way."

I tug at the collar of my shirt, resisting the urge to rub a hand over my sternum. It won't ease the ache. "Yeah, I guess it is."

"We would have been there," Grey adds tearfully.

"We *wanted* to be there." Lex sniffs. "I mean, not at this exact wedding, since we didn't know it was happening. But generally speaking, we wanted to be there on your wedding day."

"Why didn't you ask us?" Callie clenches her jaw. Even so, I don't miss the slight wobble.

Fabulous. Now I've made my sisters cry. Even the one who guards her tears like a dragon keeps its gold.

I lean back, drag my hands through my hair, and then press the heels of my hands into my eyes until I see stars. "You know I would've wanted you there. It literally was the most impulsive decision I've ever made."

The thing is … I would make the same decision again.

Only if I could do so in a world where Amelia wouldn't regret it.

"An impulsive decision about something so *big*," Callie says, like she's disappointed in me.

"Why?" Grey asks. More like *pleads.*

I close my eyes, remembering. Not just Amelia's bright eyes and wide smile as she told me she had an idea and started dragging me toward the reception on the beach.

I remember her face at the zoo when she told me I'm not just a casual, fun guy and the way she laughed when she kicked off a platform to zoom over ponds full of gators.

The way she told me I'm more than the surface everyone sees.

I recall her eyes fluttering closed as I kissed her. How her body folded so perfectly against mine.

Then I remember the note and how it felt when I realized what she wrote.

"It happened so fast."

"So fast you couldn't even call us," Callie says, and Lex shushes her. "I mean, we talked to you, what—the day before?"

"I don't mean just the wedding happened fast. I mean that with Mills—Amelia—I felt everything fast. I … *fell* fast."

"You fell," Lex says, sniffling again. "Like, in love?"

"No, dummy. Into a pit of snakes. Yes, in *love*."

This is the first time I've admitted this out loud to someone other than Amelia. It feels just as true as when I said it to her, under the stars and twinkle lights, reciting the classic wedding vows before the officiant pronounced us man and wife. I said it again and again that night, and I remember how it felt saying those words to her when I'd never said them to a woman before.

My stomach sours.

"I never thought this day would come," Callie says, pressing a hand to her heart. She definitely has tears in her eyes, though she hasn't yet allowed one to fall.

Grey beams. "I could tell on the phone when we talked to you."

"Why wasn't I on this call?" Callie complains.

"You were busy," Lex says. Then to me: "You really do love her?"

I nod, trying to unclench my jaw. "It's not like it only happened in those four days. There was the night we met, when I wanted to ask her out on a real date—until I saw her dad. I kept thinking about her, though it was like a back of mind thing. Until Coach invited us to her wedding." Even now, my lip curls. "I've been a mess ever since. It's impacted my mood, my game, and my *other* game."

I say the last part mostly to get a reaction, and sure enough, a pillow flies by my head.

"No one calls it *game* anymore," Lex says. "It's gross."

"And demeaning," Callie adds.

"I was kidding." Mostly.

"It's rizz now," says Greyson. "Not game."

"Then it affected my rizz."

"Or lack thereof?" Grey suggests with a smile.

Grey is quickly becoming my least favorite sister. But it's

hard to get too annoyed when I can still see camo paint inside the shell of her ear.

"So, you haven't been dating anyone else?" Lex asks.

"Not for a long while."

I actually don't remember the last date I went on or the last time I went out with the guys, hoping to meet someone. It's been like it was with the reporter today—I just haven't *seen* other women. Haven't wanted to. The guys had teased me about it a few times, but it's not like I could tell them I had a thing for Coach's daughter after meeting her once and talking for an hour.

Also, a lot of my closest friends on the team have been distracted finding their own women.

"I don't like her," Lex says with a frown. "She left you."

"With just a note. After *marrying* you." Callie shakes her head. "Wait—was it really her idea?"

"It was. But I was on board."

"What I don't understand is *why*," Grey says, lip trembling. "Why she wanted to get married so soon after her engagement ended. But more—why you agreed to it. To a *marriage*, Robbie."

She doesn't need to say more. We have an understanding, the four of us.

Mom and Dad really did a number on us as far as marriages go. Torching their own and then going through rapid-fire speed marriages wreaked havoc on our formative years. We've all internalized in different, unhealthy ways.

Callie wouldn't date at all for *years*. I dated anyone and everyone, but wouldn't commit. Grey went through a thankfully short period where she embodied the daddy issues stereotype—latching onto a series of total losers, desperate for someone to love her. Lex poured herself into work. Had

Mitch not really pursued her, she'd probably still be married to her job.

A few years back, the four of us sat down and hashed out our issues with marriage. Over a few bottles of wine, which seems to be the best way to ease into a conversation about the trauma your parents caused, we agreed to look out for each other. Point out any unhealthy behaviors and coping mechanisms. Offer support as needed.

And, above all, NOT repeat our parents' mistakes.

Which meant when and if we got married, we would do our level best to make it *forever*.

"Do you think she loves you?" Grey's question comes with uncharacteristic softness.

Doesn't soften how it lands.

"I don't know. She was still reeling from what her fiancé did, and probably wasn't in a place to know for sure."

Lex leans forward. "So, why'd you marry her? If you knew she wasn't in a good place mentally or emotionally, *why?*"

I've asked myself the same question. A lot.

The thing is … I don't like the answer.

"I think because I wanted it to be true," I admit. "I wanted Amelia to love me. And maybe I thought …" Now I'm the one holding back tears. I breathe through it until I can speak again. "Maybe I thought she'd change her mind if we waited."

There's a little sound from one of my sisters. A squeak, followed by a sniff. I can't look at them, so I stare at the rug.

"Should I have waited on the marriage part? Yeah, probably. But I also don't know that I regret it. I went to talk to the team lawyer about getting it annulled. But then, I couldn't go through with asking. I realized it's because … I don't want to."

333

"You want to stay married to her after she *left you?*" Callie asks.

"In her defense, that text was pretty damning," Lex says. "But I'm still mad at her."

Grey sniffs and offers me a watery smile. "Poor Amelia. And poor you. I would have paid all the cheese to come. A whole giant wheel of cheese." She stretches out her hands on either side of her head.

I can't help but chuckle. "I'm sorry, Grey. All of you—I'm sorry. No one needs to pay me in cheese for something like this. I should have told you. I would have wanted you there."

It's true. I wasn't thinking about my sisters while I was marrying Amelia—which is a good thing when you think about it—but now that I'm looking back, it's wrong they weren't there. As bridesmaids or my best women or just as my *sisters*.

I may not regret marrying Amelia—not completely, anyway—but I absolutely regret not having my sisters there.

"What do you need?" Lex asks. "How can we support you? I know Parker flew us in for the playoffs, not knowing any of this, but the timing is perfect."

"You needed us, but you wouldn't have called," Grey adds. "But now we're here!"

And then she crosses the room to throw her arms around me, giving me the hug I didn't know I needed. It's a little awkward since I'm slouched in a chair, but still perfect. I close my eyes, as much to hold back the tears as anything.

Soon, there are more arms going around me, the weight of another sister and then another.

"This doesn't mean I fully forgive you for not telling us," Callie whispers in my ear. "Or Amelia for leaving you."

"Same," Lex says. "But I'm getting there."

"Thanks."

Grey chimes in. "I'm not mad at anyone. I just want to help you fix this so we can have another sister and then you can have a bunch of babies and we can be the best aunts ever."

"A little too soon to talk about babies," Callie says.

"They're married," Grey points out. "I can talk about babies if I want."

"They probably need to work this out before they think about kids," says Lex.

We're still in the middle of a messy, four-person hug turning into a close-up bickering match about babies when there's a knock at the front door.

I freeze. No one ever comes by my house.

My first thought is that it's Amelia.

Which can't be right. She may be my wife, but she doesn't know where I live.

What's more likely—Alec is coming to talk to me about my decisions and how they're affecting the team. Or it'll be the whole group of guys, staging an intervention of some kind.

As long as it's not Coach, here to take another swing at me.

"Expecting someone?" Callie asks.

My sisters pull away, Grey patting me on the head like a dog.

"Nope." Standing, I rub my hands down my thighs before walking to the door, trailed by my sisters.

When I open the door, it's not the guys.

"Hey," Amelia says, giving an awkward wave.

She's standing on my front porch surrounded by multiple bags and a rolling suitcase so full it looks ready to explode.

"Hey?" I try to keep my voice steady, not betraying the wild way my heart is beating in my chest. I don't want to allow myself any kind of hope. Especially not when I'm still hurt. And angry.

But Amelia looks shy and more than a little unsure.

She clears her throat and drops her gaze to her feet. "Things aren't great with my dad right now, as I'm sure you can imagine and … I hoped maybe I could crash on your couch?"

CHAPTER 27

Amelia

GROVELING AT MY ESTRANGED—*can I call him estranged???*—husband's door was not in my plans for the day. Or the week. Or the year.

But after the conversation with my dad in his office, there's no way I can stay at home. I only hope Van says yes.

Otherwise … my next stop is a hotel.

He leans in the doorway, looking practically edible. If not aloof. I fidget with the handle of my rolling bag, waiting for a response.

"So, you came to me because you're desperate," Van says. "Was I your last option?"

I hesitate. "The second," I admit.

"Ah."

The truth, which I can't quite get myself to confess to Van, is that I *wanted* to come here first. He was the very first person I thought of running to when I left the Summit in tears. Not only because I need someone, but because I want that person to be *him*.

Plus, I couldn't stop worrying about how he was after everything that happened. I wanted to make sure he's okay.

I convinced myself that Van wouldn't want me to come—which so far, seems accurate—and that I was being ridiculous. Morgan, my very best friend in the world, might have been the first person I asked, but she was the second person I thought of.

Going to Morgan meant finally coming clean, and I didn't know how she'd feel after learning what I kept from her.

As it turns out, Morgan's reaction was amusement—which I never would have predicted. She laughed for a solid minute. I actually watched the seconds tick by on the phone while she cackled.

"You married him. *Married*. On a beach. On a whim! A hockey player even *I* know your dad hates. This is too good," she said, and it sounded like she was wiping tears from her eyes. "*So* good that there's no way you can do anything other than run into your husband's arms. Also, I need some time to process you not telling me, your very best friend, that you got *married*."

So now I'm here. Feeling more alone than I ever have. More unsure. And for a conflict-averse person, there is pretty much no one in my life I *don't* have issues with right now.

Or, I think, looking at Van, *who doesn't have issues with me*.

Van has still not moved. Not smiled. There is zero sign of his trademark smirk.

I take the tiniest step backward, already running through a list of hotels in my mind. My bank account will hate me, but so be it. I care less about the money and more about being alone.

"Honestly, don't worry about it," I say, dropping my gaze as I reach for my bags. "I shouldn't have come."

In one big step, Van is beside me, taking my bags. "Get inside, Mills. Of course you should have come."

My throat grows tight, and my chest feels warm. I can't manage words, but I nod.

"If you can't crash at your husband's place when your life falls apart, where can you go?"

His tone is teasing—which is the perfect response right now. I want to wrap him up in a hug, but I don't know if he'd want that. He did call himself my husband, even if teasing. Feels like a tiny olive branch. Maybe a puny one with no leaves and no olives.

The moment has passed, though, and he's already walking inside, carrying all my bags.

"Come on, slowpoke."

I scurry after him, blinking back tears of gratitude. Well— a mix of gratitude and a whole lot of other things too.

"How did you find out where I live, you little stalker?" he calls as I close and lock the door.

"Don't flatter yourself. I'm not stalking you," I say, trying to match his playful tone. If my voice is a little wobbly, he doesn't comment on it. "Parker told me."

The entryway isn't open to the rest of the house, and as I step through the doorway to the living area, I immediately halt.

I did *not* anticipate Van's sisters being here.

We have not gotten off to a good start, and I can see that we aren't off to a good middle either. At least, based on Callie's narrowed eyes.

Grey steps forward and hugs me, though, and I'm so surprised I don't react, which means my arms are trapped against my body. "I promise they'll love you just as much as I do," she says. "As long as you don't break Robbie's heart. Then … all bets are off."

"Thanks?" Even with the mild threat in her words, I appreciate the physical comfort of the hug.

Earlier today Parker walked out of the press room with no idea what she dropped me in the middle of. As soon as the door closed behind her, Callie smiled—the kind of smile I imagine serial killers offer their victims before getting down to business.

"Hello, Amelia," she said, steepling her fingers on the table, Godfather style. "We've been looking forward to meeting you."

Meeting is a loose word for what happened next, which was more of a verbal annihilation. Grey kept trying to cut in and, from the sound of it, soften things, but she didn't get a chance to speak.

She and I had that in common. I didn't even try to talk. What does etiquette say about talking to the sisters of a guy you married, then ditched? I'm not sure even the expanded edition of Emily Post addresses this.

So, of course I'm nervous when Grey finally releases me and steps back in line with her sisters.

Where is Van?

"Mills?" he calls from somewhere deeper in the house. Somewhere behind his sisters. He emerges and stops, huffing out a breath. "Oh, right. Your welcoming committee is here. Ladies—would you mind stepping aside so I can show Amelia to her room?"

"Do you mean your room?" Grey says hopefully. "In your bed?"

I think even my eyeballs are blushing.

Van sighs and shoulders his way between his sisters until he reaches me. Then, with hands on hips and eyes on mine, he says, "Yes. Mills will be in my bed. I will be on the couch."

"Boo," Grey says.

I feel the same way. Even if I shouldn't.

"Do you even fit on the couch?" Callie asks. "That can't be comfortable. Or a good idea with playoffs tomorrow. What if you get a crick in your neck?"

I'm not sure if she's trying to make me feel bad for taking Van's bed or trying to get us into bed together. From the way she's been looking at me since I walked inside the house, probably the latter.

"I should take the couch. I don't want to kick you out of your room."

"You two are married," Grey points out. Like we didn't know. "Married people share beds. It's a whole thing."

Van closes his eyes like he's searching his eyelids for some extra patience. He must find it because when he opens them, he meets my gaze again and gives me a little smile. It may be small, but I feel that grin all the way down to my pinky toes.

"We are also adults," he says. "Stop trying to meddle."

Then he reaches out and takes my hand, guiding me through the gauntlet of sisters and into a back hallway leading to the bedrooms. I fist his shirt in my other hand and lean close to his back.

"Thank you," I whisper, not wanting his sisters to see any sign of weakness. They're like jackals. And despite Grey's kindness, I don't for a second think they wouldn't turn on me.

He doesn't answer, but his thumb strokes over my knuckles one time. The tiny gesture has me grinning, burying my face in his back. He smells divine.

And then we're alone.

In his bedroom.

Van swings me out and releases me like some kind of ballroom dance move and I careen forward, ending up half sitting on his enormous bed as he closes the door behind us.

Gulp.

The last time we were in a bedroom together, it was right after we recited vows and danced in the moonlight. By the way his eyes darken, I can tell he's thinking about the same thing.

He clears his throat and his expression, shifting from a heated gaze to cool and detached.

Van also looks handsome, but that's irrelevant. Van never *doesn't* look good. Even with the slightly swollen cheek, which reminds me of how he also looked good the last time he had a bruised face.

Crossing his arms, Van leans back against the closed door like he's waiting for me to speak. It makes sense, considering I basically invited myself into his place.

Which, for the record, is really nice.

I didn't notice much on the way in, too nervous and excited—before I saw his sisters. Then I was slightly fearful for my life. Maybe once they all leave I can snoop around—respectable snooping—and see what the rest of his house is like.

His bedroom is neat almost to a frustrating level. I want to crack open one of his dresser drawers just to see if he'd immediately walk over and close it. I bet he has one of those feather duster things for the blades of his ceiling fan.

"You make your bed?" I feel stupid the second those words leave my mouth. But my palms are flat on his comforter, which is a charcoal gray. It's a great fabric: soft, but it feels like it wouldn't be too hot at night.

I'm stalling. I'm fully aware.

Van raises one dark brow. "Is that really what you want to talk about right now—my comforter?"

I don't want to talk about anything, honestly. I'd like to curl into a tiny ball—maybe in the corner of his closet—and hide for the next ten years until I've matured into the kind of person who can face up to her mistakes or even recognize a mistake from a miscalculation or a misconceived notion. Maybe in ten years, I'll be better at knowing what I want, unabashedly reaching for it, and being able to handle conflict like a mature person.

"I'm just a little surprised. By your room," I say stupidly.

"There's a lot you don't know about me," Van says. A challenge. "And clearly, a lot I don't know about you."

"What should we do about that?" I ask, and it comes out way huskier than I intend.

Van's detached expression immediately gives way to surprise and then a wolfishness that makes my insides quiver. He doesn't say the words but I swear his eyes are saying something like, *I could present a list of ideas. Some suggestions. Perhaps a syllabus.*

I am all ears.

But slowly, the look fades into something more somber.

"You can stay as long as you need to," he says. "Is everything okay with you and your dad?"

My eyes start to burn. I shake my head slowly. "No."

"I'm sorry," Van says, and even though he's talking about me and my dad, not the two of us in this room, hearing his words releases something in me.

I've been practicing an apology for days. All kinds of versions. Now … it just kind of drops out of me.

"I'm sorry too. About leaving you in Florida with just a note. I should have stayed. I should have asked you about it."

"You could have yelled at me about it," Van says. "I

wouldn't have blamed you if you'd thrown my phone over the balcony." He laughs at my expression—a kind laugh. "Somehow, I can't picture that."

"Did you watch *The Office?*"

"Do bears beat *Battlestar Galactica?*" he asks with a smirk.

I throw my head back and laugh. "I think the line was 'bears, beets, *Battlestar Galactica.*'"

"I like mine better. Yes. I watched *The Office*, Mills. Why?"

"Do you remember the season where things get really ugly between Jim and Pam? They have the horrible counselor who makes them speak their truths and it's super cringey?"

"Are you going to suggest we try that?" Van makes a face.

"No! Definitely not. I'd rather eat beets. Or even bears. I was thinking today of the episode when Jim gets frustrated by all that and is going back to Philly. But Pam tells him to stay so they can fight."

"I remember," he says.

I slide my hands over the fabric of his comforter again, then curl my hands into fists and drop them in my lap. "I don't think I know how to do that."

"Do what?"

"Fight," I admit. "I'm realizing I don't know how to deal with conflict at all. I think I'm allergic. Or just … chicken."

"Most people don't deal with conflict head on. Not well, anyway," Van says. "Then there are the people who dive straight into it head first when they should have worn a helmet."

"You seem very much like you belong in the second category."

His smile is wry. "I can when it's with someone like your dad. Or my teammates."

He pauses, and I catch him tapping his index fingers on

his arms, which are still crossed over his chest. A tell, maybe?

"But this is the first real relationship I've had. This is uncharted water for me, and I did some avoiding of my own. Not telling you the second your dad offered me his deal." Van shakes his head. "I was already walking to the airport. Before his call. Your dad had absolutely nothing to do with me getting on that plane."

This shouldn't matter to me as much as it does. "Really?"

"Promise. I just … didn't tell *him* that. And then I didn't tell *you* what he said. Stupid," Van says, shaking his head. "I made multiple stupid decisions, and I'm sorry."

"Like marrying me." I mean it as a joke, but Van's face closes down. He straightens, dropping his arms and shoving his hands in his pockets. I scramble to fix it somehow but come up empty.

"You're welcome to stay as long as you like," Van says finally. "Make yourself at home."

I want to take back my words, but it's like all the talking I've done has leached all the bravery from my bones. So, I just follow his lead, stepping back into the shallows.

"Really—I don't need to take your bed, Van. Just put me on the couch. It's fine."

A smile curves one side of his mouth. "You're safer in here. With a lock." He must read the look of alarm on my face, because he chuckles darkly. "I don't mean safe from *me*. You don't need to worry about *that*."

"Oh." Worry isn't the word for how I was feeling about that. But I guess after my failed joke about our marriage, I shouldn't be surprised.

"My sisters," he explains as color rises in my cheeks. "I wouldn't leave you out there unattended." Van glances toward the door. "They're as protective of me as I am of them. But"—he raises his voice, again glancing behind him—"I'm sure they'll be on their best behavior now, *won't they?*"

There's a thump outside the door. Then a giggle.

"They're listening to us?" I whisper, horrified.

Van rolls his eyes, but I can see the barely restrained amusement. "I'm sure my sisters would *never* stand outside my bedroom door, eavesdropping. But if they were, they'd bring me a bottle of water from the fridge."

"Yes, sir!" a faintly muffled voice calls from outside the door. More giggling. Footsteps move away along with whispered voices.

"What's that look?"

"I just … I thought I'd meet your sisters under different circumstances."

I still vividly remember the phone call with Grey and Lex in Florida. Hearing them bicker back and forth, arguing about their tradition of trading cheese points for information.

I'd felt a sense of longing, an ache to be part of a close-knit group like this. A family.

Or to be part of *their* close-knit group. Their family.

Van clears his throat. "So did I," he says, and we exchange a weighted glance.

It's weird because it's like we're staring at each other across an ocean or some deep gorge, not across his bedroom. We're sharing a look and the same sentiment. Regret is etched into his face, same as mine.

The thing is … I'm not sure if it's a shared regret or an opposite one.

What I know is that I'm no longer certain of what the path forward should be. I had started to think maybe we should undo what we did—starting with talking to Summer about an annulment—and then consider dating. Like normal people do. Getting to know each other. Taking it step by step with all the normal milestones in their proper order.

Then, if there is still this tug and pull between us, the sense of rightness when we're together, *then* we get married. The right way—with our family and friends and the whole thing.

But I'm not so sure that's what I want, and it makes me feel like the bottom is dropping out of my life. It's the first step off the zip line platform, only right now, I'm not entirely sure I have a harness. One step might be the most exhilarating ride.

Or it might be a messy death.

"Van," I say, digging deep to find the words. "Do you want to get an annulment? If … it's even possible at this point."

The word annulment seems to bounce around the room between us like a slow-moving screen saver.

His jaw flexes, and he glances away, then back at me as he says, "No."

Relief practically makes my bones shiver. Or is that fear? Maybe a little bit of both.

Van takes one step forward. Then another, until he's standing right in front of where I'm still perched on the edge of his bed. He towers over me.

"I don't want an annulment or a dissolution or a divorce," he says, and I have to crane my neck to stare into his inky dark eyes. "I want more than the one night I had with you. I want all your days too. I want to come home knowing you'll be here. I want to look up from the ice and see you there, wearing my jersey, shouting my name."

Van lifts his hand and slowly, tenderly cups my face, his thumb lightly brushing over my cheek. "I want to watch you find out what a life without following the rules looks like. Or, maybe—to find out which rules are worth following and which ones are worth breaking. On *your* terms. I want to be the one cheering for you and your dreams, wearing *your* jersey. Figuratively speaking."

He smirks, then his expression slides into serious again. I think my heart is lodged permanently somewhere in my throat as he bends. His other hand flattens on the bed, fingers splayed next to my hip. He presses his forehead to mine.

"I want it all, Mills," he says. "I want *you*. But only if this is what you want too. Only if *I'm* what you want. I have no idea what I'm doing," he confesses, and the vulnerability in his voice makes me curl my fingers into my palms.

I want to wrap my arms around his waist, to press my ear to his chest and hear the sound of his heart. But I stay still like the little coward I am, breathing him in, focusing on the featherlight brush of his thumb on my cheek.

"And if this isn't what you want—" He pauses, and I close my eyes. "If I'm not what you want, then yeah. Let's talk to Summer."

There is a deep, thrumming ache in my chest. My thoughts whir, stopping and starting like a printer with a paper jam.

I want you gets caught in my throat, swallowed up by a yawning panic.

I could kiss him instead, leaning forward barely an inch to press my lips to his. The instinct is a thousand acre forest fire, urging me to kiss him. To show him what I can't seem to say.

The thing is … I don't know which instincts of mine to trust anymore. I'm beginning to think my wiring is faulty. Do I need to be reset? Or maybe reprogrammed all together?

I open my mouth—to say what, exactly, I'm not sure—but

there's a bang on the door. And with the smallest kiss ghosted over my cheek, Van steps away.

"Your water as requested, sir," a voice says in a terrible British accent.

Van opens the door a crack and a hand thrusts a water bottle through. As soon as he takes it, the hand disappears, yanking the door closed.

"Don't do anything I wouldn't do," Grey singsongs.

Van pinches the bridge of his nose, clutching the water bottle in his other hand so hard I can hear its plastic groan. *"Greyson Kimberly."*

Her laughter echoes in the hallway, moving away from us. After a moment, Van sighs heavily, opens his eyes, and holds out the water bottle. "Here."

I stare at it a little too long, feeling a sad sort of desperation. When our fingers brush, I almost burst into flames.

"Thanks." I wish my voice were more than a rough whisper, but the day has been long and my emotional cup overfloweth.

Van steps closer to the door, glancing at me, then away. "If you need anything …" He blinks a few times, like his eyelids are hitting a reset button. "Just let me know," he finishes, then leaves the room.

And as I fall asleep hours later when my brain finally shuts off, it's with Van's warm, masculine scent wrapping around me.

CHAPTER 28

Amelia

"WHY ARE YOU WHISPERING?" Parker whispers into the phone too, like the need to speak quietly is a virus I've passed on.

"It's a long story," I whisper back, not wanting to admit that I'm staying with Van and his sisters might be listening outside his bedroom door again. "But you're *sure* I can work from home and don't need to come in?"

Home is a general term. I'm not lying, exactly, even if I'm not at the house where my current bedroom is. What *is* home, anyway?

Would a home by any other name smell as sweet?

I'm not sure Shakespeare's question makes sense in this context, but I *do* know that no other comforter would smell as good as the one I'm wrapped up in.

In any case, I've spent the morning wrapped in Van's

comforter and his scent. Afraid to come out of his room, honestly. He left for the Summit early, and without him, my safety buffer is gone.

I woke up when he slipped into the room when it was still dark. Guess the lock wouldn't have stopped his sisters anyway if it was easy enough for Van to pick.

I pretended to be asleep while he tiptoed in, using his phone as a flashlight. When he went into the closet, I watched him through slitted eyes, slipping them closed again when he came back out, duffle bag in hand.

He hovered by the bed for a moment while I tried to breathe slow, steady, sleeping breaths even as my heart pounded.

What was he doing? What was he thinking?

He probably stayed less than a minute but it felt much longer. Just before leaving, he gently tugged the comforter up to my chin, and I swear, I felt his lips brush my hair.

It left me wired, my brain tumbling over anxious thought after anxious thought. I fell back asleep, only waking when I started hearing his sisters move about the house. The idea of running into them—here in Van's house of all places—means I'm trapped in here. Unless I want to face them, and right now, I don't want to face anyone.

Possibly not even myself.

"It might be better if you don't come in," Parker says with a sigh. "All things considered."

"Have you seen my dad after … everything?"

"Only from a distance, and he's kind of a holy terror. I just hope he'll channel his feelings into helping the guys win tonight."

Or, at least, that he won't channel his feelings into punishing Van.

"I'll send an updated list of things to work on." Parker's

voice returns to normal, like she started her day off with a breakfast of sprinkles and sunshine.

She doesn't bother asking me if I'm coming to the game tonight, and I'm both disappointed and relieved.

I feel like a coward, hiding in Van's room. From his sisters. From work. From my dad. From *him*.

"I'm sure you're really glad you hired me now, huh?" I ask.

"I *am* glad." Her answer is immediate and fierce. "I only wish I'd been aware of the circumstances so I could be mindful for your sake. I mean, I was trying to play match-maker with a guy you're already married to." There's a pause. "For now."

I hear the slightest question in her voice. She's offering me an open door. One I could walk through, trusting Parker with how I'm feeling now, and what's going on with me and Van.

"Just know that I'm here," she says after the moment of silence stretches on. "For anything you need. Are you ... okay after everything?"

"Not really," I admit. "But I will be."

And if I keep telling myself that, even with no idea how it's possible, maybe it will become true.

———

I spend the day locked in Van's room like I'm a curmudgeonly hermit. And it's starting to feel like a tiny prison cell. One with the most comfortable bed ever.

While I did do enough actual work to justify being paid for this job, I also spent time googling and reading stories of people who fell in love fast.

Turns out there are a *lot* of people out there who have

352

ridiculously quick love stories. Couples who got married within a few weeks or a few days of meeting. People who claim they fell in love at first sight. Arranged marriages, Vegas weddings on a whim, elopements.

While I didn't shy away from stories that didn't end happily, I found way more firsthand accounts than I thought possible of couples who are still together after years despite a quick courtship.

Love stories with a super fast timeline definitely aren't the norm, but reading so many accounts convinced me that it's possible.

The real question—is it possible for me? For *us*?

Voices carry down the hall and I hear the sounds of keys jangling, feet stomping, and then the front door slamming. I peek through the blinds, watching their rental car back out of the driveaway.

I don't know if Van's sisters are running out for fast food or if they're leaving this early for the game. But my stomach is about to eat itself, so, I make a break for the kitchen.

Just outside Van's bedroom door, I find a tray of food covered in foil along with a note from Grey.

Thought you could use a little fuel. Don't worry; my sisters didn't poison it. I checked. -G

And sure enough, when I lift the corner of the foil, both the sandwich and the cookie have a bite out of them.

I gobble them down anyway.

Technically, we're family. At least for the time being. Family members swap germs, right?

Then, I snoop. Respectfully.

Van's house is tidy. I think if his sisters weren't here, immaculate would be a better word. But I find signs of them everywhere—makeup scattered on the guest bathroom counter, a pair of flip-flops in the middle of a room like someone just walked out of them and disappeared.

There isn't really decoration—no paintings on the wall or picture frames, or curtains. It seems like maybe he just moved in? Or like he's running for the Minimalist of the Year award. The furniture though is comfortable and the colors he's chosen are masculine. It fits him, though I feel like what's missing is a touch of the irreverent—the sort of smirky, snarky attitude Van has in spades.

When I return my dish to the gorgeous, updated kitchen, I find a bright green betta fish on the counter. I remember Van talking about having a fish while we were in Florida. I'll admit—I thought Van made him up.

"But you're real, aren't you?" I ask, leaning my elbows on the counter. I swear, the little guy struts for me, swimming with a little flounce that makes his tail billow. "Just like your daddy, huh?"

They do say pets often resemble their owners. It definitely seems true in this case. I probably shouldn't feed him, since I have no idea whether Van or his sisters or both already did. But he's practically begging, and I can't help giving him a tiny pinch of food.

"Our little secret," I tell him as he gulps down the little red flakes. "Can you keep another one? I think I made a big mistake."

And I don't mean the wedding.

The mistake, the one I woke up thinking about and haven't been able to stop thinking about since, was not being fully honest with Van last night.

Not being brave the way he was when he flat-out told me what he wanted.

Because I think I want the same thing, and it terrifies me.

The part of me that's always done things by the book is

354

scandalized by this. My dad would lose his mind. I think telling him I want to stay married to Van is the only thing that would shock him more than saying I married Van in the first place.

But I think it's time I learn how to love my dad without doing everything according to what he thinks is right for me. Without living for his approval or at the very least, trying to keep the peace.

Something I've done since Mom died.

I wish she were here. Though she died when I was barely old enough to ask for dating advice, somehow I know she'd have the exact right thing to say. Or maybe she wouldn't say anything, but would just listen and offer me support either way.

What I do know is that she'd tell me I shouldn't make decisions based on what makes my dad happy.

She'd tell me to be brave.

Which is the exact opposite of what I do when I see the rental car turn back into the driveway. I bolt for Van's room and dive into his bed, grabbing my laptop and pretending to work.

I hear them come in, then head into their rooms. Music comes on, something poppy and upbeat, and I strain, listening to the lilt and fall of their conversations, their laughter. I should go out there. I should make peace or make friends or … maybe make a fool out of myself?

But I stay in my room, forcing myself to type words that will need to be heavily edited later. The American Marketing Association says writers should aim for an eighth grade level in online articles. Right now, my writing is more like a first grade level.

I jump when someone starts banging at the door.

"Open up or we'll break the door down," a voice calls.

"We can just unlock it," another voice says in a whisper I can still hear.

"That's an invasion of privacy," the first voice whispers.

"But we're literally *trying* to invade her privacy. In a nice way."

More knocking. "Amelia?"

"You can come in," I call. "I didn't lock it."

I'm not prepared for how the sisters look as they walk into the room. They stop at the end of the bed while I stare.

The three of them are decked out in Appies gear or colors head to toe. Which is a lot, but it would be fine.

The turquoise, white, and gray paint covering every inch of their faces, however, is startling. Callie is almost all turquoise, with what I guess is Van's number on her forehead in white. Lex has half her face painted turquoise and half white, and Grey has painstakingly done white, gray, and turquoise camo from her forehead all the way down to her chin.

They look like a mini troupe of Appies clowns.

"What are you doing?" Callie asks with a frown.

"I could ask you the same thing," I say.

"We're about to go to Robbie's game," Lex says.

"Okay." I nod, my fingers twisting in the blanket. "I mean, I guessed that much. Um, have fun?"

There's a beat of silence, then Grey says, "Unacceptable."

"What?"

"Unacceptable," she repeats. "We're not letting you do this."

"Do what?"

"Sit here and wallow in my brother's bed," Lex says, but it's Callie who walks over and tugs on the comforter. I tug right back.

"What are you doing?"

Grey leans over the end of the bed, grabbing another part of the comforter and giving it a good yank. I'm now playing a full-on game of tug-of-war with Van's sisters. I'm not sure what the stakes are, exactly, but I know I don't want to lose.

"Hey—let go!" I tighten my grip.

"It's not yours," Callie cheerfully points out.

"Actually," Grey says, "depending on state law, technically, it might be fifty percent hers."

Callie groans. "Watching Judge Judy does not make you an expert on legal matters."

"I learned it from celebrity gossip sites," Grey says loftily. "Look, Amelia. Just let go of the comforter. We're not going to hurt you." She pauses. "You are wearing pants, right?"

"Yes. But what are you doing?"

"Helping," Grey says simply.

Doesn't feel like helping to me. I curl my fists tighter around the comforter.

"We didn't have to do this the hard way," says Lex, grabbing another side of the comforter.

I have *no* chance when it's three versus one. Honestly, probably any of the three could take me. Van's sisters are *scary*. I'm holding on by sheer force of will right now but I start to get fabric burns on my hands as the comforter slides more and more quickly through my fingers.

And then—it's gone.

Grey stumbles back into Van's dresser with the force of it, and the television rocks precariously before Lex steadies it.

"Now," Callie says, crossing her arms. "Was that so hard?"

Grey, however, is staring at me with wide eyes. I scoot back against the headboard, knees to my chest in a protective ball.

"What?" I ask.

"You're …" She sputters.

The other two are now studying me too, but Lex figures out whatever it is first and gasps. I glance down, wanting to be sure I'm still clothed and that I haven't grown a second head or something. Being gasped at by a person whose face is fully painted is kind of an ironic moment.

"Those are Robbie's pants," Callie says.

I look down again, my cheeks warming. "Oh. Yes."

I'm practically swimming in the sweatpants, which I pulled out of a drawer to sleep in last night. Desperate moment? Possibly. I mean, I *did* have my own pajamas. I can't really explain why I felt the need to go through Van's drawers to find a pair of pants to sleep in.

I just … wanted to wear something of his.

And I'm aware this probably makes me both hypocritical and sad but this is where I'm at in life: wearing the sweatpants of a husband who I haven't been completely honest with while his sisters gape at me in full face paint.

Not exactly part of my life goals.

"I can take them off," I say.

"No!" both Lex and Grey practically shout.

"Okay," I say slowly.

Grey's expression softens, but it's Lex who sniffles. I glance between them, still trying to understand, my body poised in fight, flight, or hide under the bed mode.

"I don't think Van has ever let a woman wear his clothes," Grey says softly. And now her eyes are brimming with tears too.

"I mean, it's not like he *let* me. I helped myself. Kind of a Goldilocks situation where I just made myself at home. These definitely don't even fit and—"

"No," Grey says, biting back a smile with teary eyes. "He

358

gave you his bed. Full access to his room. I bet he'd love to see you in his sweatpants."

"And take you out of them," Lex says with a smirk that's all too close to Van's.

Callie elbows her. "Gross."

I glance down at the fabric pooling around my body. My toes are practically the only part of my feet visible. "He really hasn't let any woman wear his clothes?" I ask. "I mean, I thought he dated a lot."

Callie snorts. "Oh, he has. Just not anyone who ever got far enough to wear his pants. All super casual."

I wrinkle my nose. Maybe I didn't want to know about his dating habits. I feel a strange lump in my throat, and I'm not sure if it's because they're emotional or because I'm thinking about Van and other women.

"But don't worry—it's not like Robbie treated women poorly," says Callie.

"We'd have killed him." Grey's tone is far too chipper to be talking murder.

"There just happen to be a number of women out there who *also* don't mind dating with zero commitment and expectations," Lex explains. "No strings. And definitely no sweatpants."

Not really helping.

I hold up a hand. "Could we, um, not talk any more about Van's dating history?"

"Right," Callie says, and she seems to regain a bit of composure. It's still hard to take her or any of them seriously whenever I look at their painted faces. "Well, let's get you up then. Come on—hop to it."

"I'm sorry?" If anything, I curl into myself tighter. Especially when the three of them start advancing toward me.

Slowly. But definitely making movement, coming at me from three sides.

"We don't have much time," Grey says with a shrug.

Lex adds, "Not if we want to be there for puck drop."

It takes me only another few seconds to catch on. "Oh. I'm not going to the game."

"Sure you are," Callie says.

I flinch as Callie reaches out, but then she takes my hand. Gently. Her eyes meet mine with the same dark espresso intensity I've seen in Van's gaze.

"You're coming with us."

"You know you want to," Lex says. She puts a hand on my shoulder.

Grey climbs right up on the bed, sitting cross-legged facing me and curling her fingers around my foot. "We're going to get you showered—okay, that part you can do alone —and dressed for the game. Like us."

My brain is a veritable spin cycle of thoughts. But I keep hearing an echo of Van's words from the night before, telling me what he wanted.

Me, at his game. Wearing his name, cheering for him.

"I don't have any Appies stuff to wear."

"I thought you worked for them," Lex says with a frown.

"I just started this week."

"No problem," Grey says, and with that, she strips off the jersey she's got on, leaving her in only a sports bra underneath. "Take this. It's Robbie's jersey. I'm sure he's got an Appies t-shirt or something in his closet I can wear."

I turn the jersey over with my one free hand, running my fingers over the name on the back. Van de Kamp. I bite my lip.

Grey rocks forward, her knees nudging mine. "Come on."

"You barely know me," I say, voice wobbly.

Lex pats the top of my head once. "We've got time to get to know you. But we don't have much time to get to the game. Let's go."

"Trust us," Grey says, and when I meet her eyes, something in me shifts.

I want to go to the game. I *need* to go to the game. I need Van to see me there in his jersey with his sisters.

He put it all out there for me in his bedroom last night.

Now, I want to put it all out there for him. Publicly.

And maybe if my dad sees me and sees how much I really care about Van—no. I stop myself. First, I need to worry about Van. Then I can worry about how to get my dad on board.

A sense of sudden urgency overwhelms me.

"How much time do we have?" I ask.

Lex glances at her watch. There's a smudge of turquoise paint on her wrist. She makes a face. "Just … hurry."

Squeezing Callie's hand and looking at each of them in turn, I nod. "Let's go."

CHAPTER 29

Van

"ARE you looking for your sisters or your wife?" Alec asks, practically shoving me through the tunnel after the second period.

Guess it hasn't escaped his notice how my head has been on a swivel, constantly checking the empty seats. Alec's voice is strained, but I can tell he's trying to be understanding. Trying to do something other than tear my head off.

Might be an improvement to my game.

"They're supposed to be here," I mutter. Meaning my sisters.

Not Amelia.

I told myself not to hope she'd come. Even if I carry a secret *hope* she does.

It's hard to keep even the smallest flicker of hope alive

when you lay it all on the line like an idiot and get basically no response.

But with my sisters MIA, I'm starting to grow concerned. Did something happen to them? To Amelia? They wouldn't come all the way to Harvest Hollow only to not be here for the first playoff game.

Maybe leaving the four of them in the house alone was a bad idea.

"If something was wrong, Parker would tell you."

I know Alec's right. Parker knows everything, and she'd find a way to tell me if there were a serious issue.

"I'm sure they'll show up soon," Alec says through clenched teeth as we push into the locker room. "But until then—how about *you* be here. Because it's obvious you're not."

It's obvious to Coach too, who plays bad cop to Alec's good cop, leaving little flesh on my bones after his scathing review of my performance so far.

Not usually a yeller, tonight he makes an exception. I'm pretty sure I saw his tonsils, and I definitely learned a phrase or two I'd never heard. I think he invented them.

Oh, and I'm also sure a lot of his rage, directed mostly at me though we're *all* playing like a peewee team, stems from personal reasons.

So, I just sit with my head down and take it. Deserved on all counts.

Yeah, yeah—Van sucks.

Yeah, yeah—I shouldn't have married your daughter when I know you can't stand me.

Once he's done tearing me apart, Coach turns on the team. I can't help but feel like it's my fault. Sure, we're all playing like trash, but we've had bad periods before. Bad games. Coach always has a way of bringing us back out of our slump in the intermissions.

Today, though, he's just unloading.

When he finally stomps out of the locker room, red-faced and muttering under his breath, the room is silent for about three seconds. This is by far the worst we've played all season, collectively. Missed passes, missed shots, penalties. It's definitely possible to turn a series around, but it's hard to come back mentally from a game like this.

Thankfully, Felix doesn't seem to have off nights, and our goaltender is the only reason we're down three nothing and not losing by more. But he doesn't look happy about it.

Alec finally stands, looking slowly around the room, intentionally meeting every eye. He holds my gaze a beat longer. Then winks before he speaks to the whole team.

"What are we?" he asks. Quietly. But firmly and with a barely contained intensity. It's the kind of voice that makes you sit up and pay attention.

"Family," Logan says. He stands too.

"And how do we play?" Alec asks, just as quietly. With just as much restrained intensity.

"Together." Dominik is the one who answers him this time.

It's such a shock that Dumbo actually chokes and Tucker has to smack him on the back.

Dominik meets my gaze, but I can't read his expression. He stands too.

"Together," Alec repeats, glancing from player to player again. "Family. That's more than how we play. It's who we *are*."

One by one, the rest of the team gets to their feet. Standing in solidarity. Except me. I'm still worried about my sisters and wondering if all of this is my fault. Like playing poorly is a virus, and they all caught it from me.

Stupid, but it's hard not to shoulder some of the blame. If for nothing else, then for Coach's mood.

"We're Appies," Alec continues. "Off the ice. On the ice. Together. Family. We play for more than wins, more than trophies. We play for *family*. Not just the people in the stands supporting us. For each other. Every man in this room is your family. And what does that make this place?"

"Home." I stand, emotion swelling in my chest.

I'm still worried about my sisters. Disappointed Amelia's not here. Bothered by Coach's blatant disapproval. Embarrassed that I put my heart on the line for Amelia only to get no response in return. Frustrated by how I've been playing—not just tonight, but honestly, for months.

The tangle of negative emotions is still there, but something greater is shoving them all down. A sense of urgency. The connection between us all. The knowledge that this is bigger than all of us individually.

It's time to stop wallowing in it. Feeling sorry for myself. Feeling like a mistake, a disappointment. I'm part of a team. A family. We're the Appies. And we aren't going to go down like this in our own house.

"That's more like it." Alec nods and shows off what we all call his Disney prince smile. Blinding. White. Perfect.

I'm pretty sure they're veneers.

Anyway.

"So, I ask you—are we going to let another team come in and take this game from us?" Alec asks, arching a brow. "Or are we going to show them what a real family looks like?"

The roar in the room is deafening, and as we head out and back through the tunnel onto the ice, I force myself not to look up in the stands.

Whether my sisters are there, whether Amelia comes with them—it can matter to me later. But right now, my focus needs to be right here—with *this* family.

———

Alec's team reset pays off.

We're monsters the next period. From the puck drop, it's like we sent out a different team.

Or, maybe, we're finally just skating like the team we *are*. Not the ones we played like the first two thirds of the game.

Nathan and Alec are absolutely brutal on defense, and the Badgers can do little more than dump and chase, getting repeated icing calls and getting nowhere near Felix. He's practically taking a nap.

Eli, who I'm pretty sure hasn't stopped smiling this entire period, scores twice in the first four minutes. I slot the puck to Logan not a minute later, who ties it up with a third. Dominik pushes us into the lead on a beautiful breakaway during his next shift.

The kid came into this period like a whole different person—and I don't just mean his playing. It's the first time his skills have been on par with his normally cocky attitude. But the attitude is gone, and he's actually playing *with* us—a first. Hopefully a permanent shift.

We play hard but clean. The Badgers are gassed, getting sloppy and dirty as we near the end of the period and end of the game.

When one of their D-men takes a swing at Wyatt, I think we're about to see things get ugly. Wyatt isn't the kind of guy you mess with. The blow glances off his cheek, and Wyatt barely flinches. He also doesn't remove his gloves, which results in another power play for us and a score from Camden to leave us up by two.

The crowd is absolutely losing its mind, but I still refuse to look. I don't look during my shifts. Not while I'm on the bench.

I'm afraid if I see empty seats again, I'll lose momentum.

But after a line change, Logan nudges me on the bench. His glove is off and he's wiping the inside of his visor, which is fogging up. "Look," he says, tilting his chin toward the stands.

I don't want to. I've been so good. So focused. Even if curiosity is a hot burn in my chest.

Shaking my head, I take a drink, keeping my eyes on the ice. "That's okay. I'm good."

"No," Logan insists, nudging me a little harder. "*Look.*"

I do, my eyes immediately going to the seats that remained empty through the first two periods.

They're no longer empty.

I'm grinning like a fool as my gaze bounces from one sister to the next to the next. It's hard to tell the three of them apart when their faces are fully covered in paint and—

Wait.

Not three. There are *four* faces painted in turquoise and white. Four practically feral women decked out in Appies gear just behind the glass.

Amelia.

She came with my sisters—and she's screaming for me, pounding her fists on the glass, looking every bit as feral as they do.

And she's wearing an Appies jersey. Backwards, for some reason.

When our eyes connect, her grin spreads. Most of her face is blue, with white painted around her eyes like a bandit's

367

mask and my number in white on one cheek. A heart is on the other.

Then she points the the jersey, gesturing wildly until I realize—she's wearing it backwards so my name is plain to see, right across her chest.

My throat gets tight, and I lift my glove. She waves back like a maniac, and one of my sisters shoves her—Grey, I think?—and then all four of them are screaming again as Nathan slams someone to the boards right in front of them.

"Nothing like a little motivation, yeah?" Eli says, slapping me on the back. "Let's go."

It's more than motivation. It's ... *everything*.

Every significant person in my life is in this building, and the thought makes warmth spread through me. More than a need to win the game, I'm fueled by the need to *finish* the game, get out of the locker room, and to find Mills.

The fact that she's here, wearing my name, my number, screaming for me just like I said last night—it makes the tiny flicker of hope roar into something larger.

I practically throw myself over the wall as our line heads back out. The Badgers have found a second wind, which is dangerous. Even with only five minutes left.

A two-point lead isn't enough. I'm sure Felix would love to hold them scoreless in this final period after our defense let him down.

And now that I know who's watching, I want a goal of my own. I want my moment. For my sisters. For Mills.

I've played well—maybe the best period I've had this season, aside from actually sending a puck into the net myself. Time to change that.

Eli sends it my way as we cross the blue line. I have a shot, but it's not a sure thing and I've got guys on me. But no one seems to notice Logan hanging quietly just outside the crease.

I have less than a second to debate taking the risky shot or going for the sure thing.

Slicing right, I line it up, but then at the last second send it behind the defensemen and straight to Logan. He tips it in.

The horn blares and the noise in the Summit is deafening. Logan skates straight to me, ramming into me with a hug that would have taken me off my skates had Eli not sandwiched me in from behind.

"Aw, Vanity gave up his glory for the good of the team," Eli says. "Mama's little boy is growing up."

"Shut up," I say through my smile.

"Nice one," Logan says. "The assist. Not whatever Eli said."

"*Very* nice," Alec says, joining the group hug. "But the game's not over yet. Think we can do it again?"

We don't.

But it doesn't matter because neither do they. Which means we win by three with six unanswered points in the third period.

The Summit goes wild. The horn goes on forever. Fans practically shake the stadium, pounding on the glass and stomping their feet. Our bench empties onto the ice in a big messy celebration.

But my gaze goes over the mass of bodies and finds Amelia.

She and my sisters are jumping up and down, hugging and screaming, but she stops when she sees me and steps forward, forehead and palms pressed to the glass.

Without a word to the guys, I sprint across the ice, never breaking her gaze.

There's no way we can hear each other over the sheer

volume in the Summit, but I line my hands up with hers and drop my forehead to the inch of plexiglass separating us.

This is easier than words.

Though right now, I crave her words. I want the reassurance. I need to know if this means what I think it means—her here, face painted, my name across her chest.

But I can't wait for that.

I love you, I mouth. *I love you, Mills.*

She nods emphatically, her eyes brimming.

I love you too, Robbie, she mouths back.

Something about seeing her lips form my name, my real name, shifts something inside me. I want to break through this plexiglass with my fists. I want to rip it away and—

"Van!"

My Hulk fantasy is interrupted by Alec summoning me back to do all the post-game stuff. I drop my hands and start skating slowly backwards. I'm vaguely aware of my sisters next to Amelia, but I can't take my eyes off her.

I'm so sorry, she's saying.

Pointing toward the tunnel, I mouth, *Later?* Hoping she'll find me, that Parker will help her get to me.

I need to see her without this between us. I need her in my arms. I need to hear the words, to feel her mouth on mine.

"Van!"

This time it's Coach bellowing my name, his narrowed gaze bouncing between me and his daughter. I'm surprised he even recognizes her with the face paint. But he clearly does. And despite the win, he's not happy.

Amelia's eyes narrow, and I nod, hoping she understands. I got this.

Hoping that I do, in fact, *got* this. I mean, Coach can't punch me again … right?

CHAPTER 30

Amelia

"I NEED to see my dad. Now."

When I grab Parker's arm and demand this, I can tell she wants to tell me that it's impossible to get to my dad, the coach, at this exact moment, which is less than two minutes after their game ended. But I saw the look on Dad's face when he glanced over at me and Van, and I strongly suspect my presence is needed.

The guys left the ice only moments ago, and fans are streaming up the stairs toward the exits. We're still squeezed in our row, and I barely managed to stop Parker before she flitted off to help wrangle all the visiting families.

"I don't think I'm familiar enough with the building to get down there myself. *Please.* Dad looked like he might punch Van again. I just don't want him to do or say something to hurt Van. Or his own career."

As far as I know, the guys didn't say anything to anyone about my dad hitting Van. I can't see a world in which he wouldn't lose his job over that.

I might be upset with him, but I don't want him to flush his career down the toilet.

A variety of emotions flicker over Parker's face like a spinning game show wheel, waiting to land on one. "Um," she says. "So, the thing about that is, usually family waits in the designated room and *right* after a game it's hard to—"

Callie steps up beside me. "I do believe the lady said *now*."

Alexandra flanks my other side and Grey squeezes in next to her. I'm not sure if we look intimidating or ridiculous or maybe a little bit of both—what with the face paint. I'm more than ready to wash it off. I swear, I can feel my pores gasping for oxygen.

Parker sighs. "I can make no promises. I'll get you there, but I don't know about the rest."

"Just get us to him."

And we're off. Parker guides us through a door with a security guard who nods to her and barely holds back a smile at Van's sisters and me. I *really* need to get this face paint off.

Once we're in the bowels of the building, it takes a minute for me to recognize the way to the locker room. Parker is practically vibrating with nerves beside me, and Van's sisters walking just behind us are giving off prison guard transfer vibes.

"Hey," I say, pulling Parker to a stop when I see the locker room door. "You can go. I don't want you to get in trouble for butting into their post-game whatever."

"Are you sure? It's just … I feel like your dad might forgive you more easily than me."

She might be surprised. "It's fine. I promise."

Parker starts to walk off, then stops and bites her lip. "Will you … tell me how things are going? Just keep me in the loop for whatever is going on with you and your dad and you and Van. I don't want anyone losing their jobs. Or faces. When you feel ready. No pressure. Mild pressure," she amends. "Or medium."

I laugh. "I'll tell you. Thanks."

"Oh, and definitely knock first!" Parker calls from down the hallway. "But you still might want to cover your eyes when you go in there."

Lex steps in front of me and kneads my shoulders like I'm a boxer about to head into the ring. "Don't show fear. Just be yourself."

"Is this really necessary?" I ask.

"I don't know," Lex says. "We're not sure what your plan is. But this kind of speech seems to work in the movies."

"One question." Callie nudges Lex aside and makes pointed eye contact. "Are you going to break his heart?"

Lex and Grey say nothing, but I can practically feel all three of them holding their breath.

I remember the expression on Van's face when he saw me with his sisters. When he skated over to me right after the game. When he pressed his forehead to the glass.

"No. Now, step aside and wish me luck." I step toward the door and knock loudly. "I need to see Coach Davis!" I call. But I don't wait for a response. "I'm coming in!"

Taking Parker's words to heart, I cover my eyes and step inside the room, peeking only between my fingers. From my limited view, I don't see tons of skin on display, so I think I'm safe. When I drop my hand, I see a few guys are out of their jerseys, but at least everyone's still wearing pants. Van is in a white tank top, showing off the tip of his dragon tattoo.

"Amelia?" My dad frowns.

I drop my hand and glare at my father, who's standing across the room. Very near Van, I can't help but notice. There's no blood, but there's definitely tension. The assistant coaches and Malik are standing close too, though, like maybe I'm not the only one worried about my dad lashing out right now.

"You two," I say, pointing between my dad and Van. "Your office. We need to talk."

When they don't immediately stop staring at each other and move, I clap my hands. "I'm serious. *Now*. Then you can get back to …" I trail off and look around, wondering exactly what I've interrupted.

Eli grins at me, flipping his sweaty blond hair out of his eyes. "Coach was just yelling at us for"—my dad clears his throat and Eli pauses—"um, sorry—he was telling us we should have played the whole game the way we played in the third period."

"Yes. That about sums it up," Dad says. "Though I did have something else I wanted to say to Van."

Oh, boy.

Van glances at me, then back to my dad. "Yes, sir?"

I'm not sure if my dad is being dramatic on purpose, dragging this out to make Van sweat, or if he's pausing for another reason. The whole room is waiting.

And I'd bet Van's sisters have their ears pressed to the door, also waiting.

"You made a good call with that assist," he says finally. "You could have gone for the glory, taken the risky shot. But you made the better choice for the team. Good job."

I almost fall over. Van looks equally surprised. Maybe there's hope after all.

"Thank you, sir," Van says.

"But as far as my daughter is concerned—"

Never mind.

"Hey," I shout across the room. "Not here. Come on."

Dad looks at the assistant coaches. Ken waves him on, telling him he's got this. Malik gives me a thumbs up, clearly wishing me luck.

I'm going to need it. Luck or bravery.

I definitely need both.

I'd rather talk somewhere more neutral than Dad's office, but there aren't many neutral spaces in the building, so I guess his office is as good as anywhere. Van urges me inside ahead of him, a hand on my lower back. He drops it when he sees my father trying to burn a hole through his bones with a look.

I close the door, but don't take a seat like my dad or Van.

Hands on hips, I remain standing in what Morgan would call a power pose. I channel the fierce directness she always uses when facing hard things head-on. I'm no Morgan, but I do feel more powerful.

Maybe it's just knowing, possibly for the first time in my life with absolute certainty, what I want.

Stepping closer to Van, I drop a hand to his shoulder, feeling the muscles bunch under my fingertips. I don't miss the way my dad's focus lasers in on that point of contact. Van shifts a little in his seat and places his hand on top of mine. Dad's eyes are practically slits, paper-cut thin.

"You always tried to keep me away from hockey players," I start, not sure if this is even the best place to begin. But it will do. "And I understand why. To a point. But you've invested your life into these guys on the team. I've spent time with them—they're good guys, Dad."

"Some of them are," he says in a tone that makes it clear he's not sure Van is one of them.

But if I'm not imagining it, his gaze softens. Slightly.

"Did you know Van and I met about a year ago?" I ask. "Neither knew who the other was, but when he figured out I was your daughter, he panicked and sort of disappeared."

"I was afraid you'd kill me, sir."

"You were right to be afraid," Dad says.

"Knock it off." My tone is so hard that Dad blinks in surprise. "While I appreciate how protective you are and how you've taken care of me since Mom died, this is too far."

"Or not far enough."

I know Dad has been through a lot. While Drew's actions mostly were hard for me, they were a challenge for Dad in a different way. I can't imagine the stress, and I do know the cost—which hopefully he'll be able to recoup from Drew. But the rift between Dad and Uncle Bobby, plus everything with Becky—it's a lot.

Then … finding out about this the way he did, on top of everything else.

I tell myself to have some compassion, even though what I'd like to do is put him into a time out since he's acting like an overgrown toddler.

"Dad, you trusted Van enough to send him with me to Florida," I point out.

"I was desperate," he says. "I didn't want you to be alone. Not after everything. Van was already with you, and I knew he wouldn't let anything happen to you." Dad's frown becomes a glower. "I also assumed he'd know not to get involved with you."

Van clears his throat. "You did make that very clear, sir."

"But it's not your choice to make," I say.

"And I was already getting on the plane before you called. Sir," Van adds.

"You can't actually think that this"—Dad points between us— "is real. This … marriage." His lip curls when he says it.

So does mine, but for a different reason. Van squeezes my hand, and I meet his gaze. We may not have spent many cumulative hours together, but I can read his expression right now.

And shockingly, I get the sense he wants me to go easy on my dad.

Almost as shocking—I feel myself soften.

Drawing in a breath, I look back at my dad. "Is it just how quickly this happened? Or is this about who I'm with?"

He blinks like he's surprised I'm asking for clarification at all. "Both. You can't possibly take marriage seriously when it happens on a whim."

Van flinches. I curl my fingers around his shoulder, squeezing.

"That's not how it works," Dad says, shaking his head. "Marriage takes time, and love is hard work and it's—"

I cut him off. "That's not what you raised me to believe."

"Excuse me?"

"You always told me about how you and Mom fell in love. You were friends first, and it grew into something more."

"Exactly," Dad says, stabbing a finger into his desk. "Over time."

"But you also said everyone has their own love story waiting to be told. If that's true then why can't *this* be my story?" I flip my palm and lace my fingers through Van's, offering him a shy smile. "*Our* story."

"But he—"

I hold up my other hand. "Stop. I won't let you disparage him. As I said before, you don't know him as well as you think. You see a part, not a whole."

"You really think you know him better than I do?"

"Yes." Firm. Concise. Sure.

I silently will my father not to press me for details. Somehow, I doubt he would want me to categorize all the ways I know Van better than he does.

Van gets it. I know from the way he tilts his head, faking a sneeze to hide a laugh.

Thankfully, Dad moves in another direction.

"You're sure this is what you want? Being with *him* til death do you part?" Dad chokes a little. "Raising babies together?"

Van chokes a little too.

"I'm … not totally sure about all the details, though that's definitely an important point to cover. For the future," I say, looking at Van. "No babies today."

"Good," he says, then gives me a little smirk that I swear tells me he's thinking about the *making babies* part of babies. I squeeze his hand hard enough to make the smirk disappear.

"I mean, I'm scared. I have doubts. I have questions," I say. "There are things to figure out."

"You barely know him," Dad protests, circling back to this argument.

I smile at Van again. Wait—did I *stop* smiling at him? "In some ways, you're right—I barely know him. Which makes this more exciting than it is terrifying. I'll *get* to know him. But I already know enough. I'm all in."

This is said more for Van's sake than my father's. And I wish I were saying it alone, but I think it actually may mean more to him being said this way, in front of my father.

"Sir, I'd like to say—" Van starts.

But my dad interrupts.

"If you're going to try to convince me you're worthy of my daughter—"

Van barks out a laugh. "I would *never* try to convince you of that. I'm absolutely *not* worthy of her. I'll never be."

"For once, we agree on something," Dad says dryly. But there's a little spark in his eyes that makes a matching tiny spark bloom in my chest.

It's not quite a baby step. What's smaller than that? A baby ... crawl? A scoot?

"It's a good start, wouldn't you say?" Van says.

"Don't get ahead of yourself there, son." Dad's eyes go wide the moment the word son leaves his mouth. So do Van's. "I didn't mean to call you son like *son* son. Literally son—or son-in-law. It was just an expression!"

He looks so panicked I cover my mouth to hide a laugh.

Van lifts a shoulder, smiling smugly. "Sorry. You said it. Can't take it back, Dad. Can I call you that on the ice? It sounds better than coach ..."

My dad tips his head back and groans, muttering something about *of all the guys I would have warned you away from ...*

But it's in this very moment I catch a glimpse of the future. I'm not sure Van will ever *not* drive Dad crazy. It seems almost like his natural setting—poking the bear. The thing is ... maybe my dad *needs* to be poked. He needs someone who doesn't just fall in line the way I always have, my whole life.

Until Van.

The two of them are already starting to bicker again. But I've lost my patience for this conversation.

I raise my voice over theirs. "Now that we've had this discussion, I'm stealing your player. Hopefully, he wasn't scheduled to do any press. Because he can't. He has a prior obligation."

"I do?" Van asks, but he stands when I give his hand a tug. "I do."

"Wait," Dad says, following us to the door. He glances at Van, then holds out his hand, even though there's a slight curl to his lip. Van stares at his hand for a moment before taking it. "I'm sorry for hitting you. Both times. But especially the one this week. It was out of line."

Van nods and shakes his hand. "Thank you."

Dad seems to be turning the handshake into some kind of competition. They're still shaking and seem to be squeezing one another's hands too hard.

"Hey," I say. "Enough."

Releasing Van, Dad shifts his expression to me. "Milly, I'm sorry for what I said."

"Which thing?" I'm almost shocked at my own question. But I don't take it back or apologize.

Dad scratches his head. "All of them. But especially the thing I said about your mom. You've never reminded me of her more than today."

I wrap him up in a hug, and I can feel his shuddery breaths as he hugs me back. My own breathing feels just as wobbly, and I blink back tears. I wait until he's steady before backing away.

"I'll be back later to get my stuff," I tell him. "I'm staying at Van's." I grin. "With my husband."

Dad drags a hand over his face. "It's going to take some time to get used to this."

"We've got nothing but time," I say, then pull Van out of Dad's office. "Is there another way out of here that doesn't involve going through the locker room?"

"I probably should change," he says.

I shake my head. "No time."

He chuckles. "Follow me." As we're about to push through a door, he says, "But close your eyes. I'll guide you."

"Why would I—"

He opens the door and steam billows out. Along with the sound of running water. Ohhhh … the shower room. And it's clearly in use.

I keep a hand firmly clamped over my head as Van pulls me through the room. There are catcalls and shouts and people making kissing sounds. Someone starts singing the chorus to Taylor Swift's "I Knew You Were Trouble."

Van slows, and I hear the sound of a door being pulled open.

"You've got a nice voice," I call. "I think the more appropriate song, though, is 'But Daddy I Love Him.'"

This earns me a chuckle from Van and roars of laughter that fade as he pulls me out into the hallway. Thankfully, I recognize where we are. Now I'm the one pulling him.

"Where are we going?" he asks.

"You'll see."

Finally, the door appears at the end of a quiet hallway, and I open it and lead Van inside.

Van grins. "The stairwell is my prior obligation?"

"It's *our* stairwell," I correct.

"Right." His gaze drops to my mouth. "I remember."

And it's only as he leans forward that *I* remember how I look. "The face paint," I say, shoulder's slumping. "I'm all blue. It will get everywhere."

"I don't mind getting a little messy," Van says.

And then we're kissing like two people who haven't for *ages*. Two people desperate for each other. Who belong together.

Who do not care that blue face paint is smearing everywhere.

"Can I put this back?" Van asks, and he takes my right hand in both of his.

It takes me a moment to realize he means my mother's

ring. My eyes well with tears, and I nod, biting my lip. Van slips it on my left hand.

"Where's yours?" I ask. "I probably should upgrade it to something that won't turn your finger green."

He blinks. "How did you know it turned my finger green?"

Giggling, I say, "It did?"

"Yep. But"—he fishes inside his collar and pulls out a thin chain I didn't even notice—"I kept it on."

He starts to take it off the chain, and I cover his hands with mine. "Keep it there for now."

He slips it back inside his tank and then goes back to kissing me breathless.

"I've got two questions for you," I say, minutes or hours later, my lips moving against his blue-tinged mouth.

"Shoot."

"Will you grow your beard back?"

"You like the beard? I'll grow back the beard." He places a lingering kiss on the corner of my mouth and I chase his lips.

A moment later, we're both breathing heavy, his hands tangled in my hair and mine cupping his jaw. Which is now half blue with a little smear of white.

I dip my finger into his tank top, touching his tattoo. "Hey, Frisky. I've missed you."

Van chuckles. "I forgot you named him that."

"I didn't forget." I give Frisky a blue stripe on his neck. "Oh! I met your fish by the way, since we're talking about your animals."

"Confession," Van says, looking guilty. "I lied in Florida about having a fish. I bought Theodore when I got home."

"Why?"

Van brushes my hair away from my neck. "I didn't like

keeping the stuff with your dad from you. The only other lie I told was about the fish. So, I made it true. Are you mad?"

"Nope. But thanks for telling me. From now on, the truth. Okay, hotshot?"

He grins at the nickname. "Truth. Didn't you have one more question?"

"Ah, yes." I wipe at the turquoise paint on his cheek. "Do you happen to know how easy your sister's face paint is to clean off?"

Van laughs, the sound rich and low. I watch the bob of his throat as he throws his head back.

"I don't think it's too bad," he says, smiling back at me. "But until we figure it out, I don't mind every person I see knowing exactly where my mouth has been."

I lean forward, leaving more blue paint on him as I kiss his neck. It's slightly damp, and his skin smells sharp and salty. But I'm starting to notice that his sweat-soaked tank top ... doesn't.

"We should probably clean up," I suggest, wrinkling my nose.

"You make a cute Smurf," he says. "But yes. We should. And then, let's go home."

Home. The word sends a thrill through me, and I grin as Van takes my hand, leading me back up the stairs—him with my face paint smudged on his skin and me wearing his name across my chest.

EPILOGUE

Van

I TAKE a last look in the mirror, adjusting my tie and running a hand over my beard. I trimmed it this morning. On a scale of five o'clock shadow to mountain man, I'm leaning toward five o'clock lumberjack.

Just the way Amelia likes it.

This *is* how she likes it—right? Or did I go a little too short?

I'm not sure why I'm obsessing over my facial hair. Or any of the other details of today. Earlier, it was my socks bunching up. Then I worried I put on too much cologne. Stupid things that shouldn't matter in the grand scheme of things.

Especially since, as far as I'm concerned, Amelia and I have been married since that night on the beach.

Even if, as it turns out, the certificate we signed was *not* legally official. I guess you can't trust every random officiant you find on the beach.

Though Mills and I could have just gone to a courthouse or signed a paper with a witness, we both loved the idea of having a do-over. A wedding where our family and friends could be with us. That is our shared regret from our first wedding. Not how impulsively we did it or anything else, but the fact that our family and friends weren't there.

So, there is no reason for me to be so nervous. And yet ...

I am. More jittery and unsure than before my very first game with the Appies. At least then I knew the adrenaline would kick in the second the puck dropped. Now, I'm afraid I might black out right in the middle of the ceremony.

And I have this nagging feeling like there's something I forgot.

"Oh, my *gosh*," Callie says, sneaking up behind me and making me jump back from the mirror. "Would you stop admiring yourself, Vanity?"

"I want to give all the guys on your team a high five for thinking of that nickname." Lex comes up beside me and leans her head on my shoulder, grinning up at me.

"Honestly, it's shocking you three didn't think of it first," I say. "I mean, it was right there—ripe for the picking. And you went instead with—"

"Robbie Bobby Baby Benjamin Bunny." Grey comes up on my other side, linking her arm through mine. "It has such a nice ring to it. And the guys really seem to like it."

"You did *not* tell them."

Grey shrugs. "They made me an offer I couldn't refuse." Lex giggles, and Callie gives Grey a high five.

I groan and step away from my traitorous sisters. "You know I will *never* hear the end of it."

"That was kind of the point," Grey says. "Anyway. Are you ready for this—your second wedding in one year?"

"A little excessive," Callie says. "But very on brand for you." Her expression and her tone soften. "We're so happy for you and Amelia. And glad we get to be here this time."

Callie suddenly looks like she's going to burst into tears, and I wrap her in a hug, shielding her from Lex and Grey, who are bickering now about their shoes.

"You're welcome," I whisper near Callie's ear.

"I owe you a block of extra sharp white cheddar," she says with a laugh that catches on what sounds like a sob.

I'm having a hard time myself. My nose is doing that tingling thing and it's hard to swallow. "Sounds good, Dr. Van de Kamp. I'll also accept payment in the form of shredded or sliced."

She squeezes me tighter, laughing.

There is a sudden commotion at the door, which can only mean one thing.

"It's time!" Eli announces, bounding into the room. "Hope you've got your pants on!"

Callie whispers, "Thanks," and slips out of my embrace.

"Why wouldn't I have pants on?" I ask as the rest of the guys file into the room.

Eli shrugs. "I don't know. Coming in here feels a little like coming into a locker room or something, all private-like and intimate."

"Speaking of intimate," Alec says. "Do we need to have a talk about the wedding night? What to expect?"

"I think I'm good," I tell him, covering Grey's ears. Leaning closer to her, I say, "You should go before the three of you get corrupted by the untoward influence of my teammates."

"Like they could corrupt us," Lex says loftily. "But we should go check on Amelia."

"Tell her hi!" I call as my sisters start to file out the door. "Actually, tell her I said, 'Shoot the hostage.'"

Logan snorts, and Nathan gives me the kind of look that would turn a grape into a raisin right on the vine. Alec is shaking his head. In appreciation or exasperation—kind of hard to tell which one.

I ignore them all.

Callie pauses, one foot halfway out the door. "You want me to tell her *that*? Right now—ten minutes before your wedding? Not very romantic, bro."

"It's a quote from *Speed*. She'll get it. It's a Keanu thing."

"You're so weird," she mutters as she closes the door behind her.

As soon as my sisters are gone, the guys descend on me.

"Went a little short on the beard, eh?"

"Could have used a little trim on the back of your hair, too. Want me to do it? I've got a pair of fingernail clippers in my pocket."

"If you're going to quote Keanu to your wife, you should really pick a better quote. Like 'I know kung fu.'"

"So, does this count as your *second* marriage? Because if so, I don't think we're obligated to give you a gift."

All the teasing has the effect of calming me down, kind of like a hockey player's lullaby. I'm not sure if that's the intent or if they're just being obnoxious, but I appreciate them, nonetheless.

I don't get a chance to say so because a voice booms from the doorway, "That's *enough!*"

Coach's booming voice has us all whipping around and standing at attention like we're military men, not hockey players.

He glares from the doorway, his eyes moving from man to man to man until they finally land and stick on me.

"Leave us," he says, and I gulp.

"Hope you're wearing your cup," Alec whispers in my ear as he passes.

"And a bulletproof vest," Eli mutters.

But the moment they're all gone, Coach's face breaks into a grin, and I relax. Mostly.

"How's my second least favorite player and first least favorite son-in-law?"

"Second least favorite? I got an upgrade?"

"Dominik is making me nuts. You look like you're about to puke."

"I might," I admit.

"Well, if you're going to do it, do it now. Not when you're standing in front of all those people." He walks over to me, circling like he's inspecting me. "You clean up pretty good."

"Thanks. You don't look so bad yourself, Dad."

He scoffs. Something he does every time I call him Dad. Which is probably why I do it so frequently. A lot of things have changed in our dynamic, but one thing has not—I still get under his skin like no one else. And I still enjoy doing it just as much.

Once he finishes circling me, he stops in front, smoothing down my lapels before patting me on the shoulders roughly. "Look, I don't want to get all sappy. I already did that with Milly, and I don't have it in me to do it twice. But I want you to know that I love you."

His words are so unexpected that it takes me a minute to really register what he's said.

"Well, don't look so shocked, son," he adds.

But I *am* shocked. "I'm just ... wow. You totally—I didn't —wow."

"It's a good thing you're not giving any speeches tonight," he says. "You suck at them. And you shouldn't be so surprised by family telling you they love you."

I stare down at my shoes. They're so shiny I can see the recessed lights reflected near my toes. But there's a scuff on the left one, and I bend, trying to buff it out with my fingertip. It only makes smudges. One tear falls with a tiny splat on the shoe, and I rub that around. It works better.

"What are you doing?" Coach asks.

"My shoe is dirty." I stand, sliding my sweaty palms down my pants and sniffling.

Coach is frowning at me. "What is it? Did I say something wrong?"

I shake my head. "I only just now realized that I don't know the last time my dad told me that."

Now, he's the one looking upset. Or like he might puke. But what Coach does is pull me into a hug. Not for too long. Because he may like me better than he did, and he may love me, but I still bug him more than anyone else.

"Thank you for trusting me with your daughter, sir."

He nods. Sniffs. Wipes one eye. "Thank you for helping her fly."

———

The deejay started playing slow songs in a steady stream about twenty minutes ago, and I'm pretty sure it has to do with putting a stop to Tucker's twerking. It seems to be his only move, and the man sure has endurance. But it's hard to twerk to "Unchained Melodies."

Something I'm grateful for.

Mills snuggles closer, yawning into my neck. "Is it time to go yet? I think I'm weddinged out."

I glance around the room, a historic theater turned reception hall in the older part of Harvest Hollow. There are more than a few couples swaying like we are, plus a few still seated at tables around the room. But it's mostly just a few stragglers—our closest friends. We decided not to do a big send-off, so we can go any time before midnight, which is how long we rented the space.

A lot of the guys are still here, though a few of the couples left an hour or two ago. Morgan is flirting shamelessly with Wyatt, who is doing his best impression of those British guards who aren't allowed to react to anything. I think that's *why* she's flirting with him—Amelia's best friend likes a challenge.

Parker and Logan are making out in a corner behind a large potted plant, which hides nothing. Summer and Alec are having some kind of intense conversation, with Nathan glowering next to her. *That* looks fun.

Coach is saying goodbye to his brother and Becky—two people I didn't particularly want to invite. But both Mills and her dad wanted to make peace. Things are tentative, but they're here. It helps that Becky sincerely apologized to Amelia. And she isn't dating Drew any longer.

It's wild to think about the two of them. What they did was awful. But if they hadn't done it, I might not be here.

"How about after this song?" I suggest, giving Amelia's earlobe a tiny bite.

She giggles, then yawns again. "Okay. Can I make a request?"

"Anything." I trail my lips along her neck.

At least, until I accidentally lock eyes with her father across the room. He's now alone, and he's glaring. Immediately, I straighten and lift my hands a little higher. Closer to her waist than where they just were. Which was … not on her waist.

"What's the request?" I ask.

"Will you carry me out when we go? Not just over the threshold or whatever. But out of this room, down to the car, and then from the car to the house. My feet hurt."

"I would love nothing more. Consider me your personal carrying service."

"M'kay." She nuzzles into my chest, becoming almost dead weight. I think she's about three minutes from falling asleep.

"On second thought, I don't think we should wait until the end of the song. You, my little Mills, need a nap."

"Just a little one," she says. "Because I had plans at home. A whole"—she yawns again—"outfit and stuff."

I chuckle. "As much as I like the sound of an outfit and especially *and stuff*, you'll have to save it for the honeymoon."

Without giving her any warning, I scoop her up into my arms. She practically melts into me, her eyelids fluttering closed. I pause for a moment, needing to remember this. Amelia's cheeks are flushed pink, highlighting her scattered freckles. Her lips are barely parted, and I want nothing more than to tuck her into our bed at home and press a kiss to those lips.

Okay, there are a *few* things I'd like more.

But not tonight. She's completely tapped out. And actually … she might be drooling on my tux.

We said our official goodbyes to her dad and my sisters hours ago, and I give them all a quick nod as we start toward the door. It only takes a quick glance at Amelia to see why we're leaving. Grey puts a hand over her heart, and Lex wipes her eyes.

Right at the door, I'm stopped by a frowning Summer, who is dragging Alec by the arm.

"We need to talk," Summer says.

I groan. "Can it wait? Is it life-threatening?"

"I mean, no one's going to *die*," she says. "But you probably want to know this now. Want to tell them, Alec?"

"Tell us what?" Amelia murmurs, barely cracking open her eyes. "Oh, and thanks again for doing the ceremony. It's nice to have a guy on the team who can perform weddings."

"About that," Alec says, and the guilty look on his face tells me exactly where this conversation is headed. "Apparently, the kind of certification I have to perform weddings needs to be renewed."

"And you didn't renew it," I state.

"He did not," Summer says. "Which means ... you just got married for the second time with*out* a valid marriage license. Which means, legally speaking, this doesn't count."

"You had one job," I tell Alec. "One." I'm honestly not really mad, but it's fun to be the one getting after our captain. Usually, it's the other way around.

"You and your paperwork," Amelia says, giving Summer a look. "Are you going to try to tell me that Van's not my husband? Because he is. He was my husband from the time I said I do and till death do us part and all the other stuff on the beach. Now, we've done all that two times. He is my husband twice over and then some. Don't you try to take this away from me. It's unconstitutional."

Amelia's head falls back against my chest, and a second later she lets out a tiny, adorable snore. She looks like a happy, sleepy, beautiful marshmallow with the fabric of her dress practically swallowing her. I have a sudden flashback to her in my SUV, drowning in a different wedding dress, and trying to throw the garter belt out the window. I still keep it in my dresser.

"How about we deal with the legal stuff later?" I suggest to Summer. "I'll pay you double your hourly rate if you can figure out the best and fastest way for us to actually get legally married."

Summer nods. "Will do."

"Glad you're not mad," Alec says. "And you know what they say—third time's the charm!"

I level him with a look. "I never said I wasn't mad. Now you owe me, and I plan to collect."

But right now, I have a sleepy bride who needs to be put to bed. We'll deal with the marriage license another day, and I can't even be mad about it. Because despite my vow that I would only get married once, I would say "I do" to Amelia a hundred times over.

TYPO HALL OF FAME

Typos are like cockroaches and Twinkies—able to survive through a literal apocalypse. Here are a few from this book that I thought were noteworthy and deserving of a moment to shine.

"Just a **hung**, but I'm not sure I'd trust any promises he makes."

[should be: hunch, not hung]

The sectional **soft** could hold almost that many.

[should be: sofa not soft]

He grunts when I lean over, my knee going into **my** stomach.

[should be: going into his stomach]

The **main** is just plain stareable.

[should be: man not main]

…where my sides are exposed and in the low **tip** of the back.

[should be: dip not tip]

… as I see the cheap **fash** wash and body wash Amelia bought at Walmart.

[should be: face not fash]

Dumb interrupts. "I'm not in a group chat."

[should be: Dumbo not Dumb]

And the king of all typos…

When I grin, his eyes **fart** briefly to my mouth, then up to meet my gaze.

A NOTE FROM EMMA

Helllllo, y'all!!!

If you are here, you are my favorite kind of person—a NOSY one.

I love nosy people. Thanks for being all up in my business.

So: Van. Vanity. Robbie.

Robbie Bobby Baby Benjamin Bunny.

While I am partial to all my characters, I LOVE characters like these—the guys who seem like one thing on the surface but have a whole lot of real estate underneath. So, while I wrote Logan's and Eli's stories, I've been low-key DYING to get to Van.

And who better to fall for the coach's daughter than the guy on the team with the reputation?

Pretty quickly, I knew where I wanted this story to go. A wedding that wasn't. And then another one that WAS.

When I talked through this idea with Jenny Proctor, my fabulous coauthor and critique partner, I asked if this was too wild. Too much. Too fast.

I think her response was: "Convince me."

I did, and I hope I convinced you.

Love really does come in a lot of shapes, sizes, and time-lines. Some are fast and some are slow. Some people start as friends and some start as enemies and some start as the coach's daughter and the bad boy.

While I love writing these bad boys (and also grumps), I married a cinnamon roll—one whose name happens to be Robbie. And his childhood nickname, given sooooo graciously by his older sister.

The funny thing is that when I asked the family how *Bobby* was spelled, they said it was oral tradition only. So, I've chosen: Robbie Bobby. It is written.

I hope you enjoyed this addition to the Appies series, and I also hope you go check out the others if you did. Jenny and I have had SO much fun creating this team, sending texts back and forth asking character questions and hockey questions, and even going to Savannah Bananas events.

FOR RESEARCH.

I hope you love this book and this family of characters as much as we do!

Thank you for reading, and I hope to connect with you on Facebook, Instagram, or on my email list if you want a free novella!

Happy reading, y'all!

-e

PS- If any of you are *Arrested Development* fans, please know I could not stop thinking of Tobias and the Blue Man Group. IYKYK.

ABOUT THE AUTHOR

Emma St. Clair is a *USA Today* bestselling author of over thirty books and has her MFA in Fiction. She lives near Houston with her husband, five kids, and a Great Dane who doesn't make a very good babysitter. Her romcoms have humor, heart, and nothing that's going to make you need to hide your Kindle from the kids. ;)

You can find out more at http://emmastclair.com or join her reader group at https://www.facebook.com/groups/emmastclair/

Her first book with Thomas Nelson will be coming out in 2025, and she is represented by Kimberly Whalen, The Whalen Agency.

ACKNOWLEDGMENTS

Jenny, we really dragged ourselves over the finish line with this one, didn't we? Thank you for everything. You are the MOE I need in my life.

And holy moly—I am so grateful to Tara, Abby, Carole, Bethany, Michelle, Jenn, Haley, Devon, Kimberly, Chelsea, Darla, Lindsay, Kristen, and Alicia for offering to help me find all the eye farts in my books. (And anyone else I might have missed!) You helped so much and, in some cases, gave me ideas to make it better.

To all my Creepers (you know who you are), THANK YOU for all the love!

Jordan, you are a precious and wonderful woman—I am SO thankful for you and your suggestions!!!

THE APPIES

Just Don't Fall- Emma St. Clair

Absolutely Not in Love- Jenny Proctor

A Groom of One's Own- Emma St. Clair

Romancing the Grump- Jenny Proctor

Runaway Bride and Prejudice- Emma St. Clair

Oakley Island (with Jenny Proctor)

Eloise and the Grump Next Door

Merritt and Her Childhood Crush

Sadie and the Bad Boy Billionaire

Other books by Emma:

Love Stories in Sheet Cake

The Buy-In

The Bluff

The Pocket Pair

Sweet Royal Romcoms

Royally Rearranged

Royal Gone Rogue

Love Clichés

Falling for Your Best Friend's Twin

Falling for Your Boss

Falling for Your Fake Fiancé

The Twelve Holidates

Falling for Your Brother's Best Friend

Falling for Your Best Friend

Falling for Your Enemy

Made in the USA
Las Vegas, NV
12 October 2024

96514879R00246